LORD
OF THE
DARKWOOD
The Tale of Shikanoko

Lian Hearn's beloved 'Tales of the Otori' series, set in an imagined feudal Japan, has sold more than four million copies worldwide and has been translated into nearly forty languages. It is comprised of five volumes: *Across the Nightingale Floor*, *Grass for His Pillow*, *Brilliance of the Moon*, *The Harsh Cry of the Heron* and *Heaven's Net is Wide*. The series was followed by two standalone novels, *Blossoms and Shadows* and *The Storyteller and His Three Daughters*, also set in Japan. Lian Hearn's new series, 'The Tale of Shikanoko', is made up of two books: *Emperor of the Eight Islands* and *Lord of the Darkwood*.

Lian Hearn has made many trips to Japan and has studied Japanese. She read Modern Languages at Oxford and worked as an editor and film critic in England before emigrating to Australia.

Also by Lian Hearn

TALES OF THE OTORI

Across the Nightingale Floor
Grass for His Pillow
Brilliance of the Moon
The Harsh Cry of the Heron
Heaven's Net is Wide

Blossoms and Shadows
The Storyteller and His Three Daughters

THE TALE OF SHIKANOKO

Emperor of the Eight Islands

LORD

OF THE
DARKWOOD

The Tale of Shikanoko

LIAN HEARN

PICADOR

First published 2016 by Hachette Australia

First published in the UK 2016 by Picador

This edition first published 2017 by Picador
an imprint of Pan Macmillan
20 New Wharf Road, London N1 9RR
Associated companies throughout the world
www.panmacmillan.com

ISBN 978-1-5098-1281-3

Visit www.picador.com to read more about all our books
and to buy them. You will also find features, author interviews and
news of any author events, and you can sign up for e-newsletters
so that you're always first to hear about our new releases.

For my family,

For my friends,

For fans of the Otori around the world.

Might it be through grief
at sight of the bush clover,
coloured by autumn,
that the stag's cries continue
until the foothills resound?

Kokin Wakashū
TRANSLATED BY HELEN CRAIG MCCULLOUGH,
STANFORD UNIVERSITY PRESS 1985

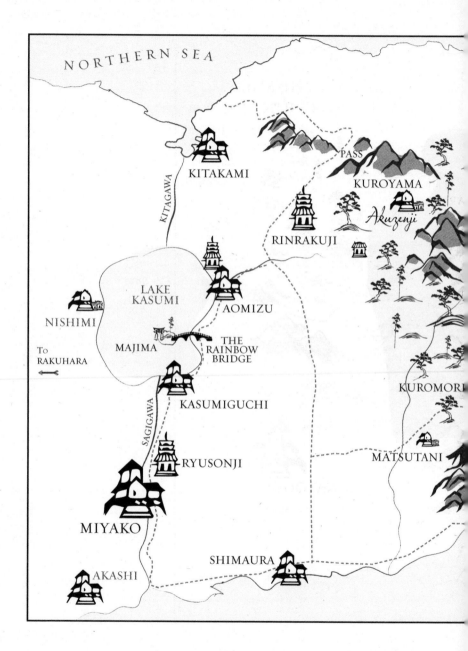

THE SNOW
COUNTRY

THE
ARKWOOD

Shisoku

MUENJI

KUMAYAMA

MINATOGURA

KUMAGAWA

ENCIRCLED SEA

------ ROADS

———— RIVERS
AND STREAMS

CONVENT
OR TEMPLE

HUT

SHRINE

ESTATE

TOWN

LIST OF CHARACTERS

MAIN CHARACTERS

Shikanoko (Shika), first known as Kazumaru, the son of Shigetomo and nephew of Sademasa, lords of Kumayama

Akihime (Aki), daughter of a nobleman, Hidetake, foster sister to Yoshimori and Kai

Kiyoyori, the lord of Kuromori

Tama, his wife, originally married to Masachika, mother of Tsumaru and stepmother to Hina

Masachika, Kiyoyori's younger brother

Hina, sometimes known as Yayoi, daughter of Kiyoyori

Tsumaru, Kiyoyori's son

Bara or Ibara, Hina's maid

Yoshimori (Yoshi), the true Emperor, heir to the Lotus Throne

Takeyoshi (Take), also Takemaru, son of Shikanoko and Akihime

Lady Tora, mother of the five children born to five fathers

Shisoku, the mountain sorcerer
Sesshin, an old scholar and sage
The Prince Abbot of Ryusonji
Akuzenji, King of the Mountain, a bandit
Hisoku, Lady Tama's retainer

THE MIBOSHI CLAN

Lord Aritomo, head of the clan, also known as the **Minatogura Lord**
Takaakira, lord of the Snow Country, friend and confidant to
    Lord Aritomo
The Yukikuni Lady, his wife
Takauji, their son
Arinori, lord of the Aomizu area, a sea captain
Yamada Keisaku, Masachika's adoptive father
Gensaku, one of Takaakira's retinue
Yasuie, one of Masachika's men
Yasunobu, his brother

THE KAKIZUKI CLAN

Lord Keita, head of the clan
Hosokawa no Masafusa, a kinsman of Kiyoyori
Tsuneto, one of Kiyoyori's warriors
Sadaike, one of Kiyoyori's warriors
Tachiyama no Enryo, one of Kiyoyori's warriors
Hatsu, his wife
Kongyo, Kiyoyori's senior retainer
Haru, his wife
Chikamaru, later Motochika, **Chika,** his son
Kaze, his daughter
Hironaga, a retainer at Kuromori
Tsunesada, a retainer at Kuromori
Taro, a servant in Kiyoyori's household in Miyako

THE IMPERIAL COURT

The Emperor
Prince Momozono, the Crown Prince
Lady Shinmei'in, his wife, Yoshimori's mother
Daigen, his younger brother, later Emperor
Lady Natsue, Daigen's mother, sister to the Prince Abbot
Yoriie, an attendant
Nishimi no Hidetake, Aki's father, foster father to Yoshimori
Kai, his adopted daughter

AT THE TEMPLE OF RYUSONJI

Gessho, a warrior monk
Eisei, a young monk, later one of the **Burnt Twins**

AT KUMAYAMA

Shigetomo, Shikanoko's father
Sademasa, his brother, Shikanoko's uncle, now lord of the estate
Nobuto, one of his warriors
Tsunemasa, one of his warriors
Naganori, one of his warriors
Nagatomo, his son, Shika's childhood friend, later one of the
    Burnt Twins

AT NISHIMI

Lady Sadako and **Lady Masako,** Hina's teachers
Saburo, a groom

THE RIVERBANK PEOPLE

Lady Fuji, the mistress of the pleasure boats
Asagao, a musician and entertainer
Yuri, Sen, Sada and **Teru,** young girls at the convent
Saru, an acrobat and monkey trainer
Kinmaru and **Monmaru,** acrobats and monkey trainers

THE SPIDER TRIBE

Kiku, later Master Kikuta, Lady Tora's oldest son
Mu, her second son
Kuro, her third son
Ima, her fourth son
Ku, her fifth son
Tsunetomo, a warrior, Kiku's retainer
Shida, Mu's wife, a fox woman
Kinpoge, their daughter

Unagi, a merchant in Kitakami

SUPERNATURAL BEINGS

Tadashii, a tengu
Hidari and **Migi,** guardian spirits of Matsutani
The dragon child
Ban, a flying horse
Gen, a fake wolf
Kon and **Zen,** werehawks

HORSES

Nyorin, Akuzenji's white stallion, later Shikanoko's
Risu, a bad-tempered brown mare
Tan, their foal

SWORDS

Jato, (Snake Sword)
Jinan, (Second Son)

BOWS

Ameyumi, (Rain Bow)
Kodama, (Echo)

Part One

LORD OF THE DARKWOOD

HINA (YAYOI)

The girl could see nothing. Her lungs were bursting. At any moment, she would open her mouth and breathe in the fatal waters of the lake. Snatches of her brief life came to her: her mother's face, her father's last words, her brother's cry for help before he disappeared. She had been one of the few survivors after the massacre in Miyako. Now her life was over, and she and Takemaru, the baby she clutched desperately, would join the dead. Tears formed in her eyes, only to be lost in the ebb and flow of Lake Kasumi.

Then suddenly there were dark shapes next to her, strong arms seized her. She was pulled upwards towards the light, miraculously still holding the baby. She retched and coughed, gasping for air, taking great gulps of it into her lungs. Hands reached down from the side of the boat and took Take from her. He was limp and pale, but, as she herself was pulled on board, she heard him scream in ragged, outraged gasps. He was alive.

The boat bucked like a living animal in the strong westerly wind. She saw the ochre-coloured sail lowered quickly, dropped on the deck, while the helmsman struggled with the oar at the stern. The men, who had plunged into the water to save her, were lifted up; they tore their wet clothes off and went naked, laughing. Monkeys screamed and chattered at them, dancing at the end of their cords. The sun in the east was dazzling. A crowd surrounded her. The men who were not naked were all dressed in red. They looked like beings from another world and she was afraid that she had drowned. But women stripped the heavy robes from her with hands that felt real, exclaiming at their fine quality in human voices. She and the baby were wrapped in furs, wolf and bear skins, and a bowl of some warm, strange-smelling liquid was pushed into her hands.

Men hoisted the sail again, the hemp flapping, fighting them, ropes snapping, snaking through the air. The monkeys screamed more loudly. In the confusion, one of the boys approached her, holding the lute. Beneath the howl of the wind, the slap of the waves, it was still playing, but more softly, its mother-of-pearl and gold–inlaid rosewood gleaming in the sun.

'Who are you?' he said quietly. 'What are you doing with Genzo?'

Fragments of memories came to her. *It is Genzo, the Emperor's lute,* Take's mother, Akihime, the Autumn Princess, had said, and she had promised to tell her where the child Emperor was, but she had not. Could this be him standing before her? It must be, the lute revealed him. But she must hide the fact she knew who he was.

She shook her head at him, as though she did not understand, and held out her hands. His eyes narrowed as he thrust the lute at her. She saw his unease, longed to speak to reassure him, but did not dare say anything. How would she address him, for a start? Words of honour and deference rose on her tongue but then the sailors shouted roughly at him to come and help them. Beside him the other boy was holding a text, made up of pages stitched together.

'Yoshi caught the lute and I caught this,' he said, holding it out to her. 'It's heavy! How did a girl like you manage to throw it so far?'

She grabbed it from him. She could not explain it, maybe it had sprouted wings and flown. She already knew the Kudzu Vine Treasure Store was enchanted. She tucked it under one arm while she turned her attention to the lute. It gave a sigh, as if it would start playing; she gripped it with her other hand.

More shouts echoed round her. The boys darted from her side and the lute quietened. It retained all its beauty, but it surrendered to her touch and allowed her to play it. It no longer played itself, in that wild irrepressible outburst of joy.

'She is a musician,' one of the men who had rescued her exclaimed. 'We must take her to Lady Fuji.'

The other looked back towards Nishimi, now barely visible over the choppy surface of the lake. 'She must be from a noble family. Someone will miss her, someone will come looking for her.'

'That was Lord Hidetake's home,' the oarsman called. 'He is dead.'

'Could this be his daughter? The one they call the Autumn Princess?'

'The Autumn Princess would be a grown woman by now,' said one of the women, who had already put Take to her breast and was nursing him. 'This one is still a girl. How old are you, lady?'

'I turned twelve this year,' the girl replied.

'And what do they call you?'

She did not want to say her name. There came into her mind a fragment of memory, a poem. 'Yayoi,' she said. It meant Spring.

'Is this little man your brother?' the woman asked, stroking Take's black hair tenderly.

She knew she must not tell them that the baby was the Autumn Princess's son. 'No, my mother died, a long time ago. He is the child of one of my maids.' She went on, improvising, 'She died giving birth to him. I like to play with him. I was holding him when I had to run away.'

'What were you running from?' They were sympathetic towards her but their curiosity was becoming tinged with anxiety.

The girl who had named herself Yayoi began to shiver, despite the furs and the warm drink.

'A bad man came,' she said, and then regretted sounding so childish. 'I was afraid he was going to kill me.'

'We should take her back,' one of the men suggested.

'Kinmaru,' the other man reproved him. 'Someone was going to kill her!'

'And that someone, Monmaru, could very well come looking for her and then who will get killed? Us, that's who!'

'Can't turn back against this wind,' the helmsman called. 'It's impossible.'

•

It was late in the afternoon by the time they came to the shore near the Rainbow Bridge. The market was almost over. Lanterns were being lit in the streets of Aomizu, on the island of Majima and along the bridge. As soon as the boat grounded, the acrobats leaped ashore with the monkeys.

'It's not too late to do a trick or two,' Kinmaru cried. Monmaru began to beat a small drum and immediately the boys threw themselves into a performance, a circle of somersaults with the monkeys, a high tower with three of the monkeys on top, a wild dance where the animals jumped from man to boy to man. A crowd soon gathered round them. Yayoi realised the audience knew the monkeys by name, calling out to them, *Shiro, Tomo, Kemuri*, and had their favourites, whom they applauded wildly. She was dazed by the noise, the colourful clothes, the shouts in a dialect she could barely understand. She gripped the lute and the text close to her chest, as though they could shield her from this strange new world.

'Come,' said the woman who had nursed Take – he was now asleep in her arms. 'You will stay with us tonight and tomorrow we will ask Lady Fuji what she thinks we should do with you.'

Yayoi slept restlessly on a thin mat in a room with three women and a clutch of children – one other young infant and three toddlers. The toddlers slept deeply like kittens. Take woke once screaming and the other baby was colicky and fretful. Every time Yayoi felt herself dropping into sleep, the baby wailed and she woke in alarm, half-dreaming something had happened to Take, he slipped from her arms underwater, he was stolen by monkeys. She heard the men and boys return later, their exaggerated efforts to keep quiet, their muffled laughter, the monkeys chattering as they were returned to their cages. For a few hours the house fell silent but she thought she heard a bird call, while it was still dark, before even the roosters had woken, a long, fluting call like an echo from the past.

The women rose at dawn to prepare the morning meal. Yayoi, who had never made a meal in her life, held Take for a while. He was nearly two months old. He looked closely at her face and smiled.

He will never know his mother, she thought and felt tears pool in her eyes. What would this day bring for them both? She felt sick and faint with fear.

'Don't cry, lady.'

'Look how pale she is, white as a spirit.'

'You need to be beautiful for Lady Fuji.'

The women's voices echoed around her.

'Will Lady Fuji let me keep Takemaru?' she said.

They exchanged looks that she was not meant to see.

'The baby can stay with us.'

'Yes, I have plenty of milk for two.'

'You cannot look after him, you are still a child yourself.'

'Then let me stay with you too!' Yayoi could not hold the tears in.

'This is no place for a young lady like you,' Take's foster mother said.

It was cool in the early morning, but, by the time Lady Fuji arrived, the sun was high in the sky and the air was warm. She came in with a rustle of silk, cherry blossom petals in her hair, the sweet perfume of spring all around her.

The women immediately started to apologise on Yayoi's behalf.

'Her clothes are not yet dry.'

'She's been crying, her eyes are red.'

'She nearly drowned yesterday; she can't be expected to look her best.'

Fuji studied Yayoi carefully, taking her head between her hands and tilting it from side to side. 'I can see how she looks. What a beautiful child. Who are you, my dear, and where do you come from?'

Some instinct warned Yayoi that her former life was over and she should never speak of it. She shook her head.

'You can't tell me? Well, that may be for the best. You have a Kakizuki look to you. Are you a survivor of the massacre in the capital?'

Yayoi did not answer, but Fuji smiled as if she had acquiesced.

'Someone hid you at Nishimi, but you were discovered and that is why you ran away?'

This time Yayoi nodded.

'Can you imagine any man wanting to kill something so precious?' Fuji said. 'Yet hundreds of women and children were put to death in Miyako, last year, when the Kakizuki warriors fled, leaving their families behind. I am of a mind to protect this one.'

She looked around and saw the lute and the text. 'You brought these with you? As well as the baby?' She picked up the lute and studied it with an expressionless face. It had lost its glowing rosewood and its gleaming inlay, yet Yayoi thought the older woman recognised it.

'So what am I to do with you?' Fuji said finally. 'Is anyone going to come in pursuit of you?'

'I don't know,' Yayoi replied. 'Maybe.' She held herself rigid, trying not to tremble.

'Someone must have seen you fall in the lake, but did they see you rescued? If anyone is looking for you, they will start their search with our boats, so I think I will take you somewhere where you can be safely hidden. We will hold a funeral service for the children who sadly drowned.'

Hina drowned and Yayoi was rescued.

'Will Take come with me?'

'How can a girl like you take care of a baby? And that would only draw unwanted attention to yourself. Take can stay here, the women will look after him. One more baby makes little difference to this troop of children.'

She called to the women to bring some clothes, not Yayoi's own robes, which she told the women to cut up for costumes, but old cast-offs that smelled of mildew and something sour like vinegar. When she was dressed, they covered her head with a cloth, which concealed her hair and most of her face.

'I must take my things,' she said anxiously. 'The lute and the text.' Clasping them to her chest, she followed Fuji into the rear courtyard of the house, where the boys from the boat were feeding the monkeys and playing with them. A young girl was with them, idly beating a small drum, laughing at the monkeys and teasing the boys when they yawned and rubbed their eyes. Yayoi wanted to stay with them, to be one of them.

She felt the lute stir and quiver and the notes began to trickle from it. She gripped it, willing it to be silent. The girl came to Yoshi's side and took his hand protectively. Yayoi wondered if they had grown up together, if the girl was a Princess like Aki.

Fuji shook her head. 'It will be safer hidden away too,' she said. 'Kai, dear, I've told you before not to hang around here with the monkeys. Go back to your own place. I'm sure you have plenty of chores there.'

'I wish I could stay here,' Kai replied.

'What nonsense! Girls are never acrobats. Be thankful the musicians took you in.'

Fuji helped Yayoi into the palanquin which rested on the ground outside the rear gate, the porters, two strong young men, beside it. They both bowed respectfully to Fuji who gave them directions in a quick, low voice before she climbed in next to Yayoi and let down the bamboo blinds.

She heard the women call, 'Goodbye! Goodbye! Take care of yourself.'

'Goodbye, Takemaru,' Yayoi whispered.

•

The lute quietened as the men jogged and the palanquin swayed. The stuffy heat and the motion made Yayoi sleepy and she nodded off several times, dreaming in brief lucid snatches, then jolting suddenly awake. She could see nothing outside, only had the sensation of moving from light into shade, splashing through water, then going up a steep hill, the palanquin wobbling alarmingly as the men negotiated the steps. Finally, the palanquin was set down. Fuji raised the blind and stepped out.

Yayoi followed her, glad to breathe the cool mountain air. Below her, framed by twisted pine trees, lay Lake Kasumi. She could see smoke rising from the villages round its edge and the tiny sails of boats, gleaming yellow in the sun. Behind her a bell tolled. It must be midday.

'This is a temple for women,' Fuji said. 'I have sent a few girls here to be looked after, until they are old enough.'

Old enough for what? Yayoi wondered, her mind shying away from the answer. She concentrated on what was around her: the vermilion wooden gate, the flowering mountain cherries, the steps that led upwards beneath pines that curved over them like a dark tunnel.

Fuji began to climb them swiftly. Yayoi had to trot to keep up with her. The stones were set too high for a child and, by the time they reached the top, her legs ached. Someone must have been told of their arrival for at the top of the steps a nun was waiting to greet them. Behind her was a garden, with a spring that filled a cistern, then overflowed and ran trickling away from them into a large fish pond.

'Our Abbess asks that you will take some refreshment with her.' She looked at Yayoi with cool, unfriendly eyes. 'You have another foundling for us to look after?'

'She is called Yayoi,' Fuji said. 'I would prefer as few people as possible to know she is here. It will not be for long.'

'No,' the nun agreed, her eyes appraising Yayoi's height and age. 'I suppose she can join the other girls in prayer and study.' She turned and began to walk towards a low building at the side of the temple. Its roof was curved at each end in an upward swoop, like wings, as if it would take flight at any moment.

The nun paused and said to Fuji, 'Asagao will want to see you. She can be this girl's friend. They are about the same age.' She clapped her hands.

A girl came from the building and dropped to her knees before Fuji, who stepped forward to take her hands and lift her to her feet. She looked carefully at her, much as the nun had studied Yayoi. The girl blushed. Yayoi thought her very pretty.

'Lady Fuji,' Asagao said. 'I am so happy. I missed you so much.'

'Sweet child, I have brought someone to be your friend. Please take care of her for me.'

'Go with her to the girls' room and show her where everything is,' the nun said. 'Give me your things. Well, well, what have you brought with you? An old lute and an even older text? The lute will be useful, but you won't need the text here. Don't worry, we will keep it safe for you. When you leave, you may take it with you.'

'Reverend Nun, may we walk a little way with you and Lady Fuji?' Asagao pleaded.

She had an enchanting manner and the nun was charmed. 'Very well, since it is so long since you have seen your benefactress. Just as far as the fish pond.'

Red and white carp swam peacefully in the large stone basin, beneath lotus leaves, from which the flower stems were just beginning to emerge.

'See how the red and the white can live together?' Asagao said. 'Why is our world so torn by war?'

Fuji smiled. 'You are very poetic, my dear. I can see you have been learning well. But it is best not to speak of the red and the white. As far as the Miboshi are concerned, there are now only the white.'

'Yet in this pond the white are outnumbered by the red,' Asagao said, so quietly only Yayoi heard. She wondered what her story was and how she had ended up under Fuji's protection. The two older women walked on and the girls were left alone.

•

Over the next few days she was able to learn more about Asagao and the other girls. Their ages ranged from six to fourteen. The oldest was gentle, rather tall, as slender as a reed and seemed shy and younger than her age. Her name was Yuri. The next oldest was Asagao, who was born the year before Yayoi. Then there were two sisters, so close in age they looked like twins, with red cheeks and a stocky plumpness that the meagre food at the temple did nothing to diminish. They were ten and nine years old and were called Sada and Sen. The youngest, the six year old, was Teru, a thin, wiry little girl who reminded Yayoi of the monkey acrobat children. She wondered if she was of the same family and if so why she had been sent away to the temple.

She mentioned this to Asagao one night as they were preparing for bed. The older girls helped the younger ones, combing their hair, hanging their day clothes on the racks. Teru had fallen asleep while Yayoi was smoothing out the wrinkles from her robe. Yuri was at the far end of the room, singing quietly to Sada and Sen who were already lying curled together. Her voice sounded thin and mournful. The plum rains had begun and everything was damp. The water fell in a steady cascade from the roofs, drowning all other sound. In the dim days, the girls became both febrile and depressed.

'Lady Fuji probably bought her from her family,' Asagao said. 'Many parents have no choice. Daughters fetch a good price. Everyone wants girls these days.'

'Is that what happened to you?' Yayoi was ashamed of asking so directly, but could not control her curiosity.

'My mother was one of Lady Fuji's entertainers,' Asagao whispered. 'I am not meant to speak of it, but I want to tell you. My father was a Kakizuki warrior. They fell in love, he bought her freedom and took her to his house in Miyako. Women on the boats don't have children – you will find out, I suppose – so I was lucky to be born at all. When the capital fell to the Miboshi, my father did not flee with the Kakizuki, but sent me to Lady Fuji, and killed my mother and himself.'

'How horrible, how sad,' Yayoi murmured, wondering how Asagao could still grow up so pretty and so charming.

'I think you would find all the women on the boats are the same these days,' Asagao said. 'They all hide tragic stories of loss and grief beneath the songs and the smiles.'

She stroked Yayoi's cheek. 'I am sure we will be friends.'

At that moment Yayoi wanted nothing more. 'Let's be friends forever,' she said, seizing Asagao's hand and pressing it.

•

The following morning Reverend Nun came into the room where the girls were practising serving tea and other drinks, with water in the place of wine, taking turns to be the male guest and the female entertainer. Playing the role of the men made the two sisters giggle uncontrollably, and Sada, in particular, proved extremely inventive in portraying drunken behaviour. Asagao was equally gifted as the entertainer, distracting and calming the guests with songs and dances. They did not have to pretend to be in love with her. Even Reverend Nun watched for a few moments, her face softening. Then she recollected why she had come and said, 'Yayoi, our reverend Abbess wishes to see you.'

This message was obviously shocking to the other girls, who all stopped what they were doing and stared open-mouthed. Sada broke off in mid sentence and began to hiccup for real. Reverend Nun gave her a disapproving look. 'Perhaps this role play is becoming a little too realistic. Asagao, put away the bedding. The rest of you can do your dance practice now with Yuri. Come, Yayoi.'

The cloisters that linked the buildings around the main hall were flooded and rain poured down on each side. It was exhilarating, like running through a waterfall. Yayoi found she was stamping deliberately in puddles, as if she were a little girl again, playing with her brother, Tsumaru, and Kaze and Chika, the children of Tsumaru's nurse.

'Walk properly,' Reverend Nun scolded her, when one unexpectedly deep puddle sent water splashing up her legs.

At the end of the cloister stood a small detached residence, not much more than a hut. On the narrow verandah a ginger-coloured cat sat with its paws tucked under it, looking morose. The hut was old and weather beaten; the bamboo blinds over the doorway hung crookedly and were black with mould. One of the steps was broken and there were several boards missing from the walls and shingles from the roof.

'Did you say the Abbess wanted to see me?' Yayoi said doubtfully.

'Yes – don't ask me why! She has never asked to see any of the girls before. It is most unusual.'

'And she lives here?'

'Our Abbess is an unworldly woman. She does not concern herself with material things. She chose this hut as her abode when she took over the headship of our community. She agreed to it only if she was permitted to live in this way, as humbly as the poorest peasant. The former Abbess was very different, very different. We all miss her.'

Yayoi was hoping Reverend Nun would expound more on the former Abbess, who sounded interesting, but at that moment a voice called from inside.

'Send the child in.'

Yayoi stepped up onto the verandah, avoiding the broken step, and pushed aside the bamboo blind. Gloomy as the day was, it was even darker inside, though one small oil lamp burned in front of a statue that Yayoi recognised, when her eyes adjusted to the dimness, as the horse-headed Kannon. A flowering branch had been placed in front of it and the sweet smell filled the room, mingling with incense, and not quite concealing the whiff of dampness and mould.

'Come here. I am told your name is Yayoi.' The woman stretched out a pale hand and beckoned to Yayoi to approach. Her head was shaved and her skull gleamed in the light, as if it were carved from ivory. Her features were ordinary, snub nose, wide mouth, small, rather close-set eyes, and her build, though not at all fat, was solid. She wore a simple robe, dyed a deep maroon. Her feet were tucked under her, reminding Yayoi of the cat outside.

Yayoi saw the Kudzu Vine Treasure Store, lying on a shabby cushion beside the Abbess.

The older woman followed her gaze. 'You brought this with you. Can you read it?'

'I can read a little,' Yayoi said. 'But it often seems very difficult.'

'I should say it does!' The Abbess laughed, a surprisingly merry note. 'Many would call it the most difficult text in the world, if they were lucky enough to get their hands on it. Do you mind telling me how it came into your possession?'

There was something about her that made Yayoi relax, as if the woman were a relative, an old aunt or a grandmother, neither of whom Yayoi had ever known. She knelt down on the cushion, moving the text aside, happy to feel its familiar touch beneath her hand.

'An old man gave it to me. I was interested in plants and healing when I was little. I used to brew up potions from dandelion, burdock roots, charcoal, and try to get the dogs and cats to drink them, when they were sick. Master . . . he, the old man, came upon me one day and asked me seriously about my ingredients and measurements and if I was keeping records of the results. Later he gave me the Kudzu Vine Treasure Store and said I would find many cures in it, but I haven't got to that bit yet.' She hesitated for a moment and then said confidingly, 'It only lets me read certain parts.'

'Oh yes,' said the Abbess. 'It is a text of great power but I can see it would be tricky. This old man, can you tell me his name?'

'Master Sesshin,' Yayoi said, and immediately wished she had not.

'Don't be afraid,' the Abbess said. 'Only truth is spoken in this hut. Truth is what I seek: true thought, true sight, true speech. This Master Sesshin, what kind of a person was he?'

'He had a lot of books. He lived in my father's house, I don't know why, but for as long as I can remember he was there. Even when my mother was alive, before Lady Tama . . .' She recalled her stepmother's cruelty and fell silent.

'What is it that Lady Tama did?' the Abbess prompted.

'She had his eyes put out,' Yayoi whispered, 'and she drove him away, into the Darkwood.'

'Poor man,' said the Abbess. 'And poor Lady Tama who has added such darkness to her life. Was she your father's second wife?'

'My mother died when I was very young,' Yayoi said. 'My grandfather took Lady Tama from her husband, my uncle, and made my father marry her.'

'Ah, what trouble these old men cause with their attempts to control everything! If only they could foresee the ripples that go on through generations!' The Abbess said nothing more for a few moments but took Yayoi's hand and stroked it gently.

'My husband died,' she said finally. 'I was still a young woman, and we had one son. I had been married at my father's command. I had not seen my husband previously. But I came to adore him, and he me, I believe. He died in the north. After his death, his brother begged me to marry him and swore he would preserve the estate for my son, but my grief was so great I could not bear to look at either of them, for they both resembled my dead husband. I chose to leave my son in his uncle's care and I renounced the binding ties of love and affection. I wanted to know the truth of this treacherous cruel world, and why humans have to live lives filled with such deep pain.'

'Did you find any answers?' Yayoi asked.

'In a way. We worship the goddess of healing and compassion here and she has helped me. But I missed my son terribly and when I was told he had died in the mountains my pain was no less intense than it had been for his father.'

A long silence followed.

'What am I to do here?' Yayoi asked, not knowing how to respond to the Abbess's disclosures. She thought of her own uncle, her own mother and father. Why were some forced to die and others permitted to live? Where did the dead go? Did they still see all that took place on Earth? How could they watch those they loved and not grieve over them and long to be with them? Why did their spirits not return more often?

'Lady Fuji has asked us to take care of you and teach you all you need to know. We do this for several girls she has sent to us. In return, she pays for the upkeep of our temple, our food and so on. And she protects us. She has many powerful friends. There are not a few, these days, who are offended at the idea of women running their own affairs. They would like to impose a male priest to keep an eye on us. Times are changing, my dear Yayoi; even in this remote place we can sense it. The Miboshi are warriors, not swayed by gentler pursuits as the Kakizuki were.'

'Can I stay here, always?' Yayoi said. She did not want to be reminded of the power struggles in the capital in which her father had died.

The Abbess said gently, 'I'm afraid Lady Fuji has other plans for you. We try to give the girls skills, both physical and spiritual, so they may live the best life they can. I see you can read and write, but do you know how to calculate?'

Yayoi shook her head.

'Well, I will teach you that. And you will come to me once a week and we will read your text together.'

•

'What did she say to you?' Asagao asked jealously. 'None of us has ever been sent for. What is she like?'

Yayoi had returned to the girls' room, puzzled by the conversation with the Abbess. Asagao was alone; the other girls were dancing in the exercise hall. Asagao had been told to put away the bedding, after which she was supposed to sweep the floor, but she was still lying on one of the mats, the broom abandoned at her side. Her face was flushed, her sash loosened.

'I am to learn to calculate,' Yayoi replied. She did not want to speak about the Kudzu Vine Treasure Store.

'Why? Are they going to marry you to a merchant?' Asagao giggled. 'You will be totting up how much rice you have sold and working out the value of the bean harvest. What a waste of a beautiful girl!'

'The Abbess will be giving me lessons herself,' Yayoi said.

Asagao pouted. 'You are going to be everyone's favourite. I shall be jealous. But what was the Abbess like?'

'She is rather like a cat. In fact she has a cat, a ginger one. She is merry and playful but you feel she might scratch at any time.' Yayoi looked at Asagao sprawled on the mat, saw the translucent white of her skin. 'Hadn't you better hurry up? Reverend Nun will be angry if she catches you with the bedding not put away and the floor unswept.'

'I have been practising for my first time.' Asagao giggled again. 'I can't help myself. It's so much fun. Yuri showed me. You know she is leaving soon? Here, I'll show you. Lie down and we'll pretend I'm your merchant husband.'

Yayoi's heart was beating fast, with a kind of terror. She could not put it into words, but she suddenly saw her future. She turned and ran from Asagao, ran from the room, out into the garden. Her eyes were filling with tears. She came to the top of the steps. Where would she go, if she did run away? The choices seemed stark. She could stay where she was, and hand control of her life and her body over to these others, or she could die. By this time sobs were shaking her. She crouched down, her head in her hands. She did not want to die. But she did not want to go where they intended she should either.

She heard someone behind her, and Asagao put her arms round her.

'Don't cry,' the other girl soothed her. 'Don't cry. I'm sorry I upset you. Our lives may be hard, but they will have pleasures too. Maybe you are too young to understand now, but one day you will. And we will always be friends, I promise you.'

They heard the Reverend Nun calling them.

'I suppose I had better finish the floor,' Asagao said.

2

BARA

A little way from the capital while they could still smell the smoke from the fires at Ryusonji, the fugitives, Shikanoko and the Burnt Twins, paused in their flight at a remote temple. Eisei insisted they bury the Autumn Princess though Nagatomo thought Shikanoko, numbed and silenced by grief, would have ridden on with her dead body until he too passed away. The temple was neglected and the monks, whom Eisei knew, were reluctant and taciturn, yet Nagatomo thought he would not mind it as a final resting place, against the side of the mountain, looking out over the narrow valley where the flooded fields reflected the bamboo groves and the clouds and the wind sighed in the cedars. The funeral was hasty, with little ceremony. The lord, as Nagatomo called Shikanoko in his mind, stayed with the horses, watching from a distance.

Nagatomo thought someone else watched too. In the next few days he was aware a woman was following them. The horses knew she was there; the foal frequently turned with pricked ears and alert eyes, staring back the way they had come, until its mother called in her fretful, anxious way. The lord did not notice. He noticed nothing.

'It's just a coincidence,' Eisei said, when Nagatomo mentioned her. 'She is on a pilgrimage or going home to her birthplace.'

'Travelling alone?' Nagatomo replied. 'And who goes into the Darkwood on a pilgrimage?'

The great pilgrim routes all lay to the south. There were no sacred shrines or temples, and no villages, in the huge forest that spread all the way to the Northern Sea. Apart from the occasional hermit, no humans dwelt there, just wild animals, deer, bears, wolves, monkeys, and, it was said, tengu – mountain goblins – as well as huge magic snakes and other supernatural beings.

When they stopped to eat and sleep – though Nagatomo knew the lord did neither – the woman hid herself. She lit no fire; he wondered what she ate, who she was, what she wanted from them.

The rain had lessened to a steady drizzle, but the trees still dripped heavily and the streams and rivers spread out, drowning the path. The fake wolf jumped from rock to rock. It did not like getting wet. The horses waded through water up to their hocks. The lord rode the silver white stallion, Nyorin, and Nagatomo and Eisei doubled up on the mare, Risu, though both preferred to walk. The mare was bad tempered and ill mannered, and bucked and bit, without provocation. The foal was still nursing and the mare stopped dead whenever it demanded the teat.

At night they removed the black silk coverings they both wore and caressed each other's ruined faces. It did not matter, then, that no one else would ever look on them with desire again or understand the terror and agony as the mask seared away skin and flesh. They were the Burnt Twins. They had found each other.

Only the lord could wear the mask. Nagatomo knew it had been made for him in a secret ritual by a mountain sorcerer. Usually it was kept in a seven-layered brocade bag to be taken out when the lord walked between the worlds and talked to the dead. But now, on the journey into the Darkwood, he wore it day and night. The polished skull bone, the cinnabar lips and tongue, the antlers, one broken, the black-fringed eye sockets through which glistened the unending tears, transformed him into a different creature.

'He cannot take it off,' Nagatomo whispered to Eisei.

'Cannot or will not?'

'It is fused to his face in some way.'

'It must be because of what happened at Ryusonji,' Eisei said, as if he had been thinking about it over and over. 'The dragon child was awakened, my former master destroyed. Finding that overwhelming power, and releasing it, came at a price.'

'Has it burned him?' Nagatomo wondered aloud. 'As it did us?'

'He does not seem to be in pain,' Eisei replied. 'Not physical pain,' he added, after a long pause.

Mid-afternoon on the fourth or fifth day – he was beginning to lose count; every day was the same: steep gorges, flooding rivers, huge boulders, the wild cries of kites in the day and owls at night, the humid air that made them sweat profusely until just before dawn when they shivered in their sodden clothes – Nagatomo noticed the woman was no longer following. The foal had been restless, trotting back along the track, almost as if it were trying to attract his attention, making its mother baulk and neigh piercingly after it.

The lord was far in front, Gen, the fake wolf, close to the stallion's heels, as always. Eisei pulled on the mare's bridle, yelling at her.

'I'll catch up with you,' Nagatomo said, and began to walk back the way they had come. The foal whickered at him. It was uncanny how intelligent it was; often it seemed on the point of speaking in a human voice. It trotted confidently ahead of him.

He told himself he was being a fool, trailing after a horse. As Eisei said, it was just a coincidence; she had not been following them and, even if she had, he should be relieved she no longer was.

After Ryusonji the lord was a hunted man, an outlaw. Any one of Aritomo's retainers might be on their trail, hoping to win the Minatogura Lord's favour as well as great rewards. Maybe it was not a woman, at all, but a warrior in disguise. Maybe it was a mountain sorcerer or a witch.

But the foal knew her. He was certain of that.

How long was it since he had last been aware of her? He could not be sure. There was no way of knowing exactly what hour it was, with the sun hidden all day behind dense cloud. He was hungry enough for it to be almost evening, but he had been hungry since he woke and the sparse dried meat and unripe yams had done little to fill his stomach. He walked for what seemed like a long time. The mare's cries grew fainter, and then he could no longer hear her, at all, but the foal still trotted forward, stopping at every bend to check if Nagatomo was following.

The woman was sitting on a rock by the track, her head low, her face buried in her arms, her hands bound together in front of her. She did not move at their approach but, when the foal nuzzled her, she put out her tied hands and pulled its head close to her. It allowed her to embrace it for a few moments, breathing out heavily. Then it nudged her more insistently. She raised her head slowly and looked at Nagatomo.

Her face was streaked with tears, her eyes and lips swollen with grief. He thought he must be an alarming sight, with the black face covering and his long sword and knife, but she showed no fear. In fact she looked as if grief had consumed her and left no room for any other emotion.

He started to speak, but at that moment the foal squealed and leaped backwards. The woman, as she fell, looked beyond Nagatomo, and he, forewarned by something in her eyes, had drawn his sword in an instant and turned to face his attackers.

One called, 'Are you Kumayama no Kazumaru, known as Shikanoko, wanted for murder and rebellion?'

'Come and find out,' Nagatomo said. He was assessing them quickly. They had emerged from the forest, while he was distracted by the woman. How long had they been following them? Was she one of them, part of the trap? The foal whinnied and horses neighed in reply. The men wore crests of three pine trees on their jackets, and held swords, but they did not appear to have bows.

'It is he,' the second man said. 'He covers his face to hide the demon mask.'

'There should be three horses,' the first said, hesitating for one fatal moment, during which Nagatomo flew at him, flicking the man's sword from his hand with a twist of his own and with the returning stroke slicing him through the neck. The blood spurted from the opened artery, and the foal screamed like a human.

The second man, his eyes dark with shock, took a step back, gripping his sword. He was more prepared and, Nagatomo guessed, a better swordsman. He and Nagatomo circled each other, assessing stance, grip, weapon. Nagatomo's sword was longer and heavier. It gave him more reach, but his opponent's lighter blade gave its owner greater speed and flexibility. The other man was fitter, and probably better fed. Nagatomo wondered about him briefly, where he was from, what his name was, what fate had led them to encounter each other in the Darkwood, one evening in summer. Then he thought of nothing, as his enemy thrust at him and he began to fight for his life.

It had started to rain again and the ground was becoming slippery. For a long time they exchanged blows, parrying and ducking, grunting with exertion, now and then uttering cries of hatred. Nagatomo was slowly forcing the other back towards the stream, which was spilling over its banks and flooding onto the track. The water splashed round their ankles, hiding roots and holes, and one of these was his opponent's undoing. His foot slipped into it, he stumbled and dropped his guard.

Nagatomo rushed forward, the point of his sword entering the man's throat and coming out the other side, skewering him. The force of the blow threw the dying man backwards into the water, his blood streaking the surface briefly, before becoming lost in the murky current.

Nagatomo put one foot on the man's chest, to pull out his weapon. Bubbles burst from the mouth and the wound. For a moment he thought the sword was stuck but then it came free. His opponent's mouth under the water went slack and air no longer came from it, though blood did.

He staggered back to the bank, gasping for breath and trembling as the tension ebbed from his limbs. Elation seized him. He was not dead; his attackers were. He saw life and death, side by side, in their raw simplicity.

The foal came docilely to his side and sniffed at the man's legs. They looked foolish, half covered by water. Nagatomo wanted to laugh; he wanted to embrace the foal. He gave it a thump on its hindquarters and turned to face the woman.

She was on her feet, her eyes fixed on him. He had hardly had time to look at her before. Now he studied her as he walked rapidly towards her, his eyes flicking over the undergrowth behind her in case there were any more men hidden there.

He stopped a few paces from her. She was tall, only a little shorter than he was, and large boned. Her face was tanned dark by the sun, her nose flat, her mouth wide. Her hair was covered by a sedge hat tied down by a scarf, but he guessed it would be as coarse as a horse's mane. It angered him irrationally that even a woman like this would never look on him with love or desire and for that reason, or maybe because he suspected she had been in league with his attackers, he addressed her roughly.

'So you thought to entice me into an ambush? Your companions are dead. Who are you and why are you following us? Answer me truthfully or I'll send you to join them in the next world.'

'They are no companions of mine,' she said angrily. 'They wear the crest of Matsutani – that means they serve Masachika. I was following the horses, and have been for weeks, ever since they were taken from Nishimi, when Masachika captured the Princess. I waited at Ryusonji. I saw you leave and watched you bury her. Then, when I realised Masachika's men were also on your trail, I stopped. I didn't want to lead them to you. I thought I might distract them, while you vanished beyond their reach.'

'And did you?' he said, unable to keep contempt from his voice.

'I think they were saving me for later,' she said, without emotion. 'That's why they tied me up.' She held out her hands; he sheathed his sword, took out his knife and cut the cords. The foal gave a low whinny and, when her hands were free, she embraced it, as Nagatomo had wanted to earlier.

'Dear Tan,' she said. 'I never thought I would see you again.'

'Tan?' he questioned. They had never given it a name; it was just called *the foal*.

'It's what my lady called him because when he was born he was as dark as coal. His coat is lightening now just as Saburo said it would.' Her eyes filled with tears.

Nagatomo felt a perverse pang of jealousy. She was weeping for someone, in a way no one ever would for him. 'So why follow us in the first place? You have not answered me.'

'My name is Ibara. I have a favour to ask of you,' she said, hesitant. 'I am sorry, I know a woman like me should not speak so directly to a great warrior like yourself, but I am beyond caring about all that now.'

One of the horses neighed from the grove.

'We should ride on,' Nagatomo said. 'Wait here while I get their horses. We will talk further as we ride.'

The two horses were tethered beneath an oak tree. They laid back their ears at his approach and swung their haunches towards him, as though they would kick him, but the foal came barging through and its presence seemed to calm them. He untied them and led them back to the track, where he stripped the corpses of their clothes and footwear and gathered up the weapons, using one of the tethering cords to tie them into a bundle and strap them behind the saddle. Then he helped the woman mount one of the horses and, still holding its reins, leaped nimbly on to the back of the other.

'They are good horses,' he exclaimed.

'Masachika is a rich man, now,' the woman replied. 'The body of the Princess gained him many rewards.'

'I imagine the favour you mean to ask is that we should kill him,' Nagatomo said.

'Not exactly. I want you to teach me to fight with the sword, so I can kill him myself.'

There was a clap of thunder and the rain began to fall more heavily.

It was nearly dusk when they caught up with Eisei who had taken shelter beneath a rocky overhang, where the stream emerged from between steep cliffs. It offered some protection from the direct rain but the walls and the boulders on the ground were dank with moisture. Further back, a kind of low cave extended beneath the cliff, where the ground at least was dry.

'You can sleep here,' Nagatomo told the woman, ignoring Eisei's disapproving look.

'Surely the lord . . .' she began.

'He will not sleep or seek shelter. We will take it in turns to keep watch.'

'Where is he?' she said, gazing out at the rainy darkness.

Nagatomo looked at Eisei who made a small movement with his shoulders and said, 'Somewhere. Not far away, I think.'

'What is wrong with him?' she said in a hesitant voice.

'He loved the Princess. She died,' Eisei said curtly.

'He wants to die too,' the woman said, partly to herself. 'I know that feeling.' And then, even more quietly, so only Nagatomo heard her, 'But we will see Masachika dead first.'

•

The horses were restless all night, upset by the two new stallions who, excited by the presence of the mare, challenged Nyorin with loud calls. Bara hardly slept and, when she did, the dead talked to her in muffled voices and wrote messages she could not read. At dawn, she crawled from the cave and went towards the bushes. The man who had rescued her was asleep on his back. The other, the monk, was tending the smoky fire. Both had removed their face coverings and, after one shocked glance, she averted her gaze.

The monk did not look at her but, as she walked past, said, 'See if you can find some dry wood.'

'I will,' she replied.

It had stopped raining and there were patches of blue sky overhead between the pink- and orange-tinged clouds. The foal came up to her eagerly and followed her through the undergrowth. Then it went ahead, while she squatted to relieve herself, turning back, when she stood, to whicker at her. The mare responded in the distance with an anxious neigh.

Bara walked after it. To her right, she could hear the endless babbling of the stream as it rushed over rocks and through pools.

On her left, the forest rose in a steep slope, thick with trees she did not recognise, apart from maples. She had grown up in the port city of Akashi and then had worked in the house in Miyako, and the Nishimi palace, on the shores of the lake. Everything here alarmed her – the strange bird calls, the half-seen creatures that slithered away, the darkness between the trees that seemed to stretch away forever, the uncanny dappled circles where the sunlight shot through.

The ground was still sodden but there were plenty of dead branches on tree trunks that she could reach easily and she was breaking these off and making a bundle in her left arm, when the foal, which had been walking ahead of her, stopped dead and snorted through its nose.

Pushing past it, she in turn halted suddenly. In the path stood the animal that she had noticed following the horses. She had thought it was a dog, but it did not look like any dog she had ever seen. Perhaps it was a wolf. Close up it did not seem quite real. Its eyes were as hard as gemstones and its movements awkward. The idea came to her that she was dreaming; she had fallen asleep, after all; she could almost feel the rocky floor of the cave beneath her. She struggled to wake. The wolf curled its painted lips, showing its carved teeth and its man-like tongue.

'Gen!' a low voice called, as if it were an angel or a demon, making a pronouncement. Shivers ran down her backbone. 'Gen!'

The wolf seemed to sigh as it retreated. She went forward slowly, Tan's nose in her back, pushing her on.

She saw the head first and thought she had come upon a stag. The antlers, one broken, were lit up by the morning sun. Then she realised it was a man wearing a mask. She recognised the shape; it matched exactly the pattern of the burns on the other men's faces. It covered three-quarters of his face, leaving his chin free. Through the sockets she could see his eyes, so black the iris and the pupil merged.

He had been sitting, his legs folded beneath him, but he stood as she approached. The antlers gave him added height and he seemed, to her, like some spirit of the forest, half-man, half-deer. He reminded her of the dancers at the summer festivals of her childhood. In Akashi they had danced the heron dance, wearing beaked and feathered headdresses. In that garb, the men had become protective, chaste, quite unlike their usual truculent, predatory selves.

She felt no fear now, only pity, for, somehow, she recognised a grief as deep as her own.

He did not speak to her but addressed the foal.

'Who is this my lord has brought to me?'

She recognised the sword he wore at his hip – it was the sword the Princess had left in the shrine at Nishimi, as an offering to the lake goddess. He also bore a rattan bow and a quiver on his back, filled with arrows fletched with black feathers. She could see traces of cobwebs spun between them. It was a long time since they had been disturbed.

The foal nudged her, pushing her forward. She fell to her knees and said, 'My name is Bara, but now I call myself Ibara. I was at Nishimi when the Princess came, with the horses and with that sword you wear.'

A stillness came over him, like a deer after the first startle. She was afraid he was going to leap away and disappear into the forest but, then, a long shudder ran through him and he sank to his knees in front of her.

'With Jato?' he touched its hilt briefly.

'If that is its name. The last time I saw it was before the altar in the shrine.'

'Masachika must have taken it. It was made for me but he had it at Matsutani. I took it back from him.'

'You should have killed him then,' Ibara said. 'Swords return for a purpose.'

He did not respond to this but said, 'Tell me what happened at Nishimi.'

She could see him more clearly now. How young he was! She had formed a picture of an older man, for that was what the word *lord* suggested to her. But he was not much more than a boy. How had he destroyed the Prince Abbot, in an act of such power the temple at Ryusonji had burned to the ground?

He loved the Princess. She died. His mouth had the same shape as little Take's, and his long fingers too. Tears welled in her eyes.

'Akihime came to Nishimi, with Risu and Nyorin. Yukikuni no Takaakira employed me to look after Lady Hina. Hina knew the horses, she knew their names.'

'Hina?' the lord said wonderingly. 'Lord Kiyoyori's daughter?' and the foal came closer, nodding its head.

'I had no idea who Lady Hina was, other than that she was his ward and that he was secretive about her and didn't want anyone to know she was living with him. I guessed he'd saved her life. I would have done the same thing – anyone would. She was enchantingly pretty and so brave. She hid the Princess, and we pretended she had been rescued from the lake. After the baby was born Akihime worked in the kitchen. We thought no one would suspect her of being anything but a servant girl.'

'She had a child?' His lips were ashen.

'A son. She wanted him to be called Takeyoshi. Lady Hina often played with him and she was carrying him when Masachika came over the mountains from the west.' She halted abruptly. 'This is the bit I don't understand. For he came with Saburo.'

Tan gave a low whinny.

'Yes, Tan, Saburo, the man who saved your life at birth. He must have told Masachika that the Princess was at Nishimi, but I cannot believe he would betray her. And then Masachika killed him, stabbing him in the back.'

'Masachika often works as a spy,' the lord said. 'Your Saburo would not be the first to be deceived into trusting him.'

He laid one hand against the foal's neck. 'What happened to Hina?'

Ibara replied, 'She jumped into the water with the baby in her arms.'

Tears splashed on her arm and hand. The foal was weeping.

'What is this animal?' she cried, half-rising. 'How does it understand every word and why is it shedding tears like a human?'

The lord said quietly, 'The foal is a vessel for the spirit of Lord Kiyoyori, Hina's father.'

'The one who died at the side of the Crown Prince? How can that be possible?'

He looked at her. The bone mask allowed no expression apart from the eyes, but they seemed to open onto a world she did not know existed. She could not hold his gaze.

'Is it like rebirth?' she said after a long silence.

'Not quite. Lord Kiyoyori's spirit refused to cross the River of Death. A man who owed him an unthinkable debt took his place. I summoned the lord back. The mare was pregnant. His spirit took over the unborn foal.'

It might have been the wild claim of a man driven mad by grief, yet, if she accepted it, so many things made sense – the foal's devotion to Hina, its ability to understand human speech, its tears.

'I don't believe Lady Hina is dead,' she said, addressing the foal. 'There was a boat. I think they saved her and the baby. Don't grieve for her yet . . .' and then, deeply uncomfortable, she added, 'Lord.'

Accepting it was true gave her new hope. 'Why can't you summon the Princess back? Or Saburo? Summon him back into whatever shape you like. He died before we even held each other. I cannot stand it.' She was twisting her hands together frantically.

'I know,' he said and, for a moment, Ibara felt their deep grief unite them. Then he said bitterly, 'Don't think I haven't tried. Night after night, I attempt to walk again between the worlds and summon up the dead. But she is gone. Maybe she is in Paradise, maybe she is reborn, either way she is forever lost to me. Your Saburo must have died even earlier. He also will have crossed the last of the rivers that flow between this world and the next. I was given much power and taught many things, but I lay with her when I should not have done, and though together we destroyed the Prince Abbot, we did not escape punishment. She forfeited her life and I cannot remove the mask. I am condemned to live half-animal, half-human, belonging to neither world. I will go without food or sleep, until I follow her into the realm of the dead. Maybe there I can find forgiveness.'

'It is not forgiveness I seek,' Ibara said in a low voice. 'It is revenge.'

The foal gave a sharp neigh of encouragement.

How strange, she thought, *I am just a girl from Akashi, a servant, but my desire for revenge is stronger than this boy's, who was born a lord, brought up as a warrior.*

'No one is to blame for the Princess's death but myself,' he said. 'It is on myself that I am taking revenge.'

'The baby looks like you. He is your son, isn't he? Don't you want to find him?'

'Better he died in the water,' Shikanoko said, 'than grow up in this world of sorrow.'

3

MU

Three of the five boys who had been born from cocoons, Mu, Ima and Ku, had been left at the mountain hut all winter. Once a messenger had come from Shikanoko at Kumayama to check that they were still alive, but after that they heard nothing of him or their other brothers, Kiku and Kuro. At first they did not worry, living day to day without much thought, like animals, but when spring came Mu began to be plagued by restlessness and a sort of anxiety. He took to roaming through the Darkwood and it was there that he saw a foxes' wedding though at the time he did not know what it was. It was the third month, when showers chased sunshine. For several days he had been away from the hut, sleeping under the stars or in caves when it was too wet, feeling almost like a fox himself. One morning he was plucking young fern shoots, cramming the tender stems into his mouth, in one of the hidden clearings on the lower slopes of Kuroyama, when he heard curious noises, the soft padding of many feet and flute music, so high he could not tell if it was really music or the wind in the pine trees, and drums that might have been rain falling. He quickly climbed an oak tree and hid in the foliage, as a procession came into the clearing.

At first, he thought they were people, dressed in colourful clothes, walking upright, playing flutes and drums, but then he saw their pointed ears, their black-tipped snouts, their precise, delicate paws. A male and a female were carried on the shoulders of the largest foxes, who were the size of wolves. Like the music, they hovered between reality and imagination, filling him with an intense longing. He did not think they were aware of him, but, as they passed beneath the oak tree, one young female looked up and smiled in his direction, a smile that seemed to be an invitation into worlds he had not known existed.

The sun shone brilliantly on the short winter grass, only recently liberated from snow, starred with flowers, yellow aconites and celandines, white anemones. The bride and groom were lowered to the ground and stood facing each other. They joined hands – *paws*, Mu thought – as the flutes played even more sweetly and the drums more loudly. Then the sky darkened, sudden rain joined in the drumming, and, when Mu could see again, they had all disappeared, as if the shower had dissolved them.

When he came home his brothers, Kiku and Kuro, had returned and were crouched by the fire, silent and miserable. He felt a moment of relief as if his anxiety had been for them, but why had they come alone and why did they look like that? The youngest brother, Ku, was sitting near them, watching them with a troubled expression on his face, a bunch of puppies, as usual, crawling over him and tumbling round him. The fourth boy, Ima, was tending a pot in which a stew of spring shoots was simmering along with some sort of meat.

Ima scooped broth into wooden bowls and offered them to Kiku and Kuro. Kuro took one and drank without a word, but Kiku refused with a gesture that made Mu's heart sink.

'What's happened?' he said.

'Shikanoko . . .' Kuro began.

'Don't you dare speak!' Kiku shouted. 'It was all your fault!' He hit Kuro over the shoulders so violently the soup flew from the bowl, scalding Kuro's face and hands. Kuro swore, grabbed a smouldering stick from the fire and thrust it towards Kiku's face.

'Stop it, stop it!' Mu cried. 'What happened to Shikanoko? He's not dead?'

'He might as well be,' Kiku said angrily. 'He has sent us away. He never wants to see us again. It was all Kuro's stupid fault. I told him to leave all his creatures behind. But he had to bring the deadliest one.'

'The snake? The snake bit someone?' Mu said.

'Only a woman.' Kuro tried to defend himself.

'Only a woman?' Kiku repeated. 'The woman we were meant to rescue, the Autumn Princess, the woman Shika loved.'

'I don't understand that,' Kuro muttered. 'I don't know what *love* means.'

'I'm not sure I do either,' Kiku admitted.

Mu thought of the fox girl and how her look had transfixed him. *Do I love her?* he wondered.

'Shika felt something for her,' Kiku tried to explain. 'An emotion so strong her death destroyed him. He has turned us away, our older brother, our father, the only one who cared for us, who brought us up.' He said all this in a bewildered voice as though, for the first time in his life, he himself was feeling some strong emotion. He brushed his hand against his eyes. 'What is this? Is it the smoke making my eyes water?'

Tears were staining his cheeks. Mu could not remember ever seeing him cry, not even when the rest of them had wept after Shisoku died. 'Where has Shika gone?' he said.

Kiku sniffed. 'He rode away into the Darkwood, with Gen, three horses, and two men with burnt faces. He performed an act of great magic and defeated the priest. He raised a dragon child from the lake. You should have seen it, Mu, it was magnificent. Balls of lightning everywhere, a roaring like you've never heard. The priest dissolved in fire.'

'Tell Mu about the price Shika paid,' Kuro said. 'Tell him about the mask.'

'The stag mask he uses,' Kiku said. 'It stuck to his face. It cannot be taken off. Now he is half-man and half-deer.'

'Is that so bad?' Mu asked, wishing he could be half-fox.

'It would not matter if he had stayed with us,' Kiku gestured towards the fake animals that the old mountain sorcerer Shisoku had created from skins and skeletons. 'He would have fitted in perfectly here. Or he could still have been a warlord like he intended. He would have been all the more terrifying. He did not need to send us away. He could have achieved anything he wanted with our help. Look what we have done for him so far! He would never have got the better of that monk, Gessho, or taken his old home back from his uncle.'

'It was my bee that killed the uncle,' Kuro added proudly.

'And then getting into Ryusonji,' Kiku continued. 'It's a shame about the Princess – my eyes are doing that strange thing again. Why is your fire so smoky, Ima? – but the Prince Abbot was destroyed. Shika could have done none of those things without us.'

At that moment one of the fake wolves gave a long muffled howl and fell over with a thump. Ku pushed away the pile of dogs that surrounded him and ran to it. The puppies yelped and snarled at it in playful attacks but it did not move. The other boys stared at it.

'It's dead,' Ku said.

'It was never really alive.' Kuro moved towards it and knelt beside it, pushing the puppies away. He looked up at Kiku. 'Whatever power was holding it together has left it.'

Kiku looked wildly around at the other fake animals, making no effort now to control his tears. Mu followed his gaze. He realised what he had not noticed before: Shisoku's creations were winding down, fading in some way. Regret stabbed him. He also felt his eyes water. Why hadn't he looked after them better?

A crow plummeted from the branch it had been perched on and lay broken and silent on the ground, its borrowed feathers scattered by the breeze.

'No!' Kiku sobbed.

'You never liked them much, anyway,' Mu said, surprised at his apparent sorrow.

'I hate them,' Kiku replied, controlling himself with an effort. 'But they are breaking down before I've had a chance to learn how they work, how to make them. How did Shisoku get them to move, to live to the extent they did? How did he and Shika make the mask? What would he have done with the monk's skull that we buried? And the horse's? I need to learn all these things, and now there is no one to teach me.'

'What's going to happen to us?' Ima said, suddenly anxious.

Kuro said, 'The old man Sesshin . . .'

Mu started at the name. 'He is one of our fathers. The only one still alive, apart from Shika.'

'Well, he told Shika to kill us. He called us imps. My snake was meant to bite him!'

'He must know some sorcery,' Kiku said.

'He gave all his power away to Shika,' Kuro said. 'I heard the torturers tell the Abbot Prince.'

'Prince Abbot,' Kiku corrected him.

'Whatever, he is gone.' Kuro stood up. 'But wasn't the dragon superb? If only I could learn to summon one up like that.'

'Well, you won't now,' Kiku retorted. 'Because Shika is never going to want to see you again.'

They looked wildly at each other. They were all crying now, even Kuro.

What will become of us? Mu thought. *There is no one in the world who cares about us.*

•

Over the next few weeks the boys sulked and squabbled as more of Shisoku's animals ran out of living force and fell to the ground. Mu wanted to burn them; they did not exactly decay like real animals but they gave out a strange smell, insects began to dwell in the hides and maggots hatched. The corpses heaved with a new movement that nauseated him. But Kiku would not allow it. He studied each one's unique make-up, committing to memory how they were put together, out of which materials.

He went through the hut, looking at, smelling, tasting the contents of all the flasks of potions and jars of incense and ointments that Shisoku had concocted or collected. The sorcerer had kept records in an arcane script, which none of them could read, but Kiku searched out every object of power, every amulet and statue and figurine. He knew their weight and what they were made from, but he did not know how to use them for his own ends. That did not stop him trying everything out, experimenting fearlessly.

Sometimes he raved uncontrollably about visions and deep insights, sometimes he seemed to work magic by accident. Once he threw up so violently and for so long the others thought he was dying.

He gathered the remains of the werehawk, from where they still lay on the roof, and made a necklace from the beak and talons. He dug up the horse's skull. Worms and insects had done their work and the flesh was stripped from the bone. The last remnants fell away when Kiku boiled the skull in an iron pot on the fire.

'You can't make a horse,' Mu said. 'Even Shisoku never made anything so large.'

'I want to make a mask like Shika's,' Kiku replied.

Mu had never seen the mask, only knew the seven-layered brocade bag in which it used to be kept, but Kiku had watched Shika wear it and had held it in his hands.

'I carried it,' he said, with a note of pride in his voice. 'He said he wanted to leave it behind, but I knew he didn't really, so I took it to him.'

He described it to Mu: the stag's skull, the antlers, one broken, the half-human, half-animal face with its carved features, smoothly lacquered and its cinnabar-reddened lips. But he did not know the ritual in which it had been created, months before the boys were born, the blending of the red and white essences of male and female.

When the horse head was reduced to gleaming bone, Kiku tried to shape it, but his chisel often slipped and the resulting skull pan was lopsided and jagged. He made a face mask from wood, carving out eye sockets and a mouth hole, and he and Kuro lacquered it without really knowing the method. The lacquer bubbled and cracked, as if it were diseased, and the result was monstrous, both laughable and sinister. When Kiku put it on, the dogs howled and ran to Ku, and two more fake animals lay down and did not get up again.

'It's useless,' Kiku said, taking the mask off and throwing it to the ground. 'It's ugly and it has no power.'

'It's only your first attempt,' Mu said. 'Imagine how many times Shisoku had to experiment and practise, before he got it right. And he was still making mistakes up to the time he died.'

'But he mostly knew what he was doing. He must have had so much knowledge,' Kiku said. 'Why do I have no one to teach me? Don't you ever feel it? That there is a huge part of our lives missing? Why is there no one like us? Where did they all go?' He sighed, and glanced around the clearing, his eyes falling on the dogs, cowering round his youngest brother. 'Maybe the skull has to come from something I kill myself.'

'No!' Ku said defiantly.

'A dog is too easy,' Mu added. 'It is not enough of a challenge for you.' He picked up the horse mask and set it on a pole near the hut. 'It'll make a good guard.'

The mask was not what Kiku had intended, yet it was not a complete failure, and some strange force had attached itself to it. At night they heard hoof beats and whinnying, and several times the post seemed to have moved by morning. Ima was fascinated by it. He patted the post and clicked his tongue at it when he went past, and brought offerings of fresh grass and water.

Weeks went by. Shikanoko did not return. Kiku continued his experiments. Kuro set about replacing his collection of poisonous creatures, and managed to capture another sparrow bee.

One morning Mu had gone with Ima to the stream to gather grass and check the fish traps. The boys were always hungry and, though they preferred meat to fish, fish were easier to get and more plentiful. The stream did not flood that spring and, in the deep pools, sweetfish hid in the shadows, while crabs could be found under every rock. Sometimes the traps would catch an eel, which was as rich and tasty as meat. They were both knee deep in the water, when they heard someone approaching. Neither of them had Kiku's acute hearing, but the sounds were unmistakable: a snapped twig, a dislodged stone and then a quickly muffled gasp as a foot slipped.

The two boys were out of the water and into the undergrowth, in one movement, as quick as lizards.

A boy and a girl came warily down to the stream. The boy looked familiar, and Mu realised it was the messenger who had been sent by Shikanoko in the winter, the boy called Chika. He was still not very clear about human ages – his own growth, like all his brothers', had been so rapid he had nothing to go by – but he knew Chika was a boy, definitely not yet a man. The girl seemed younger, but maybe not by much. They were both thin, legs scratched and bleeding in several places, barefoot, burned brown by the sun. Yet the boy carried a sword, and the girl a knife, and, Mu thought, they both looked as if they knew how to use them.

The boy knew his way, leading the girl across the stream, helping her jump from boulder to boulder. When they reached the bank, they walked downstream towards the hut. Mu picked up the fish they had already caught, still flapping on the grass stem threaded through their gills, and gestured to Ima to bring the bucket of crabs. They followed the pair, silent and unseen.

The boy halted near the horse skull, hand on sword, and called, 'Is anyone there? I am Chikamaru, son of Kongyo, from Kuromori. I am looking for the man known as Shikanoko.'

Kiku emerged from the hut, blinking in the sunlight. 'We know who you are, Chika. Shikanoko is not here.'

Slowly the other boys appeared and surrounded the pair. The girl held her knife out threateningly but Kiku brushed it aside and stepped close to her, touching her face and her hair, in a gentle way, that both astonished and alarmed Mu.

'Kongyo?' Kiku said finally. 'He was the man who came with the horse.' His eyes flickered to the horse mask on the pole.

Chika said, 'That's Ban? My father said he died. He was our last horse. But what have you done to his skull?'

Kiku made a dismissive gesture. 'It doesn't matter.'

The girl began to cry silently, as if the sight of the horse, once no doubt magnificent and prized, now a hideous replica, had unleashed all her grief.

'I've done that,' Kiku told her. 'Water has come from my eyes. It will dry up, don't worry.'

His face had taken on an intense fixed expression, like a male animal about to mate or kill.

'Cook the fish,' Mu said to Ima, to break the uncomfortable silence, and then addressed the boy, Chika. 'Sit down, we'll eat something. Are you hungry?'

They both nodded. The girl slumped down, still weeping. Chika said, 'Our mother told us to flee. After our father died she was afraid his murderers might seek to kill us too. I don't know what will happen to her. My sister is still in shock, I think. She hardly speaks and the slightest thing sets off her tears.'

'Our mother is dead,' Kiku said, sitting down next to the girl. 'She died just after we were born.'

'Lady Tora?' Chika said.

The boys stared at him. 'You knew our mother?' Mu said.

'She came to Matsutani with Akuzenji, the King of the Mountain. Shikanoko was with them too.'

Mu remembered the name, Akuzenji. Shika had told them he was one of their five fathers.

'What does that mean, King of the Mountain?' said Kiku.

'That's what he called himself. He wasn't really a king, he was a bandit. Merchants paid him so they could travel safely along the northern highway. If they didn't pay, he robbed them and usually killed them. He set an ambush for Lord Kiyoyori, whom my father served, but he was captured and the lord beheaded him and all his men, except Shikanoko. Then Lord Kiyoyori fell madly in love with

Lady Tora and made her his mistress, even though she was said to be a sorceress.'

'One of our fathers took the head of another of them,' Kiku murmured. 'That would be a skull worth having.'

'The bodies were burned and the heads displayed at the borders of the estate,' Chika said. 'You should have seen it – thirty men separated from their heads in as many minutes. It was brutal. I've been in sieges and battles but nothing was as horrifying as that day.'

'You say you have been in battles,' Mu said, 'but you are not yet a grown man.'

'I still know how to fight with this.' Chika tapped the sword that lay beside him on the grass. 'I have just escaped from the battle in which my father died.'

'Why have you come here?' Ima said from the fire. The sweet smell of grilling fish rose in the air.

'I could think of nowhere else to go. Our father is dead, along with all Lord Kiyoyori's men and their families. We held out for months in the fortress at Kuromori but after Shikanoko left for the capital, and never came back, Lord Masachika attacked for the second time, took the fortress and put all the defenders to death. Then he did the same at Kumayama. He holds a huge domain now for the Miboshi. No one is left to oppose him in all the east.'

'It sounds very complicated,' Kiku said. 'You'll have to explain it to us. We need to understand all these things, if we are to live in the world.'

'No one understood why Shikanoko disappeared,' Chika said. 'They felt betrayed and abandoned. At first we thought he must have died, but then we heard that he destroyed the Prince Abbot at Ryusonji. He could have dominated the capital himself, but he rode away, no one knows where.'

'Someone died,' Kiku said, glancing at Kuro who sat a little way off, letting a snake slither up his arms and round his neck. 'A girl Shika liked.'

'Loved,' Mu said.

Kiku frowned. 'Loved,' he repeated and bent forward to look in the girl's face. She squirmed away and said to her brother, 'I don't want to stay here.'

'You spoke,' he said in delight. 'You see, we will be safe here. We can stay, can't we?'

'Of course,' Kiku said. 'You are welcome, you and your sister. What did you call her?'

'Kaze.'

'And your name, Chika – that's like the other lord you mentioned.'

'Masachika. I wish it were not. I hate him more than any man alive. It's one of the clan names – Chika, Masa, Kiyo, Yori. Many of us are called some variation of it. Masachika is Lord Kiyoyori's younger brother.'

So he is some relation to us, Mu thought. *If Kiyoyori is one of our fathers, this Masachika is our uncle. Kaze is Chika's sister. He will be uncle to her children. And if I have children my brothers will be their uncles.* He thought of the foxes and the girl he had seen, thought of having children with her. The blood rushed to his face and he trembled. In the following weeks he often went back to the clearing, looking for her, but he did not find her.

•

During that time Kiku and Chika had many conversations about the realm and governance of the Eight Islands: the Emperor, the nobility, the great families who held roles of state, the warlords and their warriors, the rich merchants who had their own sort of power. Kiku's frustration increased daily, until finally he announced his intentions to go out into the strange and enticing world Chika described. 'You can't be a sorcerer without someone to teach you,' he said. 'We can't live in this stinking place forever. We must find some way of having power in the world.'

'Maybe we should be bandits,' Kuro said. 'I would like to be called King of the Mountain.'

'King of the Insects, that's what you are,' Ku jeered.

'And you are King of the Dogs,' Kuro countered.

'Bandits are like crows,' Kiku said. 'They swoop down and steal, they scavenge. But if you are rich you don't have to scavenge.'

'Others steal from you, then,' Mu said.

'Then you could be a bandit, in secret, as well as a merchant,' Kiku suggested. 'Yes, that's what I would like to be.'

'Being a warrior sounds very fine,' said Ima, who had been entranced by Chika's tales of heroism and sacrifice.

'You can't be a warrior,' Chika told him. 'You have to be born into a clan.'

'Lord Kiyoyori was our father,' Ima reminded him. 'And so was Shika.'

'Well, if Shikanoko had stayed around he might have brought you up as warriors. But he's disappeared and Lord Kiyoyori is dead, and no one's going to believe you're sons of either of them.'

'Why not?' Ku asked.

'You don't look like it,' Chika replied.

'What do we look like?' said Kiku.

'Not like anyone else, really,' the warrior's son said.

The brothers exchanged glances, seeing each other's coppery skin, their sharp bony faces, their unkempt black hair.

'I have no intention of being a warrior,' Kiku declared. 'They all end up being killed or killing themselves. I am going to be a merchant, by day, and a bandit, by night. And maybe a spy or an assassin, but only for the highest reward.'

Chika laughed. 'To be a merchant you have to have something to sell, and ways of either making it or buying it.'

Kiku laughed too, but more loudly. 'I have something that I think will get me started. Come into the hut.'

They crowded into the hut after him and watched as he pulled a pile of old rags away from the wall. Beneath it lay a large flat stone.

'I'd never been able to move it,' Kiku said. 'Then, one day, it shifted. Something I did must have unlocked it. Help me lift it – Kuro, you're the strongest.'

Together, they raised the stone and slid it aside. A wooden chest had been buried under it. Kiku removed the lid and plunged both hands in, pulling out pearls, golden statues, silver prayer beads, copper coins, jade carvings – all small, light things that could be easily carried. 'They must be valuable,' he said.

'Where did it come from?' Kuro asked.

'Maybe Akuzenji got the sorcerer to hide it for him?' Mu suggested.

'That's what I think,' Kiku said. 'Our fathers provided for us, before they knew of our existence. It's touching isn't it, Chika?'

Chika said nothing, just stared at the treasure.

'What should I deal in, Chika? You know what men buy and sell. What are the things people cannot do without?'

'Wine, I suppose, and the things you make from soy beans: paste, curds, sauce.'

'I imagine I'll find out what all that stuff is,' Kiku said. 'Chika and I will go to . . . what's the best place?'

'Maybe Kitakami,' Chika said. 'I've never been there, but it has the reputation of being a city where anyone can make a fortune. It trades with countries on the mainland. It is said to be rough and wild.'

'Then we will go to Kitakami.'

'I don't mind coming with you,' Chika said. 'But what about Kaze?'

'Kaze can stay here. I'll come back for her, once I've started making my fortune.'

'I'm coming with you too,' Kuro announced.

Kiku stared at him for a moment, and then nodded. 'Yes, I'm sure I'll need you.'

Kuro grinned. 'Me and my creatures.'

•

After the three left, Mu, Ima and Ku went back to the peaceful life they had been leading before their brothers returned. Yet it was not quite the same, for now they had a girl living with them. She followed Ku and the dogs around and joined Ima in bringing offerings to the skull of her father's horse. She ate what they ate and slept alongside them, outside on fine nights, inside the hut when it rained. It did not rain often – even though the plum rains should have set in – and the days and nights were very hot.

Shikanoko had taught all the boys to use the bow. One day, Kaze took up Mu's bow, went off into the forest and returned with a hare and two squirrels. They could all move silently, and could take on invisibility, but she was a better shot than any of them. She still did not speak much, but now and then at the end of the day when they sat around the fire watching the flames grow brighter as night fell, she would sing – lullabies that made the dogs sigh in their sleep, ballads of love and courage that filled the boys with yearning.

They were fascinated and intimidated by her. She ordered them around, as if it were her right to be served. Ku and Ima adored her. Her presence, Mu thought, made them all more gentle, more complex – perhaps more like real people. He remembered Shika's wolf companion, Gen, who had been as artificial as the ones whose remains now littered the clearing, but who had grown more and more real, because of its attachment to its master.

He began to pay more attention to the fake animals, tried to revive their strange spark of life.

Even objects need attention, he thought. *Even the lifeless need love.*

Some nights he saw green eyes shine in the darkness under the trees and he imagined the foxes had come to listen to the singing. He heard vixens scream at midnight. One day, when he went to the stream to get water, a fox was drinking from one of the pools. It ran into the undergrowth at his approach. He called, without knowing why, 'Come back! I won't hurt you!' and a few moments later the leaves rustled and the fox girl stepped out.

They stood and gazed at each other, the stream flowing sluggishly between them. She seemed less like a fox than before and more like a human. Her ears were only slightly pointed and her feet were small and delicate but they were definitely feet, not paws. Beneath her robe, which was dyed red and tied with a yellow sash, was a hint of a tail but, at second glance, it was not a tail at all but just the way the robe fell.

'I saw you,' he said.

'I know. You were in the oak tree.'

'What was it?'

'A wedding,' she said gravely. 'I'll show you if you like.'

He held out his hand. 'Come across.'

'No, you come to me,' she commanded.

He leaped the stream in a bound and found himself so close to her he could smell her faint animal scent. She smiled at him and, reaching up – she was much smaller than he was – kissed him on the mouth.

The effect on him was so surprising he broke away from her, crying out, which made her laugh. Taking his hand, she led him into the bushes and pulled him down, so they were lying side by side. The sunlight dappled the moss with tiny circles. In the distance a warbler was calling. She loosened her robe and guided his hands to her body, then reached under his clothes to caress him.

•

She lived in the hut with him as his wife. She combed and braided Kaze's hair – the girl responded as if the fox woman were her mother, climbing on her knee when they sat by the fire, though Kaze was really too big to be cuddled. The dogs growled at her at first but she rubbed their ears, picked off their fleas and won them over. She was always merry; everything made her laugh. She liked to dance in the twilight, while Kaze sang. And every night she lay down with Mu and made him happy in a way he had never dreamed of.

Once he said to her, 'Why did you choose me?'

'Your mother was one of the Old People.'

'I don't know what that means,' he said.

'They were here before the horsemen came. They are more like us, both animal and human. Shisoku was one too. The Old People know many things about other realms that the horse people have never learned.'

Mu thought about the mask and the skulls. 'Can you teach me those things?'

'I am teaching you already,' she said, laughing. 'Didn't you notice?'

SHIKANOKO

Throughout the summer the Burnt Twins and Shikanoko kept travelling north, following the tracks of deer and foxes through the tangled forest. Not knowing where else to go, Ibara went with them. They saw no one nor was there any sign that they were being followed.

That first autumn the rain ceased and though the following winter there were heavy snowfalls, the seasonal summer rains failed. They had found shelter in an abandoned building, where a solitary hermit had once lived. It stood near a spring, from which water flowed constantly, and the former occupant had made a garden, which still existed wild and overgrown. Yams and taro had self seeded, as well as pumpkins, and there were fruit trees, an apricot and a loquat. They found his bones in the garden, in a tangle of grass and kudzu vine, scattered by scavenging birds and animals. Eisei gathered them up and buried them.

Animals came to drink at the spring, foxes, wolves and deer. The deer lingered to graze on the sweet grass in the clearing, which, thanks to the spring, flourished all through the hot summers while the rest of the land dried up. Nagatomo trapped hares and rabbits and shot birds – pigeons mostly and the occasional pheasant – but the lord would not allow them to hunt deer. Consequently the deer became more and more tame, allowing him to mingle with them and feeding from his hand.

'That is why he is called Shikanoko,' Nagatomo said. 'The deer's child.'

Ibara had not known his name, though she had heard it once, a long time ago it seemed, from the mouth of the man with the Matsutani crest whom Nagatomo had killed. In the long months when there was little to do, Nagatomo taught her with that dead man's weapons and now she carried his sword at her hip; she wore his clothes and tied her hair back. She had fallen a little in love with Nagatomo, almost overcome with desire when he held her hips or shoulders to correct her stance, but he never responded. She knew he and the monk were lovers, twinned in some way by their shared suffering. In time she recovered her equilibrium, but she did not lose her desire for revenge. Every day she thought of Masachika and how she was going to kill him.

Shikanoko spent hours in meditation but he began to eat. Ibara could feel how little by little grief gave up its grip on her heart and she thought she could sense the same in him. When the deer came in the evening he moved among them as if he were following the steps of an ancient dance. When she had first seen him she had recalled the heron dancers. Now he danced with the deer – they all did – and in the dance created the ties that bind Heaven and Earth, humans and animals, the living and the dead.

The foal grew to its full size and its dark coat turned to silver. It looked like its father, but it had a black mane and tail. Nagatomo introduced it to the saddle and bridle but it did not need breaking in. It accepted the saddle but did not like to be bridled. However, no one felt comfortable riding it. There were enough horses for the three men and Ibara took Risu. Tan followed close by her side and she talked to him about Hina, feeling sorry for the man trapped in a horse's body, wondering what good it had done him to be summoned back.

The mare lay down one cold winter night and did not get up again. The death rekindled Shika's grief and he wept bitterly. The two stallions mourned like humans.

Something about Ibara's presence goaded Shikanoko. She was like the thorn she had named herself. She pricked and scratched away at the armour he was building around himself. Perhaps it was that she often talked of Hina to the horse, Tan, and then she would mention Tan's twin, his own son, Takeyoshi. So he heard of the baby's birth, and Hina's beauty, her great intelligence, her kindness, and it filled him with a longing to see them both.

It was not magic or sorcery, nor did she do it deliberately, but little by little he awakened and began to emerge from grief. He took out Jato and cleaned and polished it, rebound his bow, Kodama, and carved new arrows, fletching them with white winter plumage.

They were in the northernmost part of the Darkwood, right up near the snow country. The snow was heavier than Shika had ever seen. After blizzards they had to dig their way out of the hut. The clearing, the grave, every branch and twig, every boulder and rock, were blanketed in white.

For weeks they were confined inside together. On the worst nights they brought the horses inside too, otherwise they would have been buried under the snow. Shika's intention had been, when winter came, to continue his meditation and fasting, in the open, which was really a slow way of killing himself, fading back into the forest, ceasing to live in a world so full of pain. But perversely his body showed signs of wanting to live. It became hungry and demanded food, suddenly it slept again, in the deep, healing sleep of boyhood. His mind awoke too. His hours of solitary meditation had revealed to him, among other things, how little he knew. He understood nothing about how the world worked, what Aritomo's motives were, why the Miboshi and the Kakizuki fought each other, what it meant to be a warrior, what was the nature of revenge, such as Ibara desired. He recalled his own upbringing, his father's death, up here in the north; the loss of the bow, Ameyumi; his uncle's brutality. And now he had a son, Takeyoshi, whom he was condemning to the same orphan state.

He saw how impetuous and thoughtless his actions had been, all his life, how he had been used and manipulated by others, for both good and bad, in his need for approval and affection, in his quest to redress his own pain.

On days when the snow fell heavily, there was nothing to do but talk. Eisei had received the usual education of a monk, could read and write, and knew sutras and other holy writings by heart. He had also absorbed, over the years, the songs and ballads that were sung in the outer courtyards at Ryusonji, and he often recited these: long intricate tales of heroes, warriors, powerful priests, warring clans, child emperors. Nagatomo and Shika had shared the rudimentary education of provincial warriors. They could read and write, and knew the history of their clan and the legends of Kumayama, but they had never learned how to conduct a careful argument or correct a false idea. Ibara could read a little, write in women's script, and calculate. She knew a great deal about her home town, Akashi, and the way the free port and its merchants operated. Since she did not defer to any of them, dressed like a man, and usually spoke like one, they forgot she was a woman. Three of them were born in the same year. Nagatomo was a year older.

One evening, Ibara said, 'Takaakira, the man who employed me to look after Lady Hina, was called the Lord of the Snow Country. I suppose his estates were not far from here?'

'We are alongside them,' Nagatomo replied. 'They begin on the eastern edge of the Darkwood and extend far to the north.'

Shika recalled the day Eisei had told him of Takaakira's death. He had not known then that it was on Hina's account. Now he felt a new interest in the man who, in disobeying Aritomo, had saved Hina's life and paid for it with his own.

'What sort of a man was he?' he asked Ibara.

'In truth, I hardly spoke to him, and then only about Hina. He knew a great deal about all sorts of things, he wrote poetry. There were two women whom he arranged to instruct Hina in history, music, and so on. He talked more to them, about her progress and her timetables. I had no idea a child could absorb so much. It used to worry me sometimes. I had to make sure she went outside from time to time, even though he didn't really approve. He wanted her to keep her pale complexion.'

'He had a reputation for courage,' Nagatomo said.

'I heard him claim once he was an adept,' Eisei added. 'There must be some strange esoteric practices in the Snow Country. He believed Yoshimori was the true Emperor and he was going to tell Aritomo that, on the day he died, and plead for your life and the Princess's. I suppose he never got the chance.'

Ibara had a remote expression on her face as if she was dwelling on the past. 'He adored her,' she said finally. 'I've never seen a man so obsessed.'

Shika was surprised at the strong emotion that welled up in him, part jealousy, part affront, but also, mingled in, gratitude and relief. Before he met Ibara, he had assumed Hina had died in the massacre of the Kakizuki women and children. Now, Ibara was convinced she had not drowned. But where had she gone? What had happened to her?

'Yet she was only a child,' he said. 'And how old was he?'

'Well over thirty, I would imagine,' Ibara replied. 'She was about eleven years old. He intended to make her his wife – but he had not touched her,' she added, maybe noticing Shika's face.

The shutters rattled as the wind howled against them. The snow fell with the lightest of sounds, like insects swarming.

•

On sunny days, when the snow did not fall, they rode out through the forest – no longer the dark wood but gleaming white. The horses plunged through the deep snow, snorting with excitement. Gen was light enough to run over the frozen surface. They took their bows and hunted hares and squirrels. Sometimes they saw wolf tracks. Every now and then, Shika caught sight of his antlered shadow, blue-black on the snowy ground. Each time he felt the shock anew.

Will I ever be rid of it?

As spring approached, the snow fell with rain mixed in. The icicles that clung to the roof began to drip in the sun. The stream melted and the water roared with its new fierce flow. The deer dropped their antlers. Nagatomo and Ibara collected them, polishing them. Fawns were born, and bounded after their mothers on long, delicate legs.

The short summer brought biting flies and heavy humid air. Violent thunderstorms crackled round the mountain peaks. In the autumn, drums sounded from far away, giving a rhythm to their own dances. Another winter passed: the same deep drifts of snow, the same long conversations in the smoky hut. They saw no one else and began to forget they were fugitives. No one ventured so deep into the forest, or so they thought, until one day in early spring when Nagatomo returned from collecting water, saying, 'Am

I going mad and hearing things, or is someone beating a drum in the distance?'

Once he mentioned it, they all heard it, a dull monotonous pounding on a solitary drum. It stopped for a while, then started up again. It was the wrong time of year for the drum festivals and, in truth, the playing did not sound skilful.

'Someone practising?' Ibara suggested.

After the drumming had persisted for a full day and a half, Shika said, 'I'm going to see what it is.'

The Burnt Twins exchanged a swift look, and said together, 'We should go.'

'You still act as if it matters if I live or die,' Shika said, with amusement.

'It matters to us,' Nagatomo said.

Shika was touched, though he did not show it. 'Well, you can come with me. Ibara, do you mind keeping guard here?'

The drumbeat was halting and uncertain, yet there was something compelling about it. The mask responded to it in some way. He felt the rhythm pass through his skull and reverberate within the antlers.

The snow melt filled the streams and the trees were just beginning to put on their first green sheen. Frogs rejoiced and birds sang, skirmished, mated, in their urge to raise young ones before the short summer ended. The horses trotted eagerly, nipping at each other and bucking occasionally for the sheer joy of being alive.

On the edge of the forest, where the huge trees gave way to bamboo groves and then to coppice, the stream widened into a marshy lake. Sedge and susuki reeds grew around it; a snipe took off at their approach with a sudden cry of alarm.

A shaggy, northern pony, dun coloured with a brown mane and tail, threw up its head from where it had been grazing and whinnied loudly. The drumbeat stopped abruptly. A young boy, about ten years old, got to his feet, took one look at the antlered man on the white horse, and ran away, shouting to the pony to come to him. But he was slowed by the drum and Nagatomo easily caught up with him, before he could reach his mount.

He tried to lean over and scoop up boy and drum together, but his horse was spooked by the drum's hollow sound against its neck, and shied, throwing its rider. Nagatomo fell to the ground, still holding the boy, the silk covering slipping from his face.

When he stood, the boy looked up at his ruined features, but did not say a word. Nagatomo's horse ran back to the others. Eisei seized its reins. The boy's eyes followed it, he saw Eisei's black-covered face, and then he saw Shika. He tried to wriggle out of Nagatomo's grasp, not to escape but to throw himself face down on the ground.

'Kamisama, kamisama,' he wailed. 'Please help me!'

Shika dismounted, and told him to sit up. It saddened him to see the fear and shock in the boy's face.

'I am no god,' he said, thinking, *But I will never be human again.*

'Then take off the mask,' the boy challenged.

'That I cannot do.'

'Then you must be gods or spirits, all of you. I was trying to summon the deer god. I didn't really think I could, but I was so desperate I didn't know what else to do. And you came.'

'Is that why you were beating the drum?' Eisei said.

The boy replied, 'People have said they've seen a figure, part-deer, part-man, in the forest. I thought I would try to call him out. I borrowed the drum from the shrine, but it's not as easy to make it speak as I thought it would be.'

'You were certainly persistent,' Nagatomo remarked. 'In what way do you need help?'

'My father died two years ago in Miyako, and now his cousins want to divide his estate between them. They say he was ordered to take his own life because he was a traitor and therefore his lands must be forfeited and I should not inherit them. When my mother opposes them, they say she and I deserve death too and we will be killed if we do not submit. But my mother thinks we will be killed even if we do. There is no one to help us. We cannot appeal to Lord Aritomo – my mother suspects he might even be supporting these false claims.'

'What was your father's name?' Shika said, though he had already guessed the answer.

'Yukikuni no Takaakira, Lord of the Snow Country. My name is Takauji. I am his only son.' He had recovered some of his composure and now studied them, with their ragged clothes and their wild hair and beards, almost insolently. 'You are so few. And you look like bandits. Is this how the deer god answers my prayers?'

Shika liked his defiant attitude and found himself inclined to help Takaakira's son. He put his hand on Jato and felt the sword quiver in response, as if it sensed his desire to fight and shared it.

'There is one more of us,' he said. 'We are not bandits, but you are right, we are few. How many cousins are there, and what forces do they command?'

'There are three of them. Each has about twenty men. There are a few hundred warriors still attached to the estate and they are mostly undecided. They don't think the land should be split up and they are loyal to my father's memory. But I am not yet a man and they are not used to the idea of serving a woman. However, round here everyone worships the deer god and would do whatever he says.'

Shika drew the Burnt Twins aside. 'What should we do?' he asked quietly.

'People obviously know we are here,' Nagatomo said. 'Sooner or later they will learn who you are. Either we move on now, further north, or we take advantage of this new situation.'

'It's an opportunity to stamp your mark here,' Eisei added. 'If you have allies and men in the Snow Country, you will return to Miyako with the east protected.'

They both spoke of the future, Shika thought, whereas he still did not consider he had a future. One action would lead to another if he started to re-engage with the world.

Tan, who had been following them through the forest at his own speed, trotted up to them, sniffing curiously at Takauji.

'What a fine horse,' the boy exclaimed.

'What should I do, Lord Kiyoyori?' Shika said.

Tan pawed the ground and neighed shrilly. Naturally, Lord Kiyoyori wanted to fight.

'We should talk to your mother,' Shika said to Takauji. 'Where can we meet?'

Takauji pointed to a small shrine hut at the further side of the lake, half-obscured by willow trees and hazel bushes. It had the high steep roof of Snow Country buildings. Above its door antlers had been fastened, some of the largest Shika had ever seen, and newly tanned deer hides were spread over the small verandah. A frayed and knotted rope hung beneath a wooden bell. 'I will bring her there at this time tomorrow.'

'We will be there,' Shika promised.

'Can I touch your antlers?' Takauji asked.

Shika lowered his head. Takauji grasped the unbroken branch and pulled sharply, jerking Shika forwards, unbalancing him.

Shika cuffed him. 'I told you, the mask does not come off.'

'You really are the deer god, aren't you?' Takauji said, with awe.

•

When they returned to the forest hut and told Ibara what they had learned, she said, 'I would like to do something to help Lord

Takaakira's son, and his wife – she has suffered a lot in her life, I think.'

'She must have seen very little of him,' Eisei remarked.

'Yet he trusted her to run that vast estate in his absence,' Ibara said. 'She is by no means a helpless woman; it may be some kind of trap. Let me go first tomorrow. I should be sorry to die before Masachika, but apart from that my life is unimportant.'

Shika smiled, though he knew no one could see it beneath the mask. 'We could argue all night over whose life matters the least.'

'I don't believe either of us has yet fulfilled our destiny,' she replied in a low voice.

'Then you and I will go to the shrine and meet her together and give Heaven a chance to prove you are right. Nagatomo and Eisei will keep watch outside.'

They rose early and were on the edge of the forest, with a clear view of the shrine, just after daybreak. They had hidden the horses further back among the trees, but Tan had followed them, picking his way carefully among the winter's dead leaves, through which blades of grass and flower stems were emerging. Under rocks the last of the snow still lingered. Gen walked stiff legged behind Shika, turning his head to favour his right ear, now and then stopping to sniff the air.

Shika settled into a meditation position, Jato on the ground beside him, his bow on his back, while Eisei and Nagatomo checked that the shrine was empty. They then melted back into the forest.

Gen crouched on his haunches, a little in front. After some time, when the sun had burned the mist from the fields, the fake wolf raised his head and gave a faint whine. A few moments later, Shika heard the muffled tread of horse hoofs in the soft earth; only one horse, he thought.

A crow called: Nagatomo had heard the horse too. A real crow replied from a tree nearby, making Shika grin.

The three figures came into sight, the woman riding, the boy running alongside. It was the same pony from the day before. It caught Tan's scent and stared towards the forest, whinnying a greeting. The other horses would have neighed back, had they been within earshot, but Tan remained silent.

The woman did not really ride the pony but rather used it as a method of transport. She had no other interest in it. He guessed she did not ride often. It stopped abruptly not far from the shrine and she slid from its back, as though thankful to get off.

The pony looked thankful too, shook itself vigorously and began to crop the new grass. The boy ran to the shrine, his knife drawn, and entered cautiously. After a few moments, he came out and beckoned to his mother.

She looked around once, took some offerings from a cloth and went forward to place them on the steps. The boy pulled the bell rope and the wooden clapper gave out a hollow, eerie sound that made Shika's neck prickle. Gen gave a muffled howl.

Shika picked up his weapons and approached the shrine. Ibara emerged from the dead bracken where she had been concealed, and followed him. At the steps she touched his arm and indicated that she should go first, but at that moment Takauji appeared on the threshold and gestured to them to come in. Bending his head, Shika stepped inside.

For a moment he could see nothing, in the gloom. He heard her gasp and could only imagine how the antlered mask had startled her. He made no bow or greeting, but she dropped to her knees, laid her palms flat on the floor and lowered her head.

'My son told me,' she whispered.

'I am not the deer god,' he answered. 'I am a man under enchantment, a curse, you could say.'

'It must make you powerful,' she said, more loudly, sitting up and gazing at him frankly. 'Yes, I can see it does. Believe me, I know all about power.'

He could see, now, the planes of her face, sharp features, pale, northern skin. There was something birdlike about her; she reminded him of a falcon, fierce and swift. Her hands and feet were very small, her wrists slender.

'Are you better with the bow or the sword?' she said, wasting no time.

'I believe I can outfight most men with both,' he said, 'but probably the bow suits me more.'

She said, 'I am glad of that. This is my plan. I don't want to plunge the whole of the Snow Country into war, brothers against brothers, fathers against sons, but until those who challenge me are dead, that war cannot be avoided. I am going to invite my husband's cousins to an archery contest, in honour of the deer god, and you will kill them.'

She gave a thin-lipped smile. 'Of course, there is no reason why you should help me. I don't know who you are or where you have come from.'

'There are bonds between us,' Shika replied. 'My companion was employed by your late husband.'

'Were you there when he died?' the lady said, turning her piercing eyes towards Ibara.

'No, lady.'

'Are you a woman?' her voice was bitter. 'Is that why you found *employment* with him?'

'No,' Ibara said simply, and then, 'I worked in his household.'

'Looking after Kiyoyori's daughter, I suppose. I heard all about it. What a foolish thing to die for, don't you think? I will never forgive him, but I will never forgive Aritomo either.' She was twisting her hands together, and then struck one fist with the other palm, and held her hands firmly so they would not move. 'I'm sorry,' she said. 'It has become a habit, since I had the news of his death. What happened to the girl? I hope she is dead too. It was an evil day when Takaakira came upon her.'

'She drowned while trying to escape,' Ibara said, levelly.

'So much the better. But you are a strange one! Dressed as a man, carrying a sword. What are you trying to achieve?'

Ibara gave Shika a look, and stepped to the open door, where she crouched down, staring at the lake.

'I have offended her . . . him . . . which should I say? I did not mean to talk about these things. Now I am upset.'

Shika could see that her life had made her self-centred and angry. He was inclined to leave her to it: let the relatives divide the estate as they desired, but Takauji interested him and he wanted to spare the boy the sort of childhood he himself had had.

She studied him as though divining his thoughts and said, 'I suppose Aritomo would be very interested in knowing about you.'

'He already knows about me,' Shika said. 'He has nightmares about me.'

'Does he know that you are here, in the Snow Country?'

'By the time he learns that, I will be somewhere else.' Her gall in trying to threaten him, in this oblique way, made him laugh.

She had the grace to look uncomfortable. 'Well, as I said, I am no friend of the Minatogura Lord. He will not hear about you from me. My men deeply resent their lord's death. They are Snow Country people. They know how to keep silent.'

She got to her feet and came close to him. For a moment he thought she was going to touch the mask, and he wondered briefly if it would come off under her fingers, but though she looked at it intently, she did not reach out. She lowered her eyes to his legs, as though appraising him, making him aware that her husband had been dead for many months, and even before that she had been more or less abandoned. He felt her hawk-like determination. He admired her but he did not in any way desire her.

•

At night, it was still cold, and sometimes there were new falls of snow but, once the equinox had passed, spring came with a rush. In the days before the competition, targets made of bundles of straw, shaped like wild boar, with large painted eyes and real tusks, were set up along the lake shore. Horses were washed and groomed, their winter coats brushed out, their manes and tails plaited with red. They caught the excitement and neighed wildly, stamping their feet and tossing their heads. From the marshes, nesting birds shrieked in response.

Takauji and his mother were given the place of honour on the steps of the shrine. All day men competed in heats, galloping past the targets and loosing their arrows. The boars' eyes were considered the winning shot. Finally there were four rivals left, the three cousins and one of Lady Yukikuni's men, middle-aged, skilful and cunning, with a clever, nimble horse. None of them had achieved the perfect score of three eyes in a row.

As they were preparing to ride off against each other, the lady said in a clear voice, 'There is one more competitor, the representative of the deer god himself. Who dares take him on?'

She beckoned towards Shika and called, 'Come out!'

Nyorin stepped out of the forest, his silver coat gleaming, his long mane decorated with flowers and leaves. A cry of surprise and awe came from the watching crowd. The other competitors fell back as the horse approached the shrine. Shika bowed his antlered head to the lady and her son and took the huge bow from his shoulder. Nyorin's nostrils flared and he uttered a challenging neigh as Shika turned him towards the starting point, breaking into a swift gallop as Shika dropped the reins on his neck and drew from his quiver one of the arrows he had made in the forest.

It was easy for him, far easier than shooting the werehawk from the sky. One after another three arrows slammed into the boars' eyes.

Nyorin came to a halt and trotted back to the starting line, where he stood snorting in triumph as though saying, *Beat that!*

Shika was about to dismount and go to the lady when one of the cousins rode towards him, shouting, 'Take off that mask and let us see who you really are!'

Several tried to dissuade him, but he had already drawn his sword and was thrusting towards Shika. Nyorin moved like lightning, striking out with his forefeet, giving Shika time to draw Jato.

The lady said in a clear voice, 'He has drawn his sword against the deer god. Let him die.'

No one saw who loosed the shaft that pierced the man's chest. It came out of the forest. Shika knew it was Nagatomo's. Within moments the other two cousins were dead. *Eisei and Ibara*, he thought. The straw boars stared with their blind eyes as the blood soaked into mud and sand.

The lady was on her feet, her pale face flushed with triumph. 'It is the judgement of the forest itself!' she cried.

People drew back as Shikanoko rode away, afraid his shadow would fall on them.

•

The next day there were offerings on the edge of the forest, and every day after that. A week went by before the lady came, riding the dun pony, with Takauji leading it. She had brought him a pair of chaps made from wolf skins. The fur was grey and white, the bushy tails still attached.

After she had given them to him she said, 'Stay with me as my husband. I know you are a man.'

'If you can remove the mask, I will,' he replied, not believing she could.

She smiled and reached out immediately, certain she would succeed, but she could not shift it from his face. Tears of disappointment came to her eyes.

'Stay anyway,' she begged. 'I will tell no one. You may hide out in the forest all summer and I will come to you at night. You have seen how the farmers are already bringing you food. You will lack nothing. I will show you my gratitude.'

Shika thanked her but, as soon as she had left, without even any discussion among them, they prepared the horses, packed up their few possessions and began to ride to the north.

5

KIKU

Once they had struck the northern coast highway and turned towards the west, the three boys, Chika, Kiku and Kuro, came across many other travellers: merchants with trains of packhorses; monks carrying stout sticks and begging bowls; officials and their retinues; warriors on horseback, in groups of three or four, offering their swords and their services as bodyguards; beggars, and probably not a few thieves, Chika thought, taking care to keep the treasure well hidden. They had divided it into three and put it into separate bags, though Kiku and Kuro had each taken a strand of pearl prayer beads to string round their necks. Kiku's entangled with the beak and talons of the werehawk.

He explained who all these people were, as best he could, adding to the knowledge Kiku and Kuro had acquired in their previous forays into the human world, but their grasp on how everything hung together was still flimsy.

'Is this the mountain Akuzenji was king of?' Kuro asked as they climbed up to the pass. The road was steep, hardly more than a track. Horses stumbled over rocks and slipped on the scree. Even high in the mountains, it was hot. Sweat dripped from men's faces, and the animals' bellies and legs were flecked with white stains.

'I suppose so, and this must have been the most dangerous part of the journey,' Chika said. 'Any number of men could lie hidden, behind the outcrops, and there is nowhere to escape to.'

The mountain rose steep and jagged on one side, and, on the other, the valley fell away, a sheer drop of hundreds of feet.

'That's where Akuzenji used to throw the bodies of those who refused to pay him,' said a man who had been walking just behind them, leading a small horse laden with baskets. 'Only they were not strictly speaking bodies, not until they reached the bottom, that is.'

Kuro's eyes brightened with interest.

'Where are you boys walking to?' the stranger went on.

'Kitakami,' Chika said.

'All alone? No family?'

Chika said warily, 'In Kitakami – we are going to a relative's house.'

'What is their name? I know most people in Kitakami.'

'I don't remember.'

'So where do they live?'

'Near the port,' Chika improvised.

The man laughed. 'In Kitakami everyone lives near the port. Well, if you find them, tell them Sansaburo from Asano says good day. May your journey be safe!'

He clicked his tongue at the horse and walked past them.

'What did he mean by all that?' Kiku said.

'I think he was just being friendly,' Chika replied.

Kiku looked at Kuro, who raised his eyebrows as if he, also, did not understand.

At the top of the pass, they paused to catch their breath. The black cone of Kuroyama rose behind them, and in front lay fold after fold of ranges all the way to the west. In the distance, to the north, Chika could see the glimmer of the sea and in the south a huge lake – Kasumi, he supposed. It was approaching evening; most travellers had hastened on to find lodging before dark. Only the friendly merchant was still on the road ahead of them.

Kiku, deep in thought, hardly looked at the view but, as they began the descent, said to Kuro, 'Let's take that horse.'

'All right,' Kuro replied agreeably. 'Shall I use the sparrow bee?'

'That'll do,' said Kiku.

They quickened their pace, until they had almost caught up with the man. Kuro took the cover from the wicker cage and the sparrow bee began to buzz angrily. He released the catch and the bee shot out, soaring briefly, then descending to attack. The man called Sansaburo from Asano gave a cry, danced around, waving his arms futilely. The bee stung him on both hands, then on the neck. Within moments he was lying in the dust, clutching at his throat.

'What have you done?' Chika cried in shock.

Kuro had grabbed the lead rope of the startled horse and was trying to catch the bee before it stung it. When he had succeeded he said, 'Let's throw him over the edge.'

'No, we'll leave him here,' Kiku said.

'You killed him!' Chika said. 'He'd done nothing to you!'

'Don't worry. I have a plan. We'll take the horse.'

'What's in the baskets?' Kuro said, curious.

They loosened the well-tied knots on one of the baskets and prised open the lid. A faint fishy smell floated out.

'Just old shells?' Kiku said. 'What use are they?'

Chika slipped his hand in among the shells and felt their smooth interiors. 'It must be mother of pearl. It's used as decoration, in inlays and so on.'

'Is it valuable?' Kiku asked.

'Very,' Chika replied.

'We'll take it to the . . . who should we hand it over to?'

'What do you mean?' Chika asked.

'Aren't we going to keep it?' Kuro said.

'We must give it back,' Kiku declared. 'We'll say we found the horse, straying. But first we need to kill a couple more merchants, so people begin to be frightened.'

Chika said doubtfully, 'We'll be caught.'

'I promise you, we will never be caught,' Kiku said, with conviction. 'Just tell me who we should take the shells to.'

'I suppose to whoever ordered them. This man probably took them to the same person, year after year.'

'Hmm. I should have asked him that, before he died,' Kiku said. 'There's so much to learn. Well, you can make enquiries when we get to Kitakami.'

They walked a little further and, when night fell, went off the track into the forest to rest for a while. Kuro sat by the horse, keeping watch, and Chika and Kiku lay down, side by side. Kiku seemed to fall asleep immediately but Chika was wakeful, and when he did finally sleep he had a nightmare that one of Kuro's snakes was slithering towards him. He tried to run but his limbs were paralysed. The snake hissed and flickered its tongue and he knew any moment it would bite him and he would die. He woke to find Kiku's arms around him.

'You were screaming. What's wrong?'

'I had a bad dream.'

Kiku said, sounding surprised, 'It feels nice, holding you like this.'

Chika lay without moving, letting the other boy touch him with exploring hands. He felt his body begin to respond to the pleasure. Their limbs entwined, their mouths joined, as they took the first steps on the journey of sex and death that would bind them to each other.

The second merchant was garrotted by an invisible Kiku. They took his horse, loaded this time with bamboo scoops and bowls. Kuro looked after the horses while Chika and Kiku fell on each other with the ferocious lust of young males, incited by their seeming power over life and death.

'Can you kill anyone you choose?' Chika asked, as he lay panting and exhausted.

'I don't know yet. I am finding out. It's fun, isn't it? The killing, and then this afterwards? I had no idea it was all so much fun. I don't understand why people don't do it all the time.'

'Some do,' Chika replied. 'But it's not so much fun for the people who die.'

'If people did not die, there would be no room for new ones. And don't they just get reborn into a new life, anyway?'

They had heard monks and priests expounding the doctrine along the road.

'Can *you* be killed?' Chika asked, a new fear seizing him.

'I suppose so. Our fathers are mostly dead, and our mother.' Kiku did not want to dwell on the subject. 'So who shall we kill next? You choose.'

The idea seemed suddenly irresistible, yet a few months ago it would have appalled him. His warrior upbringing was being corrupted and tainted by Kiku. He tried not to think of his father's stern teachings. He knew he was enthralled by Kiku, as by no one else in the world. He wanted to please him; he could not resist him.

'I bet you cannot kill a warrior,' he challenged.

•

He was not much of a warrior, a solitary, grizzled man with only one eye, the empty socket yawning disconcertingly. He sang ballads in a monotonous, melancholy voice outside a lodging place not far from

Kitakami. Chika and Kiku watched him, while the horses rested and drank, and Kuro procured food. Chika found the strains of his voice, in the summer evening, curiously moving. He wondered where he had come from, what had reduced him to this.

He wore a faded green hunting robe and under it a corselet, missing much of its silk lacing; at his hip was a long sword. He did not earn enough for a meal, let alone a room, and began to walk away, his measured gait and the set of his shoulders indicating he was resigned to another night on the road.

The two boys sauntered after him, and Kuro pulled the reluctant horses along behind them. Kiku waved at his brother to fall back out of sight.

'Attract your warrior's attention,' he whispered to Chika. 'I'll grab him from behind and then you can use your sword.'

Chika watched, with all the shock and thrill it always gave him, as Kiku faded into nothingness, and then, hastening his steps, called, 'Hey, sir, wait a minute!'

The man turned. The sunset behind him made him appear solid, black and featureless, and for a moment Chika felt afraid, but as he came closer he saw the lines in the face and the grey hair. The remaining eye was clouded, two fingers were missing from the left hand. When the man finally moved, it was stiffly – no doubt he was troubled by old wounds.

'What do you want, boy?'

'I am travelling alone. I thought we could walk together.'

The warrior gave him a shrewd look. 'What happened to your companions and the horses?'

Chika said, 'They have gone their own way. Maybe they stopped for the night.'

'You carry a sword; you look like a warrior's son. Were you not taught to speak the truth, at all times?' His tone was forbearing but the words flicked Chika like a whip.

'You are an expert on the life of a warrior, are you, you beggar?'

The man turned. 'Walk by yourself. I am a little fussy in my choice of companions. If you ever learn any manners, you can approach me again.'

Chika's hand was on his sword. At the same moment the warrior drew his own, turned as fast as a snake and struck out.

Kiku gave a shriek, breaking into sight, grasping his arm, blood beginning to drip from it.

'What are you?' the warrior cried. 'Forgive me, you should not sneak up on a man like that. It's instinctive, you see. I can't help but react. Now I have cut you!' His eyes went back to Chika's sword. 'What? You were intending to kill me? Two shabby boys like you? You must be desperate! I have nothing but these clothes and my sword. I'll die before I hand that over!'

'I'm bleeding,' Kiku said.

'It's not fatal,' the man assured him. 'Unless you are unlucky enough to get wound fever. Wash it well, that's my advice. And now, my young friends, unless the warrior's son wants to fight me, I'll be on my way.'

'Wait,' Kiku said. His brow was taut with pain and concentration. 'What are you planning to do in Kitakami?'

'None of your business, brat.'

'You must be hoping to find someone who can feed you, someone you can serve.'

The warrior laughed. 'And if I am, what's it to you?'

'How would you feel about serving me?'

He laughed again but more bitterly. 'The first requirement of anyone I serve, is that they be rich!'

'We are rich,' Kiku said, pulling out the pearl prayer beads and fingering them. 'But we don't know what to do in Kitakami and we are afraid of being cheated. We found these horses, wandering. We want to take them to their rightful owners. Not for any reward, we don't actually need it. Just to do the right thing.'

Kiku had been turning paler and paler while he talked and now he swayed as if he were about to faint.

The warrior sheathed his sword. 'Come, let me take a look at that cut.'

Chika knew he had a chance of killing him, now, while he was unprepared. He saw the exact place in the neck where his blade would open the flesh and the blood vessels within. His hand flexed and clenched, his sword quivered. He was not sure if Kiku's faintness was a ploy to get the man off his guard.

'Put the sword away,' the man said. 'I may be one-eyed and crippled but you still wouldn't stand a chance against me. Here,' he tore a strip from his under robe. 'Run to the spring and wet this. We'll bind his arm.'

'What is your name?' Chika asked after the wound was bound and Kuro and the horses had caught up with them.

'Yamanaka no Tsunetomo. And yours?'

'Kuromori no Motochika.' He used his adult name.

'Huh? Everyone at Kuromori was slaughtered. So why are you still alive?'

'That's my business,' Chika said, making Tsunetomo laugh.

'That's right, my friend. Some of us are called to die and some to survive at any price. If that's your path, embrace it, without regret or shame.'

'Has it been your path?' Chika asked.

'Maybe it has,' Tsunetomo said. 'At any rate, I am still alive. Now let's see what those horses are carrying.'

It was almost dark, a warm night with no moon, the starlight diffused by the hazy air. Kuro made a fire and unloaded the baskets from the horses' backs. Tsunetomo inspected the contents.

'You found the horses straying, you say?'

Kiku nodded. His eyes were a little brighter in the firelight and his cheeks were flushed, but he no longer seemed faint, nor otherwise affected by the wound.

'What happened to the owners, I wonder?' Tsunetomo's face was expressionless, his voice bland.

'No sign of them,' Kiku said.

'Maybe someone murdered them?' Kuro suggested.

'That's what people are saying,' said Tsunetomo. 'I've already heard one or two rumours – Akuzenji's ghost, or some new bandit chief, or ogres who kill people to eat them. If such rumours continue to spread more people will become afraid and soon no one will want to travel alone.'

'That's good,' Kiku said. 'We can offer them protection – you and your sword.'

'Am I to guard the whole length of the highway?' Tsunetomo laughed.

'You must know other people you can hire to help you.'

'As a matter of fact, I do.'

'So will you serve me?' Kiku asked.

Tsunetomo stared at him. 'I will,' he said finally. 'You're a strange creature, but there's something about you . . . keep me in food and shelter, and a little extra for wine, and my sword is yours.'

6

ARITOMO

The fiery death of the Prince Abbot had not only shocked and grieved Lord Aritomo but had also alarmed him. His hold on power was weakened, his authority shaken. With his usual clear-sightedness he knew it would only take one more blow to dislodge him. He strengthened the capital's defences, while making plans to retreat to Minatogura, preparing boats at Akashi, in case attacks came from Shikanoko in the east and the Kakizuki in the west.

But his enemies did not take advantage of his momentary weakness. Shikanoko vanished into the Darkwood, Lord Keita and his retinue made no move from Rakuhara. Within a few weeks Masachika, whom Aritomo came to depend on even though he could not forgive him for Takaakira's death and some days could hardly bear to look at him, finally captured Kuromori and went on to take Kumayama. The east was once more secure.

Hoping to placate the vengeful spirit of the Prince Abbot, Aritomo gave orders for Ryusonji to be rebuilt, exactly as before, and for the dragon child to be worshipped there, yet the construction progressed slowly. After a series of inexplicable accidents the carpenters refused to work, saying the place was occupied by ghosts and untethered spirits whom no one could control now their master was gone.

The Imperial Palace, which had burned to the ground in the Ninpei rebellion, was also being rebuilt. In the meantime the Emperor, Daigen, and his mother were living in a nearby temple. The treasures that had been destroyed were slowly being replaced, but expenses were high and even Aritomo's new taxation system could not produce enough revenue. It was his custom to visit Daigen weekly, to take part in the rituals that bound Heaven and Earth through the sacred person of the Emperor. Daigen had been the Prince Abbot's choice and Aritomo could not fault him. He was intelligent, courteous and, most important, biddable, seemingly resigned to his role as a figurehead and happy to play it in return for beautiful companions, wine and poetry. There was no reason for harmony not to be restored but, as the years passed, the drought worsened; rain hardly fell, the lake shrank and the river dried up.

Aritomo tried to wipe Takaakira's dying words from his mind: *Yoshimori is the true Emperor.* Yet they haunted his dreams and he often woke suddenly in the night hearing a ghostly voice speak them in the empty room.

On one of his visits the Emperor's mother sent a message through a courtier that she wanted to speak to him. He had to obey, yet he went with reluctance, fearing she was going to grumble about their living conditions or demand some new luxury for which he would have to find the money.

Lady Natsue received him alone. He prostrated himself before her, as was required, feeling a twinge of pain in his hips, regretting his sedentary life, longing for a horse beneath him, a hawk above, the brisk air and huge skies of the east.

It was a warm spring day and water trickled through the garden. The room was not unpleasant; it faced south and was elegantly appointed with flowing silk hangings and a few exquisite pieces of lacquered furniture. He could not see what she had to complain about.

'Please sit up, lord,' Lady Natsue said.

He dared to look directly at her. She had been the late Emperor's second wife, always, it was whispered, jealous of the first, Momozono's mother. Yet surely no one could have surpassed her in beauty. Even now, in apparent middle age, she seemed perfect, still youthful. She spoke at length about the joys of the season and the various flowers and birds of the garden, then told an amusing anecdote about a court lady and a mouse which His Majesty had turned into a poem. When she fell silent he said, half-irritated, half-charmed, 'What can I do for your Majesty?'

'I need to speak to you about Ryusonji.' She gestured that he should come nearer. The tone of her voice changed though it was no less attractive. 'My late brother and I were very close,' she whispered. 'He shared many of his secrets with me. Under his rule Ryusonji became a place of great power. Now he is gone it lies empty; its power leaks from it.'

'I am trying to rebuild it,' Aritomo replied. 'But the work is proving difficult and slow. No one can replace the Prince Abbot.'

'I had heard about the problems. Last week I went to see for myself. I wanted to prepare for the anniversary of my brother's death, pay my respects and mourn him. Women, as you know, are not usually permitted to enter into spiritual mysteries, yet my brother recognised that in me dwelt an ancient soul that had acquired great wisdom. He often sought my advice and he promised me that if he died before me he would attempt to reach me from the other world. When I knelt before the half-completed altar I felt him call to me. He wants me to move into Ryusonji. I will be able to ensure that the repairs progress smoothly and the various disruptive spirits are appeased. My son will come with me. It is fitting that the Emperor should be in the spiritual heart of his capital.'

'I am not at all sure that it is fitting,' Aritomo said, wanting to speak with his customary frankness yet fearing to offend her. 'How shall I put it? The events that took place there, the deaths, the dark forces unleashed . . .'

'I can handle any darkness at Ryusonji. The shadows are a source of power just as much as the light. When the new palace is finished maybe my son can live there. But it is imperative that I move quickly, for someone else is about to take possession of the temple.'

'What do you mean?' Ever since he had been told of the details of the confrontation between the Prince Abbot and Shikanoko, he had had nightmares in which a masked half-human figure confronted him in judgement. Now the Empress's words summoned up that image. He feared it was what he would find at Ryusonji. Yet Shikanoko was surely far away, in the Darkwood.

'An old man is there, camped out in one of the cloisters. He plays the lute and sings. I was told he was harmless, wandering in his mind, but his presence seemed offensive so I ordered him to be removed. However, no matter how many times he was thrown out, he always returned. Finally the guards lost patience with him and beat him to death, they thought, but the next day they heard the lute and his voice – he was back in the cloister. Now no one dares approach him. I believe I know what he is doing there. He has obtained the Book of the Future and means to erase my son's name and inscribe that of Yoshimori.'

Neither of them spoke for a moment. The trickling of the stream seemed suddenly louder and birds called from the garden.

'Who is he?' Aritomo whispered.

'The monks who survived told me he is Sesshin, once many years ago a fellow student of my brother. He became a great master who gave his power away to the evil man they call Shikanoko.'

'Gave his power away?' His skin was crawling. He had heard of Sesshin before, some connection with Matsutani and Masachika. And then he remembered, and the terrible day Takaakira died came back to him.

'So he could pass as a foolish old man,' Lady Natsue explained. 'But little by little he is gathering knowledge again. He has all the time in the world since he has made himself immortal.'

He stared at her in disbelief, wondering if he had misheard.

She repeated the word, 'Immortal.'

'What is his secret?' Aritomo said hoarsely.

'That interests you, Lord Aritomo?' Her gaze pierced him. 'Would you steal it from him? Would you wish never to die?'

'I want more time,' he replied. 'I don't want to die before I have achieved all I strive for.'

'None of us can know the hour of our death,' she said, her eyes not leaving his face. 'The water from the well at Ryusonji is reputed to prolong life. My brother and I have both drunk from it. I am much older than you think, but I am still as mortal as my brother proved to be.'

The wind had risen and leaves rustled from outside, a branch scraping against the roof. A crow called harshly as if it were sitting directly above them. He felt parched, almost feverish. Surely it was hotter than it should be?

'Lord Aritomo,' she said. 'Are you unwell?'

'No!' he replied, his voice suddenly loud. He was never sick; he denied illness access to his body. Even battle blows glanced off him, hardly leaving a wound. But the idea of an immortal at Ryusonji, slowly rewriting the Book of the Future, had struck deeply inside him. He struggled to regain calm.

'I will inspect Ryusonji myself,' he said. 'If I consider it suitable you and his Imperial Majesty may move there.'

'Let us not waste any more time.' Lady Natsue inclined her head graciously.

•

When Aritomo returned to his own palace, the one abandoned by Lord Keita when the Kakizuki fled from the capital, he sent for Masachika who, he knew, had just come back from Minatogura. It was not long before the Matsutani Lord was kneeling in front of him, apparently in perfect submission. Aritomo studied him for a few moments. Masachika was undeniably a handsome man, and he had gained great popularity and respect since the discovery and capture of the Autumn Princess, but Aritomo thought he could read his deeper character clearly, seeing how opportunistic and self-serving all his actions and words were. He did not trust his loyalty, yet, though he did not like admitting it, Masachika had made himself indispensable.

First he told Masachika of the Empress's request and asked him to inspect the temple and make all necessary preparations.

'I will come with you. I have not visited Ryusonji myself since the Prince Abbot died. But what news do you bring from the east? I hope you have sorted out your personal life.'

Masachika smiled, a little embarrassed. 'I finally convinced Keisaku and his daughter that I was never going to marry her. I could have taken her as a second wife but I did not want to distress Lady Tama, after all she has suffered. I found a suitable husband for the young woman, and released Keisaku from all obligations to me. They will hold Keisaku's estate in vassalage to you, which protects Minatogura from the north. It seemed an acceptable solution all round, provided Lord Aritomo agrees, of course.'

'It will be good to have someone loyal in between the port and the Snow Country. I had hoped Takauji would be removed. I cannot trust him not to challenge me sooner or later. But I hear the cousins failed in their efforts to get rid of him?'

'Yes, and they are all dead now. The mother arranged an archery contest. An unknown archer, who she claimed was the deer god, came out of the forest to win it, and the challengers were all killed. She said it was the judgement of the forest. Takauji is, unfortunately, more secure than ever.'

When Aritomo made no response Masachika said, 'He is the son of the man who betrayed you. You cannot trust him.'

'I am fully aware of that,' Aritomo snapped, enraged that Masachika should speak so of Takaakira who had been so superior to him in every way. Yet he knew he was right. Unless he was removed, Takauji would be a continuing threat. 'I cannot deal with him now,' he said, more calmly. 'First we must destroy the Kakizuki. Did you find out the identity of this so-called deer god?'

Masachika said, 'All the evidence – the antlered mask, the skill with the bow, the fake wolf-like creature – suggests it was Shikanoko.'

Aritomo kept his face still, his expression impassive, yet a kind of dread was welling up in him.

Masachika went on. 'By the time my men investigated he had disappeared again. The archery contest took place weeks ago. Shikanoko could be anywhere by now. Takauji was extremely hostile and my men were lucky to return alive. Unlike those I sent immediately after the disaster at Ryusonji, who never came back. Remember we are not dealing with an ordinary fugitive but with a sorcerer.'

'Is it his power that makes the rain dry up? How do I combat that? I don't mind facing a thousand men on a battlefield, but this one sorcerer keeps evading me.'

'Shikanoko has no men, no army,' Masachika said. 'All were destroyed at Kumayama. If he had been going to challenge you he would have done it immediately after the death of the Prince Abbot. I don't think he will ever emerge from the Darkwood. If you don't provoke a snake it will not bite you.'

'Is he completely alone?'

'He has a few companions, I believe: the ones they call the Burnt Twins, one is a former monk from Ryusonji, the other from Kumayama, and one other whose name and identity I have not been able to discover.'

'So some survived from Kumayama?'

'These were already with him. But there are always some survivors. Some hide, some run away, some are left for dead but recover from their wounds.'

'I will never eradicate all my enemies,' Aritomo said.

Masachika nodded in sympathy. 'But we will do our best to control and weaken them. I did find out something else, probably not very important. One of the women left at Kumayama told me. Shikanoko's mother became a nun, after her husband Shigetomo died. Apparently she is still alive and is in a convent a little way from Aomizu, on Lake Kasumi.'

'What would she know about anything? It must be years since she forsook the world.'

'As I said, it's not likely to be important.'

'Well, follow it up anyway,' Aritomo said. 'Arinori is in Aomizu now. He can look into it. There's no need to go yourself. Write a message.'

Arinori had served him for years and had been rewarded with Lake Kasumi and the surrounding districts. He was an experienced seaman, ambitious and determined. Aritomo trusted him far more than Masachika, though he had to admit the latter was considerably more intelligent.

•

The next day they rode in an ox carriage to Ryusonji. Both had dressed carefully and soberly in formal clothes, each with a small black hat on his head. A large retinue followed on horseback. Aritomo travelled frequently around the capital, inspecting new buildings and repairs, overseeing merchants and craftsmen, keeping an eye out for excesses of luxury and extravagance which would attract new taxes to pay for horses, armour and weapons.

People dropped to their knees as he went by, but he inspired fear not love. The city ran smoothly, his officials keeping every section meticulously administered, but neither he nor they could make the rains fall at their appointed time or save the crops when they failed.

The lake at Ryusonji had shrunk; the exposed bed was muddy and foul smelling. A charred spiral of black across rocks and moss still showed where the burst of flame had scorched the ground and set fire to the buildings. Most of the blackened beams had been removed and new lumber was stacked in the courtyards. There seemed to be some desultory activity, workmen sawing planks, and preparing floors, but it was still far from finished.

'The Empress wants to move here as soon as possible,' he said to Masachika as they descended from the carriage. 'See if there is anywhere suitable for temporary lodging. If she is to be believed, her presence here will speed the completion.'

Masachika went to speak to the head carpenter. Aritomo waited in the shade of the cloister, trying to sharpen all his senses, to discern what was really going on at Ryusonji.

The sound of a lute came to him, its mournful, plangent notes turning his spine cold. Masachika came back, saying enthusiastically,

'This hall is nearly finished. It could be ready before the end of the month. I will start arranging furnishings and servants.'

'They will need many rooms,' Aritomo said. 'And priests, guards and so on. What happened to all the priests and monks who were here before?'

'Some died in the fire, I believe. The rest must have run away.'

'Well, the Empress will bring her own, no doubt. Consult the steward of the Imperial Household.'

Masachika inclined his head. 'I will, lord.'

If he resented being given this tedious, if prestigious, responsibility he gave no sign of it. Aritomo knew he could rely on him, that Masachika would complete the task swiftly and efficiently as he did everything. Yet, no matter how competent he was, Aritomo would never warm to him.

The notes of the lute trickled through the air as if they were summoning him.

'Let us inspect the other courtyards,' he said.

The sun beat down on the blindingly white stones, making his head ache. The new moss was an unnaturally brilliant green. The shadows under the cloisters were deep black.

The lute player sat cross-legged, the lute in his lap, his face turned towards them as if he had been waiting for them.

Aritomo saw the hollow eye sockets, the shrivelled lids.

Masachika exclaimed, 'It is Master Sesshin!'

'The one whom your wife had blinded?'

'Yes, it was his eyes that I replaced at Matsutani and so subdued the guardian spirits.'

'I remember,' Aritomo said coldly. He could not take his eyes off the old man. So this was what immortality looked like! When the physical body could not die, did it simply mean endless pain and suffering? The deformed frailty before him tempted him briefly, savagely. He had often seen how under torture life persisted longer than he would have believed possible, but eventually it was extinguished. The Empress had told him the old man could not be killed and he wanted to put her claim to the test.

'Your lordship should not concern himself with the old lute player.' The head carpenter had followed them into the courtyard and stood beside them, regarding Sesshin with an indulgent smile. 'He is our talisman, aren't you, grandfather?'

He spoke in a loud voice and Sesshin nodded and smiled with senile glee.

'As long as he is left alone to play and sing, our work progresses. I bring him some food every day, not that he takes more than a mouthful. Since he returned there have been no accidents, no fires. The men say the dragon child must like his songs.'

'Does he have any books?' Aritomo said, remembering what the Empress had said.

The workman shook his head. 'I don't think so. What use would he have for books since he cannot see?'

Aritomo leaned over Sesshin and said loudly, 'Where is the Book of the Future?'

'I will show it to you, one day,' Sesshin replied, his voice low and rational. 'And you will see whose name is written in it. There is no need to shout. I am not deaf.'

Then he took up the lute and began to pluck the strings with his long fingernails.

'That's the way,' the head carpenter said approvingly. 'Keep playing for us!'

'I will come back and talk to him again,' Aritomo said. There was so much he did not understand, it was unsettling him. The feeble old man who was somehow immortal, the Book of the Future: none of it made sense. And it was too hot, the wind was too dry. He longed for the grey skies and constant drizzle of the plum rains. He decided he would make sure the old man stayed here so he knew where he was, and he would come and question him, alone, and discover his secrets.

HINA (YAYOI)

Yayoi grew taller and, in her third spring at the temple, her body began to change. Her breasts swelled and she bled monthly, like all the women, attuned to the cycle of the moon. She had seen first Yuri, and then Asagao, become women in the same way – indeed, Asagao made sure there was not a single detail in the process that Yayoi did not know about – so she was not shocked or frightened as young girls sometimes were. Mostly she accepted womanhood – what else could she do? – but she also grieved for that girl-child, single-minded and courageous, now gone forever.

Yuri left the temple one spring, making the journey on her own, the palanquin waiting at the foot of the steps. Sada and Sen, the two sisters, wept for days. Asagao was now the oldest girl. She did not sing them to sleep as Yuri had. She teased them for their red eyes and, when no one else was around, she bullied them. She left the following year. Lady Fuji herself came for her, bringing another young girl, whom she entrusted to Yayoi's care.

'You, yourself, will be ready soon,' she said with her familiar, appraising look.

The girls missed Asagao, her high spirits, her teasing ways. Even Sada and Sen wept for her, while Yayoi felt bereft as though she had lost a limb.

In the sixth month of that year, when they had given up hoping for the plum rains, men came on horseback, demanding to speak to the Abbess. Their leader was obviously a warrior of high rank, though the nuns did not know him. He wore a crest of a sail above waves and the white stars of the Miboshi.

Men's voices, their heavy tread, their sweaty smell, were so unusual, it threw the girls and the nuns, even the ginger cat, into a state of anxiety and agitation. The men spoke politely, yet there was an undertone of menace. The lord made it clear that the women's temple survived only on his sufferance. One word from him and it would all be destroyed.

The Reverend Nun tried to hide the girls but the men demanded to see every person living in the place. She rapidly tore off the robes they usually wore and made them put on nuns' habits and servants' clothes, rubbed dirt and ash on their faces and hands. They had never seen her so distressed and it alarmed them into silence.

Yayoi was terrified one of the men might be Masachika, her uncle. Would she even recognise the man who had killed Saburo in front of her eyes? Would he know her, after all these years? But all the men seemed strangers to her and, though they studied her intently, she did not think any of them knew her.

They did not lay hands on the girls but they touched the older women, patting their breasts and feeling between their thighs, and one nun, taller than the others and somewhat masculine in look, was forced to disrobe to prove she was not a man.

Since the men hardly spoke, no one knew who or what they were looking for. They searched every corner of the temple, from the chests that held the sacred sutras to the woodpile stacked on the southern wall.

'Why did they spend so long at the fish pond?' Yayoi asked after they had left.

'People hide underwater,' the Reverend Nun replied, 'and breathe through hollow reeds – or so I have heard.'

She helped the girls clean themselves, her hands shaking. 'I suppose we were lucky. None of you has been harmed and nothing has been damaged that can't be mended.'

Torn manuscripts, a broken statue, ripped hangings, a shattered ceiling, doors forced out of their tracks – the tall nun, weeping silently, set herself to repairing them.

Yayoi, now the oldest, undertook the task of calming and consoling the other girls. They all, like her, had fears from the past that had been reawakened by the armed men. She took out the lute and forced it to play soothing music, wondering where Yoshi was and if she and Genzo would ever be in his presence again. Several sutras needed recopying; Sada had quite a gift for writing and she and Yayoi worked on them together, Yayoi reading them aloud.

When they were finished, she took them to the Abbess for her approval, kneeling quietly while the older woman read through them, reciting each syllable under her breath. Yayoi felt as if peace was being restored with every precious word. Even the cat was calmed; she could hear its loud rhythmic purring.

The Abbess said suddenly, 'They were looking for a man whom they called Shikanoko.'

Yayoi felt shock run tingling through her limbs. Her heart thumped.

'I did not understand why they thought such a man, an enemy of Lord Aritomo, a warrior and a sorcerer, would be here at our insignificant temple. They told me they had recently discovered he was my son, and therefore there was every reason to suspect I was hiding him.'

Yayoi said nothing, silenced by astonishment.

'My son, whom I have not seen since he was a young child, whom I believed to be dead. Not a day has passed that I have not prayed for him, but all my prayers, it seems, have gone unanswered. They say he has become a monster. He murdered his uncle through dark magic and then destroyed the Prince Abbot and the temple at Ryusonji. Now, these men say, Lord Aritomo believes it is his evil power that has cursed the realm and caused the rain to cease and the rivers to dry up. I told them if I knew where he was, I would have handed him over to them. But I do not know.'

She stopped speaking and stood abruptly. The cat, alarmed, ran out of the room.

'And now our temple has come to the attention of Lord Aritomo. He sent Arinori to investigate me. I could tell Lord Arinori was shocked that we had no priests overseeing us. He asked how we ran our affairs and I was forced to reveal our benefactress, Lady Fuji. She will not thank me for that. No doubt she will come under his scrutiny next. They also enquired to whom we paid tax and I had to admit that we pay no tax to anyone.' She went to the door and gazed out on the garden. 'I cannot believe he has grown up to be so evil, but he had a fierce temper even as a baby. He screamed and bit my breasts. My women said that meant he would be a powerful warrior. But how did he fall into sorcery?'

Yayoi longed to reveal all she knew of Shikanoko, how he had served her father for a while, his kindness to her and her brother, the way he had cared for Sesshin after the old man had been blinded. She remembered the day he had arrived at Matsutani, riding Risu, the bad-tempered brown mare, and how he had been able to shoot down the werehawk that no one else could. But she did not dare open her mouth. Waves of emotion swept over her, so violent she feared she would faint. *What is this? What is wrong with me?*

'I must renew my prayers,' the Abbess was saying. 'I will fast for the next week, while I endeavour to restore tranquillity to myself and my temple. Let no one disturb me.'

Through the next few weeks, Yayoi became aware that what had been a childish fantasy about Shikanoko – that she would grow up to marry him, cherish him, make him smile, wipe the sorrow from his heart – had become a true adult emotion. The knowledge sustained her. It was a secret as precious as a sutra to be carried in her heart, binding her spirit to his, in the same way the sacred words bound the earthly and the divine.

Lady Fuji came unexpectedly at the beginning of autumn. The typhoons had brought some rain, but less than usual. Summer crops had been sparse, and the shortage of food and the approach of winter had caused unrest among the farmers. It was being harshly suppressed, Lady Fuji told them, and Miboshi warriors were everywhere.

'That is why I need you, Yayoi my dear,' she said, with a sigh. 'It is earlier than I planned, but only by six months or so. And look at you, you are ready. Something has awakened you.'

The other girls wept bitterly and Yayoi could not prevent tears forming in her own eyes. She went to bid farewell to the Abbess and received back the text, the Kudzu Vine Treasure Store, that Master Sesshin had given her all those years ago.

'Let us read it together one last time,' the older woman said. 'Really it is an honour that it has dwelt with us all these years. It has blessed us and so have you.'

Yayoi let the pages fall open where they willed.

The Abbess was studying her face. 'What has it shown you today?'

'It tells of a stone that reveals sickness,' Yayoi said, deciphering the faded gold letters on the indigo dyed page. 'Here is a picture – but now it is gone again!'

It had given her a tantalising glimpse: a surface of perfect smoothness, a dark mirror that had allowed her just one brief glance into its depths.

'Ah, I wonder,' the Abbess murmured.

'What is it?' Yayoi asked.

'If you were staying here I would tell you, but there is no point now.' The Abbess could not hide her distress. 'How I will miss you! I deeply regret the path you are being forced to follow.'

'I still don't understand the truth of the world and why there is so much pain!' Yayoi could feel tears threatening. She did not want to leave; she wanted to stay and learn more about the mysterious stone but she knew the peace and seclusion of the temple were no more than an illusion. Ever since the Miboshi warriors had come to search for Shikanoko, none of the women had felt entirely safe.

'I will always pray for you,' the Abbess continued.

'And I for you,' Yayoi replied.

'Use what you find in the text only for healing. Do not follow my son into sorcery.'

Yayoi bowed without speaking. *I would follow him even into the realms of Hell,* she thought.

Fuji had brought a second palanquin with her. When Yayoi had arrived, she had been a child, small for her age. Now she had reached her adult height she would no longer fit inside a palanquin with the other woman. But she also felt Fuji was glad to keep her distance, that she was not entirely comfortable with whatever plan she had for her. She did not look her in the eye or embrace her spontaneously as she had when she had come to collect Asagao. Alone in the palanquin, Yayoi had plenty of time to imagine what might be going to happen to her and to dread it.

It was dusk when they arrived at Aomizu and the boats on the dock were bright with red lanterns, the lights reflected in the still waters like a host of fireflies. The moon was a crescent in the sky, waxing towards its ninth-month fullness. Music was playing and Yayoi could hear singing. She thought she recognised Asagao's voice and was slightly comforted. She longed to see Take, and then thought of the boy called Yoshi, and felt the lute in her lap begin to stir.

One of the women whispered to Fuji as they stepped on to the boat. 'He is here.'

'What, already?' Fuji exclaimed, biting her lip. 'We hardly have time to prepare her. Quick, bring some water. Let me wash her feet at least. How impatient these Miboshi are,' she muttered as she brushed dust from Yayoi's robes and combed her hair until it fell silky and tangle-free down her back.

'Yayoi,' she said, her voice serious and cold. 'You are a clever girl, they tell me. You know what is expected of you. Charm this warrior, do whatever he wants, please him in every way. My future, the future of all of us on the boats, depends on it.'

She led Yayoi to the stern of the boat where the bamboo blinds surrounded the largest of the separate spaces. She dropped to her knees, raised the blind on one side and, bowing to the ground, said, 'My lord, I have brought the one you requested.'

Yayoi found herself on her knees shuffling forward. The blind unrolled behind her with a slight rustle. The lanterns outside threw wavering shadows as the boat rocked slightly on the water of the lake.

A lamp burned in one corner, the scent of oil strong. By its light she saw him sitting cross-legged, a flask of wine and a bowl beside him. It was the lord, Arinori, who had come to the temple.

'Don't be afraid,' he said. 'Here, drink a little wine, it will relax you.'

She took the bowl and sipped, the liquor flowing like fire into her throat and stomach. It did not relax her but had the opposite effect, making her heart pound with fear. Her whole being recoiled from the idea that this stranger, enemy even, should have intimate access to her body. How is it possible, she thought, that men have such power over women? That even Fuji was complicit in this transaction, that probably bought her privileges, that was pleasing to all parties, except Yayoi herself, without whom the transaction would never have taken place?

'They could not really turn such a little pearl into a serving girl,' he said, coming closer, putting his hand on the back of her neck, feeling her hair, pulling her face towards his. His other hand was inside her robe, caressing her breast, and then reaching further down, forcing her thighs apart.

He had the hard body, the iron muscles, of a warrior. He was nearly twice her size. When he thrust into her it was like being knifed. She could not help crying out from pain and fear. It excited him and she felt the gush of his release, alien in its smell and wetness.

Afterwards he was kind to her, in a way. He stroked her hair and called her his little Princess. He held the wine bowl close to her lips so she could drink, and kissed the tears from her eyes.

He wanted her to know he was a prize, how lucky she was to have attracted him. He was rich and powerful, he would always take care of her. Lord Aritomo himself had named him, he boasted. They were as close as brothers. That week he came every day, expressing his pleasure with gifts of silk robes, casks of wine, and the fine quality rice that was otherwise almost impossible to obtain. Fuji was delighted and showered Yayoi with compliments and affection, any remorse she might have felt dispelled by the success of the transaction.

'Lord Arinori has become our protector. It is just as I hoped. But, Yayoi, you look so thin, you must not lose weight. Eat, eat, it's the sweetest rice we've had all year. Don't fret, don't dwell on what might have been. This is your life now and, while it may not be what your parents might have hoped for you or what you would have chosen, it is better than being dead. Enjoy it, strive to please Lord Arinori, and one day he may even buy you from me for his own.'

Yayoi could not imagine anything worse. When Arinori's duties took him back to the capital, she began to choose men from the visitors that came aboard at Majima, Kasumiguchi, Kitakami and the other market towns around the lake. She learned their desires and their foibles, their needs and their strengths. Some she liked more than others, some became almost friends. But not one of them ever knew that, when she embraced him and gave herself to him, in her heart it was not him she was holding, but the wild boy who had ridden into her father's lands on a brown mare all those years ago.

8

MU

The fox girl laughed when Mu asked her name, as she laughed at most of his questions.

'You can call me Shida, if I have to have a name,' she said, tickling him with a dried fern. She liked to drape herself in the leaves and flowers of the forest as they came into season, making garlands from strands of berries and the brown fronds of bracken for herself and Kaze, and for the child, when it came.

They had been together for four winters. The child was a girl, as slight and delicate as a fern leaf herself. They called her Kinpoge, after the celandines that starred the forest floor around the time of her birth. She did not seem to have any fox attributes, apart from her animal-like agility and her rapid growth, though in certain lights her thick hair had a russet gleam to it and her eyes were amber.

During those years, Shida taught Mu the bright playful magic of the fox people. It seemed to have no purpose other than to make life amusing. She cast a spell on Ban's skull, to Kaze's utter delight, that sent the horse flying through the air. She summoned up shape-shifters, tanuki, cranes, turtles and snakes, just for the fun of startling

Ima or Ku. They never knew if an iron pot was really a pot or a grinning fat-bellied tanuki, or if an old robe, thrown on the ground, might not suddenly sprout wings and launch itself, squawking, into the air.

Her presence seemed to revive many of Shisoku's fake animals. One of the creatures, a cross between a dog and a wolf, which had been Shisoku's water carrier, raised its head from where it had fallen by the stream and Shida ran to help it to its feet, chuckling at its awkward gait.

'You should make a companion for it,' she said, when it tried to lift the water vessel on its own and the water spilled out lopsidedly.

Mu had to admit he did not know how to and that all he did not know overwhelmed him. The forest and the mountain were home to thousands of plants, flowers, trees, grasses and myriad creatures, insects, birds, small animals as well as deer, monkeys, foxes, bears and wolves. There was no one who could teach him their names. Shida did not understand his need to label them. They were all instantly recognisable to her, she did not need words. Mu realised she lived like an animal, in each single moment, observing, feeling, enjoying, but not reflecting or recording. Sometimes he felt himself slipping into the same way of being and days would pass when he hardly had a single thought. Then he would wake in the night from a bad dream in which a stranger who was at the same time familiar accused him of wasting his life. He would lie there in the dark, hearing the others breathing around him, alarmed and uneasy at what he was leaving undone, yet ignorant of what it might be.

He became preoccupied and silent. Shida accused him of being gloomy and turning into an old man before his time. There were no mirrors to look in; he could not check his appearance, yet he felt she was right. He was ageing rapidly. He could see the same thing happening to Ima and Ku. Kaze grew like a human child, but the brothers seemed fated to have lives as short as insects.

And as pointless, he thought.

Even before Kiku returned, Mu and his fox wife quarrelled. Her playful magic no longer enchanted but irritated him. She began to spend time away, with her own people. He missed her with a kind of agony, but was angry with her when she came back.

And then one day Kiku rode into the clearing with Chika and an older man, a warrior with missing fingers and one eye.

They had an air of prosperity about them; their cheeks were fat and their hair sleek. The horses were sturdy, with bright eyes and round haunches. Mu saw the hut and the clearing through his brother's eyes and felt ashamed.

Kiku made no comment, hardly even greeted his brothers, but said as he dismounted, 'I have come for the skull.'

'Do you remember where we buried it?' Mu said, thinking of the day when its owner, the monk, Gessho, had died.

'Oh, yes!' Kiku said.

'What will you do with it?' Mu asked.

Kiku cast a look at Ban, the horse skull he had tried to infuse with power, which stood on its post, motionless. 'I know what I'm doing now. Our father, Akuzenji, had other sorcerers in his service. Tsunetomo took me to one who was familiar with these old matters. He taught me what I have to do. I'm going to try again.'

'Ban can fly,' Kaze told him. 'Shida did it.'

Kiku turned his gaze on Shida, who sat by the fire staring at him with frank interest. 'You can do magic, Lady Shida?'

'A bit of this, a bit of that,' she said carelessly. 'Why do you call me *Lady*?'

'You're a beautiful woman. Are you my brother's wife?'

'No!' she said, laughing, even as Mu said, 'Yes!'

Kiku said, 'I need a beautiful woman to infuse the skull with power.'

'Find your own wife,' Mu said.

'I have come for my wife,' Kiku replied. 'I am going to take Kaze as my wife, sister of my dearest friend. Isn't that right, Chika?'

Chika nodded without speaking. Mu noticed he stayed by Kiku's side, as close as a dog.

Kiku went on, 'But the ritual demands something different, some other woman, one more like our mother.'

'If you touch her, I will kill you,' Mu said.

'Don't be silly,' said Shida. 'You can't dictate what I can and can't do. I don't belong to you. If he wants me to join him in some magic, where's the harm in that?'

Kiku said to Chika, 'Go and dig up the skull. Ima will show you where it is. Then boil a pot of water, Ima. We will clean it tonight, and tomorrow we will start the ritual.'

'No!' Mu cried and leaped at his brother, not knowing what he intended to do, driven only by fear and frustration. But his arms were seized by the warrior, who up to this time had not spoken and who moved faster than Mu would have thought possible. He was strong, too, and held Mu with no effort. Mu struggled to use the second self, to turn invisible, but it was so long since he had used either he was not quick enough.

'What shall I do with him?' the warrior asked.

'I don't know,' Kiku said impatiently.

'Do you want me to kill him?'

'No, not really. I don't want him interfering or distracting me.'

'He won't distract you if he's dead,' the warrior said with a laugh and tightened his grip on Mu's neck, as if he would break it with his bare hands.

'But it would be an inauspicious start to the rituals,' Chika said.

'Take him to the other side of the stream, Tsunetomo, and tie him up there.'

Tsunetomo picked Mu up and strode across the stream. Then, despite his struggles, he trussed him like a goose, in a kneeling position, his hands tied to his feet behind his back. His knots were expert; there was no way Mu could wriggle out of the ropes. After an hour his joints and muscles had set up a scream of pain that dulled his hearing and his senses to everything else.

As night came Ku brought water and stayed beside him, helping him to drink, whimpering like a dog.

'Untie me,' Mu begged, unable to keep himself from whimpering too.

'They say they will kill you, if I do.'

'I would rather be dead, for then I would not feel.'

He could hear all night long the hiss and bubble of the water that was boiling the skull clean.

•

The rituals lasted for several days, during which time, as far as he could tell, Kiku and Shida were alone in the hut, with the skull. Every now and then Mu heard the others talking, smelled the food Ima and Kaze prepared – he himself refused to eat – and saw the horses come to the stream to drink. The sight of him alarmed them, as if they could not determine what he was, and they gazed at him with huge eyes and pricked ears. Often, a silence descended on the clearing, a sudden hush as if the whole forest held its breath in awe at what was taking place within the hut, the transformations that were occurring. Nothing, no one could help being affected by it. When sounds and voices returned, they were solemn and muted. Under Mu's tormented eyes, the hut seemed to glow with light, transformed into an enchanted palace in a garden of wisteria.

Kiku finally emerged and held the skull aloft. It was lacquered now and gleamed black and red with brilliant green jewelled eyes and cinnabar lips, the teeth inlaid with mother of pearl. Mu saw it clearly, because his brother brought it to the side of the stream to wave it in his face.

It was midday. The sun sparkled on the water, on the wet stones, on the mother of pearl.

They began to make preparations to leave. Mu heard Kiku's voice.

'Ku and Ima, you will come with me. From now on we must all be together. I have taken everything I need from this place, its treasure, its knowledge.'

'What about Mu?' Ima said.

'He can stay here and become like Shisoku,' Kiku replied.

'I'm not leaving the animals,' Ku said stubbornly.

Kiku turned the skull towards him and went closer. 'I am your older brother and you will obey me.'

Ku tried to take a step back, but Kiku lowered the skull, grasped his arm and forced him to stare into his eyes. Mu could not see what happened but within seconds Ku had slumped to the ground.

'Pick him up and put him on your horse,' Kiku ordered Tsunetomo, and the warrior obeyed, screwing up his face in a sort of unwilling admiration.

'Now you,' Kiku addressed Ima, but Ima shook his head.

'I need to look after things here. I'll stay with Mu and Kinpoge.'

Mu saw Kiku repeat the same process, and stare intently into Ima's eyes. But Ima stared back. Whatever power the skull had given Kiku did not work on him.

Kiku's eyes flashed with anger and for a moment Mu feared Tsunetomo would be ordered to kill them both. The warrior had his hand on his sword, as eager as a hunting dog.

Kiku turned to the horse, which Chika held ready for him. As he mounted, and Chika lifted Kaze up behind him, he said, 'Stay then. You can untie Mu now.'

Mu screamed as the blood flowed back into his cramped legs. It was a long time before he could stand. When he finally managed it, on ankles that kept bending the wrong way beneath his weight, the clearing was empty, apart from Ima, and Kinpoge who flitted around him like some ghostly spirit.

'Where is your mother?' he said to her, and her amber eyes filled with tears.

'She is in the hut,' Ima said awkwardly. 'I have tried to rouse her but . . .'

Mu hobbled slowly towards it, seeing it clearly in the afternoon light. The magic had all fled. It looked as dilapidated as usual, the roof sagging, the walls subsiding, revealing no trace of what had happened within it. He slid the door and stepped in, his eyes adjusting to the dimness.

Shida lay on the ground, half-naked still, her legs apart, her arms above her head. He thought for a moment that she was dead, but when he knelt beside her she stirred and said something he did not understand. He took her in his arms, helpless to avoid his own clumsiness and the pain it caused them both, but even as he held her he knew her shape was changing.

The fox snarled and snapped at him. He embraced all its loveliness for one last time and then he released his grip and the creature ran from the hut and from his life.

He crawled out after her and saw her disappear into the forest, her tail burning as if with foxfire. He collapsed on the threshold.

Kinpoge knelt beside him, her hand like ice on his brow.

Ima brought rags steeped in hot water to bind the joints, and rocks from the fire to lay against his muscles. The heat seemed to enter his entire body and he burned like the fire itself, until it fled from him, like steam evaporating, and a chill followed that made him shake and shiver uncontrollably. When the fever subsided, it left him weak and in despair. At first he did not recognise this new emotion, but then he realised it was grief and he knew that he had loved her and love had changed him.

•

For a long time, he limped like a cripple and had to use a cane. Winter came early, with the first snow in the eleventh month. It drifted waist deep round the hut and continued to fall for the next two months. If Ima had not been there, Mu and his daughter would have starved, or frozen to death, drifting into their long sleep without noticing. But Ima kept them both alive, going out daily to track hares or rabbits, occasionally bringing down, with an arrow, a squirrel or a pheasant, once even a serow, whose skin made a warm cape for Kinpoge. In some ways, hunting was easier, for against the white snow there was nowhere to hide and neither humans nor animals could conceal their tracks.

Ima kept the fire going too, coming home with armfuls of dead wood, and cooked meals, roasting the tender joints, stewing the rest. Maybe it was the tempting smell of food, or Ima's tracks clear in the snow, that showed the tengu where they were.

The tengu came in the late afternoon, when a blood-red sun was sinking rapidly behind the western mountains, and it was already freezing. The light from the fire and from the lamps in the hut looked tiny against the great snowy mass that the Darkwood had become.

Kinpoge must have seen him first, lurking in the shadows just beyond the firelight, for she cried out and jumped into Ima's arms. Mu looked into the darkness and saw two red eyes glaring at them. He felt for the knife that Ima had been using to cut up the rabbit that would be their supper. Ima slid Kinpoge off his lap, pushed her behind him and reached for his bow.

The tengu was dressed in bright blue leggings and a short red jacket. He had a long beaklike nose and, when he sat down opposite Mu, he made a curious shrugging movement to adjust something feathery between his shoulders, which, at first, Mu thought was a dead bird and then realised was wings. The wings were greyish white and shaggy, almost indistinguishable from the tengu's thick shock of hair. He pulled out a sword and a bow, which he had been carrying on his back between the wings, and laid them down, the sword on his left, the bow on his right.

He gave Mu a long penetrating look and said, 'We would really like to know what's going on. And that rabbit looks good. Give me a piece. I love rabbit.'

He reached out to the embers. He had only three fingers and a thumb.

Ima said, 'It's not cooked yet.'

'I don't mind,' the tengu said, and crammed the half-raw rabbit's leg into his wide mouth.

'He's your brother, isn't he?' he said indistinctly.

'Who?' Mu said, thinking for a moment he meant Ima.

'So-called Master Kikuta, who claims to be Akuzenji's son and the new King of the Mountain.'

'Kiku?' Mu said, with pain, after a long pause.

'Is that his name? Kiku meaning the flower, or Kiku meaning listen?'

'Listen, I think.' Mu had never heard of the flower.

'Well, he writes it like the flower these days, with a fancy crest to go with it, a crest that now appears on the robes of fifty warriors and is stamped on tons of goods going between Kitakami and the east, by road and by sea.'

He had said all this while chewing vigorously, blood and grease running down his chin. Now he swallowed and reached for another piece.

'You know more than we do,' Mu said. 'Why have you come to ask us? We can tell you nothing you don't already know. We have not seen or heard from our brothers since they left in the ninth month. Before that, they were away for years.' He pressed his lips together, trying to master the agony of remembering.

The tengu watched him intently over the rabbit bone he was chewing. He bit into it with his powerful teeth and sucked out the marrow noisily.

'And what were you doing all that time?' There was a note of accusation in his voice that Mu did not care for.

'What business is it of yours?'

The tengu hissed through his teeth in annoyance. 'If I am informed correctly, you are the son of several powerful men and a sorceress of the Old People. I daresay you have many talents. Yet you are skulking here with the half-dead – and even they are ceasing to live – only kept from death yourself by the efforts of your brother, who may not have your abilities but is a lot more practical than you.'

'How can you tell that?' Mu said. 'You've only known us for five minutes!'

'I know many things. I am not without some supernatural ability myself,' the tengu said smugly. Then he addressed Ima in a kind voice. 'This rabbit is delicious. Well caught! Well cooked! In fact, well done, all round.'

Ima narrowed his eyes and said nothing. Kinpoge peeked out from behind him.

'Ah, a little child!' the tengu exclaimed. 'I love children!'

Not in the same way you love rabbit, I hope, Mu said to himself.

'So, what have you been doing?' the tengu repeated.

'Nothing,' Mu admitted. 'What should I be doing?' He recalled his nightmares and immediately wanted to defend himself. 'I have no one to teach me anything. Those you say are my fathers are either dead or distant – either way, they are no use to me and never have been. So I can do certain things real, ordinary people can't, but, as you pointed out, here in the Darkwood Ima's skills are more useful. I can take on invisibility to surprise my daughter, or use the second self to make her laugh, but even that I don't do often, and when I needed to, seriously, I was too slow. I was tied up for days, and now I am half-crippled.'

'Your brother tied you up?'

'Not himself, but on his orders. A warrior who serves him, called Tsunetomo.'

'I know Tsunetomo. He leads the band they call the Crippled Army.'

'Who are they?' Mu said. 'Maybe I should join them.'

'Well, it's a possibility,' the tengu replied. 'But that's some time ahead. They are a bunch of warriors, both Kakizuki and Miboshi, seriously injured in battle, mutilated, scarred, some blind, some without arms, some legless. They became ugly and imperfect and were turned out by their former masters, to starve to death or become bandits. Most of them are thickheads, but one or two among them have picked up some knowledge of this and that. Tsunetomo is not a complete idiot. Now they serve your brother, Master Kikuta. At first he seemed just another ambitious merchant, good at seizing opportunities and ruthless in eliminating his rivals – there are many men like that in Kitakami, but this year something changed.' The tengu had been staring into the flames as he spoke. Now he fixed Mu with his glittering eyes and said, 'He has acquired some magic object from which he derives extreme power.'

Ima looked across at Mu and their eyes locked. Mu raised his eyebrows slightly and Ima made an almost imperceptible movement with his head. The tengu intrigued Mu, and, somewhat to his surprise, he felt he could trust him.

'It is a skull,' he said slowly. 'The head was taken from the monk, Gessho, by Shikanoko when he killed him, and after Shisoku was killed in the same fight. Shisoku was the sorcerer who lived here, and made the creatures.'

'I know Shisoku,' the tengu said impatiently. 'Or knew, I should say.'

'It was buried for years,' Mu went on. 'Kiku returned to retrieve it and invest it with power in secret rituals.'

'Were these rituals conducted by himself alone?'

'With a woman,' Mu forced himself to say. 'A fox woman.'

'Mu's wife,' Ima explained.

Mu steeled himself to meet the tengu's eyes. He felt they saw deep into his heart, even into his soul. They examined him without pity, saw through all the defences he might erect, all the excuses he might make.

'Your name is Mu?' the tengu said. 'Is that Mu written as warrior or Mu written as nothing?'

'I don't know. I have never seen it written.'

'Well, when I have finished with you, you will be both. You will be a great warrior but you will be as nothing, free from all attachments. That is what I am going to teach you.'

The tengu spoke with such assurance Mu could not help laughing. 'You speak as though I have no choice in the matter.'

'That is correct.'

'What is your purpose?' Mu asked.

'I'm not going to tell you.' The tengu cackled with sudden brusque laughter. 'Not yet, anyway.'

The tengu started the next day, waking Mu before it was light. There had been a deep frost in the night and the surface of the snow crackled beneath their feet when they walked outside.

'Since it is winter, we will start with a lesson on how to stay warm,' the tengu announced. He surveyed Mu by the light of a flaming branch he had plucked from the fire. 'Look at you! There is nothing to you. You are as frail as a dead spider. Don't you eat anything?'

'I eat plenty,' Mu said, trying not to shiver.

'I saw you last night, toying with a tiny bit of rabbit, drowning your appetite with that vile twig brew. You should have grabbed that carcase and shoved the whole thing in your mouth. That's what Master Kikuta would do!'

'My daughter and my brother needed to eat too,' Mu said. He had intended his voice to be mild but it came out whiney. 'Not to mention you, Sir Tengu, our honoured guest.'

The tengu cackled. 'Sir Tengu! That's a good one. No one's called me that before.'

'Do you have a name?' Mu said.

'You can call me Tadashii, because I am always right. Now, to work. Watch this.'

He handed the burning torch to Mu and began to breathe in a rapid rhythm. The snow beneath his feet melted immediately, steaming as he sank through the frozen surface down to the buried grass. Standing next to him, Mu felt the heat radiate from him, making him believe for a moment winter was over and spring had come.

'Now you do it,' Tadashii said.

'Just like that? You aren't going to give me any instructions?'

'It should be second nature for you, just like the other skills that you've neglected. Imitate my breathing and think of the warmth of your own blood. That's all I'm going to tell you.'

Tadashii took the smouldering branch back from Mu, waving it in the air so sparks flew from it and it crackled into flame again.

Mu began to breathe in the same rapid way as Tadashii had. He was watching the branch's fiery arc when suddenly he felt its heat inside his belly. His blood began to boil, racing through his veins. The snow steamed around him as he sank through it to the grass beneath. He felt mud under his feet.

'Ha! Ha! Ha!' Tadashii's laughter rang out through the silent forest. 'Easy as breathing, isn't it?'

Mu did not reply at once. Within himself something was melting like the snow. He saw a life beyond the great drifts of grief that had all but buried him, a life where warmth and laughter – and power – were all possible again.

'What else am I going to learn?' he said.

'Everything,' Tadashii promised. 'I am going to teach you everything. It will be very hard work, but fun too.'

•

It was hard work such as Mu had never known, but he revelled in it. All that he had felt was empty was now filled. He no longer dreamed of Shida or yearned after the foxlights that flickered in the marsh. He had a new purpose: to meet every challenge Tadashii threw at him and to master it. He stopped caring what the tengu's intentions might be. The training had no end other than itself. By the time summer came he could use his own innate skills flawlessly and he had learned much more: the art of sword and bow; the roots and herbs of the forest that poisoned or cured; the names and properties of trees, plants, animals, insects; how to trap a stoat, whose meat when dried was a source of courage; how to track bears and wolves; how to recognise scorpions, spiders, snakes and toads, and milk their venom.

His physical strength increased, as Tadashii showed him how to use his muscles and how to build them up. For hours he carried boulders the length of the stream and back again, and while he would never approach the tengu in strength – Tadashii could lift great rocks with one hand – he surpassed most ordinary men, despite his slight build and appearance. He was no longer lame. He kept the stick, but as a weapon. Tadashii forged a sword for him.

Tadashii could not give Mu wings but he showed him how to leap to great heights, how to swing from treetop to treetop like a monkey, how to stride the crags like a mountain goat. He seemed to have an inexhaustible patience, which he also taught to Mu. Indeed Mu thought he must have a different sense of time for though he had spoken with some urgency on their first meeting, now he seemed to be in no hurry, either to solve the problem of 'Master Kikuta', or to leave.

The seasons passed. It was winter again, and then another winter. Often in the long dark nights they played Go or checkers or chess, for the tengu loved all games, but still he gave no indication of what his original purpose might have been.

•

One spring night, two years after the tengu arrived, he took Mu by the shoulders and flew with him high above the forest towards the side of the mountain. It was the night of the full moon of the third month and they could see as clearly as if it were day. Mu caught a glimpse of water that was Lake Kasumi, and the river that flowed from it all the way to the capital, and, in the other direction, the Northern Sea.

Tadashii landed on a ledge, where rocks had been placed in a circle, dropping Mu gently in the centre of them. On each rock perched winged tengu; some, like Tadashii, had beaks, others long red noses. They were all armed with swords and bows. To see so many at once was alarming. Mu had landed on his hands and knees and he now turned this into a deep, reverent bow.

'Welcome,' said a number of voices, all low and gruff, like Tadashii's.

'So this is your pupil?' said one long-nosed being.

'It is,' Tadashii replied. 'His name is Mu, the warrior of nothingness.'

'Does he understand the principles of being and non-being, of form and no-form?' the tengu asked.

'That's not as important as being able to play a good game,' another tengu interrupted. 'Is he going to be a player or a stone on the board?'

'That is not yet decided,' Tadashii said. 'I am hoping you, my masters, will look on him favourably and instruct him.'

'If he is able to learn we will teach him. Let us see if he can survive our lessons.' There was a ripple of laughter as if the tengu did not really believe that was possible.

Tadashii touched Mu's head. 'Be strong,' he whispered. 'I hope we meet again.'

Mu shivered slightly. The uncharacteristic affection alarmed him as much as Tadashii's words. There was a faint rush of air against his face, as Tadashii flexed his wings, followed by a greater rush as all the tengu rose into the air, leaving him alone on the mountainside.

Alone, but not alone. Physically the tengu might have departed but they were still present in some way, observing Mu, as the moon set and the stars wheeled overhead. He settled, cross-legged, in the meditation position Tadashii had taught him, reminding himself he had been tied up for a week, in a far more uncomfortable way, and had survived. The first light of dawn filled the sky and birds began to sing piercingly. The mountain air was cold, heavy with dew. Mu warmed himself, almost without thinking. The hours passed. He was neither hungry nor thirsty. He had no needs and no desires.

He knew only the eternal being that includes all life, all death, in which each person exists for a tiny moment and is then absorbed back into the endless void of all and nothing.

He knew he had great powers; he saw they were meaningless. He embraced the nothingness of his name.

He lost all track of time. He seemed to take leave of his body and fly above the land. At first it looked like a Go board and then more like a vast scroll, presenting various scenes to him. He left the Darkwood behind and soared over Lake Kasumi. He saw the lake was shrinking, its marshlands drying out, a rim of half-dried, foul-smelling mud clogging its beaches. He was above a city, to the north of the lake. Could this be Kitakami? He peered down, through buildings that seemed to have no roofs, so he could see straight into them. He saw Kiku, grown older, surrounded by servants and retainers. Mu perceived the network of his business empire, spreading like a spider's web over the land.

Then the wind took him and blew him towards the south. He saw a young woman on a pleasure boat, entertaining a man who looked like a merchant, one of Kiku's rivals perhaps, and he looked deep down into the lake, where someone lay hidden, breathing through a reed. To his surprise, he recognised Chika. On the shore red lanterns denoted a festival. A troupe of acrobats were performing with monkeys. Mu noticed a strong well-built boy, about twelve or thirteen years old, and an older lad, maybe in his twenties, wiry and flexible, a natural performer, with attractive expressive features, who kept the crowd spellbound. A young girl of the same age beat time on a drum, her eyes fixed on the performer. A large black bird with a sprinkle of gold feathers hovered above him and it suddenly soared upwards, as if it sensed Mu's presence. He saw its bright yellow eyes searching, but it did not see him.

Now he was over the capital, floating above mansions and palaces. In a sumptuous room a great lord, his face grey tinged and gaunt, was retching into a silver bowl. Outside, warriors and noblemen gathered anxiously. Along the river bank were strewn corpses. Dogs scavenged among them. The river was a thin, dirty trickle. He was above a temple, newly built from gleaming cypress and cedar. Again he could see straight down into the halls and cloisters. An old man sat with a lute on his knees. He seemed to be dozing but as Mu passed overhead he startled and turned his face upwards, listening. Mu saw into the depths of the lake where a sleeping dragon lay coiled, its scales shimmering dully in the murky water. A swirling motion began, a whirlpool formed, the dragon stretched and flexed. In the main hall of the temple a figure knelt, chanting sutras, before an altar where golden statues and painted deities kept watch. A woman's voice rose and circled around the lutist's song. The notes vibrated and echoed against each other until the friction became unbearable. At the edges of the land, smoke was rising, as when a scroll is first thrown on the fire. Its edges blacken, it begins to contort in the heat, scorch marks appear here and there, finally flames seize hold.

The land is about to burn, Mu realised.

Only the Darkwood seemed untouched. With a sense of gratitude and relief, he turned back to its dark green mass. He and Tadashii had made many journeys through the forest, but now Mu went further than he ever had before. He was shown a building hidden among the trees, high in the mountains, a small shrine perhaps, or a hermit's retreat. Looking down through the canopy of leaves he saw two silver-grey horses grazing in a clearing. Nearby a wolf-like creature kept watch.

Gen!

In the clearing were four figures involved in an intricate dance. One was clearly a woman, though she dressed like a man. Two wore black cloths over their faces, covering everything but their eyes. The fourth wore a mask, a stag's head with one broken antler.

'Shikanoko!' Mu cried.

Shikanoko looked up, the only person to notice Mu's presence. Unlike the bird, he could see him. Mu felt their eyes meet and lock, but before he could speak he sensed he was losing the power of flight. For a moment he thought he would plummet to earth, and he almost blacked out as he rushed through the air, but he calmed himself and summoned his concentration, and found himself with a thump back on his mountain ledge.

Tadashii was sitting waiting for him. 'Not a very elegant landing,' he said. 'But otherwise, my masters have reported you did quite well. You have seen the state of the board. I hope we will soon be ready for my next move.'

'Do you think you could explain a little more clearly?' Mu said. The tengu did not reply.

'I saw many strange things that I don't understand,' Mu persisted. 'Meditate on them.' Tadashii refused to say anything else.

•

Her father was so preoccupied during the years of the tengu's training, he hardly noticed Kinpoge growing up. She turned more and more to Ima, who took care of her, fed her and taught her how to hunt and to cook. She liked to catch fish, taking them out of the water with her bare hands; she knew where to gather fern heads and burdock, mushrooms and chestnuts. She looked after the fake animals that remained and, particularly, the skull horse, Ban. She gave it grass and water every morning and, in the evenings, rode it through the air. She wove reins for Ban from the green rushes, and tied two cross pieces onto the pole, one as a hand hold and one for her feet. In spring and summer she made garlands of flowers and decorated the skull.

Sometimes she wished she had a real horse but, as Ima pointed out, a real horse could not fly and it would grow old and die, whereas Kiku had, unwittingly, given Ban another kind of life.

Ban responded to her attentions, turned its head towards her when she approached and leaped joyfully into the air when she untethered it.

She did not go far from the hut where she had lived all her life. Mountains surrounded it and she did not think Ban could fly that high. But she often followed the course of the stream that flowed past the hut. After a few miles, it divided into two, one branch continuing to the west, the other turning southward. Once, she had gone south, but, after a while, the land became cultivated and there were too many people around. She knew instinctively that she should keep hidden and that she should never give away the location of the hut.

So, instead, she and Ban explored the west branch, which flowed through a steep, thickly wooded valley. Occasionally she saw movements in the trees and she realised monkeys lived there.

The monkeys fascinated her. She watched the mothers and babies with a kind of hunger – she who had hardly known her own mother. The mothers took such good care of the babies. In the summer they roamed carefree through the forest, leaping from tree to tree like her father, and in winter they gathered around the pools of the hot springs. Kinpoge spied on them through the branches of the leafless trees. Once or twice they noticed the skull horse and shrieked in alarm, as they did when eagles flew overhead.

One day, near sunset, it was maybe her tenth or eleventh spring on earth – like her father she had matured quickly and was nearly an adult – she and Ban were hovering over the thick canopy, hoping to catch sight of the monkeys, when a boy's face popped out through the leaves, staring at her in astonishment. She could not tell his age, but he seemed taller than she was. His eyes were long and narrow, his nose rather sharp, his cheekbones high. The sun's rays shone round him like a halo.

'Hello!' he exclaimed, and then, hurriedly, 'Don't be frightened! Don't leave!'

Ban was quivering beneath Kinpoge's hands. She knew she should escape quickly, but then the boy pulled himself a little higher so his feet were planted firmly in the crook of the branches, and stood up. Two monkeys pushed through the leaves. One climbed onto his shoulders, peering at Kinpoge and Ban and chattering excitedly. The other sat beside the boy, holding onto his leg with one hand and scratching his own belly with the other.

'Who are you?' the boy said. 'Are you some magic creature? You must be, for you are so small and you are riding a very strange-looking steed. Do you understand human speech?' When she did not reply he persisted. 'Do you speak some fairy language?' He began to mime his words with extravagant gestures that made her laugh.

'I understand you,' she called across the space between them.

'What's your name? Mine is Takemaru – everyone calls me Take – but that's a child's name. Soon I will take an adult name, for I am nearly grown up.'

'Kinpoge,' she said.

'Like the flower? That is so beautiful. And it suits you, you are so small and bright! Where do you live? In the treetops?'

'I live with my father and my uncle. A little way upstream. I must go now.'

'Come again,' he said. 'I will look out for you.'

'Goodbye!' Kinpoge cried, turning Ban's head to the east.

She did not tell her father or Ima about the encounter. Both had warned her never to let herself be seen, never to talk to anyone. But she could not stop thinking about the boy, Takemaru, and she wanted very much to see him again. The next day she wove a fresh garland of spring flowers for Ban and, in the afternoon, she set out again. She knew she should not fly towards the west but somehow she could not help it.

The days were lengthening and there were still several hours before nightfall. The sun in the west dazzled her. It made the shiny new green leaves glisten as they danced in the breeze. It was the fourth month and already very hot. There was no sign of rain and even the dew, which usually soaked the forest every night, had dried up. Every tree was familiar to her and she could tell each one was suffering. They had responded to the demands of the season and had put out new leaves but it had cost them; they were becoming frail, their roots no longer held firmly by the embracing earth.

She guided Ban to the same tree and there was the boy, alone this time. His face lit up when he saw her and he held out his hand. Kinpoge took it and, still holding Ban's bridle so the skull horse could not fly away, stepped nimbly onto the branch.

The tree swayed in the wind, the leaves rustled, the humming of insects rose around them. There was a strong, heady smell of blossoms and catkins. Take held her firmly.

'I'm all right,' she said, easing herself from his grasp and sitting down astride the branch. 'I won't fall.'

'You should be an acrobat,' he said, sitting down facing her. 'You are so light and adroit. But, I don't know why, girls never are, only boys. Even Kai who is agile like you has to be content with playing the drum.'

'I don't know what you're talking about,' she said. They were so close their knees almost touched. 'What's an acrobat? Is it something to do with the monkeys?'

'In a way. We do tricks with the monkeys. People like to watch us. They give us food, clothes, even coins sometimes. We go to all the markets and every year, at this time, we come to the forest to look for suitable monkeys to train – do you know what train means?'

'I do!' Kinpoge screwed up her face. 'My father is being trained by a tengu. It's been going on for years. I hope your monkeys don't take as long!'

'A tengu?' She could tell this interested Take very much. 'A real tengu? What is he teaching him?'

'Everything. But mostly how to fight with sword and bow.'

'How to kill people?' Take's eyes gleamed.

'I suppose so, though I think it's more about not letting them kill you, as far as I can see. And then there's a lot of meditation and spiritual exercises. My father is often absent for weeks and when he comes back he seems like a different person.'

'Different in what way?' Take asked, and then added quietly, 'I have never known my father.'

'You haven't missed much. Fathers are very tiresome, at least mine is. He has seen and learned things most people don't know about. Well, I can't really say what most people do or don't know, as you are the only real person I've met. But the tengu teaches him secrets and shows him hidden things.'

Take sighed. 'I'd give anything for that kind of instruction. I feel I should have been born to the way of the sword and the bow. But the acrobats I grew up among follow a different path. They will not kill anything. They eat only fruit and plants.'

'Come back with me,' Kinpoge said eagerly. 'Ima, my uncle, will make you roast hare or a meat stew. And we'll ask my father if he will share the tengu's teaching with you.'

•

Ima was out in the forest, somewhere. Mu was alone, going through the rigorous exercises he followed every day. The tengu no longer lived at the hut – he had gone away on a mission he did not reveal – but Mu continued to work as if Tadashii still breathed down his neck with his hot peppery breath and clacked his beak in admonishment.

He was inside the hut, in front of the altar that Shisoku had made years before. The tengu had shown him the meaning of all the objects the old hermit had collected: the augury sticks, the reed arrows, the protective carvings made of peachwood, the panels depicting the twelve cardinal points, the twelve month guardians, the twelve animals of the cycle of the years. He had explained how to use them, and access their power, just as he had explained the curses that lay sealed, with the five poisonous creatures, in their jars – curses that killed an enemy and then controlled his soul.

Mu had grown up among these things and had never appreciated their power, though Kiku had. His brother had known enough to perform rituals in this place, with the fox woman, Shida. After that time, Mu could hardly bear to enter the hut and at one time had wanted to burn it down. Through Tadashii's teaching, he had faced that pain and humiliation and seen them as illusions of heart and mind. The memory no longer touched him.

He did not like to be interrupted or even watched. Usually, Kinpoge and Ima kept out of his way. But now his daughter's voice broke into the clear well his mind had become, sending unwelcome ripples through it. At first he ignored her, wanting to stay in that removed state of concentration that had become the source of knowledge and power for him, but her voice was as sharp and insistent as a crow's.

'Father! Father, where are you? I've brought someone to meet you.'

He heard steps right outside and leaped to his feet. He did not want to let any stranger in. Taking on invisibility, he slipped through the doorway. For a moment, unseen, he studied them: the girl, his child, her ragged clothes and unkempt hair, her small face appearing like the pale moon among dark clouds, her bare arms and legs, scratched and scarred. And alongside her the boy, tall, handsome, he supposed, with the face of a young warrior, but wearing strange red clothes, his hair tied in a topknot, his shoulders unexpectedly broad for his age, his arms and legs as muscled as a grown man's. He recognised him, and after a moment remembered he had seen him on his flight over the land. What did that mean? That he and the other acrobat and the girl drummer were all somehow connected to him and Tadashii? Despite this, the sight of him filled Mu with a kind of unreasoning anger. It would be a pleasure to kill him.

He was surprised by the anger. It was a long time since his peace of mind had been disturbed by emotion. He looked at it dispassionately and let it slip away.

Then he said quietly, 'Kinpoge. I am here.' He let himself be seen.

They both turned at the sound of his voice, the boy with a startled expression on his face, the girl more exasperated.

'Don't play tricks on us, Father!'

'Surely we walked right past . . . how did we not see him?' the boy whispered in Kinpoge's ear. Mu heard him clearly.

'It's just something he does. I told you he was tiresome.' Kinpoge held the skull horse by the woven reins. She gave it a perfunctory pat and thrust its pole into the ground.

'Did the tengu teach him?'

'He's always been able to do it. But he's got better at it, since the tengu came.'

It amused Mu to hear Kinpoge's assessment of his progress. He was smiling, as the boy approached him, which must have encouraged him, for he bowed his head and said boldly, 'Sir, my name is Takemaru. There's no reason why you should show me any favour but your daughter has told me about your great skill and, well . . .' His formal tone deserted him and he dropped to his knees. 'I have no one to teach me how to fight with the sword and the bow. Please let me become your pupil.'

'What a ridiculous idea,' Mu said, neither moving nor bowing. 'Go away. Don't come back. Kinpoge, you are not to meet him again.'

As the boy raised his head Mu saw the disappointment in his face. Kinpoge said, 'Father, please!'

'Don't argue! It's impossible. Now go away.' Mu settled himself, cross-legged, and pretended to tend the fire.

'I'd better go,' Takemaru said.

'I'll come and see you again.' Kinpoge's voice was thin with emotion.

'No, if your father forbids it, you must not,' he said seriously. 'You must obey your father.'

'Quite right,' Mu remarked. 'Now get going!'

'Goodbye, sir. Goodbye, Lady Kinpoge.' He bowed formally and began to walk away, his back straight, his stride proud.

'Wait!' Kinpoge cried. 'I'll go with you. I'll show you the way.'

'Stay here,' Mu ordered.

He sensed the conflict within her between desire and obedience. He saw her struggle and then, suddenly, with no warning, the second self emerged. He had seen it so often in his brothers and, since the tengu's arrival, he had used it himself, with increasingly refined mastery, but he had not really expected his daughter to have the same skills. The shadow Kinpoge began to flit after the boy who walked resolutely on, ignorant of what was happening behind him. The real Kinpoge wavered for a moment. Her eyes began to roll backwards. Mu caught her as she fell.

The other Kinpoge faded as the two selves merged. He splashed water on her face and rubbed her wrists. After a moment she opened her eyes.

'What happened?'

'You did one of my tiresome tricks,' Mu said.

'Was I invisible?'

'No, there were two of you. You discovered your second self.'

'Really? It felt strange.'

'You will learn to control it,' he said, 'and use it when you want to.'

'How exciting!' Kinpoge's eyes gleamed. 'But I'd really like to be able to become invisible.'

'Maybe that will come too.' It made Mu sad. She was almost grown up. What would become of her? Who would marry her? Who would look after her when he and Ima passed on? The tengu had promised he would be free of all attachments, but this one for his daughter obstinately remained.

She lay in his arms, in a way she had not since she was a child. They were still sitting like that when Ima returned carrying a large dead hare. He looked at them but said nothing, then began to build up the fire, which had almost burned out, with exaggerated care.

'Uncle, I used the second self,' Kinpoge announced.

'You did? I thought you would sooner or later!'

'You expected it?' Mu said. 'I didn't. It took me by surprise.'

'You only have to consider who her father is, and her mother, for that matter,' Ima replied.

While the fire burned brightly, producing the glowing embers that would roast the hare, Ima skinned the creature and removed the entrails. Kinpoge took the skin down to the creek. Two of the dogs followed her hopefully. Mu could hear the scrape of the knife on the skin. The fur was thick and soft. They sewed the hides together to make blankets for winter.

The meat smelled fragrant as it began to roast. He thought it would bring her back soon; she was always hungry. Then his sharp ears caught another voice. The dogs barked and fled back to the fire.

'Hello, little girl. That smells good. I think I will stay for supper.'
The tengu stepped out of the shadows and jumped nimbly across
the stream.

Kinpoge dropped the skin and the knife, and hugged him.
Tadashii picked her up with one hand, set her on his shoulders,
and walked towards the fire.

'It's not cooked yet,' Ima warned before he could say anything.
'Don't touch it!'

'You know I don't mind raw meat,' Tadashii replied sulkily.

Kinpoge slipped down to the ground. 'Let's play a game while
we wait.'

'Maybe later,' he said. 'I need to talk to your father.'

'Did you finish cleaning the skin?' Ima said to Kinpoge.

'Nearly,' she replied.

'Well, go and finish it. Then string it up where the animals can't
reach it.' Ima's voice, as always, was kindly but firm. Kinpoge usually
obeyed him, without question, whereas she tested her father, arguing
with him endlessly. Now she went back to the bank of the stream
and picked up the hare skin. From the way she shook it, Mu guessed
it was already crawling with ants.

'Let's go inside,' the tengu suggested.

Mu looked at Ima before he agreed, but his brother was staring
at the hare as it sizzled in the embers, and did not return his gaze.

When they were in the hut, the tengu bowed respectfully in
the direction of the altar and sat cross-legged on the floor. Mu sat
opposite him, just where he had been a short time ago when Kinpoge
had called him.

'Don't feel sorry for him,' the tengu said.

'Who?' Mu's thoughts had progressed to the boy, Takemaru.

'Your brother, Ima.'

Mu shrugged. 'I don't, on the whole. But sometimes it seems a little unfair. We were all born at the same time from the same mother. None of us chose our parents or our circumstances. Yet Kiku, Kuro and I have talents our brothers don't have.'

'Fair, unfair, these words have no meaning for me.' Tadashii dismissed the idea with a contemptuous wave of his four-fingered hand. 'Your brother Ku is perfectly happy being a servant to Master Kikuta in Kitakami. And Ima has talents you still don't appreciate. He plays a very good game of chess, for example. He is content with his life, isn't he?'

'I don't know. Is he?'

The tengu scowled, as though he was unable to answer this. 'That's not what I've come to talk to you about,' he said.

Mu raised his eyebrows and remained silent.

'I sent you a pupil,' said the tengu. 'And you sent him away.'

'You sent him?'

'Well, not in so many words. But I intended him to come.'

'You could have told me,' Mu replied.

'I expect you to discern this sort of thing,' Tadashii said, sounding irritated. 'Didn't you recognise him and guess who he might be?'

'He told me his name was Takemaru.'

'Takeyoshi is his real name. He is the son of Shikanoko and the Autumn Princess. He has come to the Darkwood with the one they call Yoshi, Yoshimori, the true Emperor. Neither of them know who they are. They think they are monkey boys and acrobats. We need you to teach Takeyoshi to be a warrior, join forces with your brother, find Shikanoko, and offer him these forces so the Emperor might be restored and Heaven placated. Then we can get back to normal.'

Mu recalled the acrobats he had seen, the girl with the drum. 'Is that what it's all been for?' he said. He gazed past the tengu's face at the objects of power clustered all around him, some on shelves, hidden in awe of their effect, beneath seven-layered cloths or in boxes within boxes.

'Well, it's part of a plan we came up with. Out of desperation, if you must know.'

'Why don't you teach him?' Mu asked.

'I might, in due course. In fact, I must. An injustice was done a long time ago that I am trying to put right. Something that was stolen must be recovered. But it is hard for me to make contact with a fully human person who has no knowledge of the other worlds. You have shown that you can travel between them. You will be my bridge to Takeyoshi. It's your turn to be the teacher. You never know how complete your learning is until you pass it on. You could call it the ultimate stage. And the other parts of your mission could not be achieved by anyone else. You alone can be reconciled with your brother. You alone can find Shikanoko.'

'I saw him,' Mu said. 'That time I flew. He is in the Darkwood, but far to the north.'

'Very good!' Tadashii seemed more pleased than Mu had ever known him before, and even though he suspected the tengu was flattering him so Mu would carry out his wishes, he still felt a warm glow from the praise.

'I thought I saw a woman there with him,' he said, 'and two men.'

'We hope the woman is going to kill the man called Masachika,' the tengu said. 'And the men are known as the Burnt Twins. Shikanoko has to be brought back to this world. If he stays much longer in the Darkwood he will become a deer-like creature and if he dies his spirit will be that of a stag, possibly a god, but he will not be able either to enter the Pure Land or to be reborn.'

'When I saw him he wore the deer mask and was dancing,' Mu said.

'He is close to the edge. Soon he will be beyond saving. Unless the mask is removed by a pure spirit who loves him, he will be lost.'

'Is there any such person?' Mu remembered the raw emotion with which Kiku had revealed what happened at Ryusonji. 'He loved the Autumn Princess but she is dead.'

'I don't know much about that side of human life,' Tadashii said. 'I've observed there are certain acts that bring pleasure and produce children – that's all very well, I suppose, but why complicate it?'

Mu said, 'There is passion, and jealousy, the desire to possess another, the fear of losing her.'

'But you have put all that behind you, haven't you?'

'I suppose so,' Mu said. 'Living here, I haven't had much choice.'

'I'm glad, though, that you seem to know something about it, for you may recognise such a person.'

'It could be any one of us,' Mu said. 'We all loved and respected Shikanoko.'

'I think it has to be female,' Tadashii said bluntly.

'What about the woman I saw?'

The tengu laughed, in a coarse way. 'No, she is not for him.'

'Which should I do first?' Mu asked, thinking about the various tasks that lay ahead of him.

'Follow your nose,' Tadashii said, tapping his own beak and cackling.

'Should I go after this Takeyoshi and bring him back?' Mu said.

'You have missed the opportunity,' the tengu replied. 'It will be another year before he returns to the Darkwood. Next time, don't turn him away.'

9

YOSHI

That was one of the best performances we've ever done, Yoshi thought as he walked towards where Kai sat with her drum balanced between her knees. It was a warm still night – too hot for early spring but the drought seemed more bearable once darkness came and the brilliant stars appeared in the clear sky. Crowds lately had been harder to please. People had more serious concerns: their crops, their children's health, shortages of food, ever-increasing taxes. It had been a hard winter followed as usual by the most difficult time of year. Spring brought more work but less food and in the warmer weather diseases spread more rapidly. Tonight at the start the crowd had been sullen, even hostile but by the end they were laughing.

I won them over! he thought with pride, for he knew it was him they stayed to watch. The music and the monkeys caught their attention but it was his performance that kept them spellbound. Saru had always been popular and had taught Yoshi everything he knew but now Yoshi's leaps, somersaults and back flips had more daring and assurance, looked more dangerous, yet never failed. The monkeys were inspired by him, would do anything he asked of them and watched him with devoted eyes.

He was not sure of his exact age but he knew he was at the height of his ability. He had seen the older men age suddenly before they were thirty. Their life was physically hard and the demands they made on their bodies huge. He himself probably did not have many years left, but at the moment he was the shining star, the sun, the moon, of the troupe.

Saru called, 'We're going back to the boat to eat.'

The villagers had been generous in the end but they had little to share: a basket with four eggs, a handful of early greens, little cakes of millet and dried seaweed. The acrobats were always hungry. Performing and travelling used up so much energy, and none of them ate meat or fish, having taken vows since childhood to take no life, not animal or insect, and certainly not human.

Yoshi made a gesture to show he'd heard him. No doubt Saru would be annoyed but Yoshi was going to speak to Kai and make sure she came with them. Nothing else made Saru jealous, but this would. Yoshi knew Saru loved him as much as the monkeys did. They had grown up together and shared everything in life. But Kai had known Yoshi in his other life, that no one else knew about, that he never talked about. She was as close to him and as essential as one of his own limbs.

He studied her as he went towards her. The torchlight fell on her face, which was flushed with the thrill of performing, and reflected in her shining eyes. A piece of material wound around her head held her hair back and hid her ears, but she pulled it away as he approached and let her hair fall around her. He was still half-drunk with the applause and the excitement and a wave of desire for her swept over him.

Lady Fuji had tried to keep Kai away from the acrobats, telling her she must stay with the family of musicians who had adopted her, but no one could stop Kai doing what she wanted, especially once she turned sixteen and came of age. She scorned any suggestion that she might marry one of the boys she had grown up with and while she still played on the pleasure boats with the musicians, she joined the acrobats whenever she could and beat her drum for them. She had no fear of water and she followed them round the lake in her own boat. A fisherman from Aomizu had vanished from this vessel one night. The next day it could be seen bobbing about on the waves. Sometimes it seemed there was a figure in it; sometimes it looked empty. No one dared go near it in case it had become possessed by the spirit who had pulled the unfortunate man into the water and who might drown them too. But Kai swam out to it and brought it back to shore, had it blessed by the old priest with whom the acrobats worshipped, and from then on navigated it skilfully from shore to shore, followed by flocks of blue and white herons with whom she seemed to have a deep connection, calling to them and imitating their harsh cries. Often Yoshi would find himself thinking of her and would soon after hear the splash of the single oar and see her shape outlined against the evening sky and feel his heart expand with sheer joy.

About a year before, on another spring evening, they had become lovers. He had seen her out on the lake and had waited for her after the others had packed up and left to find shelter for the night. She had jumped out of the boat straight into his arms as though the moment had been preordained by the gods. He had pushed her hair back and kissed her tiny unformed ears. The boat had drifted off into deep water and Kai had broken away from him to swim after it and pull it back to shore. They were both laughing with happiness as she took off her wet clothes and he pulled her close to warm her, feeling all the curves and planes of her body and marvelling at how he fitted perfectly against them, then within them.

Now he held her again, remembering that time, recapturing its thrill and ecstasy. She was trembling and her eyes were full of longing as she led him to a deserted part of the beach and they lay down together under the stars.

Afterwards as he rested, spent, against her, caressing her silky skin, there was a sharp call and he heard the beat of wings as Kon settled on a rock nearby.

'He never leaves you,' Kai said. 'I would worry more about you if Kon were not always watching over you.'

'He doesn't actually do anything,' Yoshi replied, 'except irritate me. He hides for a while among other birds, and I think he's gone, but he always reappears again.'

'Kon bears witness to who you are,' Kai said quietly. 'I think I would have forgotten if it weren't for him.'

'Better if we all forget it.' Yoshi eased himself away from her a little.

'How much do you remember?' They had never spoken about their past, their childhood in the palace, their flight from the burning city. 'Do you remember the day the werehawk came? It was after that that everything began to change. It knew you, then. It bowed to you. Was that Kon, or another one?'

'Let's not talk about it,' Yoshi muttered.

'We need to.' She took his hand and laid it on her belly. 'Your child is growing inside me. Can you feel how my body is changing?' She guided his hand to her breasts. 'See how they are heavier and fuller. It will be born in the winter of this year.'

He wanted to make love to her again, but she hesitated. 'If you are the true Emperor,' she whispered in a tiny voice, 'you cannot be kept from the Lotus Throne. Who are we to try to defy the will of Heaven? But then we will be separated. What will become of our child?'

'I am just Yoshimaru, the monkey boy,' he whispered back. 'We have kept it secret for so long, we will continue to do so. We will be a family. You are my wife. It's what I've always wanted ever since we were children. You must know that.'

'I do,' she replied. 'I remember being told all the time that I would never be suitable for you because of my ears, and I used to cry myself to sleep at the thought of you marrying someone else.'

'We had the luck to end up together in a world where these things don't matter,' Yoshi said. 'If your ears were not misshapen Fuji would have taken you for her own trade.' He kissed first one, then the other. 'We should be thankful to them.'

'It's only that when Akihime saved your life and we fled from the palace, you said, "If I am to reign, I cannot die now." Do you remember that?'

'I was just a child,' Yoshi said. 'I didn't understand anything. After Saru and the others found me in the forest, for a long time I expected Akihime to come back for me. I dreaded it. When I heard she was dead I grieved for her, but then I realised she had died without giving me away, and I was profoundly grateful, but most of all relieved. I've never wanted to be anything else but an acrobat, to be with you, to follow the teachings of the Secret One, and now to have our child. If anyone finds out about me I'll be put to death. The Miboshi have their own Emperor, my uncle Daigen. My death would legitimise him.'

Kai pulled him close. 'Then we will never breathe a word, and we will pray that Heaven continues to ignore us. No one else knows, do they?'

He did not answer her but he was thinking of the girl pulled from the lake, the girl who had the lute, Genzo, who was now one of

Lady Fuji's most popular pleasure women. She had never spoken of his secret to him and she had kept the lute hidden away. But she had known who he was in that moment on the boat, for Genzo had told her. And then there was Shikanoko. Yoshi did not know if he was alive or dead, and had never mentioned him to Kai. But he still relived that moment on the edge of the stream when he had thought he would die, and Shikanoko still strode through his dreams with his antlered mask and drawn sword.

HINA (YAYOI)

Lake Kasumi was drying up. Villages that had been on the water's edge were now half a mile away, and often boats ran aground as the channels became shallow. This was not the only way life had become harder for the riverbank people. For years they had escaped scrutiny, living and working as they did between the worlds, on thresholds, in the spaces between high and low water, which are neither inside nor outside, neither land nor sea. They considered themselves different from ordinary people and therefore not subject to the same laws. Everything they did had a kind of magic to it: they created wares that had not existed before and transformed them into other things by way of exchange and barter, increasingly for coins, which were themselves a numinous creation. They trained animals for entertainment and lived alongside them. They controlled and dispensed the ephemeral ecstasies of music and sex, both inexhaustible, given away freely and constantly renewed, never drying up.

These gifts were not paid for, as such, but were reciprocated with other gifts, silken robes, bolts of cloth, the finest teas and wines, ceramic bowls, carvings, parasols, prayer beads. Eventually, this came to the attention of Lord Aritomo, who could not rest unless every part of his realm was brought under his control. He made a law that all entertainers and traders should be licensed. His own officials would issue permits, in return for a share in the gifts, which suddenly turned, in a quite unmagical way, into taxable produce, providing income for Aritomo's armies, his roads, and fortifications.

Because Yayoi could not only read and write, but also calculate, and because her charm was famous, it fell to her to deal with these officials. Lady Fuji, who had built up a floating empire of pleasure boats, and who was most reluctant to share the results of her good fortune and business skills with anyone, relied on her more and more.

'I wish I could come upon some scheme to stop them bothering us,' she said after one difficult encounter, when they had finally managed to make an official forget why he had paid them a visit. 'I don't know what I would do without you. Truly, it must have been Heaven that sent you. Wasn't it a miracle how the wind drove the acrobats' boat across the lake to gather you up, you and Takemaru, and then changed to bring you to me?'

They had often talked about that day, twelve or more years earlier, when Yayoi had fled from Nishimi, a baby in her arms, along with the lute and the Kudzu Vine Treasure Store. It was almost like a ritual or a ballad. Yayoi gave the expected response, hardly needing to take her attention away from her calculations, thinking fleetingly of the child she had been, when her name had been Hina.

'You and the gods saved my life that day.'

'It was surely our fate, for now you are as close to me as the daughter I never had.'

'I will always look after you, as if you were my own mother,' Yayoi replied.

'You were not the only young girl I rescued,' Fuji mused.

'I know, you have helped many who would otherwise have died.'

The girls Yayoi had known at the convent had grown up like her to become the women on the pleasure boats: Asagao, still her dearest friend, Yuri, Sada, Sen and Teru, and all the others selling their songs and smiles.

'One came like you, with a boy and a younger girl.'

Yayoi marked her place with her finger and began to pay attention. Fuji was a woman of many secrets and divulged them only when it served her purpose.

'She said he was her brother. He was about six or seven, a proper little princeling. I remember explaining the sacred and the profane to him. He was afraid of pollution. And now look at him – he has lived with the monkeys for so many years, he has almost become one of them. And the little girl is Kai, the drummer.'

'Which boy is that?' Yayoi said, striving for calm. 'I can hardly tell them apart.'

'Yoshimaru. His older sister carried a lute just like yours, though she did not have your talent. I don't believe she could really play at all, yet the lute played itself, the sweetest music you've ever heard. I suppose it was enchanted in some way. Which reminds me, I haven't seen your lute for years. Do you keep it hidden away?'

Yayoi said nothing until Fuji had fallen silent for so long it seemed unnatural not to respond. 'What happened to her?' Yayoi asked, though she knew better than Fuji.

'Kai was too ill to travel when the other two left us to go to Rinrakuji. We heard the temple burned down around the same time. Yoshimaru turned up with Sarumaru, and the monkeys, a few months later, but there was no sign of his sister and he's never mentioned her. I often wondered what became of her. She was not as beautiful as you, but she had a sort of wild charm, like a young boy. Her father had laid a condition of purity on her, which I would have respected. It suited her. She was to be a shrine maiden.'

Neither of them spoke for a few moments. Yayoi looked out across the lake. The mountain ranges beyond were beginning to turn hazy and mauve as the sun passed over them towards the west. It would have been a perfect spring afternoon were it not for the turbid water and the exposed stretches of mud.

Fuji said, 'A few months later I heard of a young girl who rode a white stallion on the roads around the lake, fighting off men, with a sword that had itself become famous. I thought it might be her, but then no more was heard of her. I suppose she is dead now. Like the Autumn Princess.'

Yayoi said nothing.

'I have been thinking about her a lot, lately,' Fuji said, leaning closer and dropping her voice. 'Yoshimaru has become such a fine young man. And you see, dear Yayoi, if he is who I think he is, some very important people might be interested – interested enough to stop persecuting us with their demands for licences and fees. I see you are astonished. You would never have guessed, would you, that Yoshimaru, our monkey boy, who is rather fond of the little drummer, is the missing Emperor?'

'It cannot be true,' Yayoi said, though she knew it was, had known ever since the lute, Genzo, had burst into melody in his presence, when she had escaped from Nishimi. The ancient lute knew the true Emperor. For years she had said nothing, had simply prayed for his safety, as she watched him grow from a child of eight to a young man of about twenty.

Like all the acrobats, he dressed and wore his hair in the style of childhood and still carried his childish name. He and Saru were inseparable, both handsome, lively young men. Take, the baby she had brought from Nishimi, adored them both, having been brought up by them, among the monkeys. And lately she along with everyone else had noticed that Yoshi and Kai were in love.

'Does he know?' she wondered aloud.

Fuji said, 'He has never given the slightest sign. He must have forgotten. He was only six years old when we first saw him.'

'We should leave things as they are,' Yayoi said. 'He will have a far happier life here.'

'But if he is restored to the throne, maybe the drought will stop and the lake will go back to how it used to be. And we would gain considerable rewards.'

'Restored to the throne? You are dreaming if you think that will happen! The Miboshi will put him to death, and probably everyone who knows of his existence!'

'You are always so pessimistic, Yayoi! You always expect the worst!' Fuji turned away, biting a hangnail in exasperation.

Isn't that how my life has turned out? Yayoi thought. *My mother passed away when I was a child, my father died at the side of the Crown Prince in the Ninpei rebellion, my little brother was killed by mistake after he had been kidnapped. My own life has been spared only through Fuji's discretion.*

Fuji spat out the nail and said in a malicious voice, 'It happened when you were away at the temple so I don't believe you ever heard of it, but Lord Aritomo forced his favourite, Yukikuni no Takaakira, to commit suicide.'

'I did not know,' Yayoi said. 'But what has it to do with me?'

'He was accused of harbouring a Kakizuki girl, Kiyoyori's daughter in fact, first in Miyako and then at Nishimi.' She looked up at Yayoi, her usual charming smile on her face. 'Aritomo saw it as unpardonable treachery. Takaakira ripped his belly. They say it took him hours to die. Nobody knows Kiyoyori's daughter survived, except me. And you, of course.'

Yayoi had not known he was dead, the man who had saved her life when the capital fell to the Miboshi. He had, undoubtedly, had his own motives, which she had been vaguely aware of as a child; he would have made her his wife, once she was old enough. But he had been kind to her; he had taught her to read and write, and so many other things. Deep grief assailed her and then she turned cold with sudden fear, hearing the threat, knowing that Fuji would not hesitate to sacrifice Yoshi to gain some advantage for herself. And that Yayoi and Take were no more than pawns in Fuji's game. The safety of all three of them depended on Fuji's silence. But how could she be prevented from betraying them?

•

Yayoi did not have time to reflect more on this disturbing conversation, for her first guest arrived, and then she was kept busy for the rest of the day. Her last visitor was one of her favourites, a merchant from Kitakami. He was no longer young, but not quite middle aged, the son of an influential family whose speciality was fermentation – soy bean products, rice wine and so on. Their name was Unagi, or Eel, and they guarded carefully both their secret recipes and the contracts they made with farmers all around Lake Kasumi, in which the promise of beans at harvest was exchanged for tools necessary in the planting season, lengths of cloth for summer weddings and festivals, drums for local temples, cord ropes and bamboo baskets.

He lived up to his family name, Yayoi thought, being intelligent, strong and enterprising, as well as able to slither out of any unpleasant situation. She enjoyed his company, as much as his gifts, and the wholehearted pleasure he took in love making reminded her of grilled eel, rich, tasty, good for the health.

But this day, though they brought considerable pleasure to each other's bodies, afterwards he seemed unusually preoccupied, almost despondent.

'Something is troubling you?' Yayoi said, and called softly to one of the girls to bring more wine.

'Forgive me, Lady Yayoi. I thought I would leave my troubles on the shore, or, at least, on the boat my servant brought me over on. It's been a strange spring . . . but I don't want to burden you with my problems.'

'You can talk to me about anything,' Yayoi said. 'Even if I can't help, voicing these concerns often clarifies the way you see them.'

'Maybe you can help, you are the wisest woman I've ever met. You know my family has been in this business for as long as anyone can remember? We've dealt fairly with people, our house was founded on mutual trust and that's the way we've always run things. This year over half our suppliers have said they can't carry on in the usual way. It appears someone else is muscling in on contracts we've had for years, taking them over, blackening our name and deliberately trying to ruin us. They call themselves the Kikuta – they have been around for some years, though no one seems to know where they came from, but now they have become much more aggressive. The head of the family lets people believe he is Akuzenji's son, though all Akuzenji's children were supposedly killed by Kiyoyori's men years ago.'

Yayoi said, 'I have never heard of them.' She remembered clearly the day Akuzenji died when she had been so afraid her father would have Shikanoko executed too.

'We have competitors, naturally, always have had, but this family is different. They use intimidation, and don't hesitate to follow through with their threats, to the point of murder. And not only of farmers, but of their wives and children too. No one dares stand up to them. Now they have started on us, demanding we sell our business, our warehouses, our stock, the vats and all our tools, as well as our secrets, to them. If we don't, they say they will destroy everything and eliminate our family. I didn't take them seriously at first, but now I don't know what to do about it. My father isn't well and I'm afraid the anxiety is going to kill him. I hate to buckle under to bullying, but I have to be realistic.'

'What can you do?' Yayoi felt a twinge of unease.

'I am trying to come to some agreement with them. After all, there are precedents – we used to pay Akuzenji to ensure safe transport of our goods overland, and we still employ seamen, who many would describe as pirates, to protect our ships at sea. It's to be expected and saves us keeping a small army of bodyguards. But the Kikuta will not discuss or negotiate; they want complete control. Our only weapon is that they cannot match us for quality, yet. My father has always had the highest standards and he refuses to compromise on that. But, even if our buyers are loyal to us, we are falling behind in supplying them because we cannot get our raw ingredients.'

Yayoi poured more wine. 'Do these people seek to control other merchant houses or only yours?'

'We are the first, I believe,' Unagi said, draining the bowl. 'However, if we go under, they will start to attack the rest. They treat it like a military campaign. They are the Miboshi with their white banners and we are the red-flagged Kakizuki.' He smiled wryly. 'And we all know what happened to them! I often wonder if we should not pack up and flee to the west, while we still have the chance.'

'But do they ally themselves with the Miboshi? Do they have their support or protection?'

'No, that was just a figure of speech. They ally with no one. But sometimes I feel we are in a kind of war and I must prepare weapons and men. Maybe the Kakizuki should not have fled but fought back, and so should I. That's what my sons want.' He sighed.

'This isn't what I'd meant to discuss with you tonight. I had another suggestion to put to you.'

He took her hand and gazed intently at her face. 'I wish I could bring you with me to Kitakami. I've dreamed of approaching Lady Fuji with an offer. But would you be willing?'

Yayoi was touched and for a moment deeply tempted. She liked and respected Unagi; she knew he would give her a good life.

'Forgive me,' he said. 'I shouldn't have brought it up at this time. Let me deal with Kikuta one way or another and then I will speak to Lady Fuji. At least let me know you will consider it.'

'I will,' she said. 'Thank you. I am very grateful.'

He stood up. 'I will send you a message. Thinking of you is going to give me courage.'

He refused Yayoi's offers of food or music, saying he preferred to return to his lodgings before nightfall. She heard the splash of the oar as his servant sculled the boat away.

•

Yayoi washed and changed her clothes. She took out the Kudzu Vine Treasure Store, intending to study it as she often did at night, but her heart was heavy. The way Unagi had, uncharacteristically, spoken of his problems had unsettled her, and her mind was full of thoughts of the dead. Takaakira must have died years ago, but she had not known of it, and the news had awakened many memories of the past. She had heard snatches of information and gossip on the boats and in the markets, but mostly men came to forget the world of intrigue and strife. If Takaakira had died without her knowing, there was every possibility Shikanoko had too. She was trapped here in Lady Fuji's world; she would never escape, never find out. Unagi's offer to buy her freedom pulled at her. She tried to imagine for a moment what her life would be like but she could get no further than the love of a good man, maybe a child, and then she heard Asagao's voice from years ago: *Are they going to marry you to a merchant? What a waste of a beautiful girl!*

She thought how useful she might be to him, since she knew how to write and to calculate. But how far removed it was from her dreams as a child, when she was a warrior's daughter. She wanted to talk it over with Asagao but it was getting late. *We will talk tomorrow*, she thought, and turned to the text, trying to calm herself in prayer. Whenever she took out the text, she began by meditating on Sesshin, who had given it to her. She did not know if he was alive or dead; she had heard nothing of him, since he had been blinded by her stepmother and turned away from Matsutani. She sat motionless, eyes closed, with one hand on the pages.

She felt them rustle, as if a strong wind had suddenly blown through the boat. She opened her eyes and saw for a moment a page that showed the mirror-like stone. Her hands curved instinctively as if they would clasp it, but then the page turned and search as she might she could not find it again.

'Well, I will not read more tonight,' she said, almost addressing it as *you wretched book*, trying to control her frustration and disappointment. As she sat back the pages rustled again. She looked down and saw the text had opened at a place it had never shown her before.

An image leaped out at her. It was a mask, carved from a stag's skull, with antlers. She had seen such things at festivals. Men wore them to dance in, becoming animals or birds, bridging the spaces between the worlds. There were living eyes behind the mask. They looked at her with silent appeal.

'Shikanoko!' she whispered.

But, before she could be sure, the text had closed the page and opened another, showing her a second mask, made from a human skull. Its eyes glittered with gemstones, its lips were painted red, black silky hair had been pasted to the bone. It seemed to turn and look in her direction, as if it were seeking her out. She felt its malevolence and its jealous, restless desire. It was not content with its own power, it could not endure anyone else's, but sought to claim all power for itself. With all her effort, she folded the text closed, feeling its resistance, and sat shaking with fear.

What did it mean? Was Shikanoko dead? Or trapped in the world of sorcery, where his mother had warned Yayoi not to follow him? She felt tears forming and struggled not to weep aloud. She remembered so clearly the evening when he had come to tell her about Tsumaru's death. And then she could not keep the tears from falling, recalling her little brother, the last time she had seen him alive, before he had been kidnapped. He had wanted to play with Chika and Kaze, but the other two children had been unwell, and she and Tsumaru had gone out alone into the Darkwood. After that she could only remember the strangers, Tsumaru's cry, her helplessness, her aching head.

Someone called softly, 'Hina!' A voice and a name from the past, a whisper, almost lost among the lap of the waves against the side of the boat and the intermittent sound of music. *Hina*, her childhood name, all but forgotten, so long had it been since anyone had used it.

'Hina! Are you awake? I must speak with you.'

Wiping her eyes on her sleeve, she hid the Kudzu Vine Treasure Store under a cushion, then lifted the bamboo blind and looked down onto the water. Unagi's narrow skiff was just below and, gripping the side of the pleasure boat to hold it steady, was his servant. She had never looked at him closely before, but now, in the light of the lanterns, she recognised him as her childhood companion, the son of Kongyo, one of her father's senior retainers, and of Tsumaru's nurse, Haru.

'Chika? Can it really be you?'

'Can you come down? I need to talk to you.'

She pulled a cloth from the rack and wound it round her head and face, then, just as she was, in her night clothes, climbed over the side and stepped nimbly into the skiff. It rocked and Chika held her to steady her. It was too familiar a touch for a servant and she wondered briefly if she had been wise, trusting a boy she used to play with, now a man, a stranger.

'Don't worry,' he said, reading her mind. 'I am not going to hurt you or force myself on you. I can't deny I've dreamed you were my wife. I used to imagine we would be married when we were children, playing at being the Emperor and the Empress. Perhaps we might have been, back then, when we were almost equals. Now, I am obliged to work for a merchant and you have ended up a pleasure woman. We have both fallen, but we are further apart than ever.'

'The great wheel turns,' Yayoi said. 'We all rise and fall with it, as we reap the harvest from seeds sown in former lives.'

'No,' he said. 'The harvest we reap is sown by those who wronged us. If neither Heaven nor Earth gives us justice, then we must seek our own revenge.'

He helped Yayoi sit in the bow, then took up the single oar at the stern and began to scull. It was a warm evening and the surface of the lake was only slightly ruffled, like twisted silk.

'Unagi is a good man,' Yayoi said finally.

'They say he is a good lover,' Chika replied.

'That is none of your concern.' She heard the bitterness and envy in his voice and pitied him. 'How did you come to be in his household, and how did you know me?'

'He talks to me about you – he's not a discreet man, he can't keep his mouth shut – and he mentioned the scroll, the one Master Sesshin gave you that you were always trying to read. I remembered it clearly.

Perhaps I was jealous that you should receive such a gift. When I managed to see you for myself, I recognised you.' His voice changed slightly, growing more tender. 'I had never forgotten you, Hina.'

'You should not serve a man you despise,' she said, feeling a need to defend Unagi.

'All men despise those they serve,' Chika replied, the bitterness returning. 'But he is not my true master. I serve him on my master's orders. I will tell you how it all came about. My father died in the battle of Kuromori, my mother sent my sister and me into the Darkwood. Masachika was searching for anyone who survived, to put them to death. I knew a place where Shikanoko used to live. I took Kaze there.'

Yayoi was momentarily deafened by the thump of her own heart. 'Was Shikanoko there?'

'No, he has disappeared. People say he is dead, or that he lives the life of a stag, somewhere in the Darkwood.' He was silent for a moment and, when he spoke again, his voice was full of contempt. 'He ran away. He abandoned us, leaving everyone to die. The only people there were the imps, one of whom I now serve.'

'The imps?'

'Lady Tora's children. Do you remember her?'

Yayoi was suddenly cold and nauseated.

'She bewitched your father. It was after she and Shikanoko came to Matsutani that everything started to go wrong. She had five children, all at one time, and they had not one father, but five. One of them was Shikanoko, another Lord Kiyoyori.'

'Does that make them brothers to me?'

Chika smiled. 'I suppose it does.'

While she was absorbing this, he related in a whisper a long account of the brothers, their fathers' names, their magic skills, their use of poisons and venomous creatures, how the Princess died, how they grew as fast as insects, and had taken wives, how they had quarrelled.

'We returned from Kitakami. Kiku dug up the skull of a man, whom Shikanoko had killed there some time ago, and, with Mu's fox-wife, carried out the rituals that have given him such great power.'

Yayoi thought, *This is what the book was showing me.* The image of the skull, its searching eyes, made her tremble again. Yet it must have shown it to her with a purpose, just as it had shown her the stag mask through which shone Shikanoko's eyes.

Chika said, 'That is why the brothers are estranged. Mu has many gifts, but now Kiku's are much greater.'

'Kiku? Are you talking about the family called Kikuta?'

'That's the name he gave himself when he became a merchant.'

My poor Unagi, you are doomed!

'So you are also under his power,' she said. 'And your sister?'

'Kaze is his wife,' Chika replied. 'And I am his closest friend, more of a brother than his own siblings. I would do anything for him. He decided I could be an informant and asked me to seek work with Unagi. It was not difficult. I had learned many things from Kiku and I knew how to make myself useful to the house of the Eel. He has come to trust me.'

'You will betray him,' she said flatly, thinking, *What can I do to prevent that?*

'If I were a servant, it could be called betrayal. But I am a warrior. I have years of disdain and insults to redress.'

'Good and evil are not defined by status,' Yayoi said.

'You have been sheltered from the world for too long. Everything is defined by status now. Do you think Aritomo does not dispense a different justice to his nobles and lords from that which he metes out to commoners?'

Takaakira's status did not save him, Yayoi thought, but all she said was, 'I know very little of Lord Aritomo.'

'No doubt he would be very interested to know more about you,' Chika said, with a flash of malice.

When Yayoi did not respond, he went on, a little awkwardly, 'I do not mean to threaten you.'

'I think you do. You have been well taught by your master.' She had been fortunate to survive for so long among the riverbank people, but now two people in one day had threatened to expose her. *I must get away. I must warn Yoshi.* But she had no idea how to do either.

Chika said, as though trying to excuse himself, 'I was afraid of what Kiku might do to my sister. I had to obey him.'

'Why have you come to tell me this?' Yayoi demanded. 'What do you want from me?'

He took a deep breath, as though he had finally reached the point of his visit. 'Shikanoko possessed a mask, made powerful by the same rituals Kiku used on the skull. After the confrontation with the Prince Abbot, apparently, it became fused to his face. That is why, after the death of the Princess, he fled to the forest, and shuns the company of men and women. I know you are a wise woman, and you have the Kudzu Vine Treasure Store, which must tell you many secrets. Furthermore, my sister had a dream about you, that you put your arms around a stag in the forest, and it turned into a man. I believe you could bring Shikanoko back.'

'What are you suggesting? That I go deep into the Darkwood to search for a man who is probably dead, certainly an outlaw?' It was exactly what she longed to do but surely it was impossible. 'You don't understand the circumstances in which I live. I'm not free to come and go as I please.'

'You're clever, Hina. You'll find a way. And I'll help you.'

Yayoi knew it was unlikely she would be allowed to go anywhere, let alone into the Darkwood on such an illusory mission. She did not trust Chika, suspecting that he, or his master, had other motives to find Shikanoko, and that they would lie to her and try to manipulate her. She remembered the skull's restless searching gaze. But all she could think of was the eyes she had seen behind the mask, their mute appeal, and the dream image of herself, her arms around the stag, her beloved.

•

She hardly slept. Whenever she closed her eyes she saw the mask. She had short broken dreams in which her hands curved around the stone and she understood everything. During the night she remembered it was the time of year when a few of the acrobats, Yoshi among them, went into the forest to look for young monkeys. The idea came to Yayoi that she might go with them. She knew she was being foolish, that the Darkwood was vast, that she was familiar with only the tiny southwestern corner of it, but she was impelled by a belief that fate would bring her to him, wherever he was and in whatever form. And, in the Darkwood, she would find a way to warn Yoshi not to return.

For years she had done nothing without Lady Fuji's permission. She tried to plan how best to approach her but as she had feared, Fuji's instant reaction was a refusal.

'It is our busiest time of year; the fine weather, the summer festivals, all the extra gifts that will need to be recorded. It is very selfish of you even to think of such a thing. Whatever reason can you have for wanting to traipse through the forest, with the monkey boys?'

'I am a little tired,' Yayoi said, fanning herself. 'I feel jaded. I will be better for a short break from entertaining.'

'Well, we will go on a pilgrimage somewhere in the autumn.' Fuji was looking at her shrewdly. 'There is some other reason, I feel. Are you planning to run away with one of our clients? It's Unagi, isn't it?'

'In truth, Unagi said last night he would like me to go with him, but naturally he would approach you first. I am wondering whether to encourage him or not. Some time away will help me think clearly. And I thought I might call in at the convent. I would like to see the Abbess again.'

'Whatever for? You can't go back, Yayoi. If you want to bury your past you must bury all of it. And put all thoughts of Unagi out of your mind. He is not as rich as he once was and he can't afford you. No, it is quite impossible!' She began to fan herself vigorously.

They were sitting in the stern of the boat. It was still early morning, but the sky was already an intense blue and the sun was hot. A shade awning protected them, but Yayoi could feel the sweat gathering on her skin. The water was green and clear. She longed to lower herself into it. She felt a sudden wave of fury that she was not allowed to act as she wished, that she would always be trapped by Fuji, always afraid that the woman would betray her and Yoshi. She pressed her lips together, not daring to let any words escape her, wishing with all her heart that Fuji were dead.

There was a small splash and a ripple of movement. They both looked over the side of the boat. Far below a shadow flickered across the lake floor.

'It is just a water rat,' Fuji said. 'Come, enough sitting around. We must get ready for the day.'

But Yayoi knew the creature underwater was too large to be a rat. She followed the ripple with her eyes and thought she saw a reed moving through the water.

•

Fuji died that night. It had been a busy day, with many visitors. Yayoi had entertained three of her special guests and had then played with the musicians, until her fingers were stiff and her head ached.

She had fallen asleep soon after the moon had risen, and had been woken at dawn, while the moon was still high in the sky, by the shocked cries and wailing of Fuji's maid.

She ran immediately to the lifeless body, slapped her cheeks, rubbed her wrists and ankles, burned incense under her nose, called her name repeatedly, but no breath returned. Fuji, so healthy and lively the night before, had departed on her final journey.

There were no marks on her body, no external wounds. Her mouth smelled faintly sweetish and Yayoi guessed she must have been poisoned, though by whom, or for what reason, no one could fathom.

The boats left at once for Aomizu. They were supposed to be heading for Kitakami, for the twenty-fifth-day market, but that would have to be cancelled. The funeral had to be held quickly, because of the intense heat, and the speed of it all somehow increased the shock and disbelief. But Yayoi noticed that, despite their shared grief, the other women and the musicians were wary of her and talked about her when they thought she could not hear.

The following day, Takemaru came to the boat, calling out to her from the shore, addressing her as *Older Sister*. She knew that he was uncomfortable on the boats, that the pleasures of love both attracted and repelled him. He was at that age, confused by desire and emotion, happiest in the company of boys his own age and the young men whom he admired excessively, yet drawn to girls. Soon, she knew, one of the women would find it entertaining to take him behind the bamboo blinds and initiate him, and then he would probably lose his mind and be insatiable for a couple of years. It amused and saddened her at the same time. She did not expect, now, to have children herself. Take was both younger brother and son to her.

He was a tall, well-built boy – too tall to be an acrobat, the others said, when they wanted to annoy him, but they could not deny that his strength made him useful, as a baseman, in the living towers they created of humans and monkeys. Already, he could take the weight of the older men on his shoulders or on his upturned feet. He was quick tempered, bold and determined in nature; if he could not conquer something he practised obsessively until he could do it perfectly. He loved listening to tales of warriors of old, their battles, their victories and defeats, and often played with a wooden pole as if it were a sword or a spear. The acrobats teased Take for his bloodthirsty and violent games, but Yayoi, who knew his parentage, saw in him Shikanoko's warrior traits as well as Akihime's nobility and courage.

The drummer girl, Kai, was with him. Yayoi had never been close to her. They had almost instinctively stayed away from each other, as though knowing they had overlapping secrets that they did not dare reveal. Because of some slight deformity, Kai had never joined the pleasure women on the boats but had been brought up by the musicians. Yayoi had seen her tiny shell-shaped ears once or twice when the wind blew her hair away from her face. Yet Yoshi had fallen in love with her, they were as good as married. Yayoi could not help feeling a pang of regret and envy.

She took her sandals in her hand, and a parasol, to protect her face from the sun's glare, and crossed to the shore. It was a relief to get away from the sobbing women – and from some other oppressive, disturbing feeling, some accusation in their eyes and the way they fell silent at her approach.

Kai greeted her warmly and the three of them walked to the end of the dock.

Take said, 'They are saying you killed Lady Fuji.'

'How can anyone believe that? Of course I did not!' *Yet,* Yayoi thought, *I wished her dead.*

'You were the last person to see her alive,' Kai said, 'and you know magic arts, fatal ones. They are saying you cast a spell on her, because she would not grant your request.'

'Where did you hear this?' Yayoi asked.

'Gossip in town,' Take replied. 'Yoshimaru told us.'

'Does Yoshi believe it?'

'No, of course not, and nor do Kai and I. But he thinks you should come away with us, in case some official hears the rumours and decides to act on them.'

'If I run away, I will be confirming their suspicions,' Yayoi said.

'Older Sister, only you can decide what is best; you are wiser than any of us. We are leaving directly for the forest. I was coming to say goodbye. Get what you want to bring, don't tell anyone, just say you are walking to the crossroads with Kai to bid us farewell.'

'You have thought it all out,' she whispered.

'Yoshi told me what to say,' he admitted.

Yoshi. Fuji had threatened to turn him over to Lord Aritomo, to expose who Yayoi really was, and then had tried to prevent her from leaving. She felt a pang of guilt. Even though she had not killed Fuji, there was no doubt she was going to benefit from her death. Was it a miracle from Heaven, or had it been the creature that was not a water rat, Chika, his mysterious master, or someone else from the Kikuta tribe?

'I will accompany you a little way,' she said in a louder voice. 'Just wait a moment.'

She knew she must act. She would never have another opportunity like this. She had to find Shikanoko, take Yoshimori to him, so that the true heir of the previous Emperor could be restored to the throne. And she had to give Shikanoko his son, Take.

She went back to the boat and collected a few things together, the Kudzu Vine Treasure Store among them. She did not dare take too much, she left her writing implements and her clothes. She was just tying the corners of the carrying cloth, when a shadow fell against the blind and a voice called quietly, 'Yayoi!'

It was Asagao, the only person Yayoi could call a friend, apart from Bara who had been her maid long ago and whom she remembered vaguely but fondly. She and Asagao were close in age, had slept side by side when they were children, hidden away in the women's temple, had caressed and kissed each other, when they had begun to learn about love. They had laughed over the ridiculous men who fell in love with them, shed tears for the charming ones who would wed other ordinary women, nursed each other in sickness, bled every month on the same days.

'Are you leaving?' Asagao said.

'No, I am just walking with Kai as far as the crossroads.' It pained Yayoi to lie to her, so she said no more.

'It isn't true, is it, what people are saying?' Asagao was watching her closely.

'No,' she said simply.

'But you are not grieving. You have hardly shed a tear. You might not have killed her but you are not sorry she is dead.'

'I am grieving. I just find it hard to express my feelings, you know that.' Yayoi strove to keep her voice light and natural.

'Yes, Yayoi, you keep everything hidden, even from your friend,' Asagao replied.

Yayoi tied the last knot and lifted the bundle.

Asagao said, 'What about the lute? Aren't you taking that?'

'Why should I? I will be back very soon.' Yayoi hated leaving Genzo, but she did not dare take it, for it had no guile. It would begin to play in Yoshi's presence and betray him.

'Can I play it?' Asagao asked.

'Of course, but it is not easy.'

'I will look after it for you.'

Yayoi looked at her and saw she had not convinced her. She took her in her arms and whispered, 'Goodbye.'

'Don't leave. Why do you have to go? What am I going to do without you?'

'I'm sorry. I can't explain.'

Asagao began to weep and Yayoi felt her own eyes moisten in sympathy. She could think of nothing else to say. She knew only that she had to take this chance and leave now, before it was too late. She joined Take and Kai on the shore and walked away from the pleasure boats, which had been her life for so many years.

II

CHIKA

Chika returned to Kitakami and immediately went to the merchant house, which was now the centre of the Kikuta empire, and his home. Kiku was overseeing the sampling of the latest batch of soy bean paste. His eyes lit up when Chika came in, he handed his ladle over to the nearest servant and took Chika into the back room, which overlooked the port, the estuary and the vast expanse of the Northern Sea.

'Lady Hina has left?' he asked eagerly.

'Yes, she has gone to the Darkwood with the monkey acrobats.'

'Were there any problems?'

'Fuji was going to prevent her so . . .'

'So you very cleverly killed her, leaving no trace?'

Chika nodded.

'Kuro has taught you something after all. Come here. You did well.'

Around him Chika could hear the sounds of the vats being weighed down with stones, to bring the soy beans to fermentation. The smell was intense, making the days of high summer seem even hotter. From the shop, he could hear his sister's voice, greeting customers, giving orders to other women, scolding the children. It should have annoyed him – after all, she was a warrior's daughter, she should not have ended up a merchant's wife, especially when that merchant was not even fully human. Yet he did not refuse to approach Kiku, and allowed the other man to embrace him, feeling the familiar stab of desire, all the stronger for being tinged with repulsion. No one else, since his father died, had met his need for approval and love, and Kiku still fascinated him, as he had since the first day Chika had spied on the boys at the hermit sorcerer's place in the forest and seen how they could split into two separate selves and fade into invisibility. He had been following the monk, Gessho, had watched the fight in which both the monk and the sorcerer died, and had longed to be like those boys, to have such skills.

He had learned everything Kiku and Kuro could teach him, but some things could not be taught. They were innate skills, and could not be acquired. His nephews and nieces possessed them in varying degrees. He had watched them develop, as the children grew, envious of them and delighted by them at the same time. There were a lot of children. Kiku had restrained his delight in killing to some extent, but not his lust. Chika's sister, Kaze, seemed to be always pregnant, as were the female servants. Kuro was the same, fathering many children, a couple of whom he brought home in a basket, handing them over without explanation to Kaze to bring up. Even Ku had found a wife and started a family.

The brothers liked the children, almost to excess, Chika thought. It surprised him, for in all other matters they showed little gentleness and no sentimentality. The children were precocious, walking at six months, talking before they were a year old, but they matured more slowly than their fathers, due to their mothers' human blood.

'There is no one like us,' Kiku often said. 'We have to make our own Tribe.' More and more frequently he referred to the three linked families in that fashion, and soon they were all calling themselves the Tribe.

Sometimes Chika envied them. If his life had not been disrupted by war, he would be married, with children of his own. But who would he marry now? He was no longer a warrior, yet he was not really anything else. Outside the Tribe he had no caste or family, yet he would never be truly one of them. He thought of Hina, as he often did, recalling her beauty and charm. *She could have been mine. What would our children be like?* The idea that Unagi hoped to take her as his wife enraged and saddened him, as did the realisation that Hina loved Shikanoko. He had seen it in her face when he had told her of his sister's dream.

One is a merchant, one an outlaw, yet they both have more chance of winning her than I do, he reflected.

Now Kiku said, still holding him close, 'You and your sister have made me more human. You came to me when I needed to learn how to relate to other people. We were the same age. I know that warriors, like the family you came from, feel strong bonds of loyalty. While I am not sure I fully understand that idea, I do feel a bond with you. I will always be grateful for that.'

'I owe you everything,' Chika replied. 'And yes, there is a bond between us.'

Kiku said, 'I used to watch the fake wolf, the one that attached itself to Shika – did you ever see it?'

'Once, at Matsutani,' Chika replied. 'And of course during the winter he spent at Kumayama it was always at his heels.'

'Affection made it become more real – it grew and changed, in a way the other animals Shisoku created could not. I often wonder what he did, when he made that one, that enabled it to love and so to grow. Do you suppose it has died, as a real wolf would have done by now, or has its artificiality extended its life?'

'With luck, we will find out before too long,' Chika said.

Kiku smiled as he released him. 'I hope so.'

'What do you want me to do now?' Chika said.

'It is the mask that gives Shika such great power. As we know, it cannot now be taken from his face. But like my skull it was created through combining male and female essences. I've learned from Akuzenji's sorcerers that in such circumstances the mask can only be removed by a woman who loves him. You told me before, after Kaze's dream, that Hina might be that woman.'

'I'm sure of it now,' Chika said, after a moment.

'You are jealous, Chika?' Kiku said with his customary acute perception. 'Do you want her for your wife?'

'Maybe I do. Maybe I always have.'

'Your family have significant dreams,' Kiku said. 'What about your father? Didn't he have a dream about Shika, that he straddled the realm holding power in one hand and the Emperor in the other?'

'My father believed it was a prophecy,' Chika said. 'But Shikanoko rejected the opportunity to take power, when it was offered to him.'

Kiku said slowly, 'The Princess's death affected him so strongly.'

'If my sister died,' Chika said, 'would you walk away from your little empire, from all you have built up?'

Kiku stared at him, trying to fathom the meaning behind the question. 'Probably not,' he admitted. 'Though I am very fond of her, in the same way I am fond of you. But all that happened years ago. Surely Shika will have recovered from grief by now.'

'There are some things we never recover from,' Chika replied.

Kiku said, 'That is hard for me to understand. The thing is, I really *need* the mask, with or without Shika.' He smiled, with the small gratification of using an exact word, whose meaning had never been clear to him till now. 'If Hina cannot remove it, we will take it, still attached to his head. He turned us away. *Let me never set eyes on you again,* he said. Once he is dead, you can have Hina.'

'He betrayed many,' Chika said, 'when he did not return to Kumayama. I'll never forget those who died as a result, and I'll never forgive him. It will be a pleasure to kill him.'

Kiku turned pale, and for a moment did not respond. Then he seemed to gather himself together. 'It disturbs me to talk of killing him,' he said. 'I am very confused. Sometimes I hate him, sometimes I feel another kind of emotion. I long to see him again.' He struck his chin with his fist two or three times. 'It is as if something is driving me to confront him, almost as if the skull wants to challenge the mask. I will have no rest until I hold it in my hands.'

After a few moments of silence, Chika said, 'So I am to go after Hina and bring her to Shikanoko, and once he is released from the mask – what then? Do you want me to kill him or not?'

'I cannot decide,' Kiku said. 'I must give it more thought. Maybe you should go first to my brothers, Ima and Mu. I have been thinking for some time that we five were born together – we should all live together, all five families. Only Mu fully understands Kuro and myself. Tell him I want to see him. I want us to work together.'

'You will have to apologise to him and beg his forgiveness,' Chika said. 'You tied him up and slept with his wife. Most people would consider that a terrible betrayal.'

'She was a fox woman,' Kiku said, 'less human than I am.'

'Mu loved her deeply, though,' Chika said.

Kiku shifted uncomfortably. 'Maybe I envied that, being able to love.'

'That's why you have to ask him to forgive you.'

'That word again,' Kiku said. 'What does it mean?'

'That you are sorry you hurt him.'

Kiku scowled. 'Very well. Tell him I am sorry.'

'Deeply sorry.'

'Whatever you like,' Kiku said, with a flash of impatience. 'Whatever it takes.'

12

HINA (YAYOI)

Kai did not turn back at the crossroads but walked on alongside Yoshi, her drum slung across her back. From time to time she brought it forward and sent its dull note reverberating through the trees. She laughed and chattered with Yoshi and Saru. Yayoi remembered how Fuji had told her that Kai and Yoshi had been taken onto the boat at the same time. Now she wondered how much Kai remembered of her previous life, and what she knew of Yoshi. Watching them together she became aware of a deep understanding between them, the sort that people described as a bond from a former life.

Occasionally she caught a glimpse of the bird that always followed Yoshi. Yayoi had long suspected it was a werehawk, like the one that had flown to Matsutani, the day the bandits were captured. Shikanoko had killed it with an arrow when no one else had been able to. It was many years ago, yet she still remembered vividly the creature plummeting to the ground, its blood sizzling, Shikanoko's stance, her father's expression.

That bird had been completely black, apart from its yellow eyes, but this one had a spangling of gold, as though its plumage were changing colour, from year to year. It did not seem to age or suffer. Yoshi did not care for it; he never fed it or spoke to it, yet he sometimes referred to it by its name: Kon. Kai was kind to it as she was to all birds. It was obvious to Yayoi that, like Genzo, Kon knew the young acrobat's true identity. Together with Kai, they were all that remained of Yoshi's former life, a link with the past that he did not – or did not want to – remember. She had left the lute with Asagao, but Kon chose where he went and whom he followed.

'Sometimes they try to trap him,' Take told her, following her gaze. 'Yoshi would love it if he stayed home in a cage. But he is too clever to be caught. I have offered to try to shoot him down but, of course, they would not allow him to be killed.'

Yayoi knew the open secret that the acrobats all belonged to a sect, a kind of hidden religion, that forbade the taking of any life. There was some divine mother and child they worshipped, which she often thought must be the reason they loved children, and remained in some way children themselves. She was also aware that they always sought a blessing before going on a journey, and that a priest of the sect lived not far from Aomizu, so she was not altogether surprised when, late in the first day, in silent agreement, Yoshi and Saru took a side track that led away to the north.

They took one monkey with them to entice the wild ones they hoped to capture to replace Yoshi's two companions Kemuri and Shiro who had both died the previous winter. Saru's favourite, Tomo, had died the year before. This monkey was a young one, captured in the forest two summers earlier. They called it Noboru. Saru led it by a long red cord and, when it was tired, it sat on his shoulders. They also had one packhorse, carrying their provisions and empty baskets for the new monkeys. Towards the end of the day, Yayoi sat on the horse, perched between the baskets. The acrobats were tireless, but it was a long time since she had walked anywhere and her legs were aching. The packhorse plodded, stumbling frequently. She wished she could put on leggings and ride as she had when she was a child, astride, freely.

After more than three hours, when it was almost dark, they came to a tiny village, four or five huts, huddled together at the foot of a tall hill, almost a true mountain. The way was overgrown and led through thick groves of trees and clumps of bamboo. Every now and then, Yoshi and Saru removed, and replaced behind them, the brushwood that had been laid across the path.

It must be a love of secrecy for its own sake, Yayoi thought, for she did not believe there was any real danger of attack. Many sects had sprung up in the years of difficulty and famine, as people sought to understand Heaven's hostility and placate it. Some were followers of the Enlightened One who taught a new, austere path, others turned to the old gods of mountain and forest. Unless they caused riots and disturbed the civil peace, they were allowed to flourish, especially if they paid contributions to Lord Aritomo's system of taxation.

The old man came out to greet them, as happy as a father meeting his children again after a long absence. A meal was quickly prepared, taro with millet, flavoured with the dried seaweed Saru had brought as a gift, followed by mulberries and loquats, picked from the trees that surrounded the small fields. Before they ate, the old man prayed over the food, speaking a blessing on the visitors and on their journey.

When he came to Yayoi he said quietly, 'You have not been here before, but you are welcome. What is your reason for travelling to the Darkwood?'

'I hope to gather herbs of healing,' she said. 'There are many that can be found nowhere else.'

'Use them only for good,' he said. 'Beware of being led into sorcery. And turn to the Secret One, for he is the source of true healing.'

She bowed her head, saying nothing, but she couldn't help glancing at the others. Yoshi's eyes were closed and his face calm and rapt. *All this has so much meaning for him*, she thought. *He believes with all his heart. But the Emperor is called upon to carry out rituals that bind Heaven and Earth. How would he be able to do that? Better he remains undiscovered and lives out his life among the acrobats.*

She prayed now, to any god that might listen, that Fuji had not had time to report her suspicions of Yoshi before her death, that they would not be pursued, that Yoshi would be able to return at the end of the summer, and then she regretted her presumption in daring to suggest that the powers of Heaven might be turned from their purpose. He was the Emperor. He could not avoid his destiny, or the sacrifices that would be demanded of him.

The sparse food and the turmoil of her thoughts gave her a restless night. For a long time she lay, eyes wide open, alongside the women and their children, dozed eventually, and awoke at dawn. When she went outside Kon was calling quietly from the roof, and Take was standing at the entrance to the path, as if on guard, his staff in his hand.

'Have you been keeping watch all night?' she asked.

'I slept for a couple of hours. Then I dreamed Kon was speaking to me, some urgent message. It woke me up and I came outside. There is some danger, I can feel it.'

'Do you think we are being followed?' Yayoi felt her world shrink again, as though she had just escaped from prison, only to be recaptured.

He gave her a measured look, mature beyond his years. 'Yoshi and Saru aren't worried. They believe, since they threaten no one, no one will threaten them. But someone could be following us – maybe the authorities investigating Fuji's death, or maybe . . .'

Lord Arinori, my so-called protector, who, if he is not going to have me executed for murder, might seek to own me completely, or Chika or his master and his brothers.

'What should we do?' she said.

'We are safer here than on the road. We should stay for a few days. I'll see what news I can discover and return by nightfall. Tell the others where I've gone and wait for me here.'

She tried to persuade him not to go alone but he was impatient and would not countenance any opposition to his plan. He set out at once before the others woke, leaving Yayoi to explain where he had gone.

Saru and Yoshi mocked his concerns, but were happy to spend at least one more day with their beloved teacher. Take returned in the late afternoon, looking pleased with himself.

'I was right,' he whispered to Yayoi. 'Someone did come after you – Lord Arinori.'

She felt a jolt of fear. If they had stayed on the road, he would have caught up with them.

'It's a good thing I stuck to my decision. He has gone to the temple where you lived for a while. He thinks you would have fled there. We will stay a few more days until he has returned to Aomizu.'

She remembered the earlier search at the temple, the destruction, the nuns' terror.

'Don't worry,' Take said, seeing her expression. 'If he does not find you there, what will he do? He is not going to hurt the nuns.'

Yayoi gave her fine robes to the village women, telling them to get rid of them or sell them at the market. She dressed in the dull, shabby clothes of a peasant, and worked alongside the women in the fields, letting the earth stain her hands and the sun darken her skin. The young men cut wood for the winter, helped build a new shed to stack it in. There was always work to do and the villagers were grateful for the extra hands. Many days passed before they were ready to move on. They laughed at the dangers that Take saw everywhere, his mind influenced by the tales and legends of the past that he so loved, their intrigues, betrayals, battles and uprisings, and teased him until he lost his temper.

The morning they left, they knelt before the old man to say goodbye and receive his blessing.

He smiled when he looked down at Saru. 'May you find a friend to replace the one you lost.' To Kai he said, 'I am glad you are staying here with us. You and your child will be safe here.'

Kai smiled, blushing a little, and reached out to touch Yoshi's hand. He grinned too, but the old man turned to him with a sombre face. 'What you seek will not be found in the Darkwood. It is not what you think, maybe not even what you desire. I told you once, all paths lead to your destiny.'

'Master your anger,' he said to Take. 'It blinds you to what is real and what is best for you.'

To Yayoi, he said, 'You may use your real name now. Your old life is finished.' And from that moment she called herself Hina again.

•

Take hurried them off the track, as soon as possible, and they began to make their way eastwards, meeting the road to Shimaura some way south of the crossroads where the highway from Aomizu went on to Rinrakuji. They slept for a short time on the edge of the fields, and were woken in the early morning by two small boys who demanded to see the monkey.

'Wait a few months and we will be back with a whole troupe,' Saru promised.

They walked all day, and then took a track that turned off to the east. The two young men and Take had been here many times, but for Hina it was completely new. The forest closed around them. Cicadas shrilled in a constant shower of sound and mosquitoes whined. The air was stifling, the track stony. For a while she rode the horse, but it stumbled often, its straw shoes slipping on the rocky ground, and she felt safer walking.

She thought they would sleep in the open air again, but, in the late afternoon, she saw they were approaching a derelict hut. Take had gone ahead to scout, and came running back.

'There are people in the hut,' he said in a loud whisper.

Hina stopped, Yoshi beside her.

'I don't like this place,' Yoshi said. 'I've been past it many times, and it always makes me tremble.'

'Did something bad happen here?' she asked.

His face closed and she knew she was right, but he would never tell her.

Saru, with the horse and Noboru the monkey, went blithely on, calling out a greeting.

There was a slight noise from inside and a tall woman stepped out, holding a broken plank of wood in both hands, as if it were a club, a look of fear on her face. Her head was shaved, her tattered robe a dull brown colour.

Hina thought she recognised her but could not believe it was the same woman. Was it a ghost or an illusion? 'Reverend Nun?' she questioned, walking forward.

Astonishment, then anger, replaced fear as the woman lowered the plank. 'You are one of Lady Fuji's girls. The one we called Yayoi. What are you doing here? It is on your account that all these disasters came upon us. What have you done?'

'What happened?' Hina said.

The monkey was screaming loudly from Saru's shoulder and showing its teeth. The nun looked at it, and then back at Hina. She swayed slightly. The plank dropped from her hands. She crouched down, her face in her palms, her shoulders heaving.

Hina knelt in front of her, the others waiting a few paces behind; Yoshi and Saru silent and concerned, Take turning constantly, his eyes raking the forest and the track they had come along, as if suspecting a trap. There was a clatter of wings and Kon alighted on the roof. It called in its fluting voice, silencing the birds of the forest. In this hush, a voice came from inside.

'Who is there?'

Hina would never forget that voice. 'It is the Abbess,' she whispered. The nun nodded, without speaking.

'Shall I go in to her?'

Take rushed forward. 'It may be a trap. Let me go.'

'There is no one inside but our lady,' the nun said, her voice hoarse with tears.

Nevertheless, Take, holding the pole ready, stepped inside. Hina followed him. There was no door – it had warped and fallen years before – and the hut smelled of damp and mildew and of something else, a sweetish, stomach-turning whiff of flesh rotting.

'She's telling the truth,' Take said. He moved back to the door, as Hina went forward and knelt beside the small figure lying on the ground. She was about to take one of the Abbess's hands, when her eyes adjusted to the gloom and she saw the injuries.

The skin had been seared away. The flesh was raw and swollen. Yellow and black streaks of infection ran up both arms. The fingers were turning dark.

'It is Hina,' she said softly. 'I used to be called Yayoi. I lived at the temple.'

'Yayoi, dear child,' the Abbess said. Her voice was calm and clear, despite the fever. 'Look at what has become of me! I am dying, but I am glad to see you. Heaven has sent you to me.'

'What happened to you?' Hina said. 'Who did this to you?'

'I did it to myself, foolish old woman that I am. Lord Arinori came to the temple again. This time he was looking for you. Of course, I did not know where you were, nor had I heard the news of Fuji's death. I could tell him nothing. He became very angry when none of his threats worked on us, and had his men set fire to the building. My little cat – you probably knew her mother – was trapped inside. I tried to save her but the flames were too fierce. Poor creature, she was the victim of human rage and hatred, and I was punished for my stupid, vain attachment.'

'Don't blame yourself,' Hina said. 'Blame the cruelty of men.'

'Men will always be cruel and destructive,' the Abbess said. 'We live with that as we live with typhoons and earthquakes. I could not reach my cat, but I was able to snatch one object from the flames. Now you are here, I understand it was for you. It is by my side. Can you see it?'

Hina groped around with her hands in the half-darkness and came upon what felt like a smooth, rounded stone. Her palms seemed to recognise it and it knew them in return, nestling into them. She lifted it and held it up so the Abbess could see it.

'Is this it?'

'Yes.'

Hina peered at it. It gleamed slightly even in the gloom inside the hut. It was reflective, like a mirror. She could almost see her face in it.

'It is a medicine stone,' the Abbess said. 'I knew it was for you when you came to the temple with the Kudzu Vine Treasure Store – do you still have it?'

'I do,' Hina said. 'I left almost everything else behind, but the text I brought with me.'

A smile flitted over the Abbess's face. 'The stone and the text belong together. I should have given it to you then, but you were only a child, and you seemed destined for another kind of life. Now you are here, like a miracle. I can only conclude the stone brought you here so you could be united.'

'What is it for?' Hina asked.

'Hold it to my mouth so it catches my breath.'

Hina did so and a mist covered the polished surface.

'Now look deeply into it,' the Abbess said.

Hina could not help crying out.

'What did you see?'

'I cannot say!'

'Say it,' the Abbess commanded her. 'I am not afraid. It revealed I am dying, didn't it?'

Hina found she could not put into words what the stone had shown her: the intricate workings of the body, all failing one after another, before the inexorable invasion that was death. Tears formed in her eyes and she wept for the incurable frailty of the human body, its passage from birth and growth to decay and death, through a brief moment of passionate, striving life.

'It will show you the fate of any sick person,' the Abbess said. 'Whether they will recover or if they should prepare themselves to cross the Three Streamed River of Death. To most people it will seem like a dull black stone. Only in cases of imminent death does it reveal itself to be a mirror.'

Her calmness added to the awe Hina felt for the magical object in her hands. She put it down carefully, leaned over the older woman, and placed her hand on the burning forehead.

'Your hands are so cool,' the Abbess said. Her eyes closed and she seemed to sleep for a few moments. Then she said, 'Where are you going?'

Hina said, 'I am going into the Darkwood to find Shikanoko.'

'Shikanoko, the outlaw?'

'Your son. You called him Kazumaru. I don't believe he became a monster, as you feared.'

'So you are going in search of him?' the Abbess said wonderingly. 'He has been much on my mind, as I lie here, dying. Why are you looking for him? Is it because you love him? But how can that be? You can't have been much more than a child when you knew him, if you knew him at all . . .' Her speech became more rambling and incoherent and Hina could not follow everything she said. She was afraid the end was near, and was about to call the nun, when the dying woman spoke more clearly. 'When you find him, tell him his mother forgives him.'

'Maybe you should ask him to forgive you,' Hina said. 'If you had not left him, when he was a child . . . I am sorry, it is none of my concern.' But then she felt strongly it was her concern and her anger and pity rushed to the surface. 'You abandoned him! That is what made him become a sorcerer.'

There was a long silence. She feared the Abbess had stopped breathing and leaned over her to check. The woman raised her head towards her and spoke with surprising force. 'You are right. I see it all so clearly now. I thought I was seeking holiness. I so wanted to be good. But in the end I gave my cat more affection than I ever gave my son, and for that I am dying.' Her voice was filled with despair and bitterness.

She must not die like this, after a whole life dedicated to the sacred, Hina thought. Take had remained on the threshold while they had been talking. Now Hina turned towards him. She had not intended to tell him who his father was, until they found Shikanoko – for all her confident words, she could not know what he might have become, what grief and loneliness might have wrought in him. She might never find him; she might find a monster. But she had to let Take meet his grandmother, now Fate had brought them so close.

'Take,' she called softly, 'come here!'

He knelt beside them, his eyes widening in pity as he saw the damaged hands.

'You know her?' he said. 'Who is she, poor lady?'

'She is the Abbess of the temple where I lived for some years, after you and I were rescued from the lake. And she is your grandmother.'

The Abbess's eyelids had closed, but now they flew open and she searched for Take's face. 'Who is this boy?' she whispered.

'He is called Takeyoshi. He is Shikanoko's son. His mother was Akihime, the Autumn Princess. He is your grandson.'

'Is it true?' the Abbess said, and Take echoed her with the same words, as their eyes locked.

'It is true,' Hina said.

Tears flowed from the Abbess's eyes. 'I want to touch his face, stroke his hair, but I cannot bear the pain.'

Take put his own hand to her face and wiped away the tears with his fingers.

'When you find your father, ask him to forgive me,' she said.

She did not speak again. Her face took on a calm and joyful expression. Little by little the smell of sickness abated and was replaced by a fragrance like jasmine.

Hina found her lips repeating one of the sutras, that she had chanted so many times at the temple, that she had read aloud to the Abbess, as her tears fell for the dying woman.

The nun came in and joined in the chanting. The hut seemed to glow with light.

'The Enlightened One is coming for her,' the nun whispered. 'He will take her straight to Paradise.'

The Abbess began to breathe rapidly. Her eyelids fluttered. She seemed to want to speak, or maybe she was praying. Then the quick breaths ceased in one last sigh. Her eyes opened, but they no longer looked on this world.

Kon called piercingly and the monkey, Noboru, screeched in response.

The nun said, 'The other nuns went to Rinrakuji, to get help. They will be back soon. I'll stay with her body but you should not linger here. Rinrakuji is a Miboshi temple now. I don't know what you are supposed to have done, or who you really are, but you don't want to get embroiled in their questions and their procedures.'

'What will happen to you?' Hina said.

'They will no doubt find a place for us, washing dishes, sweeping floors. There are many ways a nun can serve.'

'But you have had your own temple, free from the control of men! You will find it hard to serve them now.'

'It could not last,' the nun said, in a resigned voice. 'All over the country, men are gaining power over women. They are in the ascendant, and will be for years to come. Women are condemned to begin their decline. It is all one, part of the great cycle.'

Hina knelt to ask for her blessing and Take imitated her. Then they bowed in farewell to the corpse and left the hut, Hina clasping the stone.

Once outside Take turned to her, his eyes bright with unshed tears.

'Tell me everything.'

'I will,' she replied, with a swift glance at Yoshi who was waiting with Saru, both sitting on their haunches. The monkey was on Saru's shoulder, searching his hair for fleas. The horse was cropping grass at the edge of the stream. 'But not now. Later, when we are alone, I promise.'

'What's happening?' Saru said. 'Are we stopping here for the night?'

'What's the matter with you?' Yoshi said to Take. 'Is something wrong?'

'A woman died in there,' Hina said.

Both young men drew the cross sign in the air.

'Let's get going, then,' Saru said with a nervous laugh. 'I'm not all that fond of the dead.'

'Shouldn't we help bury her?' Yoshi said.

'People will be coming soon,' Hina said. 'Really, it's best if we leave without delay.'

Take seemed about to speak but Hina shook her head at him. He ran to the stream, surprised the horse with a whack on its rump, jumped from rock to rock and disappeared into the forest. The horse flung up its head and galloped after him. The others had to follow.

•

They walked until well after nightfall, the three-quarters moon of the seventh month lighting their path, and slept briefly on the ground, until the forest birds began to call before dawn.

Yoshi and Saru went on ahead, but Take, alongside Hina, walked more and more slowly until they were a long distance behind.

'I thought my father must have been a warrior,' he said, when the others were out of earshot. 'It would explain so much about me. But what else do you know about my parents?'

She told him all she remembered from her childhood, the day Shikanoko arrived on the brown mare, his unparalleled skill with the bow, how he brought down the Prince Abbot's werehawk, and had been able to ride the stallion Nyorin that no one else could, after the death of its master, Akuzenji.

'He was born at Kumayama, and is the true heir to that estate. It lies a little further to the east from my father's twin estates of Matsutani and Kuromori.'

'Kuromori? The Darkwood?'

'Yes.'

Take gestured at the huge forest through which they were walking, the mossy trunks, the twisted roots, the fern-fringed stream beds. 'So all this was your father's?'

'If the Darkwood belonged to anyone, it was to him. But we lived on the southwestern corner. All this part is completely wild.'

'What happened to your father?' Take asked.

'He died at the side of the Crown Prince, along with your other grandfather, Hidetake, in the Ninpei rebellion.'

Take absorbed this silently, glancing at Hina with new concern. She wondered how much he had heard of the legends, rumours and ballads that had sprung up around Lord Kiyoyori and his son, the dragon child, and what he knew of the struggle between the Miboshi and the Kakizuki.

'Who owns the Darkwood, now?' he said. 'Weren't you his heir?'

'My uncle, Masachika. He had been sent to join the Miboshi when he was a young man, so he ended up on the side of the victors. He thinks I am dead, and must never find out otherwise. It was he who came to Nishimi and discovered the Princess, your mother, hiding there, not long after you were born. That's when I ran away with you, and the acrobats rescued us.'

'Did he kill her?' Hina saw in his face that he was already thinking of revenge.

'Not directly. He had her transported to Miyako and she died there.'

'And my father – what is his name?' he said after a long silence.

'Shikanoko. He was always called just that. It means the deer's child.'

'Is he still alive?'

'It seems so, for they are searching for him. Unless he died in the Darkwood. But, as I told the Abbess – I don't know if you heard – I am also looking for him.'

'My grandmother,' he stated. 'The first of my family I have ever met, and then she died within moments. I lay awake all night, thinking of her, praying for her soul.'

'Yes, I did too,' Hina replied.

They walked on slowly. Yoshi and Saru were out of sight ahead, but from time to time they heard Kon calling and Noboru chattering.

'A little while ago,' Hina said, thinking she should explain her reasons more fully, 'a man came to visit me. I knew him when we were children. He was the son of my father's senior retainer, and the same age as me. After my father's death he fell on hard times, but was taken in by a man who has become powerful in the north, in Kitakami. This man and his brothers were the children of a woman who came to our house at the same time as Shikanoko. She bewitched my father and he fell in love with her.'

She was surprised how hard it was to say this. Her face was burning.

'They are his children? Your brothers?' Take said, puzzled.

'There was some sorcery at work. They were all born at one time, they had several men for their fathers. My father was one, Shikanoko another.'

'So they are my brothers too?'

'In a way, yes.' She did not want to tell him everything she had learned from Chika, how the brothers had gone with Shikanoko to Ryusonji and caused the Princess's death. 'This man, my childhood friend, Chika, begged me to go and find Shikanoko. There are many forces at work and I don't understand them all, but I believe they are converging, with the purpose of restoring the true Emperor to the throne.'

'People say this terrible drought and the other disasters are all a punishment for the Miboshi's arrogance in choosing the Emperor they wanted,' Take said.

'You can say such things here in the forest,' Hina said, 'but never utter them where anyone else can hear you. Your tongue would be ripped out! But certainly in Heaven's eyes there is something grievously wrong. I feel we are being called to set it right. I don't know what to do, except go into the Darkwood in search of your father.'

'So my father knows who and where the true Emperor is?'

Hina said nothing, not sure how to answer.

Take was frowning as he persisted, 'Or is it that you are going to tell him? Are you the only person who knows?'

'Maybe I am, apart from the gods,' Hina said quietly. *And Kai,* she thought, but she did not voice this.

Part Two

THE TENGU'S GAME
OF GO

ARITOMO

'Yoshimori has been found?' For years Lord Aritomo had both dreaded and longed for this news. Until he saw Yoshimori's corpse with his own eyes he would never feel secure about Emperor Daigen's reign. Once Yoshimori was dead, preferably executed in public as the son of a rebel and traitor, no one would be able to question the legitimacy of Daigen. Even Heaven would have to concede.

He noticed Masachika recoil very slightly as he leaned towards him. Aritomo knew his breath smelled of decay and that his men feared he was grievously sick, even dying. He saw it in their sideways glances, their nervous voices. Yet not one of them had the courage to confront him with their fears. They did not understand he would outlive them all, that this passing illness was the price he was paying for immortality. He used white powder to mask his yellowing skin and madder to give colour to his cheeks and lips. He drank wine to dull the pain and took many other potions, concocted for him by his physicians. Nothing could alleviate the night sweats and the vomiting, or restore healthy flesh to his gaunt frame, but it would all be worth it in the end.

'It may be just another rumour,' Masachika replied. 'Arinori reported it. Messengers came from Aomizu this morning. One of the owners of the pleasure boats, Lady Fuji, hinted that she knew where Yoshimori was.'

'Is it worth investigating? It could be a ploy to ingratiate herself with Arinori. They will do anything to avoid paying their dues, these women.'

'Indeed. And as we know the Aomizu Lord is susceptible to such women, and inclined to be fanciful himself.'

Aritomo raised his eyebrows. He did not encourage his men in criticism and backbiting. It corroded their loyalty to each other and eventually to him. But he was always interested in their opinions. He wondered what Arinori would have to say about Masachika in return. He would probably not be so quick to criticise, for Masachika had a reputation for acting swiftly against any perceived rival, wiping out offences in blood.

Masachika said, 'However, the woman died, probably poisoned. The most likely suspect, one of her entertainers, disappeared the next day, fleeing into the Darkwood. What if Fuji really did know something and was silenced?'

Aritomo shifted his jaw from side to side as he did when he was thinking. The dull clicking was the only sound in the room.

'You had better go and take a look,' he said finally. 'Wear unmarked clothes and don't draw attention to yourself.'

He noticed with some satisfaction that Masachika was galled by this. Masachika had acted as a spy for both the Miboshi and the Kakizuki, but Aritomo knew he would have preferred to leave all that in the past and play the part of a great lord and that he liked riding at the head of his retinue, with the pine trees of Kuromori and Matsutani emblazoned on surcoats, robes and banners. Aritomo made a point of giving him minor errands, as though he were some insignificant underling, to keep him in his place. He saw Masachika hesitate as if he would refuse and continued to stare at him until the younger man submitted, bowed deeply and took his leave.

He thinks he will bide his time and outlive me. But he will not. None of them will.

Yet he had to admit that he did not feel well. Often he passed sleepless nights, during which he recalled his years as an exile and fugitive, the murders of his young sons as hostages, the breakdown in health of his wife, leading to her early death. He knew he was seen as cold and unfeeling but he had made himself so out of necessity, vowing he would never allow either love or grief to weaken him again. The last person he had cared for was Takaakira, who had hurt him so cruelly and made him weep for what he swore would be the last time.

Now hundreds served him in the capital and thousands more in the provinces and not one of them meant anything to him other than the means by which to impose his will. His scribes kept meticulous records of men, horses, weapons, ships as well as all the various means of acquiring, maintaining and transporting them. The administrative departments he had established kept the city running smoothly, supervised the different markets and guilds, burned rubbish, carried out investigations, imposed imprisonment and other punishments. But all the time the Kakizuki loitered in Rakuhara, preventing him from bringing the entire realm under his control. Hearing of Yoshimori's existence would only embolden them.

Surely I am strong enough to annihilate them, he thought. *It is time to put my plan into action before these rumours reach them.* For some months he had been preparing ships and men, with the assistance of Arinori. Masachika's attempt to undermine his rival had had the opposite effect, confirming Aritomo's high regard for the seaman's qualities. He dictated a message to one of his scribes, telling Arinori to make the final preparations. If he sent it by boat it would reach Aomizu well before Masachika did.

•

He was still pondering the details of the attack when later that day he went to Ryusonji, as he often did since the Emperor and his mother had moved there. The halls and courtyards of the temple had been rebuilt, as well as the prison cells, and two spacious residences added, one for the Emperor and one for Lady Natsue. Daigen could have moved into the Imperial Palace, which had finally been finished, but the time never seemed right, and a string of excuses was made until it became obvious to Aritomo that Lady Natsue wanted to keep her son close by and under her control. She entertained Daigen and his court with many artistic pursuits, poetry contests, games of incense guessing and shell matching, and kept them amused with intrigues and gossip. Yet Aritomo knew that there was another side to her life, and it was this that interested him.

He also made time to visit Sesshin who still sat in the cloister, played his lute and sang to the dragon child. The old man rambled when he spoke at all and did not seem to know who Aritomo was, yet occasionally his gaze from under his sedge hat turned lucid, and then he let fall some fragment of ancient wisdom. Aritomo thirsted after these, collected them in his heart and brooded on them.

Once Sesshin had spoken of the dragon essence in the water of the well and, remembering what Lady Natsue had said, Aritomo drank it each day, even though his physicians feared it might have traces of poison in it. Another time Sesshin had seized him by his clothes, pulled him forward and speaking directly into his face had told him a recipe for lacquer tea, which Aritomo had made up, and swallowed as much as he could stomach every night. He interpreted Sesshin's utterances like prophecies, seeing in him a man who had no fear of death since he knew he would live forever. He could not be bullied or coerced but was free in a way no one else was.

I will be like that but I will not waste my immortality plucking a lute and singing songs. I will use it to impose my will on an entire realm.

•

It was a very hot afternoon. The Empress and her ladies sat in a pavilion by the stream. From a distance they made a pleasing picture in their light robes of summer colours of blue-green and mauve, brightly dressed attendants standing around with sunshades, but the stream had dried to a trickle and the moss was reduced to dust. When he looked more closely the women seemed enervated and under the white powder their faces gleamed with sweat.

Aritomo waited in the shade of the cloisters listening to the deafening drone of the cicadas. The Empress caught sight of him and made a sign to her ladies. They rose like a flock of dispirited plovers and prepared to move within. After a few moments one of them appeared at his side and asked him to follow her.

Inside the temple it was even hotter. He felt suddenly dizzy. The mingled scents of incense and lamp oil threatened to bring on nausea. The Empress was not in the reception room where he was usually taken but further inside, in the very heart of the temple, a place devoted not to pleasure but to meditation and worship.

A few lamps burned on an altar, adding to the stifling heat of the room. Among the statues and images of deities he could make out a depiction of the Prince Abbot, the features shifting as the flames sent flickering shadows over the priest's face. So she worshipped him here, his sister, the Empress? She was still a beautiful woman but was becoming more like her brother as age melted the flesh from her bones, hollowed her cheeks and domed her forehead.

She sat with her back to the altar, a carved arm rest at her side. She barely acknowledged Aritomo's greeting before she spoke hurriedly.

'I am glad you came. I was about to send for you. I have something to show you.'

She ordered the attendants to leave the room and then said in a low voice, 'There is a text on the altar. Bring it to me.'

He had knelt before her. Now he rose and, bowing again as he passed in front of her, did as she commanded. The text seemed very old, the pages dark indigo, the lettering gold. Dropping to his knees, he held it out to her.

She did not touch it but said, 'Can you read it?'

He looked at the page he had opened. In the dark room it was like peering into the sky to read the stars. The characters were in an ancient style that he had trouble deciphering.

A voice spoke out of the darkness, from the ceiling, startling him for he had thought they were alone – but surely it was no human voice that croaked harshly, 'Yoshimori!'

Then the characters resolved themselves and he could read the name.

Yoshimori.

'It is the Book of the Future,' Lady Natsue said. 'With great difficulty, my brother had inscribed my son's name there. Now Yoshimori's name has appeared and Daigen's has been erased.'

Aritomo stared at the text in his hands. 'Who has done this? Who has been allowed in here?'

'There is no need to come physically into this room to control the Book of the Future,' she replied. 'Or to write with the hands. It is with the power of the mind that the Book is rewritten.'

'Can it be changed? Can your son's name be reinstated?'

'Believe me, Lord Aritomo, I have been trying. But I have not succeeded yet.'

Aritomo pondered this for a few moments and then said, 'Some creature spoke just now. I heard Yoshimori's name.'

'It was a werehawk. Two hatched out ten days ago. The eggs must have been lying beneath the altar for years. One day one of my priests noticed they were giving out heat. Soon after, cracks appeared in the shells. The birds came out fully fledged and within days were able to talk. They are insolent and aggressive, and too cunning to catch and kill. It is hard to bend werehawks to your will. My brother could do it, but I don't suppose anyone else is able to now.'

There was a fluttering of wings and he felt the air move against his face.

'How do you train them?' He longed to have them at his command.

'I do not know. There is nothing written down. My priests have been searching, but so many records were lost in the fire.'

'Maybe the old man knows,' Aritomo said. 'I will ask him.'

'He must be made to leave.' Natsue's voice was an angry hiss. 'He may pretend to be witless but every day I feel his powers increase and clash against mine. As fast as I learn, he learns faster. I am sure it is he who has rewritten the Book of the Future. You must get rid of him.'

'It is hard to get rid of a man who cannot die.'

'Then cut off his hands so he cannot write! Gag his mouth, tear out his tongue so he cannot speak. Tie him up and throw him in a well!'

'I will have him confined somewhere else,' Aritomo promised, thinking it would be to his own advantage to have Sesshin close by.

'Why have the werehawks hatched now?' Lady Natsue whispered. 'Why has Yoshimori's name replaced Daigen's? What has changed? Can it be that Yoshimori has appeared? That he is alive?'

Above their heads the birds cackled as if they were laughing.

'There have been rumours,' he said. 'Masachika has gone to investigate. Yoshimori will be found, captured and executed.'

'Masachika, Kiyoyori's brother?'

'He delivered the Autumn Princess to us. If anyone can bring us Yoshimori, it will be him.'

'Yet you neither trust nor like him,' she said. 'You have made that clear many times in our conversations.'

'He has served me faithfully for many years. If he finds Yoshimori he will win my everlasting affection.'

She was silent for a few moments. He wondered what was passing through her mind.

'You have no children, Lord Aritomo?'

The change of subject surprised him. 'I had two sons but they both died many years ago.'

'You must know there are concerns about your health. What will happen to the realm after . . .'

'I can assure your Majesty, I have no intention of dying!'

He could see his bluntness angered her, but all she said was, 'I look forward to hearing the news of Yoshimori's capture. I trust you will inform me immediately.'

He promised he would. As he left the werehawks swooped clumsily from the rafters and flew after him. On his way back through the many halls and courtyards he had been half-listening for the sound of the lute and now he heard it, coming from the cloister that overlooked the lake.

Sesshin sat plucking the strings idly. He did not seem to play consciously and yet a tune emerged. The werehawks landed in front of him and opened their beaks, singing as if in harmony.

'Good day, my friends,' Sesshin said, his fingers still. 'What have you come to tell me?'

He turned his head towards Aritomo and even though Aritomo knew the old man could not see him his sightless attention unnerved him.

The birds warbled. Sesshin cocked his head, listening.

'The leaves are turning red,' he said. 'Yes autumn is coming and all will be red.'

Red was the colour of the Kakizuki. It seemed hotter than ever in the cloister as the sun sank towards the west. Aritomo's mouth was parched. He swallowed hard and said, 'I could have you confined and tortured. It is by my grace that you are free.'

'You could, you could,' the old man agreed amiably. 'But it will make no difference. The leaves will still turn red.'

2

MASACHIKA

Masachika's spirits rose as he rode towards Aomizu. It was true Aritomo had been more than usually scornful to him and he had been made aware yet again that the lord to whom he had devoted his life disliked him intensely. Moreover his head ached from the wine he had drunk the night before and his eyes, which had always been weak since the bees attacked him at Matsutani, were playing their usual tricks on him, one moment darkening as if he were going blind, the next perceiving people and animals, surrounded by flashing lights, that were not really there. Yet he felt the stirrings of confidence and hope. Maybe it was only a rumour, that Yoshimori had been found, but it could just as likely be true. If he were the one to deliver Yoshimori to Aritomo, as he had delivered the Autumn Princess, his standing would be assured and his rewards great. His secret desire, which he had never shared with anyone, not even his wife, Tama, was that Aritomo would make him his heir. Surely that would be a reasonable price to pay for the missing Emperor?

But then I must also have heirs, he thought. Tama had fallen pregnant twice, but had not been able to carry either child to term, and now she was almost past childbearing. He still loved her and depended on her, but his lack of sons troubled him. Without them what was the point of being lord of three flourishing estates, let alone becoming Aritomo's successor? At times he regretted not having taken his former betrothed as a second wife; he feared Tama's jealousy and rage, but the idea of marrying another woman still persisted.

His reflections wandered to Kiyoyori's children, though he had not thought about them in years. Perhaps it was riding alongside Lake Kasumi that brought Hina to his mind, for she had drowned in its waters. It had been reported to him that a funeral was held and his messenger had been shown the grave in Aomizu. And Kiyoyori's son had died at Ryusonji, though some strange legend had arisen about him and the dragon child. There were similar legends about Kiyoyori whose body had never been found. Was it possible he had not died but was waiting to return and take his revenge? He often remembered reluctantly his dream of the foal. He had sent the young horse to Ryusonji with the others. After the Prince Abbot's death, Shikanoko had taken all three into the Darkwood. Was Kiyoyori still there, still Lord of the Darkwood? Would he come back with Shikanoko?

He shook himself and urged his horse on, riding fast as though he could escape these memories of the dead.

It was a week since the funeral, but the pleasure boats were still tied up at Aomizu. It seemed no one had taken charge since Lady Fuji's death. Masachika inspected the boats and then retired to a nearby temple, where he used Lord Aritomo's authority to commandeer a room and prepared to question the entertainers. It amused him that even though Aritomo had told him not to draw attention to himself, everyone was aware of his identity. He heard his name repeated through the courtyards and knew faces would pale, bowels loosen, and limbs tremble.

Most of them claimed they knew nothing, and he concluded they were telling the truth. They were divided in opinion over Lady Yayoi's guilt, some swearing that she had loved, even revered, Lady Fuji and was not capable of carrying out such an act of revenge, others claiming she had always been strange, different, too clever in some way, and had secretly resented her mistress. They had quarrelled over a request. Moreover, she had many unusual skills, often treated people for all kinds of diseases, and was familiar with a wide range of herbs, both healing and dangerous.

Arinori attended most of the meetings. From the way he spoke of them, Masachika suspected he had some fondness for both women, probably had been intimately involved with them. There was nothing wrong with that, unless questions of regulations and tax had been overlooked, but he would keep it in mind. Arinori might not be quite so close to Lord Aritomo as he pretended, but Masachika liked to know as much about his rivals, and their weaknesses, as possible. He could already see several ways in which he could further undermine the Aomizu Lord.

One young woman, Asagao, seemed to have known Yayoi best, and he questioned her at length.

'She said she was just going to the crossroads,' Asagao said, tears trickling down her cheeks. She had wept almost continuously, her eyes were red, her lips swollen. Masachika felt the stirrings of attraction for her.

'But I knew she was lying.' Asagao wiped her face with her sleeve. 'When she said goodbye, I knew it would be forever.'

'You had known her for a long time?'

'We were at the temple together when we were children. She must have been about twelve.'

'And how many years ago was that?'

Asagao flushed a little and said, 'I am now twenty-five, so twelve years ago.'

'So long?' Masachika said, letting his eyes linger on her face, making her colour deepen more. Then he addressed Arinori. 'What do we know about this temple?'

'Lady Fuji kept young girls there until they were old enough to serve on the boats. I first went to it about twelve years ago as it happens. It's probably just a coincidence, but the Abbess is the mother of the sorcerer they call Shikanoko.'

'Oh yes, I remember now,' Masachika said. 'You went there to investigate. Was Yayoi there then?'

'She was,' Arinori said. 'As a matter of fact, she caught my eye. She was an exceptionally beautiful girl. I asked Lady Fuji to arrange that I might be her first . . .'

'And in return?' Masachika demanded.

'I have looked after them both, I admit, but there's been no conflict with my loyalty to our lord.'

'I am sure,' Masachika said smoothly. 'I am not questioning your loyalty.'

'As soon as Fuji hinted to me that she might know where Yoshimori was, I sent messengers to Miyako. I would have questioned her further myself, but unfortunately . . .' Again he let his sentence trail away, as though there were things he did not like talking about, words he feared uttering. Masachika noted this reluctance, but said nothing, simply waited for Arinori to resume his account.

'When Yayoi did not return I assumed she had gone with the acrobats. I followed immediately but there was no sign of them on the road. They had vanished. So I went on to the temple. I thought there might have been some kind of collusion between them. I knew Yayoi had been a great favourite of the Abbess.'

'And?'

'I was angry. I'd always suspected that pack of women of subversion in some way. They offended me again and I learned nothing. I had the temple set on fire and the nuns fled. The Abbess was injured but they took her with them.'

Masachika turned his attention back to the young woman who was crying even more. 'Did either Fuji or Yayoi mention Yoshimori to you?'

'Who is Yoshimori?'

'The deceased Emperor's grandson.'

'No,' Asagao said. 'Why would they or anyone else here talk about any of the Emperor's sons or grandsons? We are riverbank people. That world is as distant from us as the clouds are from the earth.'

'Who was Yayoi?' Masachika questioned. 'Where did she come from?'

'I can't tell you for sure. Most of us never talk about the past. But people used to say she was found in the lake – the acrobats pulled her and a baby boy from the water. The boy was brought up by them and still lives with them.'

Pulled from the lake. Twelve years ago. Masachika said nothing for a few moments. His heartbeat had picked up. Was it possible? Had she not drowned after all? *I must have known. That is why I thought about her earlier.* Sometimes even he was amazed at the accuracy of his intuitions. And the boy – could he be the son of Akihime, the Autumn Princess? He remembered telling the Princess her son had drowned with Hina – how she had wept! But he had never told Aritomo about the child.

His voice when he spoke was made stern and cruel by these memories. 'Where are these acrobats now? Why have they not been brought in for questioning?' He addressed Arinori but it was Asagao who answered.

'They always go to the Darkwood at this time of year, to capture young monkeys.'

'Do you think Yayoi went with them?'

'I suppose so,' Asagao replied. 'I don't know where else she would go – but I can't imagine her living as they do in the forest. She is like me, delicate, refined.' She gave Masachika a look that was part challenging, part submissive, which he found quite charming. She was a truly beautiful young woman. He returned her look openly.

'Did she leave anything behind?'

'Almost everything. That's why no one thought she was going to vanish. She even left her lute – she gave it to me and said I could play it. I brought it with me.'

'Show me,' Masachika said, but the shabby old instrument did not really interest him. Asagao, however, interested him very much. He liked the way sorrow and fear had bruised her. It made him want to grip her, leave his own imprint on her flesh. His wife's face floated for a moment in front of his eyes. He was away from home for long periods and had often taken advantage of the many women offered to him. They satisfied his physical needs, though none had ever touched him deeply. But this girl was different. He had always liked the riverbank women and she seemed both exotic and vulnerable. She would be his reward for the inconvenience of the journey, for Aritomo's coldness and scorn. And the idea that she would give him a son fuelled his desire.

'The Darkwood is part of my estate,' he said. 'As it happens, I plan to return to Matsutani to arrange a great hunt for Lord Aritomo, in the autumn. But men cannot spend all day and all night hunting – we need entertainment too. I will take you and your lute with me. And Lord Arinori will pursue these acrobats and make sure Yayoi is not with them. Then we will arrange for the acrobats to be brought to Matsutani, as well. Lord Aritomo might find them amusing.'

Arinori chuckled, and after Asagao had left to collect her belongings he said, 'You have a taste for riverbank women, I see. I've had many a discussion as to which is the most beautiful, Yayoi or Asagao. I always had a slight preference for Yayoi.'

Masachika cut him off, not wanting to consider they were on the same level. 'Just how much did Fuji tell you?'

'Only what I said. She was going to propose a business deal; that's the sort of woman she was. She would not reveal anything more until she had settled the terms of the contract.'

'All we can conclude then is that Yoshimori might be somewhere in the neighbourhood?'

'Or anywhere round the lake. The boats travel great distances.'

'No one has seen him for twelve years or more,' Masachika said. 'How would we even recognise him?'

'We could arrest and question every young man of the right age,' Arinori suggested.

Masachika dismissed this with a wave of his hand. 'Better to try to find Yayoi and question her.'

'Well, I would undertake that but I have other commitments. I am sure our lord has told you of the planned attack. I can't say too much. It's all highly secret.'

Masachika struggled to hide the fact he had no idea what Arinori was talking about.

'You may have noticed how few ships I have on the lake,' Arinori said in a low voice. 'They have all been sent to Akashi. And we have been building war vessels there for many months – but I must say no more. You never know who might be listening. There seem to be more spies and informants than ever. Everyone's always hoping to overhear something they can sell or use to their advantage.'

'It is probably better that you are otherwise occupied,' Masachika said, spitefully. 'You have already done enough damage with your clumsy pursuit of Yayoi. We will send a message from Asagao, by means of those older men we already questioned, to bring the acrobats in the Darkwood to Matsutani, with the monkeys. Let's see if they can find Yayoi and report where she is without scaring her further away. It's a shame your secret mission will prevent you from taking part in the hunt. It will be unlike any ever held in the history of the Eight Islands.'

3

TAKEYOSHI

At first, Take's spirits were lowered by the death of the old woman, the grandmother he had never known. For a day or more he grieved, but then, the further they walked, the more excited and elated he began to feel. He had always thought of himself as an orphan, a foundling of unknown parents. Now the idea that he might have a living father, and that his mother, though dead, had been a Princess, thrilled him. Suddenly he seemed to understand everything about himself; his character and instincts all made sense. He felt the heft of the pole, the responding muscles in his arms and shoulders.

I am a warrior, born to fight. But now I need a teacher more than ever.

He felt he had grown taller. His gaze, as it continually swept the tangled trees for signs of danger, was more acute, his stride longer and more tireless, even his understanding was more perceptive. He was just thinking that the Emperor could be anywhere, and that the woman he knew as Lady Yayoi, or Older Sister, was the only person who knew, when Kon called from a high tree a little way ahead.

Take turned to watch the young men following. Noboru, the monkey, had switched to Yoshi's shoulder, and was affectionately grooming his hair. Saru was talking loudly and rapidly. Take could not hear what he was saying but he could guess what it was, some involved anecdote, a ribald dream, a tale of seduction. Both young men laughed loudly, the sound ringing through the forest.

They should not laugh so loud! Take thought, as though trying to blind himself to the knowledge that had already pierced him like a ray of light. But it was blazing inside him and could not be ignored. *Yoshi!*

I have a warrior's insight now, he thought. *How should I not know my lord, my prince, the ruler of this earthly realm I walk on?* And then he felt shocked and almost offended. It was an outrage that the son of Heaven, the heir to the Lotus Throne, should be ambling along a rough and dusty track, swapping dirty jokes, a monkey on his shoulder.

I will see him restored or die, he vowed solemnly. He could hardly prevent himself from running back and hurling himself at Yoshi's feet, swearing allegiance, offering him his life. It seemed the green light of the forest took on a new translucence, the birdsong became ravishingly beautiful. He gazed on Kon, finally understanding the bird's persistence. He heard nobility in the call now, and admired Kon's perseverance. The young Emperor had been lost, abandoned by everyone. Only Kon had stuck by him.

Kon and now me. I will take him as my example and be as true.

He found it hard to treat Yoshi naturally and over the following days grew shy and deferential in his presence. Saru noticed it and teased him.

'Take has a crush on you,' he whispered to Yoshi, loud enough for Take to hear. 'I bet he has some juicy dreams! Why don't you share them, brat?'

It was obvious Saru had no idea – he could never have teased and insulted Yoshi if he had known who he was. It made Take decide that Yoshi could not know his true identity. If he had the slightest inkling he would not allow such familiarity. Saru's behaviour upset and offended Take, but he said nothing, unsure what to reveal or when.

Yoshi became silent and withdrawn, as though a great weight had settled on his shoulders.

A feeling of coldness, almost enmity began to grow between Take and Saru. All his life Take had admired the young acrobat, as if Saru were his older brother. Now he became aware of the immense gulf between them. He could not help seeing himself differently: his father was a warrior, his mother a Princess. Saru was a nobody from the insignificant village of Iida. Yet these thoughts troubled him and he was half-ashamed of them, for in the world of the acrobats talent and ability were all that mattered and in these Saru far outstripped him. He still admired him, but he found Saru crude and resented his friendship with Yoshi, seeing how demeaning it was.

They drew near to the hot springs and began to notice signs of the monkeys' presence – broken twigs and half-eaten fruit on the ground, chattering in the treetops. Noboru became agitated and screeched most of the day. The young men set up camp. They swam in the hot pools, climbed trees, and every day practised acrobatics, tumbling across the clearing, swinging from branches like monkeys. Take joined them, but his old carefree exuberance was gone.

I will never be an acrobat, he thought, looking at their slight, wiry frames. He was already as tall as Yoshi, taller than Saru. *I will never perform again.*

The lady – he did not really want to use her old name and she had not told him her true one – retreated from them, telling them she would spend the days reading, fasting and meditating. He wanted to talk more to her, to question her about everything, but her reserve discouraged him. She came every morning to collect fresh water, but otherwise stayed out of sight. Occasionally Take heard her chanting but he did not know what the words meant. He had only ever heard her sing ballads of love before. He took to sleeping nearby in case anything threatened her in the dark, but both day and night were peaceful. Nobody came.

Saru was enjoying the holiday and was in no hurry to make their capture and go home. But Yoshi's silence increased and Take knew the lady was waiting for something, someone, some sign. He himself was restless. He wanted to start his new life as a warrior. But who could teach him all he needed to know? He had never stopped thinking about Kinpoge and her father. *He turned me away once, but I was too easily discouraged. Maybe it was a test of some sort. Now I am back in the forest I should try again.*

The tension between him and the two young men became almost unbearable. He was over-polite to Yoshi, over-rude to Saru, irritating them both equally. There seemed to be no way to resolve the situation. The knowledge that the Emperor of the Eight Islands lived, ate, slept alongside him was too momentous to contain. He knew he was in danger of blurting out a secret that was not his to tell. One night, after Saru's teasing had turned particularly malicious, he made the decision that he would go back to the man who had been taught by the tengu and insist that he teach him – this time he would not be refused.

He set out very early the next morning, before anyone else was awake. He walked swiftly, imagining all the things he longed to have: red-laced armour, a helmet crowned with stag antlers or boar tusks, a long sword forged by a master, so sharp it would slice through silk, a bow with nineteen arrows in a quiver, a white stallion for a warhorse. He practised declaiming his name as warriors did at the onset of battle.

I am Kumayama no Takeyoshi, son of Shikanoko, grandson of Hidetake . . .

His voice, just beginning to change to its adult timbre, echoed through the forest, but the chorus of cicadas was the only response. Now and then there was the sound of a large animal crashing through the bushes. *Wild boar*, he thought, hoping to kill one and take its tusks but also fearing its ferocious power. He knew the boar was the most dangerous animal in the forest.

At first, he followed the stream as he had done previously. It was not long before he came to a tree, which he was fairly sure was the one where he had met Kinpoge. After that, a landslip of several boulders blocked his way. The stream, reduced to a trickle, came seeping out under them, but the gap was too small for Take to squeeze through and, furthermore, it looked like the sort of place where water spirits might dwell and he did not want to be seized by one and kept captive for years and years. The rocks' surface was perfectly smooth, with no handholds or footholds. There was nothing he could do but leave the stream and try to walk around them. He walked until nightfall, slept restlessly, and then rose at dawn.

It was a dull, overcast day and in the dim greenish light it was impossible to be certain of the right direction. The forest had changed in a year. Trees had fallen, new ones had grown rapidly, vines had spread, undergrowth had thickened. Take would not admit to himself that he was lost; he kept walking, slashing at the undergrowth with his pole, listening for the sound of water. The air was thick with moisture and one bird kept piping monotonously. Excitement had kept him awake the previous night and now his eyes began to feel heavy, as if he had fallen asleep and was dreaming. Into his mind came a series of pictures; he thought he heard someone call his name, his feet stumbled. As he recovered his balance, he saw a woman standing a short distance ahead of him.

'Kinpoge?' he said uncertainly. It was so long since he had seen her he could not be sure of recognising her. At first he thought it was her, grown taller and older, and then, as he came closer, he knew it was not. He remembered Kinpoge as bright and pretty, but this woman was the most beautiful he had ever seen, with pale skin, red lips, and hair so long and thick it covered her like a silky shawl. Her tiny white feet emerged from it like little flowers and he felt an almost uncontrollable urge to kneel before her and touch them with his lips.

'A young warrior!' the woman said, her voice as charming and melodious as a songbird's. 'Come, let me take you to my house. I will give you food and wine.'

Take refused politely, saying, 'Thank you, I must not inconvenience you. But I am looking for a girl and her father. They live somewhere round here – do you know them? I'd be very grateful if you could direct me to their place.'

The woman made a sound like a hiss and her tongue flickered in her perfectly formed mouth.

'Come with me and refresh yourself. Then I will set you on your way.'

She held out her hand and Take, suddenly realising he was unbearably hungry and thirsty, was about to take it, when there was a clattering overhead, a shower of leaves and twigs fell, and the skull horse, Ban, with Kinpoge clinging to it, landed on the ground in front of him.

'Don't let her touch you!' she shrieked, as she let go of Ban and pushed Take back. He lost his footing and dropped the pole, but turned his fall into a backwards roll and came up on his feet, grabbing the pole and brandishing it. Kinpoge turned to face the woman and said a few words that Take did not understand. The woman's head flattened, her body stretched out, sucking her limbs and her tiny feet up into it. She hissed again, her snake tongue spitting at them, before her huge brightly patterned shape slithered away between the vines.

'She will be very disappointed,' Kinpoge said. 'She probably hasn't run across a young man in years.'

'What was she?' Take said.

'A snake woman – a sort of ghost. She has an insatiable appetite for sex, but she sucks her lovers dry and then casts them aside like snake skins. Luckily for you Ban and I came along when we did.'

'I wasn't taken in by her,' Take said. 'I would never have gone with her.' But his heart was pounding with fear and regret.

'Fine! You can look after yourself. That's why you're wandering around lost. I suppose you were coming to find us? I'll meet you at home.' She grabbed Ban's reins and clicked her tongue at him. As the skull horse rose into the air, Take cried, 'Wait! I'm sorry. It's true, I am lost. That is, I'm not sure of the way. Please go with me.'

The horse hovered. She called, 'Say, "Thank you, Kinpoge, for saving me from the snake woman."'

He repeated the words and added, smiling, 'I am very pleased to see you again.'

'Really? Or is it just that you want my father to teach you?'

'I am pleased, really,' he said.

Ban came slowly down and Kinpoge slid off. 'So you don't want to learn from my father?'

'Of course I do! Can't both be true?'

'Once you start learning from my father, you won't care for me anymore,' Kinpoge said, giving him a mournful look.

'He'll probably turn me away again,' Take said, as they began to walk back the way he had come.

'No, he has been waiting for you,' Kinpoge said.

'He has? What made him change his mind?'

'You'll have to ask him,' she returned.

•

The hut was still a long day's walk away. Mostly he followed Kinpoge, but where the forest allowed they walked side by side.

'My real name is Takeyoshi,' he said on one of these times.

'I know, and your father is the one they call Shikanoko.'

'How did you know that?' he exclaimed. 'I only found out a few days ago myself.'

'The tengu told my father. Tengu seem to know most things.'

'I hope I will meet the tengu,' Take said.

'Be careful what you hope for,' Kinpoge replied.

They crossed the stream and walked into the clearing. Take stood still for a few moments, looking around, taking in the carved animals, the rock shapes, covered in moss, that suggested bears or wild boars. Then he saw the dogs, both real and fake. They looked back at him, the real dogs yapping, the fake ones voiceless. He felt a strong revulsion for their moth-eaten coats, their awkwardly angled limbs, their gemstone eyes.

Two men sat by the fire. The sound of rasping echoed through the clearing. He saw they were sharpening tools: axes, knives and – his heart bounded – swords. They worked in silence, swiftly and competently. They were very similar in build and appearance. Both had long wispy beards and moustaches, and their thick hair fell to their shoulders. They used their feet, with thin, flexible toes, as much as their hands. They wore only loincloths and their skin, turned copper by the sun, glistened with sweat.

'Come on!' Kinpoge said, and then called out, 'Father! Look who I found!'

One of the men got to his feet, laying aside the tools unhurriedly. He moved a few paces away from the fire and stood waiting for Take to approach him.

Take went forward warily. He gripped the pole, wondering if he should prostrate himself before the man he hoped would be his teacher, deciding it would do no harm, but, before he could bend his knees, the pole flew from his hands, struck him on the head, and landed some distance away. The man he had been about to kneel to was now behind him. He spun round, but caught only a glimpse of him before he disappeared.

The man by the fire was grinning and Kinpoge was doubled over with laughter.

'You've no idea how funny you looked,' she cried.

Her father reappeared beside her. 'It could be quite amusing to have a pupil,' he said.

Take felt rage building within him. He struggled not to let it overcome him. He remembered the old priest's words the day they had left Aomizu. *Master your anger*, he had said. Here, he would need more than ever the wisdom and the ability to discern what was real.

'If you do permit me to become your pupil, I will be forever grateful,' he said, using formal speech, 'and I will endeavour to continue to amuse you.'

Kinpoge's father chuckled again. 'You look like a strong lad, agile too. I think you will learn quickly. And you will have to, for my friend, Tadashii, tells me we do not have much time. Of course, it's hard to tell as time moves differently in the world of the tengu, but nevertheless . . . You've already met my daughter. I am Mu, this is my brother, Ima. We are your brothers too, in a way, but I'll explain all that later. Who are you travelling with?'

'The lady who was called Yayoi, and the acrobats, Sarumaru and Yoshimaru.' He did not want to say anything that would give away

Yoshi's true identity, but Mu said, as if he already knew, 'Yoshimaru? Well, he should be as safe in the Darkwood as anywhere, for the time being. Kinpoge, go with Ban and find them. Tell them Takeyoshi is staying with me for a while. Reassure the lady that he is in no danger. And now, Takeyoshi, since we have no time to waste, let's get to work.'

4

MASACHIKA

Masachika gazed on Lord Aritomo with an emotion close to pity, not one he often experienced. It was indeed cruel for the lord to be attacked by what appeared to be an incurable illness at this time when so much power lay in his hands. No one seemed to be able to diagnose it or treat it. Aritomo himself spoke of it lightly, brushing aside his retainers' concerns, all the while smiling as if he had a precious secret that he would tell no one. Masachika knew his lord had special teas brewed – Aritomo was sipping one now – but he did not know what was in them and had never been invited to share them.

Aritomo had deteriorated in the weeks Masachika had been away in Aomizu, yet as usual he made no mention of his failing health nor, his aides whispered to Masachika, had he allowed it to interfere with his devotion to government. He rose while it was still dark and did not retire until late at night. The best way to win his gratitude, people joked, was to donate lamp oil or candles, or fireflies in cages. But no one made jokes in his presence.

Masachika had written a report for Lord Aritomo, which the lord was now perusing carefully, but it was not as detailed and comprehensive as it might have been nor had he lingered over its telling. He said there was no way to assess the rumour, but he was taking steps to have the fleeing suspect tracked down. He did not mention that she might be Kiyoyori's daughter. He would save that valuable piece of information for the right moment. He told himself he did not want to tire or place additional strain on his lord but the truth was he was impatient to get back to the girl called Asagao, who had cast a spell over him. He had been afraid it would not last, that since she was just a woman of pleasure he would tire of her as quickly as he had been ensnared by her, but, during the hot summer nights when the skies were like velvet and the stars like pearls, she aroused in him an intoxicating ecstasy, an insatiable thirst. She made him feel like a young man again. From time to time he wondered with feelings of dread what would happen if Tama were to find out about her, and he recalled all his wife's fine qualities with regret, but his new passion had rendered him helpless. He would never give Asagao up.

He tried not to think of her now, shifted uncomfortably in his formal kneeling position, summoned up images of snow, icy waterfalls . . .

Aritomo had put the report down and was scrutinising him with his shrewd gaze. Masachika feared the lord might see right through him and, hoping to distract him, said, 'Lord Aritomo will be well enough to ride to Matsutani in the autumn? I am arranging a hunt in your honour. The air, the excitement, the hot springs will restore your health, I am sure. We will have deer, and wild boar, bears, possibly, and wolves. I will also provide hawks and falcons – anything you might desire.'

He decided to keep the entertainment he had in mind, the musicians and the acrobats with their monkeys, to himself for the time being. He wanted it to be a complete surprise.

'I will come,' Aritomo said. 'I feel a longing for the forest and the open air. It will be an opportunity to reward those loyal to me and to assess my warriors' skills.' He paused for a moment, then gestured to Masachika to come closer. He said quietly, 'I am going to deal with the Kakizuki before winter comes. It will coincide nicely with your hunt. We will let their spies think we are fully occupied with sport and entertainment, but I have already dispatched a fleet of ships, carrying hundreds of men, to take them by surprise. Arinori is in command.'

He grinned at Masachika. His breath smelled of his illness. 'They think the old badger is finished, but he is still craftier than them.'

So that was Arinori's secret mission!

'It is a brilliant idea, but I should be leading such an attack force,' Masachika said with feigned enthusiasm. 'I can delegate the hunt to someone else.'

'If you and I seem otherwise occupied, we will allay suspicions,' Aritomo replied. 'Besides, Arinori has skills as a sailor and an admiral. Once the Kakizuki are eliminated, these rumours about Yoshimori will disappear.' He tapped the report with his forefinger. 'Rumours arise all the time. Usually there is no substance to them. An Emperor with no one to fight for him is hardly an Emperor.'

'Indeed,' Masachika agreed.

'Don't be disappointed. You will have your chance in land fighting soon enough. When the Kakizuki are gone, we will take care of Takauji.'

Masachika shuffled backwards out of Aritomo's presence, touching his head to the ground once more as attendants slid open the doors behind him. Outside, in the wide corridor, he stood and adjusted his robe. Then, trying not to look as if he was hurrying, he began to walk back to where his grooms waited with the ox carriage.

However, as he left the outer courtyard, passing through the great gates with their carvings of lions, someone approached him. It was a man he knew vaguely, though he could not recall his name, He was a minor official in the Emperor's household. Masachika suspected he probably wanted to discuss something about money. The Emperor never seemed to have enough and was always asking for more. Then he remembered, *Yoriie*.

Masachika's bodyguards had also been waiting outside and now began to move closer to him, their hands on their swords. Surely they did not suspect old Yoriie of an assassination attempt? He made a sign to them to hold back and greeted the official as curtly as he could, without being downright rude.

Yoriie replied more fulsomely. 'If it is not too great an inconvenience, would Lord Masachika accompany me to Ryusonji?'

His manner was obsequious but his small eyes were sharp and seemed to flicker upwards to scrutinise Masachika. The residences at Ryusonji were luxurious and expensive, yet ministers received a stream of complaints about the accommodation. It was too hot or too cold, the roof leaked, the nearby river stank, there was an invasion of biting fleas, owls hooted all night.

Masachika assumed it would be another of these and groaned inwardly, but he reminded himself that no one survived in an official position in the capital without brains, courage or wealth, preferably all three, and that he should not underestimate Yoriie nor refuse the Emperor. Regretfully he again put aside his desire and agreed to go with Yoriie, inviting him to ride in the ox carriage.

They did not speak much as the ox made its slow, laborious way through the crowded streets towards the river. The Sagigawa had all but dried up and lay in a series of stagnant pools that, Masachika noted, keeping his mouth firmly closed, did indeed smell noxious. The townspeople threw refuse in the river, which normally would be washed away rapidly, but which now lay decomposing, picked over by scavenging crows and wild dogs.

Outside Ryusonji's gates, people milled – beggars seeking alms, the sick and crippled praying for healing, amulet sellers, and pilgrims. Since it had become the Emperor's residence, the whole temple had taken on an increased aura of sacredness. Slivers of wood were carved from the gates, pebbles stolen from the paths, leaves gathered from the ginkgo and sakaki trees, all with the hope they would provide talismans against ill health and misfortune. Partly for this reason, the buildings and gardens had a dilapidated and untended look.

Two large black birds perched on the roof and peered down at Masachika with golden eyes. One of them made a derisive cackle and the other echoed it. They sounded uncannily human. Their excrement had whitened the gate and the ground below.

The luxury of the inner rooms tried to compensate for the exterior decay, but nothing could remove the stench from the river. The great shutters were all closed, presumably to keep it out, and the dim interior was lit by oil lamps, the smoke making the rooms even hotter.

There was a large hall within his residence, where usually the Emperor received visitors, sitting on a raised dais behind a thin, gilded bamboo screen, his courtiers ranked on the steps beneath him, but, this time, Yoriie indicated Masachika should follow him to the other side of the temple where he had never been before.

The official stepped up on the verandah of another beautiful residence and called softly. 'Lord Masachika is here.'

The door slid sideways, opened by unseen hands. Masachika dropped to his knees on the threshold and bowed his head to the ground.

There was a rich scent that he could not quite identify, and for a moment he thought with a surge of emotion that it must be the

Emperor, himself, kneeling on an embroidered silk cushion, not five paces from him. Then the figure removed the covering from its face and spoke. It was a woman.

'Lord Masachika, thank you for coming. I presume you know who I am?'

He could only guess, never having seen her before. 'Our sovereign's noble mother,' he said, raising his head briefly and then lowering it again. Natsue, the Emperor's mother, sister to the Prince Abbot. 'In what way can I serve you, your Majesty?'

'Can I trust you to keep this conversation secret? Will you swear to me that you will speak of it to no one?'

He hesitated, aware of Yoriie just behind him, of the courtiers, the servants in the background, any one of whom might be a spy. Was it some kind of trap, some test of his loyalty? 'I can have no secrets from Lord Aritomo,' he said guardedly.

'How is our dear lord and protector?' she said. 'We have heard his recovery is slow.'

'Alas, slower than we all desire, but he does not allow his illness to impede him in any way. No man has a stronger will.'

'A strong will means nothing if Heaven is against you,' Lady Natsue replied. 'My son and I are deeply concerned for the welfare of the country and the people. Is it possible that Lord Aritomo's illness is a punishment of some sort?'

'I cannot speak for Heaven, your Majesty. Let your priests do that.'

'But they have, Lord Masachika. Oh yes, indeed they have. We have heard rumours that Yoshimori might still be alive. People have the audacity to say he has greater legitimacy than my son.'

'We are doing our best to stamp out such treason,' Masachika murmured.

'Yet the drought continues, and with it the unrest. But Yoshimori's death, if it were confirmed or better still publicly witnessed, would make my son the rightful Emperor. Why has Lord Aritomo not achieved this?'

When Masachika did not reply she went on, 'I believe his illness is making him less than capable.'

He dared to raise his eyes and stare at her. She held his gaze for a moment, smiling slightly. 'I had thought . . . but you are a loyal man, Masachika. I will not trouble you further.'

Now he was intrigued. He very much wanted to know what she had thought. 'Lord Aritomo does not need extra burdens,' he heard himself say. 'I will keep whatever you want to confide in me to myself.'

'My son and I admire you,' Lady Natsue said. 'We wonder if Lord Aritomo fully appreciates you. It is wrong that he should not trust you. The Emperor would like you to be closer to him. We are both worried about Lord Aritomo's health. That is the only reason, you understand . . .'

That you are choosing me to replace him? The idea was preposterous, yet he was sure it was what she was hinting at. The heavy scent, the stifling room were making Masachika light-headed.

'It is a shame Lord Aritomo has no sons,' Lady Natsue said. 'Were he to pass away there is grave danger the realm would once more be torn apart by war. We must make the succession clear.'

It was exactly what Masachika hoped for but he did not trust himself to speak.

'My son is not happy with his circumstances. He is bored. He is intelligent, you know, and thinks deeply. He does not want to be someone else's figurehead. He wants to feel he is truly the ruler of this great country, like the warrior Emperors of ancient Shin. He needs loyal men like yourself to serve him, in positions of influence and power.' She spoke obliquely, leaving essential things unsaid. Masachika had to fill in the gaps himself – but was it truly her meaning or was he allowing his own desires to interpret her words?

'I am forever his servant as I am yours,' he said. 'But what will you have me do? I have only a few men at my command . . .' There was no way he could mount a full-scale rebellion and he was not such a fool, or so ambitious, that he would hint at such an act, even if only to deny it.

'Do nothing for the time being,' Lady Natsue said. 'Simply make sure Lord Aritomo's sickness is well managed.'

Does not improve, he translated silently.

'And be ready for our instruction. That is all.'

He bowed again to her and prepared to leave, but she made a sign to her attendants. Two women shuffled forward silently and helped her stand. One of them took the shawl, the other adjusted her many-layered robe, pink lapped over green, green over red and so on through twelve or more different coloured layers. She was a tiny woman, made all the more tiny by the mass of clothes. Her hair reached to the ground, adding even more weight to bow her down. She had grown thin but her skin was still white, her lips red. He remembered that in her youth she had been a beautiful woman who had won the deceased Emperor's heart.

'Follow me,' she said. 'My son wishes to let his eyes rest on you.'

She moved smoothly and swiftly, as though not walking at all but carried by unseen beings. As she passed him, Masachika, still prostrate, smelled her perfume even more strongly. It seemed to suggest infinite possibilities.

He walked at a respectful distance behind her down the long corridor. It was open on one side, giving out onto a courtyard. In the centre was a large fish pond fringed with reeds and lotus leaves.

I must discuss all this with Tama, he thought, as he followed Lady Natsue into the private chambers of the Emperor.

After a short enigmatic interview in which the Emperor spoke obliquely of poetry and the weather, Yoriie accompanied Masachika to the gate where the birds again looked down at him and seemed to jeer. He even thought he heard one speak his name.

'What are those birds?' he asked. 'Where did they come from?'

'The priests tell us they are werehawks,' Yoriie replied. 'The eggs hatched recently. The deceased Prince Abbot used to own several and they flew far and wide at his bidding, but none remained after his death and now no one knows how to train them.'

'What about Master Sesshin? He would know.'

'He is in his dotage and useless,' Yoriie said, his mouth curling in irritation. 'He found their antics amusing and spoiled them, giving them food. I suppose he might have been able to command them, but he is no longer here.'

'I thought I had not heard him playing. Where is he?'

'Her Majesty disliked him and wanted him removed. Lord Aritomo's men took him away.'

Masachika frowned. His intuition told him there was something strange going on, that he should look into it further, but then he thought of Asagao, longed to be with her, and could not bear any further delay.

5

MU

Take was a quick learner. It was as if the knowledge lay hidden within him and all Mu had to do was bring it to the surface. Mu was as fierce and as strict as the tengu had been with him, but Take accepted his discipline without question. He seemed to soak up everything; no challenge was too great. If he could not master some technique with the sword, or some practice of meditation, he worked obsessively at it, until he understood what Mu was asking of him and could achieve it.

Mu admired his pupil and had become fond of him. Ima liked him, and the animals, fake and real, came to accept him. Take in return treated them all with respect and kindness.

'Everything's going fine,' Mu told Tadashii on one of the tengu's visits. Take had not yet met him, as the tengu always came after the boy had fallen into one of the short sleeps of exhaustion Mu allowed him. 'Except I am worried about my daughter. She likes him too much. What will I do if she falls in love with him? We share the same father – the relationship is too close. He is a young warrior and she is the daughter of a fox woman. I don't want her to be hurt.'

'I told you, I am no expert in these matters,' Tadashii said. 'It's easy enough to separate them. I'll take Shikanoko's son away with me, for a while. And, since you will be visiting your brother soon, you can take Kinpoge with you. If she wants a man, let her marry one of her cousins.'

'I will be visiting my brother?' Mu repeated. 'I can tell you, that's not going to happen.'

'I believe it is,' Tadashii replied. 'Where is Shikanoko's son?'

'Asleep by the stream. You're not taking him now?'

'No time like the present,' Tadashii said, unfurling his wings and flexing them. 'He must be ready for us.'

He flew as silently as an owl to the stream, picked up the sleeping boy with one hand, called out a farewell and disappeared above the treetops.

Even Mu, who had come to know Tadashii well over the years, was startled by this abrupt departure. Kinpoge, when she woke the next morning, was inconsolable.

'Where did the tengu take him? Why? When will he come back?' She was fighting back tears.

'It's part of his training.' Mu tried to reassure her. 'He will be fine. You remember Tadashii often took me away. Didn't I always come back?'

'You are an adult. You can look after yourself. Take is only a boy,' she argued.

'Take can look after himself very well,' Ima told her. 'He has grown up in the weeks he has been here.' He tried to take Kinpoge on his knee to comfort her but she struggled from his grasp.

'You sent him away to spite me!' she accused her father angrily. 'You don't want us to be friends!'

'Maybe I don't, but so what? You are too young to know what is best for you. And anyway, girls should obey their fathers.' Mu tried to maintain his composure. Only Kinpoge could unsettle him so much. He closed his eyes, breathed deeply, seeking to enter the state of no attachment that made him the warrior of nothingness. He heard Kinpoge sigh in exasperation and walk away. He heard the clink of Ban's bridle and the slight rush of air as the skull horse took off.

Tadashii is right. If she is to be married the only appropriate bridegroom will be one of her cousins.

A dog began to bark. Ima said, 'Someone is coming.'

Mu heard the sounds at the same time: twigs breaking, leaves rustling, the four-beat step of horses. He opened his eyes.

Chika rode into the clearing on a tall brown horse, leading another smaller grey, laden with baskets. He was wearing a green hunting robe with a chrysanthemum crest, a bow on his back, a sword at his hip. Despite his moustache and beard, Mu recognised him at once, though years had passed since the day he had last seen him when Tsunetomo, the one-eyed warrior, had slung his youngest brother Ku, unconscious, over the back of his horse and had ridden away with Kiku, Kaze and Chika, leaving Mu destroyed in body and heart.

Mu let the memory re-form in his mind, looking at it dispassionately, observing how he had recovered from it and how it had given him the strength he now possessed. At the same time, he studied Chika, seeing the boy he had been, the man he had become. Kiku, he thought, had given him something he needed, some love or approval. He supposed they were now brothers in law. Yet there was still an emptiness within him, some unfulfilled longing that was on the point of hardening into bitterness. Nothing would ever satisfy him, no honours or rewards would ever heal the wound dealt to the heart of a child.

It was frustrating, to know there was so much he could teach Chika, and to recognise at the same time that Chika was unteachable.

I am thinking like a tengu! The idea surprised and shocked him.

Ima had walked towards the visitor. Chika dismounted, greeted him briefly and handed the horses' reins to him. Then he came close to Mu, standing somewhat defiantly in front of him.

Mu acknowledged him with a slight inclination of his head. 'What are you doing here, Chika?'

His familiar tone seemed to annoy the other man. Mu could see he had become touchy and proud. Chika glanced around, surveying the clearing and the hut.

'Not much has changed, I see.'

'Not much,' Mu agreed. 'And yet, everything.'

'And you?' Chika turned his gaze back to Mu. 'You seem to have suffered no lasting harm.'

'I did and I did not.'

'It was I who saved your life, you know. I think I deserve some gratitude. Tsunetomo wanted to kill you.'

Mu bowed. 'You were indeed the instrument of Heaven's will.'

'So don't forget, you are indebted to me,' Chika said.

'If there is a debt it will be paid,' Mu replied. 'But by the same currency, if there is an offence it will be avenged.'

Chika stared at him blankly.

'What can I do for you?' Mu said.

'Let's sit down and talk,' Chika said. 'Perhaps Ima could make us some tea. I've brought leaves with me, if you have none. We import them from Shin. I also have presents for you and your daughter. The grey horse is yours. Ima, tether the horses and unpack the baskets. They are all gifts from Kiku, your brother.'

'I know very well who Kiku is,' Ima muttered under his breath as he set a pot of water to boil on the fire. The tea leaves were of the highest quality, fragrant and sharp-flavoured. Among the gifts were green ceramic cups, much finer than anything Mu had ever drunk from.

'Your brother is deeply sorry for what happened,' Chika said, after taking a sip. 'He asks you to forgive him. He wants to see you.'

'If he is so sorry, why did he not come himself?' Mu replied. The moment he spoke he regretted his pettiness. He was going to visit Kiku, he knew that: the tengu had said so. There was no need to pretend he needed persuading. On the other hand, it would do no harm to seem reluctant.

'You don't know what Master Kikuta has become, or you wouldn't suggest that,' Chika replied. 'His empire is now so great he can't just leave it to travel to the Darkwood.'

'Where is this empire?'

'In Kitakami, on the Northern Sea.'

'From whence he summons his subjects into his presence,' Mu said, with a hint of sarcasm.

'He doesn't consider you his subject, Mu.'

'Then what does he consider me?'

'His brother, whom he wronged.'

'Those were his words?'

'Exactly as he spoke them,' Chika said, with such sincerity Mu knew he was lying.

'I will come with you,' he said finally. 'We should meet again, Kiku and I, and Kuro and Ku as well. What about you, Ima? Will you come too?'

'Someone has to look after the animals,' Ima said, 'and keep an eye on the hut. I have no desire to leave the Darkwood and go to Kitakami. Besides, Kiku did not send a horse for me.'

Was he hurt by the oversight? It was impossible to tell. As always, Ima's calm expression gave no hint of his true feelings. Mu remembered what the tengu had said. *Don't feel sorry for him.*

He was pierced by an emotion that was not pity, though pity was included in it. *I love him*, he realised. *Is this what brothers feel for each other?*

'We'll have to wait for Kinpoge to return,' he said.

'She'll come back soon,' Ima said, smiling. 'She took off without eating; she'll be hungry.'

As Ima predicted, Kinpoge appeared not long after. Chika produced presents for her: a robe of cream silk embroidered with celandines and aconites; sweet bean paste; a small bronze mirror into which she gazed in wonder; an exquisite carving of a horse, one foot raised, with a long mane and tail. Mu was astonished at the luxury and wealth that the gifts indicated and also at how well chosen they were, how apt for Kinpoge. He asked who had been responsible.

Chika addressed Kinpoge. 'My sister, Kaze, chose them for you. Do you remember her? She knew you when you were a little girl. She always kept a fondness for you. She has many children herself – your cousins. You will meet them in Kitakami.'

'Can they do the things Father and I can do?' Kinpoge asked.

Chika looked at Mu, eyebrows raised.

'She means invisibility, the second self, that sort of thing,' Mu explained.

'Oh, they are all experts in that!' Chika laughed. 'You never know who is who or where any of them are.'

Kinpoge whispered to her father, 'I do want to meet them, but what about Take? He'll come back, and we won't be here.'

'Ima will tell him where we've gone. Anyway, we don't know how long he will be away with the tengu. We're not going forever, just for a visit. It will make time go faster until you see Take.' He knew he was not being completely truthful with her. The reality was he hoped she would never meet Take again.

'Can I take Ban?' she asked.

'Ban is going to stay with me,' Ima said. 'You are going to ride a real horse, that pretty grey.'

Kinpoge looked at the horse, with shining eyes. It seemed to notice her gaze, raised its head and whickered to her. She went to it and patted its neck.

'Let's get going,' Chika said. 'It's not yet noon. We've several hours of daylight left.'

Kinpoge ran to Ban and gave the skull horse a pat. It quivered all over and its eye sockets seemed to widen. Then she hugged her uncle. Mu embraced Ima too.

'Take care of yourself,' he said.

As they rode away, he saw an old vixen on the edge of the forest. He did not know if she was Kinpoge's mother, Shida. Was it possible that she was still alive? All that day, he was aware she followed them, but the next morning she was gone.

•

A week later they were in Kitakami. Autumn came early to the northern city and already red leaves were falling and a cold wind blew off the grey sea. Kiku's residence resembled a fortress in its size and defences, and was high on a slope on the northeast side of the city, with watchtowers that looked out to the north and the south, following the course of the river that linked Lake Kasumi to the sea. Beyond that, far in the distance, lay the capital, Chika said, adding he had never been there. Mu had flown above it, had seen its lord in his sickness, but he did not mention this.

The river cut a narrow valley through mountains that rose sheer from the shoreline, their peaks already white with snow. Its estuary formed the port, the only secure harbour on the Northern Sea. Whoever controlled Kitakami controlled trade with Shin and Silla, and the lands of the barbarians in the north.

And, from the first impression of Kiku's home, it was clear to Mu who that was.

The imposing gates on the west side stood open, but he could see how they would close at a moment's notice, making the place impregnable. Guards stood in front of them, acknowledging Chika as they rode in. They all had some deformity: a missing eye, hand or leg, twisted limbs, scarred features. Yet Mu was aware of hidden abilities that compensated for their handicaps.

Kinpoge had sat behind him most of the way, except when pain from the unfamiliar act of riding forced him to walk for a while, and she took the reins. She liked being in control of the horse and begged him not to lead her but let her canter after Chika. Now she slid down from the grey's back and was immediately surrounded by a clutch of children of all ages, chattering at her, pelting her with questions.

A man came to lead the horses away, a couple of large dogs at his heels. He smiled shyly at Mu, who realised it was his youngest brother, Ku. They embraced, Ku awkward and seemingly embarrassed.

'You can talk later,' Chika said. 'I'm sure Ku is very busy and Kiku is waiting for you.'

Mu raised his eyebrows, but Ku merely bowed deferentially without meeting his gaze. It was obvious that, as the tengu had told him, Kiku had made Ku his servant.

Chika urged him forward.

'Stay with your cousins,' he told Kinpoge who looked as if she was going to follow them. 'They'll take you to meet your aunt, Kaze. You'll meet your uncles later.'

Apart from the men at the gate, Mu's sharp hearing told him others were concealed in the guardhouse, and when they were shown into Kiku's presence, he knew there were more, in alcoves and behind curtains around the room.

He is afraid I'll attack him! The idea amused him. He did not often need the cane to walk with, but he had brought it with him and now leaned on it, a little more than was necessary.

From the verandah they entered an anteroom where screen doors slid open silently to allow them into the main hall. It looked out over the cliffs to the sea and the restless surge of the waves below was a constant background noise. On this bright autumn day the sea was calm, its colour deep indigo. In the distance, several white-fringed islands could be seen. One had the red bird-perch gate of a shrine; the others seemed uninhabited except by sea birds. Twisted pines had been carved into grotesque shapes by the northeasterly wind. Mu tried to imagine what it would be like in winter, when snow covered the town and gales lashed the fortress.

The room was spacious, sparsely furnished, the floor dark polished cedar, the shutters cypress, their inner surfaces carved with scenes of life in Kitakami. One side was covered with woven wall hangings of exotic landscapes, dragons and sea serpents.

Kiku sat at the far end, his back to the sea. The brightness of the light made it hard to see his face. On his right was his brother, Kuro, on his left the warrior, Tsunetomo, who had tied Mu up and left him crippled. Both Kuro and Tsunetomo had moustaches and beards, unkempt like wild men, but Kiku was clean shaven. Mu studied all three of them, glad to realise he felt nothing, no anger, no resentment.

Chika had entered the room after him and now went down on one knee, bowing his head low. Mu remained standing. To his surprise, both Kiku and Tsunetomo placed their hands palm down on the matting and leaning forward, touched their foreheads to the floor. After a moment's hesitation, Kuro followed them.

Chika shuffled forward and indicated a silk cushion. Mu sat down, cross-legged. Kiku raised his head. Tsunetomo and Kuro stayed low.

'Welcome, brother,' Kiku said. His voice had changed, had become deeper and more cultured, yet the same hard edge was still there and still menacing. His eyes were gleaming, but at the same time expressionless. His skin had lost its copper tone and was pale, as though he rarely went outside. 'I am very glad to see you again. I believe our old friend, Chika, has conveyed to you my deep regret for the past.'

Mu wondered how genuine he was and how much of it was part of some deep elaborate scheme. What were his true intentions? At any moment, his brother might make a signal and the unseen guards would emerge and fall on him. He felt his right hand edge closer to the cane he had placed beside him. They might not be expecting to fight a man trained by a tengu.

The movement, slight as it was, did not escape Kiku. 'I can understand that you don't trust us. We treated you very badly.'

Kuro raised his head and said, 'Not me. I wasn't there. I don't see why I should have to grovel.'

Kiku made a gesture to silence him. 'Those old rituals demand a high price. We have all paid it in different ways. But it was worth it. You will see the power I have drawn from the skull. Gessho was an extraordinary man.'

'In other words, you would do the same thing again,' Mu said, more amused than angry.

'Well, I suppose I would. I am glad we can be honest with each other. Tsunetomo, you may sit up now. My brother understands, and to understand is to forgive.' He addressed Mu again. 'Really, Tsunetomo has nothing to apologise for. He agreed to serve me, he was obeying me. Any offence was mine alone. But I thought you would like to see such a warrior prostrate before you. It is quite a pleasing sight, isn't it? I never tire of it. From now on, you and I are as one, in his eyes and the eyes of all his men. You only have to say the word and they will grovel at your feet. They will thrust their swords into their own throats, if you command it.'

'Why have you summoned me here?' Mu said.

'So we are reconciled?' Kiku exclaimed. 'Come closer so I can embrace you.'

'We needn't go that far,' Mu returned.

'It's what people do!' Kiku's face was more animated now, as though he, too, found their situation amusing. 'We embrace to show we are reconciled and as long as one of us doesn't take advantage of the hug to stab the other in the back, we are friends, from now on, as brothers should be.'

Mu began to laugh. He understood Kiku perfectly as no one else ever would. He went forward and they embraced briefly. As he held the thin wiry frame so similar to his own, he felt he could read every thought that arose within his brother's mind.

'Let's drink!' Kiku clapped his hands to summon servants and wine.

After the first cups were filled and emptied, Kiku told Chika and Tsunetomo to leave, and take the guards with them. The wall hangings rippled as though a mild earthquake had struck, and an assortment of warriors poured out. Like the guards at the gate, many had limbs missing, a leg made from carved wood, a metal hook in place of a hand. Some had lost part of their skull and covered the wounds with a variety of masks, some had terrible scars or had suffered burns that left the skin seared white. Each made a reverent bow to Mu as they filed past him.

'That's just a small part of them,' Kiku said. 'Aren't they hideous? My crippled army. Hideous in the eyes of men but beautiful to me. I like looking at their scars and their injuries and contemplating their courage and their endurance, all now dedicated to my service.'

'How do you do it?' Mu asked. He couldn't help admiring Kiku's effrontery.

'Men are not hard to manipulate,' Kiku replied, pouring more wine into Mu's cup. 'Especially warriors who are so proud and so single-minded. Loyalty and courage are everything to them. Give them the opportunity to risk their lives a couple of times a month and they are happy.'

'But who do they fight against?' Mu said, draining the cup and holding it out for a refill.

'That's a very good question. Now that we've wiped out the bandits on land and subdued the pirates at sea, we are running out of opponents. My cripples are getting restless. Their old wounds ache at night and remind them of ancient grudges. Cleaning up a pack of outlaws is all very well but what they yearn for is the chance to confront those in whose service they got those injuries and who then disowned them: the Miboshi in Miyako, the Kakizuki in Rakuhara.'

'You cannot take on both those forces,' Mu said.

'I think I can,' Kiku replied, 'though it would be easier if I had a warrior as a figurehead and a cause.'

Kuro laughed loudly and emptied his cup.

'The warrior would be Shikanoko,' Mu said, after a pause, 'and the cause the true Emperor?'

'Exactly!'

'But . . . Shika has even more reason to hate you than I have. If it had not been for you, the Princess would not have died.'

'That really was not my fault,' Kiku said. 'It was Kuro's snake.'

'Well, I've lost count of how many times I've told you I was sorry,' Kuro said sulkily.

'I know, I know,' Kiku said. 'But wait till Shikanoko sees what we can offer him. The chance to fulfil his destiny, just as Chika's father dreamed.'

'Is that what this is for?' Mu said. 'You want to impress Shika and win his respect, and his gratitude?'

For the first time a vulnerable expression came over Kiku's face. 'He is one of our fathers,' he said. 'He brought us up and taught us everything. Now I have children of my own I understand what that means. I want to see him and thank him. What's wrong with that?'

'Shika has a son,' Mu said. 'A fully human boy, the child of the Princess. I am acquainted with him. He is a true warrior.'

Kiku had gone pale. His hand as he refilled his cup trembled. 'I did not know that,' he murmured, and fell silent for a long time.

He is jealous, Mu thought. *He mocks people for their emotions but he is no more immune to them than I was, and still am.* Then he wondered if Kiku's emotion was genuine, if he were not acting out something he had learned in order to hide his true motives. What did he truly want from Shika?

'You are deluding yourself if you think Shika is going to treat us as sons,' he said. 'If he does return it will be as a warrior, and no warrior family will admit to the taint of blood like ours, Old People from the Spider Tribe, born from cocoons.'

Kiku leaned forward and spoke in a hiss. 'I have made my own Tribe. I can make or break the mightiest of warlords, even the Emperor. No one is safe from me and mine. My power is based on fear and on wealth – there are no forces stronger than these. Tell Shikanoko I will place all this at his service.'

'You want me to find Shika in the Darkwood?'

'If you don't go I will send Chika, and the outcome may be very different.'

'What do you mean?'

Kiku whispered, 'Chika hates Shikanoko.'

Mu was thinking of the vision he had seen when he flew above the land, as if it had been a scroll or a Go board. All the pieces were in their positions, and flames were charring the edges. It was time to act. It was his turn now to be a player and all his training had prepared him for this. The tengu had already told him what he was to do: *join forces with your brother, find Shikanoko, and offer him these forces so the Emperor might be restored and Heaven placated.*

'I will go and find him,' he said.

6

TAKEYOSHI

Take woke, the wind rushing against his face. He thought he was still asleep, for he often flew like this in his dreams. But this was many times more real and more vivid. Something gripped him firmly and painfully by the shoulders, the chill air brought tears to his eyes and, though his vision was blurred, he could see enough to perceive below him the treetops, ranges and rocky crags of the Darkwood.

He had no idea what had happened to him, and for a moment terror churned in his stomach. He had put all his trust in Kinpoge's father, setting aside his misgivings, above all his suspicions of the sorcery in which the hut was steeped, and accepting the casual spells that Mu and Kinpoge used daily, even though at times they made his skin crawl. He had learned to conquer his distaste and discern the magic, though he would never be able to use it himself. Now he feared Mu had betrayed him, had handed him over to some evil being, maybe like the snake woman he had met in the forest, or had himself been overcome in some epic struggle that he, Takeyoshi, had slept through and of which he was the prize.

He tried to banish his fear and assess the situation, as Mu had taught him.

I am alive, he thought, *but I have no weapons. The first thing I must do is arm myself.*

Blinking hard, he began to search the terrain below for something suitable. At the same time, he was noticing landmarks, trying to orient himself. It was early evening, the moon rising in the east, the evening star just over the jagged mountain peaks. They – he and whatever creature had him in its grip – were heading north. He could see the distinctive cone shape of Kuroyama, wreathed in white steam clouds. In the west the sky was still pink and orange from the setting sun and the clouds flamed like dragons.

Was it a dragon that carried him? The wings that beat above his head, the gripping claws suggested it might be. He tried to turn his head to look and caught a glimpse of blue cloth. Leggings? Surely no dragon ever wore leggings, blue or any other colour.

A harsh deep voice sounded in his ear. 'Don't wriggle. I don't want to drop you!'

He caught a whiff of its smell, meaty, peppery. So it could speak, and it did not want to drop him?

The tops of the trees came closer. A flock of roosting green pigeons flew out, startled. Take drew up his knees instinctively as they cleared the canopy. The ground rushed up towards him. There was a huge beating of wings as the creature slowed and hovered. He felt it release its grip. He had already spotted the rock he was going to use. He rolled in a forward somersault, grabbed the rock, stood, gauged the distance, and threw, all in one rapid movement.

'Ow!' the creature exclaimed as the rock caught it in the chest. It reached over its shoulder and drew the long sword from the scabbard on its back. Take did not want to reveal how much the sword impressed him. Leaping backwards, his eyes not leaving his opponent, he reached behind him for a branch he had noticed in his first forward roll. He picked it up and stood, taking in clearly, for the first time, the sight of the tengu – for he realised that was what it must be.

It looked furious. Its eyes were bulging, its shock of dirty white hair stood on end, and its wings thrashed above its head. He thought steam was even coming out of its nostrils, but possibly it was just its breath in the chill mountain air.

He gripped the branch more firmly, remembering Kinpoge's warning. *Be careful what you hope for.*

The sword came whistling down and cut the branch clean in half, sending a jarring pain through Take's right hand. He dropped the branch and jumped backwards to avoid the sword's returning stroke.

'There,' the tengu grunted. 'I could have got you *there* and *there*.' The sword struck in, out and in again, in the direction of Take's throat. 'You're quick, though, that's good, and strong. I didn't expect you to be able to throw that rock so hard and so far. Now, shift your weight and come forward, under the blade. If you are unarmed, your hands and feet, even your head, must become weapons. Go for the soft parts, the eyes, the throat, the privates.'

Take stood still, his breath panting. He held up his hands. 'I'm sorry, I didn't mean to attack you. I didn't know who you were.'

'And now you do?' the tengu said, amused.

'You are the tengu who taught my teacher,' Take said. 'And I hope you are going to teach me.'

'Well, maybe I am. Yes, it looks like that's the way it's going to be.' The tengu sheathed the sword. 'You can call me Tadashii.'

He opened his red jacket and inspected his hairy chest. 'Look at that!' he exclaimed. 'You gave me a bruise! I haven't had a bruise like that for a century or more. Oh, I am going to enjoy myself! But tell me, how did you get to be so strong?'

'I've been an acrobat all my life,' Take replied. 'I grew too tall to be a tumbler, but I've carried adult men on my shoulders, two or three at a time, for years.'

'Hmm.' Tadashii looked pleased. He took Take's hands and looked at them. 'Great strength here, too. I suppose you can climb?'

'As well as any monkey,' Take said.

Tadashii pointed at a pine tree that rose, bare trunked, about sixty or seventy feet tall. It was the last in a line of trees that stopped abruptly on the edge of an old lava flow.

'Climb that!'

Take went to it and shinned up it, using his hands, clasped behind the trunk, and his strong toes. When he got to the branches he continued to climb. Above him rose the huge mass, the cloud-fringed cone, of Kuroyama. There was a strong smell of sulphur, and steam rose from vents in the ground. It was how he imagined the entrance to Hell. He could see Tadashii far below, and waved to him. Then, smelling smoke and hearing voices, he looked in the other direction. Beneath the sulphur was a rank odour of meat, and some animal scent, like a fox's den.

He could see down into a space between the trees where a group of creatures like Tadashii gathered round several large flat tree stumps. Torches lit their long noses, their beaks, their furled wings. He could hear the clack and rattle of stones.

The branches parted as Tadashii flew up to sit beside him.

'What are they doing?' Take whispered.

'They are playing Go,' Tadashii replied. 'I sometimes play myself.' He waved his hand towards the edge of the clearing where a huge long-nosed fellow sat hunched, contemplating the stump in front of him. 'I have a game going on over there, but I've been waiting for what would seem like months, to you, for my opponent to make his move. He's always been a slow player. He's got himself into a bit of a pickle and he's trying to plan a way out. Still, we're some way from the end game.'

Kinpoge had been trying to teach Take to play Go, but he had not yet grasped its essence or its intricacies. Now, watching the tengu play under the moon and the torchlight, he was seized by a desire to learn to play properly.

'Will you teach me?' he said.

'If we have time,' Tadashii replied. 'Let's fly over their heads. I want him to see you. I think it will unsettle him.'

His clawed hands and feet gripped Take's shoulders again and lifted him off the branch. Together they swooped low over the clearing, making several of the tengu look up. Some raised their arms in greeting, some muttered a welcome, but mostly they remained absorbed in their different games. Tadashii's opponent looked up with a scowl as Tadashii circled above him, showing Take off and cackling with laughter.

He shook his fist and bared his teeth at them before returning to his scrutiny of the board. Take just glimpsed enough to see the grid was carved into the surface of the stump. The light showed bowls of white and black stones. Kinpoge played with seeds, pebbles, berries, on a board Ima had made for her.

'Back soon!' Tadashii called, as they soared over the trees to the place they had landed before. 'He will take even longer to make up his mind now,' he said, in a smug tone of voice.

'I don't quite understand what you are talking about,' Take said, politely.

'Don't worry about it. One day you will, if you live that long. And I think you will, for I intend to make use of you. When it comes to the end game. You may rest for a little while, until dawn. Would you rather sleep on the ground or in the tree? I myself will take that branch. I find it quite comfortable. Don't walk around in the night – there are pools of scalding water. It's dangerous.'

Take looked at the ground beneath his feet. It was too dark to see clearly but it seemed to be covered in stones, both large and small. Yoshi and Saru often slept in the crook of branches, but he did not like it much, his legs being too long to fold up comfortably.

'I'll lean against the trunk,' he said, and began to clear away some of the stones so he could sit down.

'You came rather unprepared,' the tengu remarked, as he settled on his favourite branch.

'I didn't know I was coming,' Take muttered. It was much colder high in the mountains and he had no covering. Mu's hut was far from luxurious but at least there was no shortage of firewood, furs and food. He was already hungry and thirsty and wondered when, if ever, they would eat or drink.

He did not really sleep, just dozed a little, waking with a start at every noise: the hiss and roar of the volcano, the wind in the trees, owls and other night birds, the distant howling of wolves. He had never felt so alone.

I could die here and no one would ever know. The tengu would probably crack my bones.

He had lived all his life among people, the noisy, milling world of the acrobats and the monkeys, yet he had always felt different from them. He had been removed from one world, but he was not yet in the next. He was determined this time with the tengu would be the bridge between his old life and his new.

He shed a few tears of loneliness, since no one could see him and then, with gritted teeth, he set himself to practise the meditation Mu had already taught him.

•

'Don't grit your teeth,' the tengu told him next morning. 'You are not lacking in strength – what you need is fluidity. At the moment you block your strength. You must learn to let it flow.'

He had been boiling two large pale blue eggs in one of the steam vents. He took one egg and shelled it, hot as it was, sprinkled it with the salt that was encrusted on the rocks, and handed it to Take.

Take crammed it into his mouth, burning his tongue.

'And don't eat so quickly, you'll burn your mouth,' Tadashii warned, too late.

The egg had been preserved in some way and tasted old, not exactly stale, but not fresh either, a little sulphurous. 'Is there anything to drink?' Take said, when he could speak.

'I always forget how needy humans are,' Tadashii said. 'Suck a pebble. I'll find some water later.' He shelled and ate the other egg, smacking his lips.

Take waited until the tengu had finished eating and then asked, 'Why have you brought me here?'

'Your teacher, the Warrior of Nothingness, has had to go somewhere. I said I'd take care of you for a while. He sends you his regards, and says goodbye on his daughter's behalf.'

'Kinpoge went with him?'

'You know, you will see Mu again, but not her.'

The thought made Take sad. He missed her already.

The tengu looked at his face as if trying to read his expression and failing. 'Well, never mind all that. Let's get to work! You're going to need a sword and a bow. You've probably seen the sword I made for Mu. I'll make one for you, once I've seen your reach and your stance. I already have a good idea of your strength.'

He flew upwards and plucked a pole from where it was concealed in the lower branches of the tree.

'It's not a bad idea to keep a few weapons hidden in your castle,' he observed, giving the pole to Take, 'where you can reach them easily. Just a little advice for the future.'

'I'm going to have a castle?' Take said, as he tested the heft of the pole, gripping it in both hands as Mu had shown him.

'Well, why not?' Tadashii replied, eyeing Take's hands but not making any comment, as he raised his sword. 'I'd want a castle if I were you. Castles invoke respect from those above you and fear from those below. They keep your men occupied while building and give them somewhere to live when completed. I'll show you how to build a proper one out of rocks and stones.'

A castle! Men! Then Take emptied his mind as they sparred for a while, the tengu setting a fierce pace but pulling his strokes before hitting either Take or the pole.

'That'll do for now,' he said finally. 'You can go and get your bow. Once that's done, we'll make the sword and some arrows.'

When it was obvious he was not going to say any more, Take asked tentatively, 'Are you going to tell me where the bow is?'

Tadashii jerked his head upwards. 'Up there.'

Take raised his eyes to the crags that marched in a jagged line up Kuroyama. The rock was black basalt, the ground old, pitted lava, covered with small, sharp stones. Here and there pools of sulphuric water and mud bubbled viscously, and steam hung around the slopes of the mountain. Beyond the tree he had climbed, broken trunks, like the spars of the wrecked ships that were exposed when Lake Kasumi dried up, showed where the fire and the sulphur had done their lethal work.

In the closest crag there was a narrow cleft, as if it had been split from top to bottom. Take squinted up to where the steam refracted the sunlight into rainbows, and for a moment thought he could see the shape of a giant bow.

'That's it,' Tadashii said. 'Ameyumi is its name. The Rain Bow.'

'I am to climb up there for it?' Take moved a little closer, assessing the rocks and the cleft. The smooth basalt offered few footholds, but the cleft reminded him of the space, a yard or so wide, between the monkeys' shelter and the outer fence of their enclosure. The young males often played in it, inventing different ways to scale it: both feet on one side, rear on the other; one foot on each side, pushing up with the hands. It had to be done quickly, so the momentum itself carried you upwards. It would be slippery from the steam and probably hot too.

'You don't think you can do it?' Tadashii said, sounding disappointed.

'I didn't say I couldn't,' Take replied, all the more determined. 'I'm just working out the best way. But couldn't you just fly up and get it?'

'Not without attracting its owner's attention.'

'It has an owner I have to steal it from?'

'In a manner of speaking. It's not really his, though. He won it in a wager from someone else, years ago, and *won* is a rather relative term since he almost certainly cheated, so you could say he also stole it.'

'Who from?'

'Some warrior who was fighting in the north and fancied himself an expert at Go.' The tengu gave a smirk as if there was much more he might say but chose not to.

'Why is it up there?'

'Too many questions!' Tadashii cried. 'Are you going to get it or not?'

'All right.' Take went closer to the crevice, laid a hand on each side and peered up. It was harder to see the bow now, the steam and the dazzle of light at the top obscured it, but he thought he could make out the arc of its shape. The surface under his palms was warm and slick. He tested it against the soles of his feet. They were rough, hardened from years of running around and climbing barefoot, and would not need covering, but he wanted to give his hands more protection.

He was still wearing the headband and short red jacket and leggings that all the acrobats dressed in. He retied the headband and took off the jacket, borrowed the tengu's knife to make the first cut, and tore off strips to bind around his palms.

He had noticed the night before that sticky resin oozed in places from the pine tree. He collected enough to rub into the balls of his feet and onto the bindings. The resin gathered a little sand and grit, which would give him extra grip.

He did not say any more to Tadashii. The preparations were helpful in themselves but mostly they were to build up the inner impulse, the coiling of the spring that the acrobats used to launch themselves into impossible feats. He could feel it mounting within him, the desire to challenge the limits placed on the human body and the pull of the earth itself.

His first ascent was quick – feet, then hands, push upwards, jump – but he had misjudged the distance. The bow was higher above the mouth of the crevice than he had expected. He could not reach it and, anyway, needed both hands to hold on to the slippery sides. He descended quickly in the same manner and rethought his strategy. He would have to continue his upwards climb into one all-risking leap, and grasp the bow with both hands.

And then? He would slide down – or more likely fall. He would have to hold the bow upright so he would not be able to use his hands to save himself. The best he could do was try to cushion the fall. He ran back to the pine tree, climbed to the first branches and broke off as many needle leafed twigs as he could carry. He spread these over the floor of the cleft.

'Hurry up!' Tadashii cried. There was an urgent tone in his voice, but Take did not want to be distracted now. Without replying, he took a deep breath and launched himself upwards. The interior of the crevice seemed hotter and steamier. But he had reached the top once already, which gave him confidence. This time he went all the way to the lip, stood, reached up through the shimmering rainbows, felt the firm wood of the real bow and grasped it. It resisted his hold and he needed both hands to pull it towards him.

Above him the volcano rumbled and hissed and through the noise he heard another sound – a beating of wings, a cry of rage. The huge tengu that Tadashii had shown him the night before was flying towards him, clearly holding a drawn sword.

A premonition came to Take that one day he would fight this tengu – but now was not the time. Holding the bow close to his chest, he dropped down into the crevice.

He slid, fell, slid again, but somehow he and the bow stayed upright until he landed on the springy bed of pine. He had had many falls as an acrobat and knew how to roll out of them but the crevice was narrow and he had to protect the bow. The shock jarred his spine and for a moment he feared he had broken an ankle. He was gasping for breath, the hot air burning his throat and lungs, but at the same time he was filled with excitement and elation.

He passed the bow through the narrow opening and slid out after it, tearing off the soaked bindings before they scalded his palms. Then he picked up the bow, marvelling at its huge size and perfect balance, the intricacies of its bindings, its many layers of compressed wood. It seemed covered in a shiny substance that must have protected it from the steam, for, though old, it was unwarped and true.

'Well done!' Tadashii was at his side. 'I think we might go somewhere a little quieter so you can practise with it and I'll get on with the sword.'

The other tengu was screaming in rage from the top of the crag. A sudden hail of small rocks began to shower down on them. Take could not see if the tengu was throwing them or if the volcano was erupting. He gripped the bow more tightly as Tadashii picked him up and they flew back to the shelter of the Darkwood.

•

'They left for Kitakami,' Ima said when the tengu brought Take back to the hut. The fire was a pile of glowing embers and a hare was roasting on it. Ban turned its head towards them in a strange questioning way.

'I know,' Tadashii replied. 'Takeyoshi and I have some work to do and then I am going to show you one or two things too.'

Ima raised one eyebrow but only said to Take, 'You must be hungry.'

Take realised he was, and very thirsty too. He went to the stream and drank deeply, then splashed water on his face. He had placed the bow by the fire and when he returned Ima had picked it up and was studying it.

'Is it Shikanoko's bow, Kodama?'

'It was his father's,' replied the tengu. 'Ameyumi is its name. What is Kodama?'

'Shisoku made it for Shikanoko. We were only children but I remember it. And he reforged a broken sword, Jato.'

'I don't know about Jato,' Tadashii said, frowning. 'Ameyumi was my concern. It was gained unfairly. Shikanoko's father staked his weapons, his own life, his son's, even the Emperor's. His opponent cheated and he lost everything. But in this new game I'm going to win. Getting Ameyumi back was a major move.'

'So it was my grandfather who played the game of Go and lost?' Take said, his voice breaking with excitement.

'That's correct,' Tadashii said. 'I thought it quite elegant to have you regain it.'

'Are we going to give it to my father?' Take asked.

'Maybe. First I'll show you how to use it. It's good that you are already so strong. Then Ima and I will make you a sword.'

Take opened his mouth but before he could ask even one of the questions teeming in his mind, Tadashii said, 'It's best if you just do as you're told for the time being.'

'Can I ask a question?' Ima said, smiling at Take's expression.

'You most certainly may.' Tadashii clapped Ima on the back.

'What do you plan to show me?'

'Someone has to take control here. You can't let this place just wind down and dwindle away. Everything Shisoku collected is still here. You have to learn how to use it and become the protector of the forest he was.'

'Mu could do that,' Ima replied. 'Or Kiku or even Kuro. I think you'll find I have no aptitude. I can hunt; I can cook; I can forge. That's enough for me.'

'I'm not giving you a choice,' Tadashii said, irritated. 'I'm telling you how it's going to be. I expect the human to be argumentative but you should know better!'

7

TAMA

'You were received by the Emperor?' Lady Tama's eyes were narrowed and the tone of her voice was sceptical. She was trying to hide her annoyance with her husband. Masachika had returned to Matsutani, after weeks away, and had immediately thrown the household into a frenzy of activity with arrangements for the great hunt. Lord Aritomo himself was to attend. Tama did not mind this so much; she was used to entertaining lords and warriors of the highest rank, and the twin estates were prosperous and well managed, their fields overflowing with fresh produce, their storerooms packed with soy bean paste, rice, barley and casks of wine. There were deep cellars where ice was preserved throughout the hot summers, and, even in the years of drought, the streams that flowed from the Darkwood never dried up. Further into the mountains, at Kuromori, there were many natural hot springs, renowned for their healing properties.

Tama loved her land and was proud of the way she had improved it. She was excited at the prospect of displaying its riches to Lord Aritomo. But she was less thrilled by the young woman Masachika had brought with him and installed in one of the pavilions on the lake, which Tama had had rebuilt, never dreaming who would occupy it.

She was aware he must have had girls before. They were separated for long periods and men, of course, had their needs. But this was the first time he had brought one to Matsutani, wounding and insulting his wife. It aroused painful memories of Kiyoyori and the woman who had bewitched him, who she believed had burned to death in the former pavilion.

'She is just an entertainer,' Masachika told her airily. 'She'll supervise the musicians and she knows some acrobats whom I am arranging to have brought here for the amusement of Lord Aritomo. She has her lute with her – you must have heard her playing.'

'It sounds like a stubborn instrument and often out of tune,' Tama said. 'Or maybe she doesn't have much talent.'

She had longed for Masachika's return. Her body still ached for him, but when they were finally alone on the first night of his visit, his love making had been perfunctory and had left her unsatisfied. Since then he had not come to her room, making one excuse after another: fears for her health; his own exhaustion; a fever.

Fever indeed! she thought. *Girl fever.*

Now he had come to her telling her they must speak in absolute privacy. She had sent her women away and they were alone together in her room, she kneeling, he cross-legged. She had had the shutters closed; the light was dim. It was the ninth month but still very hot with the lingering heat that was the hardest to bear.

At first she found it hard to believe him and then she was alarmed. Was Masachika really thinking of betraying Aritomo, of taking his place? It seemed impossible that the Emperor and his mother would have such a scheme in mind and would suggest it to him. She felt he must have misunderstood, was endangering himself and her.

'Lady Natsue herself sent for me,' Masachika said.

'What was . . . *he* . . . like?' she said, hardly daring even to speak of him.

'I did not set eyes on him. He remained behind the blinds. It seems he wanted to see me, to see for himself what kind of man I am.'

'Who else was there?' Tama asked. 'I imagine he would be surrounded by attendants and some of them, at least, must keep Aritomo informed of everything the Imperial Household says and does. I hope you were discreet.'

'Well, you know I am often beset by complaints from the Household. I was simply investigating one of them. My conversation with Lady Natsue was so veiled as to be barely comprehensible. To the Emperor, I said little beyond platitudes, to which he responded with a few lines of verse. He is quite a good poet, they say. His mother intimated I might correspond with them in this way. Both of them are known to love poetry.'

'But you know nothing about poetry,' she exclaimed. 'Have you ever written a poem?'

'One or two, in my youth. I thought you could do it for me.'

'You still need me for some things, then?' she replied, both pleased and angered.

'I need you for everything,' he said. 'You know I am nothing without you.'

'Then send the girl away.'

'Is that what's bothering you? You can't think she is a rival in my affection for you?'

'You seem over-fond of her,' Tama said, embarrassed to admit her jealousy.

'I don't care for her at all. I will send her away, immediately the hunt is over. She and the acrobats can go back to where they came from. We will give Lord Aritomo the finest days of his life, and if they turn out to be his last ones . . . everyone knows how sick he is even though no one admits it.'

She stared at him coolly.

'Look what you have achieved here,' he said. 'Imagine what you could do with an entire country.'

He knew exactly how to tempt her. 'If we are to undertake this endeavour we must trust each other completely,' Tama said. 'No secrets, no lies must ever be between us.'

'I hide nothing from you,' he said, moving closer to embrace her.

'I love you, Masachika,' she said. 'I always have, even when I was married to your brother. But I will never forgive you if you lie to me. Let's go and swear by Sesshin's eyes that we will always be true to each other.'

'We will,' Masachika promised. 'But first I must tell you another secret.'

She pulled away from him a little, staring into his eyes. 'A good secret or a bad one?'

'I don't know yet. I believe Kiyoyori's daughter is alive.'

'Hina? It can't be true! You yourself told me she drowned.'

'I am sure she is the woman I was sent to investigate in Aomizu – the one who was accused of poisoning Lady Fuji.'

'I always feared that girl would end up poisoning someone, with all the potions and ointments she used to concoct,' Tama said. The news that Hina might have been alive all these years disturbed her. Memories of her stepdaughter returned suddenly, assailing her with their clarity: the girl's pale, serious face; the eyes that lit up only for her father; the manuscripts she was always trying to decipher; her undeniable beauty.

'It is another reason Asagao has come with me. She and Hina, whom she knew as Yayoi, were close friends. I am hoping I can track Hina down through her. If it is true that Yoshimori is still alive Hina must know where he is. She poisoned Fuji to silence her and has gone to warn Yoshimori. I am going to find her once the hunt is over and bring them both either to Lord Aritomo or to the Empress, whoever offers the greater reward.'

Asagao! Now she knew the girl musician's name Tama disliked her even more. But if she was only a pawn in this greater plan she could tolerate her.

●

The eyes lay in their carved recess in the west gate, as bright as the day when they had been torn from Sesshin's head. For years they had watched over Matsutani as their owner had promised. The guardian spirits that had occupied the house and caused chaos and destruction after the earthquake had remained in the gateposts all that time. Tama visited them daily, bringing offerings of flowers, fruit and rice cakes. In the summer she brought ice to cool them and in the winter lit fires in braziers and wrapped the posts in straw to keep them warm. On this hot afternoon, in early autumn, she brought the first persimmons of the season, their orange waxy skin smooth beneath her fingers, and branches of purple bush clover. Masachika carried a flask of rice wine and two bowls, for the spirits liked to share a drink with whoever visited them. No one ever saw them but the bowls emptied mysteriously, between one moment and the next.

She thought Masachika looked uneasy and it troubled her further. They both knew the power of the eyes. They had wept together before them on more than one occasion. The spirits had not misbehaved for years, but then they had had no cause. She was under no illusion that they would not recognise falsehood.

Tama's attendant had brought a mat, which she spread in the gateway. The entrance was paved with flat river stones, powdered with the dust that blew everywhere in the hot, dry wind. It covered their clothes and stung their eyes and throats.

Husband and wife knelt side by side. Tama divided her offerings and placed them equally before each gatepost. Masachika filled the wine bowls and they both drank. Then he refilled them and offered them to the spirits. Tama watched him carefully. He performed all his actions flawlessly, but he kept his head lowered as though he did not want to meet the gaze of the eyes.

She said in a low voice, 'Master Sesshin, I mistreated you badly. I shall never cease to regret my rash action. I ask you to forgive me.' Her face, which was turned upwards, was streaked with tears.

'Hidarisama, Migisama,' she went on. 'I thank you for your diligence and devotion in protecting our home. Please always continue to do so. In your presence, I swear that I will always be true to my husband and I will support him in everything he does.'

Masachika was silent for a few moments, making her fear he was going to refuse to speak but eventually he said quietly but firmly, 'I thank you for the protection you have given this place for years. I hope we will see no disturbances from you while Lord Aritomo is here. I think you know my devotion to my wife and I swear I will never betray her.'

Yet despite his steady voice Tama was aware of his inner conflict. His fists were clenched, sweat formed on his brow. She could do nothing but pray with all her heart that he was sincere. She was about to stand when a voice came from the left gatepost.

'Is it Matsutani Lady?'

'Yes, with our offerings. Let's drink,' the other spirit responded.

'Wait a moment. Who is with her?'

'Matsutani Lord, so-called.'

Tama whispered, 'It's years since they have been heard. What can it mean?'

'It must be a special day,' Masachika replied with forced light-heartedness. 'It's a good omen. They are not saying anything bad, they are just recognising us.'

There was a faint burst of mocking laughter.

'But what if they misbehave while Lord Aritomo is here?' Tama stood, and led him away from the gateway. She stopped and studied his face with her intense gaze.

'They will behave themselves,' Masachika replied. 'What reason can they have not to? The eyes are in place. We are their masters now. They must obey us.'

Tama had been whispering but Masachika spoke more loudly. A bee came buzzing between them, making him flinch. It must have been attracted by the clover blossoms, Tama thought, and watched as it settled on one of them. It was an ordinary bee, nothing supernatural. Yet she feared it might be a sign.

'I am just going to speak to the musician for a moment,' Masachika said as they walked towards the house.

Tama stopped and stared at him. Before she could speak he said hurriedly, 'Don't misunderstand me. I need to send for the acrobats and she will know where they are.'

Tama watched with fury as he strode swiftly to the pavilion on the lake. When she turned back to the gate, the wine bowls were still full. She went back to check once or twice during the rest of the day, but the spirits would not drink.

8

MU

'Before you set out to find Shikanoko,' Kiku said to Mu. 'I have something to show you. I'm going to give you a little demonstration of how I've used the powers you and I have, to build our empire.'

'And me,' Kuro put in. 'I have powers too!'

'You do, my dear brother, ones of your own that are very useful.' He looked from one brother to the other and smiled. 'Kuro's children have inherited his talents and so have mine.'

It was early evening, a few days after Mu had arrived in Kitakami. He was already preparing to leave again and had expected to have an early night to be on the road by dawn. Now it seemed Kiku had other plans. Mu was curious to see what he had in mind, but Kiku seemed content to sit and talk.

'Kinpoge, your daughter, is very skilled too. I've already seen proof of that. Of course, her mother was a fox woman and had magic powers of her own. I'm sorry, I don't want to wound you by bringing up the past, but I feel it has given her something special, superior even to my eldest son, Juntaro. I propose they marry and we will see how their offspring turn out.'

'Kinpoge is too young to marry,' Mu said.

'She will soon be old enough,' Kiku replied. 'We are five brothers, not like anyone else. We must establish our five families, and arrange our children's marriages carefully, to preserve what we have been given. After the first generation, we will not mingle our blood with that of outsiders, unless there are sound reasons of policy. We must maintain our Tribe.'

Mu had noticed how often Kiku used this word, the Tribe. It amused him but he liked it too. He liked the feeling of belonging to a family and had no compunction in leaving Kinpoge here. He felt her future would be secure among people like her. Far better for her to marry Juntaro, when they were old enough, than to yearn for Take.

'I've no objections,' he said, 'but give her time to settle in before you mention the idea.'

'They may not have much time,' Kiku said. 'We don't know how long their lives will be. Look how quickly we have grown and how fast we are ageing.'

Mu looked at his brother and saw the image of himself: the fine lines appearing on the skin, the grey hair at the temples. They had matured as fast as insects and now frailty was coming on them as swiftly. How brief a lifetime was!

Kiku was studying him. 'How about you? Did you ever take another woman? There are plenty here if you feel inclined.'

Mu made no response, but Kiku's words and the talk of marriage had awakened something within him. Here, among families and children, he realised how lonely he had been, and how much lonelier he would be if Kinpoge left him. Since he would rather die than let Kiku find him a wife he would have to find one himself. He had not considered such things for years, but now the idea did not seem displeasing. However, he changed the subject. 'What do you propose to show me?'

Kiku shook his head slightly and grinned, as though he knew all that Mu had been thinking, but he did not comment. He said, 'There is a merchant who has tried to compete with me for some time. His name is Unagi. Chika was employed by him, but Unagi became suspicious of him after a death in Aomizu. A pleasure woman, who was obstructing my wishes in several ways, died. One of the girls was suspected of murdering her and ran away. Unagi fancied she was special to him and wants to find her, prove her innocence and marry her. He insulted Chika, accused him of lying, and dismissed him.'

'So what are you going to do?'

'Stop his meddling, once and for all,' Kiku said, smiling even more widely. 'In fact I will be dealing with several problems at once. I will rid myself of a rival, Chika will have some very pleasant moments of revenge, and our sister will be spared becoming the wife of a merchant.'

'Our sister?' Mu said, not understanding.

'The woman who fled, who everyone knew as Yayoi, is Lord Kiyoyori's daughter, Hina. She has gone into the Darkwood to find Shikanoko. You are aware Kiyoyori was one of our fathers? Chika was acquainted with the lady when they were children. To tell you a secret, I believe he has feelings for her. Doesn't he deserve to have her? He will marry no one else and I don't like to see him lonely.'

Mu stared at Kiku without saying anything. He had not expected to be going out to commit an assassination. It seemed like an unnecessary distraction from his more important mission. Despite the tengu's training and the sword he had been given he was yet to kill anyone. He was puzzled by his brother's words and felt there was much Kiku was keeping from him. He calmed his breath and emptied his mind in order to perceive the truth of the situation. Was Hina the woman who loved Shikanoko and would be able to remove the mask? Did both Kiku and Chika know this?

He had thought Kiku was going to show him the skull and demonstrate its power. He wondered where Kiku kept the sacred object that had been taken at such great cost and made powerful at a greater one to him, death, pain, betrayal and loss all bound into it, along with ecstasy and lust. He realised he was longing to set eyes on it and dared to say, 'Will you show me Gessho's skull?'

Kiku stared at him. 'If you like. I thought you might not want to see it, that it might arouse painful memories, even though we have put all that behind us. Come, follow me. I'll prove to you that I have no secrets from you, that everything I have is yours.'

He pulled aside the wall hangings, nodded to the two warriors who were on guard behind them, and pressed a carved boss that opened a sliding door. Stairs led down the outside of the fortress, fastened into the rock face on which it was built.

'Be careful,' Kiku said. 'The spray makes the steps slippery.'

Below them the sea surged, grey, green and white. The wind was numbingly cold even though it was not yet winter.

At the bottom of the steps a wooden grill, reinforced with iron, covered the entrance to a cellar. In the shelter of the rock Mu heard Kiku whistling through his teeth, and as if at a signal the grill was lifted aside by two more of the crippled warriors. He followed his brother inside.

Once they had moved away from the entrance it became very dark, but Kiku like Mu had the vision of a cat, and went forward without hesitating.

Following him, Mu became aware of some force that was pulling him towards itself. He stopped for a moment, to see if he could resist it. He felt he could, but he did not want to. It was both a physical attraction and a seductive emotional one, offering everything he had ever wanted, unlimited power to exercise his will.

'Don't worry,' Kiku said. 'I won't let it absorb you.'

It was a strange choice of words, but aptly described his misgivings.

'You feel its power?' Kiku asked. 'You will be able to see it soon, for it shines, day and night.'

No sooner had he spoken than Mu saw the glow in front of them, and then he saw the shape of the skull, the gem eyes, the mother-of-pearl teeth. For a moment he was transported back in time to when he had last seen it, and he felt again in his limbs the excruciating pain, and in his heart the immense sorrow. Then he recalled the tengu's teaching and made his will firm against the skull's power and felt it surrender and recede.

'It is beautiful, isn't it?' Kiku murmured. 'That is why it needed the beauty of a woman in its making, as did Shikanoko's mask.'

Mu looked at it and saw its beauty, dispassionately, and remembered he had loved Shida.

The skull floated upwards as Kiku lifted it.

'How is it used?' Mu said.

'It is not used. It just *is*. Its power flows through me and into everything I do. Gessho must have been an extraordinary man. Only the mask comes close to this in power.' Kiku's voice was reverent. 'I have often wondered which would be the stronger.'

He placed his lips on the cinnabar lips of the skull and stayed without moving or speaking for several minutes. The skull's glow pulsed slowly, lighting Kiku's rapt face.

'It nourishes me,' he said, as he lowered it. 'Every day it makes me stronger.'

When they returned to the steps the wind had increased to a howl and they did not speak until they were inside again.

'You can tell Shika about the skull,' Kiku said then, pouring a bowl of wine and handing it to Mu.

'You think he will be impressed?' Mu said, with a trace of sarcasm.

Kiku flushed slightly. 'I want him to be with us. Maybe I want him to be free.'

Mu was thinking about the tengu's words. The mask would be removed by a woman who truly loved Shikanoko. But if that woman was Hina, why did Kiku speak as if she was his to bestow on Chika?

He knew where Hina was – in the Darkwood not far from where the brothers had been born. Kinpoge had taken his message about Take to her. But should he tell Chika and his brother this? Kiku might have any number of motives for bringing Shikanoko back from the Darkwood – wanting to impress him, wanting to free him, wanting him at the head of his army – but to Mu the most obvious one was he wanted to get his hands on the mask and its power.

•

'It's been a long time since I've done this myself,' Kiku confessed, as they prepared for the night attack. 'I've missed it. I usually dispatch Kuro, who has become a supreme assassin. He doesn't have many feelings, which is a help. Follow my lead. Whatever I do, do it too.'

They dressed in leggings and close-fitting tops of tightly woven hemp, dyed dark indigo, wrapped cloths of the same colour round their faces so only their eyes were exposed, and took up various tools and weapons, leather garrottes, flasks of poison, thin sharp knives. Mu carried the sword the tengu had given him, and Chika also brought his sword.

'Unagi's sons are sword fighters,' he said. 'They like to think of themselves as warriors.'

'We hope to kill their father without rousing the household,' Kiku remarked mildly.

'Better to clean out the whole barrel and not let the young eels escape,' Chika replied. 'There's an old man, too. I'll take care of him. You do your thing and I'll do mine. I see no reason why you should have all the fun.'

'I suppose you have earned it,' Kiku said, with the strange tenderness he often displayed towards Chika.

It was a dark night with no moon, the middle of the ninth month. Again Mu's eyes dilated like a cat's. Kiku's did the same. Chika kept close to them, stepping carefully in their footprints. Even the stars were dim, obscured by a low-hanging haze. Mist rose from the river as the air chilled in the hours before dawn. From the harbour came the sounds of the lap of water against hulls and the creak of boats as they shifted with the tide.

Unagi's house lay on the opposite bank. There was no bridge across the Kasumi river; during the day narrow flat-bottomed boats sculled across and back, but at this hour they were all moored on the bank, their owners and sailors asleep in the flimsy huts or in the boats themselves.

The men moved without a sound. As Chika went to untie one of the boats, a figure rose from a pile of ropes and sailcloth within it. Fuddled by sleep, he did not have time to call out before Chika leaped into the boat and had him by the throat, turning his face towards Kiku. His desperate eyes, wide open, bulging, searched for help and found Kiku's gaze. They seemed to register something, a mixture of surprise and relief, and then rolled backwards in the head, as the man went limp, just as Ku had in the forest all those years ago. *I must remember never to look Kiku in the eyes*, Mu thought.

Chika slid the sleeping body over the side of the boat, letting it go with barely a splash. Mu watched it drift away, rolling in the current, the face showing pale in the darkness.

'Live or die, there will not be a mark on him,' Chika whispered in satisfaction. 'He's known to drink too much.'

Everything had been planned meticulously, Mu realised, from the drunkard's boat to the exact time of the tide, which carried them across the river without their having to use the oars. The boat nudged gently against the opposite bank. They stepped out and waded through the water, carrying their swords above their heads. Chika knew Unagi's house intimately. There was a dock where boats were berthed. Two men lay slumped on the boards.

Kiku breathed in Mu's ear, 'Kuro was here earlier.'

A little way up a bamboo grid covered an arch through which water flowed into the garden of the residence. As Chika lifted the grid aside so they could pass through, Mu felt something brush against his legs. Fish, or maybe eels: the household must keep them here, alive and fresh.

The water lapped at a series of shallow steps, leading up to a kitchen. Ashes smouldered in a stone oven and he could smell soy and sesame oil. A small girl crouched on the highest step, her head on her knees. Mu feared she had been poisoned too, but she stirred as they went past, muttering something in a dream, not waking.

Silently they entered the main rooms of the house. The smell changed to sandalwood, mixed with the odour of people. Mu could hear the soft rise and fall of their breath. From beyond the gate a dog barked. They froze for a few moments, but no one in the house wakened. If there were any more guards they were at the outer gate.

Here and there lamps flickered, giving Mu glimpses of the rooms as they went through them, each opening into the next. The wooden floors gleamed, wall hangings shone with patches of red. Along the southern side ran a wide verandah, but most of the shutters were closed.

From the middle of the house came the sound of snoring. Chika's teeth showed white as he grinned and mouthed *Unagi* to Mu. He slid open the final door and let Kiku go in first.

Kiku took on invisibility immediately and Mu copied him, as he had been told. He could just perceive his brother's faint outline approaching the sleeping man.

Unagi lay on his back, his head on a wooden headrest. Kiku's movements were so swift Mu hardly followed them. For a moment he wondered why the merchant began to twist and kick, why he was making that strange muffled grunting. Then he saw the garrotte in his brother's hands. Unagi was a big man and it seemed impossible that Kiku should be able to hold him down, but Kiku's invisible hands were like iron and relentless.

There was a trickle of water, a foul smell, and Unagi's struggles ceased.

In the silence that followed came a rustling and an intake of breath as the old man, Unagi's father, stirred. Mu saw the gleam of Chika's knife, heard the soft sigh as it entered flesh and the gurgle of blood.

Kiku slowly became visible again. Mu could see his expression as the lamps flared. It was both stern and gentle, as if he had undergone a spiritual transformation. He smiled at Chika with that unfathomable emotion.

'That was for you.'

Chika smiled back, pulled one of the hangings from the wall and placed a corner of it against the flame. As it began to smoulder he lifted the shutter open; the breeze fanned the sparks into fire.

Jumping from the verandah, they ran across the garden to the main gate. A woman screamed from the house behind them. Shouts followed, pounding feet, the crashing of doors and shutters as they were flung open, the ever fiercer crackling of flames.

Kiku leaped for the top of the wall, scaling it easily, and Mu, still invisible, was right behind him but Chika had turned back and drawn his sword. Running figures came from the guardhouse at the gate, their own swords glinting through the mist.

Two young men, barely into their twenties, came at Chika, attacking without hesitation. In the dark it was impossible to see their faces clearly but their build and movements were so similar they had to be brothers. They possessed both courage and skill and Chika was forced back to the foot of the wall.

'Go and help him,' Kiku ordered.

There was no time to argue, to plead that he had nothing against these young men and no reason to take their lives. Mu dropped down beside Chika, letting visibility return, surprising the man on his left. The tengu's sword swung once and cut clean through his opponent's forearm. The other sword fell in a shower of blood, startlingly warm in the dawn chill.

With a cry of rage and pain, the man drew a knife with his left hand and stabbed at where Mu would have been, if he had not used the second self to avoid the blade, letting it pierce only his shadow. The man stumbled, and with a returning stroke, the tengu's sword cut him across the side of the neck, severing the artery.

Jumping over the dying man as he crumpled to the ground, Mu turned his attention to Chika. He became one person, fully visible. The surviving brother caught sight of him out of the corner of his eye and thrust at him. Mu made one of the lightning fast feints the tengu had taught him.

'Leave him!' Chika cried. 'This one is mine!'

Mu took a light step back, as the man swung at him again. He could have killed him then but he heeded Chika's command.

'Your brother's dead,' Chika shouted. 'Your father too! Go and join them!'

Unsettled, enraged, his opponent hurled himself forward. Chika's sword tip found his throat.

Kiku gave a cry of appreciation. Mu could see him. Day was breaking.

'Let's go!' Chika said to Mu and, side by side, they leaped onto the wall. All three dropped soundlessly down to the other side. They did not go back to the boat but ran swiftly away from the house, which was now ablaze, through the narrow streets, following the river upstream. By the time the sun rose they were walking along a high dyke that separated the rice fields from the river. They strolled in a leisurely way, as though they had risen early to enjoy the autumn morning air. Eventually, they came to a pier jutting out over the water. The mudbanks were exposed by the low tide, and herons and plovers patrolled the shoreline, feeding. Under the pier, Kuro was waiting in a small boat, similar to the one they had crossed over in.

They did not speak as they climbed in. Kiku went first, followed by Mu. Chika handed his sword to Mu and pushed the boat into deeper water, then jumped nimbly in and took up the scull. His face was calm, almost rapt, as though some deep need had been fulfilled.

When they disembarked at the opposite bank, Kuro fastened the boat and looked up with an expectant expression.

'Well? How was it? Success?'

'Unagi and his sons are dead,' Kiku replied. 'His father too.'

'Well done! By what method?'

'Garrotte and swords,' Chika replied. 'We set fire to the house.'

'I saw that.' Kuro looked downstream to where the smoke was rising. 'I still think poison would have been better.'

'It depends if you want to send a clear message or not,' Kiku replied. 'With poison, or with snake or scorpion, there is always an element of uncertainty. This time there will be no doubt. The house of Unagi is finished and the same fate awaits all our competitors unless they submit to us.'

As they walked back into the town the smell of fish being grilled for the first meal of the day wafted through the streets, mingled with the sweet odours of soy bean paste and curds.

'I'm hungry,' Chika said.

'We can eat here.' Kiku stopped in front of a low-roofed building whose back room had been extended over the river and turned into an eating place. A large cheerful woman was gutting fish that still quivered with life. She called out a greeting to them as they entered.

'Master Kikuta! What an honour! Welcome!'

They sat down on cushions, a low table between them. The breeze from the river smelled of salt and smoke. A young girl, so shy she did not once raise her head, brought sharp green tea and set the bowls before them.

'What a shame it is not the season. I feel like eating eel!' Chika remarked, making Kuro chuckle.

'Wasn't that fun?' Kiku said to Mu.

Fun? It had been shocking and elating. It had demanded a new level of single-mindedness and concentration. For the first time he had combined the tengu's training and his own talents. It made him feel alive and reckless, aware of his own physicality in a way he had not felt since Shida. But four people he did not know and with whom he had no quarrel were dead.

'I suppose it was,' he admitted. 'I've not used the sword in a real fight before.'

'You fight well,' Chika said. 'Not that I needed your help – I'd have dealt with them both alone.'

Mu allowed himself the slightest smile of mockery, but did not speak.

'Now you've seen for yourself what we can do, you can tell Shikanoko,' Kiku said. 'No one is safe from us, no matter how cautious or how heavily guarded. Give him this.' He placed a small piece of carved jade in front of Mu: a fawn in a bed of grass.

'Where did you get that?' Mu said, taking it up and caressing it with his fingers.

'It was among Akuzenji's treasures. I kept it because it reminded me of Shika. Whoever he wants to get rid of we will do it. Tell him that, tell him we are his to command.'

But beneath the words, in spite of the gift, Mu sensed his brother's lust for power.

9

BARA

Shikanoko had spent years in the north, living with men who chased narwhal through stormy seas, and hunted seals on rocky shores. Sometimes they treated him as a god, for he had many powers that he made useful to them, and sometimes as an idiot, for he knew nothing of boats and fishing, and could not understand their speech so they had to repeat everything three times or more. Then, like the migratory birds that came and went, summer and winter – the local people believed they were crabs that transformed into birds and then back into crabs when it turned cold – instinct told him it was time to take flight.

The Burnt Twins and Ibara followed him, as they had done for years. After a journey of several weeks they found themselves back in the old hut on the borders of the Snow Country.

One morning, Ibara thought she saw a stranger on the edge of the clearing but it must have been a trick of the light for when she looked again there was no one there. Still, she told Nagatomo and they began to notice signs: Gen, the fake wolf, howled at night, the deer were more nervous, there were footprints, smaller than any of theirs, round the pools. She felt she was being watched and began to take her sword with her when she went away from the hut.

When the figure finally came through the forest one evening while they sat around the fire, Nagatomo said, 'It is Takauji,' and Ibara recognised the young man, who had been no more than a boy the last time they had seen him.

'I realised you had come back,' Takauji said, kneeling before Shikanoko, and holding out his sword. 'I came to offer you this. The Lord of the Snow Country will serve you loyally with all his men.' Then he added less formally, 'And if you are going to the capital take me with you for I want to kill Aritomo.'

'What makes you think I am going to the capital?' Shika said. 'Maybe I will just stay here in the Darkwood.'

Takauji scowled, saying forcefully, 'My right to my land is still being disputed on the grounds my father was a traitor. Every year some new claimant tries to take the domain from me. I am tired of these challenges, of fighting skirmish after skirmish. They are provoked from Minatogura. I will never have any peace unless I control that city or Aritomo is dead – preferably both! I hoped you would support me.'

'What does your mother advise?' Shika asked.

'She died last winter.' Takauji suddenly looked much older than his years. 'But before she died she revealed to me my father's final words. No one dared repeat them but one of his men had told her in secret: *Yoshimori is the true Emperor* is what he said before he ripped his belly open. People say the true Emperor will return, but he will never reign unless Aritomo is dead.'

'Once, a long time ago, I made a vow,' Shika said. 'That I would find Yoshimori and restore him to the throne. But then the mask became fused to my face and I felt I was condemned to live out my life outside human society, like an animal in the forest.'

'But even masked you can achieve great things,' Takauji said. 'Look how you helped me and my mother before. I would be dead by now without you.'

Nagatomo leaned forwards and spoke seriously to the young man. 'Everything you desire must be fought for. And once it is won it has to be defended. You are young, it's true, but you are a warrior. Act like one.'

'I will,' Takauji promised, his face lightening.

Ibara felt Nagatomo's words had been directed at Shikanoko as much as Takauji. Shikanoko made no outward response, neither encouraging Takauji nor rebuffing him.

After that the young man came every few days to talk to them. Ibara could see that Shikanoko welcomed his visits. They must have made her careless, for the next visitor took her by surprise. Even though she carried her sword it was no use to her when the stranger let her see him, for he used some kind of magic to paralyse her arm. He appeared on the path in front of her, coming out of nowhere and she had hardly drawn the sword before it slipped from her useless fingers.

'Don't be afraid,' he said. 'I don't want to hurt you.'

She went for her knife with her left hand, surprising him, but when she lunged at the figure before her the blade struck empty air. His voice came from behind her and as she whirled around she lost all feeling in her left hand and the knife fell beside the sword.

'Gen!' she called, for the wolf had come with her.

'Gen,' the man repeated, a note of delight in his voice. The wolf came bounding out of the undergrowth, sniffed the air and then approached the stranger, its ears flat, its tail wagging.

'Gen,' he said, stroking its head. 'You're still alive? Do you remember me? Mu?'

'Gen knows you?' Ibara said wonderingly. 'Where have you come from?'

'I've been sent to find Shikanoko. It's an added pleasure to meet a beautiful woman.' The compliment sounded awkward as if he were not used to making them. Or was it just that she was not used to hearing them?

'I have never been beautiful and I am hardly a woman anymore,' she replied. 'I live like a man and I can fight like a man, unless people use cowardly magic tricks!'

'I fight like a tengu,' he said, laughing. 'For that's who taught me. And it's by the tengu's command that I've come for Shikanoko. Let's go and find him. Unless you feel like doing something else first?'

'No I certainly don't! Release my hands so I can slap your face!'

Mu picked up her weapons and she felt her hands return to normal. He came closer and thrust his face towards hers. He was thin and ordinary-looking, not very tall, of slight wiry build, with rather small feet. His features were regular, his black eyes gleamed, his skin was copper coloured, beginning to show signs of ageing.

'A slap is better than a kiss to a tengu,' he said and laughed again.

It seemed a long time since she had heard laughter. She gave him a slap that made him stagger; in some ways it was as intimate as a kiss.

'What business do you have with the lord?' she said.

'Apart from anything else, I've come to pay him my respects. He is my father.'

'Don't talk nonsense,' she said. 'He is no older than you.'

'My brothers and I age fast,' Mu said.

'Is that a tengu thing?'

'It's the opposite. Tengu age very slowly and, if they die at all, it's after hundreds of years. Presumably my life will be short. That's why I must never waste a moment or an opportunity.' He raised an eyebrow at her.

He intrigued and repelled her in equal measure.

•

Nagatomo and Eisei were waiting with drawn swords. Mu halted and bowed deeply. 'The Burnt Twins,' he said, 'I am honoured to meet you. Your fame is widespread.'

'Hand over your weapons,' Nagatomo replied, unmoved by the flattery.

'I could give you my sword, but my true weapons are not the sort that can be handed over. But I have not come to hurt any of you, least of all Shikanoko.' He looked around. 'Where is he?'

'In the forest,' Nagatomo said.

'Then I will wait for him.' Mu perched his bony behind on one of the boulders in front of the wooden hut and grinned up at Ibara.

'Come and sit next to me and tell me the story of your life.'

Her palm still tingled. 'There is nothing to tell.'

'Well, get me something to drink, then.'

'Get it yourself,' she replied, her own rudeness delighting her.

'We drink only water,' Eisei remarked.

'In that case it's lucky I brought my own liquor.'

From a pouch at his waist he produced a small bamboo flask, removed the stopper and held it out to them. The two men declined but Ibara grabbed it and took a sip and then, as all her senses welcomed the fiery liquid, another, deeper gulp.

'Ha! You've missed that!'

The last time she had tasted alcohol Saburo had been alive.

She handed the flask back to Mu and he raised it. 'To the dead!' he said, mocking and serious at the same time.

Gen turned his head and whimpered. When they followed his gaze, they saw Shikanoko on the edge of the clearing. Mu rose to his feet, taking a swig of liquor and handing the flask back to Ibara. She watched as the two men approached each other. They seemed about the same age. Shikanoko was the taller by a head, even without the antlered mask. Mu's demeanour was humble, and he dropped to his knees and lowered his forehead to the ground.

The lord hesitated for a moment and looked around. Then he stepped past the kneeling man as if deliberately ignoring him and continued walking towards the others. Gen ran, in his stiff awkward way, to Shikanoko's side, licked his hand and then went to Mu, barking anxiously like a dog.

Shikanoko turned and went back. He knelt in front of Mu and taking him by the shoulders drew him into an embrace.

Ibara drank quickly, taking no notice of Eisei's disapproving glance.

The horses, grazing in the clearing, raised their heads to watch. Tan walked with an inquisitive air towards the stranger.

Shikanoko said something to Mu that Ibara could not hear, but it made him stop dead and look at the horse. She heard his laughter as Tan sniffed him. Mu sniffed back; they breathed into each other's nostrils.

It calms a horse, Saburo had said, long ago. Tears sprang into her eyes.

'I suppose I had better prepare some food,' she said to hide them.

There was a rabbit, caught two days before, pods of wild beans, a little dried fish, burdock and other mountain vegetables. All through the meal she watched Mu. Usually they shared the cooking between the three of them, but the arrival of the stranger had somehow turned her into a woman again and she undertook women's tasks like she used to. She was annoyed and beguiled.

The food was sparse, the meal quickly over. The sun slipped behind the western mountains and the shadows turned mauve. The air cooled slightly. Frogs croaked from the stream and night insects began to call. Mosquitoes whined around their necks and Nagatomo threw green twigs on the fire to make it smoke.

Mu said, 'Things cannot go on as they are.'

'It is not my fault that Heaven is enraged,' Shikanoko replied.

'But it is in your power to restore.'

'Restore what? The Kakizuki are in exile. The Miboshi rule the whole country. Their choice of Emperor sits on the Lotus Throne. I have nothing.'

'Lord Kiyoyori is at your side and you have his sword, Jato, reforged for you. You have the Burnt Twins, and, in this woman, the instrument of Masachika's death. You have your son, Takeyoshi, who is becoming a fine warrior. I have taught him myself, so I know what I'm talking about. You have the true Emperor.'

'Yoshimori? I most certainly do not! I have no idea where he is.'

'But I know,' Mu said with a smile. 'And that is why I have been sent to get you. He is with Lady Hina. I will take you to them.'

Ibara's blood rushed through her veins and her whole body tingled. *The instrument of Masachika's death! And Hina! Hina is alive!*

Mu gave her a grin as if he read her thoughts and then continued, to Shika, 'And you have my brother, Kiku, who has wealth, power and an army of his own, which he has promised are all yours to command. He sent this as a sign.' He took the jade carving from the breast of his robe and held it out.

Shika took it, gazing on it in wonder.

'It was in Akuzenji's hoard. Kiku kept it for you.'

'I am surprised,' Shika said slowly. 'He must have changed.'

'He has. In some ways for the better, in some for the worse. Do you remember Gessho?'

Shika nodded. 'But what does Gessho have to do with Kiku?'

'Kiku turned his skull into an object of power. It has made him almost invincible.'

A long silence followed. Neither man moved until Tan neighed shrilly from the darkness and Shikanoko turned his head as if he was listening to a message.

'I would come,' he said finally. 'If I could come as a man. But I cannot appear before the Emperor as this creature, half-stag.'

His hands went to his face. His fingers touched the smooth bone.

'Remove the mask, Mu, and I will accompany you.'

'It can only be removed by someone who loves you,' Mu said, after a pause. 'I'm not saying I don't love you. I think I do. But I can't take the mask from you, and nor, I think, can any of us here.'

'Do you think we haven't tried?' Nagatomo said out of the darkness.

Shikanoko laughed bitterly. 'I destroyed my one chance of love.'

'We never do that,' Ibara said. 'We are always given another chance.' Mu looked over the flames at her and she hoped he didn't think she was talking about him. Then she hoped he did.

'I believe I know who can remove the mask,' Mu said.

Tan walked up and put his head over Shikanoko's shoulder, rubbing against him. He stroked the horse's face.

Ibara said boldly, 'It looks like Tan is telling you what to do.'

'Maybe he is,' Shikanoko said. 'I will know in the morning.'

10

SHIKANOKO

He went away from the fire towards the small clearing by the spring. The long grass was dry and dead. Ragged holes showed where deer had been digging to get at the roots. The spring's babble was muted. It had not rained all summer and whatever source fed the spring was drying up. He knew they could not remain there without water. It was one more reason to leave with Mu. If Yoshimori came to the throne would the drought end and the land recover?

The others had fallen silent. Maybe they were asleep, though he knew they would take turns in keeping watch as they had done for years. They had sacrificed their own lives to stay with him, they had kept him alive, nourished him with their friendship.

What did I do to deserve that? What am I?

He felt the mask as he had done earlier, let his fingers caress the bone of the deer's skull, touched the lips, longed with all his heart to be free of it.

Should I stay here and die in the forest? But then I condemn those who have been loyal to me to the same endless exile.

Apart from the stags who cried in loneliness and yearning, the autumn forest had been emptying of sound. Birds flew south, insects chirped their final songs and buried themselves in the ground, or died. Scarlet and gold leaves covered the ground, rustling and dancing when the wind scattered them. Pine cones fell with a thump, and beech mast lay thick under the bare trees.

An owl hooted. Shika could feel the frost taking hold. He pulled the bearskin around his shoulders. How long was it since Nagatomo had killed it? The years merged into each other. Had he been away for ten winters or a hundred?

He thought about all Mu had told him. First his son, who had had to grow up alone, just as he had. When he had first met Ibara, he had told her, *Better he died in the water than grow up in this world of sorrow.* But the boy had somehow raised himself, had managed to find Mu and learn the way of the bow and the sword. He imagined him like Takauji, a young warrior.

An unfamiliar feeling came over him, stimulating and intense. After a few moments he identified it as curiosity. He said the boy's name aloud, listening to how it sounded: *Takeyoshi.* He wanted to discover how he had turned out, he wanted to look in his face and see whom he resembled. Takeyoshi could not escape the fact he was a warrior, the son of a Princess.

Next Akihime came into his mind, as strongly as if she stood before him. He thought he heard her say, 'It was not you who killed me or caused my death. We disobeyed the gods; we were punished for it. Masachika took me prisoner, Aritomo ordered my torture, the Prince Abbot carried it out. Punish them if you will, but don't punish yourself any longer. I was dying before the serpent bit me – maybe it saved me days of suffering. And although what we did together was wrong – we were so young, we knew nothing about the world – our son came from it.'

He recalled Sesshin's words: *This is why you should never concern yourself over your fate; everything follows the laws of destiny and therefore happens for a purpose.*

He saw all his faults and mistakes, his temper, impulsiveness, greed and pride.

He had carried her memory in his heart, day and night, for years, and yet he had hardly known her and now he could not see her face, only her defiant stance as she faced him on the road. And at that moment he finally accepted he would never see her again. His grief had run its course. *Farewell,* he said, *I will find our son.* Then he turned his thoughts to the other children whom he had tried to bring up, the ones Sesshin had warned him about. He had spared them, he must accept the consequences. He stroked the carved fawn, feeling its smooth jade surface. The gift touched him. He wanted to see Kiku and his brothers again.

Mu had told him that Kiku had gained his extreme power from the skull of the monk, Gessho. Shika let this idea come into his mind and contemplated it for a long time. He slowly became aware of the power spreading out from Kitakami, seeking ever greater control and domination. He had ignored Kiku and the others for too long. His own spiritual power, honed by the years of solitude and denial, stirred in response, stronger than ever.

A little way from him, the horses moved and stamped, restless in the cold, their silver coats gleaming faintly in the starlight, their breath floating in small clouds. Sparks from the fire flew upwards. Shika heard a low murmur of voices as Ibara took over the watch from Eisei.

He thought about the horses' lives, so entwined with his own, first Risu, then Nyorin whom he had acquired after Akuzenji's execution. He had wept when Risu died, both for her and for the boy he had been when she came into his life. And then the other stallion, Tan, who carried the spirit of Lord Kiyoyori within him. Shika might have died with Akuzenji and all the other bandits, but Kiyoyori had spared him. Had he repaid that debt or did he still owe Kiyoyori his life?

He recalled his own voice saying, *She is in love with Nyorin. I think she will have a foal next year,* and a girl's voice replied, *I wish I could live with you and Risu and Nyorin and their foal. Why don't we get married when I am old enough?*

Hina had loved him then. She must have saved his son, kept him hidden for years. He should at least thank her for that. And he should take Tan to her, so father and daughter could be reunited. He dared not hope for anything more.

He could no longer ignore the truth: Heaven would not relinquish its stubborn desire to see Yoshimori restored to the Lotus Throne. And Shika could only bow to its will and accept that he was its instrument. He had within his grasp everything he needed for victory in that cause, and for his own revenge. He remembered Kongyo's dream so many years ago.

I saw you as tall as a giant, Kongyo had said. *Your head rested on the mountains of the north and your feet on the southern islands. I woke convinced Heaven has a plan for you. Why else should you have escaped death so many times?*

Kongyo was dead, but his words remained. Then he heard Nagatomo's voice as if he had had spoken directly to him: *You are a warrior. Act like one.*

Finally, as if in a dream, Shisoku's words came back to him: *When you have mastered the dance you will gain knowledge through the mask. You will know all the events of the world, you will see the future in dreams and all your wishes will be granted.*

The great power he had been promised hardly interested Shika, except in so far as he would use it to control and contain Kiku, while bringing Yoshimori to the throne. In that case, it did not matter if he was condemned to wear the mask forever. He would crush the Emperor's enemies and then retire again to the forest.

The night passed. He did not sleep. Just before dawn he saw eyes shining round the edge of the clearing. The deer had come to graze. He stood and moved among them. They did not startle but circled him as he danced, for the last time, the deer dance in the Darkwood.

One by one the others woke and came to join him. As the light strengthened he saw Takauji was among them. The young man must have known the movements of the deer dance since childhood. Shikanoko followed him in the autumn part of the dance, mastering the final ritual that he had never known. In the circling, interweaving patterns he saw his whole life and the part each of them had played in it, and the part he had played in theirs.

When the dance was finished, he called Takauji to him and said formally, 'I accept the service you offered me.'

Takauji's face lit up as he fell to his knees.

'I am going to Miyako,' Shika said. 'I am relying on you. You must hold the Snow Country for the Emperor.'

'I will do more than that,' Takauji promised. 'I will take Minatogura!'

II

HINA

The acrobats had caught two suitable young male monkeys and were preparing to go back to Aomizu, but they were reluctant to leave without Take. The strange girl had come, in the eighth month, to tell the lady that he was staying with her father, but since then there had been no other messages, nor had Take returned.

Hina did not know whether she should leave with them or stay. The images of the face in the mask and the skull had never left her mind, but they did not reappear in Sesshin's book, and despite her daily study of it, along with fasting and meditation, no other sign was revealed.

The captive monkeys screamed all night and their families hovered anxiously in the surrounding trees, crying in forlorn voices. Hina felt like adding her own voice to theirs. *Come back, Take! Where are you? Come back!*

One morning she heard the sound of men's voices, and went swiftly to hide herself behind the rocks around the hot spring. The packhorse raised its head from the grass and neighed in welcome.

She caught sight of a splash of red through the trees. Yoshi dropped down from the branch where he had been sitting, chewing on a twig and playing with Noboru.

'It's Kinmaru and Monmaru!'

Saru was soaking in the hot water. He leaped out naked and ran to the two men who were walking into the clearing. 'What's happened?' he called. 'Why are you here? What's wrong?'

The older men still behaved like children, Hina thought, and from a distance they still looked childlike, but when she approached she saw that the sudden ageing common to acrobats had fallen on them. Their joints had succumbed to the demands made on them over the years, their faces were lined, they moved like old men.

'Lady Yayoi,' Kinmaru said, and Monmaru bowed his head, yet she sensed a reserve in them towards her. She wondered what accusations had been made of her in her absence. Had they been sent to bring her back to be punished for murder?

'A message came from Lady Asagao,' Monmaru began immediately, not even waiting to sit down. 'She was taken to Matsutani by Lord Masachika. She must have made a good impression; maybe she spoke on our behalf. Anyway, the lord has summoned us, with the musicians, to entertain a great assembly, including Lord Aritomo himself, at a hunt in the southern Darkwood. Saru, you and Yoshi must go with us. We are halfway to Matsutani, there is no point in going home first. The others will meet us there. They've already set out with the monkeys and all our equipment.'

'It's a great honour,' Kinmaru said. 'And we will be richly rewarded, Asagao says. These lords know how to give generously. But we must leave at once, we have less than half a month.'

'What about them?' Yoshi said, indicating the captive monkeys.

'You'll have to let them go,' Kinmaru said. 'We can't risk taking young, untrained monkeys with us.'

Saru looked upset. 'Then we've wasted the whole summer here. These are really promising ones too.'

'You can come back next year,' Monmaru consoled him. 'This is too good an opportunity to miss.'

'Yoshi should take the young monkeys home with the horse,' Hina said. She had been listening to the conversation with mounting dread.

They all stared at her. 'We can't perform without Yoshi,' Saru said.

'Where's Take?' Kinmaru looked around. 'He'll need to come too.'

'He's gone off somewhere,' Saru replied. 'We can manage without him, but that's all the more reason why Yoshi must come.'

He flung an arm round his friend's shoulder and hugged him. 'Exciting, isn't it?'

'Yoshi,' Hina said. 'I need to talk to you alone.'

Yoshi shrugged his shoulders slightly. His usually cheerful expression turned sullen as he followed Hina. Kon swooped overhead, calling piercingly.

Yoshi looked up. 'I hate that bird,' he muttered. 'I wish it would go away.'

When they were out of earshot, Hina said, 'You must not go. You will be in great danger.'

He made no response, just stared at the ground.

'Yoshi! Look at me! Do you understand what I am saying?'

He looked at her then, his expression unreadable.

'Do you remember anything about the past, where you came from, who you are?'

'I am an acrobat. I work with monkeys. That's the only life I've ever known.'

Hina wondered if she should tell him: would he be safer if he knew or would ignorance protect him?

Yoshi said, in a low rapid voice, 'I do remember one thing. A woman telling me I must never reveal my true identity. Kai knows, for she came with me from the same world, but she has never said a word to anyone else. That's why I love her and why she's the only person I could love. I know why Kon follows me day and night. I saw how Take's attitude changed towards me – you told him, didn't you? You have known since the day we met, for the lute betrayed me. I'm grateful to you for keeping my secret all these years. But I will never admit it to anyone. You can't make me. I will deny it to the end of my days. I am not interested in power or position. I will live and die an acrobat and nothing you can say will make me change my mind.'

Even as he denied it he spoke with all the true authority of the Emperor. She found she could not argue with him.

The young monkeys were released, and were greeted by their families with cries of relief and excitement.

'You'll come with us, Lady Yayoi?' Kinmaru said, when they were ready to leave.

'I will wait for Take,' she replied. 'He will be back soon.'

Monmaru said nervously, 'We were told to bring you back with us. We will certainly be questioned about you.'

'You must say nothing!' Yoshi declared and then, taking Yayoi aside, said quietly, 'I promise I will not give you away, and you must make the same promise to me.'

'I will,' she whispered.

They did not try to persuade her further, fully aware she faced arrest if she was found. Better to starve to death in the Darkwood or be killed by wild animals than fall into the hands of Aritomo's torturers.

•

The monkeys disappeared. After the two young ones were released and the excitement had died down, they all began to hurry away towards the northeast, deep into the forest, as if each member of the group had received a hidden signal.

Hina missed their chatter and their activity. The trees seemed to press around her more densely and she heard strange noises that alarmed her. Kon had flown after Yoshi, adding to her fears – surely Masachika or one of his men would have the skill to shoot the bird down? Yet there was no way she could prevent him from following Yoshi, just as she could not stop Yoshi from going to Matsutani. He was the Emperor, he would go where he willed and Kon's destiny was to follow him.

Kon's presence must have intimidated the other birds and animals, for after he had departed they began to come more boldly into the clearing. Crows alighted on the ground beside her, cawing loudly and pecking at scraps of food left behind, peering at her with their fearless eyes, as if they hoped the flesh that covered her bones would soon become carrion.

Some animal, either a small wolf or a very large fox, lurked every evening on the edge of the clearing. She heard it hunting in the night, heard the sudden short scream of its prey. She was wary of it, knowing that, when winter came, wolves would move southwards through the Darkwood. She remembered hearing them howling on snowy nights when she was a child at Matsutani. Sometimes, made desperate by hunger, they would attack the horses. Being awakened by the screaming horses, the snarling wolves and the shouts of men running to drive them away, was one of her enduring memories. In the morning there would be dead wolves to skin – their furs made warm winter coverings or chaps for riding – and wounded horses to put down, with the promise of fresh meat for days to come.

But she was most cautious of the wild boar, which, as autumn drew into winter, she often heard crashing through the undergrowth. She had seen dogs and men ripped open by their tusks. They were aggressive, seemed half-mad, even when they were not being hunted. She did not dare venture far from the clearing in case she was attacked by one. Yet staying where she was made her anxious too. Yoshi had ordered the acrobats to say nothing about her but they could so easily let slip a casual word and betray her.

The acrobats had left her food, and wood for the fire, which she kept going diligently. There was a grove of chestnut trees near the spring and the nuts were ripening. She collected them, storing them like a squirrel. But every night was a little colder than the last. Soon it would begin to freeze and then it would snow. *I will have to spend the winter in the hot spring if Take does not return,* she thought, but the reality, she knew, was she could not survive there.

Sometimes her passive waiting infuriated her. She longed to act. For so many years she had been told what to do by Fuji, had submitted to everything asked of her and suppressed all her own hopes and desires. Now she was free of all constraints, except those imposed by the weather and the changing seasons, and the frailty of her own body. Yet she did not know what action she could take.

In the short hours of daylight she took out the medicine stone and the Kudzu Vine Treasure Store. The Abbess had been right. In some way that Hina did not fully understand, the stone made the text readable. If she kept her left hand on the stone, she found she could not only read but understand what she read. As a child she had longed to make people and animals well, riven by pity for their suffering. Now that childish pity had turned into a mature, all-encompassing compassion.

So she made a virtue out of her solitude, overcoming her fears and her hunger, until she had completely absorbed the teachings of the text. She had grown so used to being alone that when a man and a tall brown horse appeared in the clearing one morning, for a moment she could not recognise what they were. They seemed one strange being, threatening and unpredictable. So they had come for her. She wanted to hide but there was no time.

The man dismounted, calling her name. It was Chika, whom she had last seen when he came to Fuji's boat – or had she seen his shape underwater, the night Fuji died? He had come then to ask her to help Shikanoko. Her heart began to beat faster with excitement. Was it, at last, the time for Chika to take her to him?

He slid down from the horse's back and came towards her, dropped to one knee and bowed his head. The horse pulled on the reins, trying to reach the grass.

'Hina! I was told I would find you here.'

Excitement and hope made her greet him warmly, despite his familiar tone. 'I am so glad to see you, Chika,' she said eagerly. 'What news do you bring?'

He stood again, not speaking for a moment, studying her face with an intense expression that made her uncomfortable. She took a step back as she said, 'I have no food to offer you, but let me take your horse to the spring to drink and I will bring back fresh water.'

'I don't need anything,' he said, dropping the reins. 'The horse can find water if it's thirsty. Let's sit down and talk.'

The sun was just beginning to clear the trees. Hina led him to a patch of sunlight on the western side of the spring. The horse went to drink deeply, snorting through its nose. The ground was still cold. Hina sat on a small outcrop of rock. Chika pulled his sword from his sash and laid it down, then squatted on his haunches next to her.

'I've come from Kitakami,' he said. 'The brothers I told you about, Master Kikuta and Mu, have been reconciled, making the Tribe, as they call themselves, stronger than ever.'

'And Shikanoko?' Hina said, his name filling her with joy and nervousness.

'Mu has gone to find him,' Chika said.

'Will he bring him here?'

He frowned as though her eagerness distressed him and did not answer her question. 'I've been thinking while I've been riding. I've had a lot of time lately to reflect on my life. I am not proud of what I have become.'

'None of us can avoid our fate,' Hina said.

'Maybe that is true, or maybe what proves a man is striving against fate and having the will to mould it to his own design. I am a warrior's son, Hina. It's a long time since I've lived as a warrior.'

He put out a hand impulsively and gripped her thigh, his touch sending shock waves through her. 'Aritomo is planning an attack on the Kakizuki in Rakuhara, to be led by your old patron, Arinori. That's why Arinori gave up his pursuit of you. Masachika knows you came into the Darkwood with the acrobats, he will find out where you are and will certainly come after you sooner or later. But Kiku, who has informants everywhere now, even in the capital, has already sent messengers to Lord Keita. The Kakizuki will be prepared and the Miboshi will be defeated. It's a chance for us to flee together. We can ride south and find the Kakizuki. We are of the same class, our families have been linked for generations. Ever since we were children I dreamed we would marry one day – I told you this before.'

'But what about Shikanoko?' Hina said.

'You asked if Mu would bring him here. He will but he will be leading him to his death. Kiku says he wants to be of service to Shika, to restore the Emperor, but what he really wants is the mask Shika wears. I told you my sister's dream. I believe it means that you could remove the mask. But if Kiku takes possession of it, you will have condemned Shikanoko to death. He has said as much to me. In fact he ordered me to kill him. Come with me and you will save not only your life but his too.'

His touch was embarrassing her with its intimacy and she tried to move from under it.

He looked at his own hand as if in surprise and lifted it away. 'I'm sorry. I should not touch you. But you have had so many men and I have wanted you for so long. Won't you look with favour on me? I will take you away to safety. You can't stay here on your own. Masachika's men will find you eventually, if you aren't killed by wild animals first.'

When she did not reply he went on. 'We killed Unagi, you know, his sons and his father. I did it partly for you, so you would never be insulted by him again. And Kiku wanted to get rid of him. But once it was done I felt that part of my life was over. Or maybe Mu coming changed everything. I thought I was as close to Kiku as anyone, but Mu has become closer. I realised I was weary to death of that world of sorcerers and imps. I will never belong in it. Can you understand my loneliness? Kiku has offered me women, but I will never be able to meet and marry anyone of my own rank and I will not accept anyone else. But if we go to the Kakizuki, you, Kiyoyori's daughter, shall be the wife of Kongyo's son.'

'That is impossible,' she said, staring at him, shocked by his words. 'I pity you deeply but I was very fond of Unagi and, as I said to you before, he was a good man. I can't marry the man who killed him.'

'I could show you I am a better man and a better lover. What's more I am offering you a chance to escape, to save your life. You have no choice, Hina.' He grasped both her arms as if he would lift her up. 'You must come with me. I'll carry you if I have to!'

There was a crashing and rustling in the undergrowth and the horse squealed in fear. It threw up its head and barged past Chika, unbalancing him and knocking him to the ground. Suddenly released, Hina fell on her hands and knees.

She looked towards the undergrowth, the sun dazzling her. The crashing noise came again and a huge boar, the largest she had ever seen, came bursting out, head down, charging towards them.

Its long tusks gleamed, its little eyes were red with rage, streams of saliva dripped from its glistening mottled snout. Each bristle stood out as sharp as a needle.

Chika lunged towards her, not looking back at the boar.

'Chika!' She tried to shout out a warning.

He saw her gaze and turned, struggling to his feet, stumbling, reaching vainly for his sword.

The boar hit him like a galloping horse, thrust its tusks into him and ripped him open with a sideways flick of its head.

It tossed him aside. There was a moment of silence and then he began to sob in pain.

'Hina!' he cried. 'Help me!'

But she did not need the medicine stone to see he was dying.

The boar pawed the ground, peered at her with its vicious eyes. She walked slowly backwards, staring fixedly at it through her tears, not daring to lift a hand to wipe them from her eyes, trying to calm her breath.

She saw its muscles tense as it prepared to charge. It seemed to gather itself up in a solid ball of aggression and rage. There was a humming sound through the air, like a giant insect, the thud of an impact, arrow into flesh. The boar squealed and hesitated for a moment, then launched itself at her, further enraged by pain. Another thrumming, a second arrow. The animal squealed again, a piercing, almost human sound, faltered, and dropped at her feet. Within seconds the light had gone from its eyes.

One shaft had hit it in the throat, the other protruded from its back, its white feathers now flecked red with blood. The arrowhead had penetrated straight to the heart.

12

MASACHIKA

Lord Aritomo travelled to Matsutani by palanquin, his favourite horse led behind by grooms, his bow and his sword carried by high-ranking warriors. Two falconers followed with his hawks on wooden perches. A monk from Ryusonji carried a bamboo cage containing the two young werehawks, which squawked and flapped their wings incessantly. The priests had managed to capture them and had presented them to Aritomo. The lord spoke to them every day and tended them with his own hands. The hawks disliked them intensely.

Aritomo's companions were all heavily armed and more than usually vigilant. Casting his eye over the procession as they rode out, Masachika, who had gone back to Miyako to escort his lord to his home, noticed there were many absent warriors, not from the highest caste, but from the ambitious middle ranks, and particularly those from the coastal estates who had some knowledge of boats and the sea. So the planned attack on the Kakizuki was going ahead, and, while Aritomo was entertained by the hunt, his old enemies would be taken by surprise and wiped out.

Yet there was little sense of celebration. Drought and famine had ravaged the land. The dead lay unburied along the roadside and on the banks of the shrunken rivers. Crows stalked among them, the only creatures to look plump and sleek. Survivors threw stones at the birds; Masachika knew only too well how easily their aim could be turned on him and Aritomo's retinue.

Sometimes women knelt in the road, holding out starving children, begging the men for food, or, if they would give them nothing, pleading with them to put an end to their wretched lives and their children's suffering. The grooms chased them away with whips.

The mood among the warriors was sombre. Death was everywhere, ignoble, insignificant and inevitable. The wasted corpses, carrion for birds, mocked their own strength and vitality.

Look at us. You too will be reduced to bones like us. You too are no more than meat that will rot and putrefy.

At night, in the private homes or temples used as lodging places, Aritomo could not sleep and those closest to him were summoned to sit up with him and listen to his thoughts on the way to live and the way to die.

'A warrior must choose his own death. Even on the battlefield, if he is defeated, it is better to die by his own hand than surrender to an opponent.'

Death for him was another enemy, like drought and famine. He would defeat all three of them. A smile played on his lips as he regarded his men, as though he knew a secret they did not. He brewed and drank the strange-smelling tea all night, but never offered it to anyone else. Watching him closely, as he did all the time, Masachika could not help thinking how easy it would be to poison him. The more he tried to put the thought from him, the more he found himself dwelling on it.

Sometimes Aritomo spoke of Takaakira, with grudging respect. 'As I grow older I admire courage above all virtues. In the end it is the only one that matters. To live without fear of death is to be a true warrior.'

Masachika knew the hunt in the Darkwood would offer many opportunities to display fighting skills. The men would compete with each other to bring down the fiercest boar, the proudest stag. They might even be lucky enough to encounter bears. There were still vast tracts of land in the west and northeast that needed to be occupied and subdued. Warriors who acquitted themselves well in the hunt would be rewarded by Lord Aritomo with gifts of these lands. It was the next best thing to distinguishing oneself in battle, and for men eager to establish themselves and their families on estates granted to them forever, it offered a better chance of survival. Yet even hunting could be dangerous.

Shortly after they headed north from the barrier on the Shimaura road, at the turn to Matsutani, Masachika, riding ahead, heard singing, the sounds of a flute and the chattering of monkeys. He saw the red of the acrobats' clothes. He urged his horse forward and ordered the entertainers to conceal themselves, for he wanted their appearance to be a complete surprise.

Obediently they pulled the packhorses over the dyke, down into the dry rice fields. There were several men and, as far as he could see, eight monkeys. There was also a group of six musicians, carrying their instruments. The flute player had been playing, as they walked, and two of the women had been singing. The way the women moved and sang, freely, easily, reminded him of Asagao, with the now familiar but still astonishing surge of desire.

'Get down!' he told them, and they all prostrated themselves. Masachika watched from the top of the dyke as Aritomo's retinue rode past. He did not want any of his entertainers shot by over-zealous warriors. He could hear the werehawks shrieking even more loudly than usual and wondered what had alarmed them. When they had all passed by, he called to one of the older men to approach him.

'Come to Matsutani tomorrow, in the afternoon. We will be out at the hunt. We will expect your entertainment when we return. A little music first, I think, then acrobats with monkeys, and music for the rest of the evening. It must be a surprise, so do not show yourselves before then.'

'I understand, lord,' the man replied. 'We will find a quiet spot to prepare ourselves and do our final rehearsals. We are all here now. Thank you for your confidence in us. We won't let you down.'

'You had better not,' Masachika replied.

Out of the corner of his eye he saw a huge black bird fluttering down to the dyke. He had come to hate with all his heart the crows that fed on carrion along the road, and was inclined to string his bow and shoot it. But it was not a crow. *One of the werehawks has escaped*, he thought and was on the point of calling to the monk, but then he saw this bird was larger and not all black but flecked with gold patches that flashed blindingly in the sun. It unsettled him. He felt it must have some significance but he could not unravel it and he must not let Lord Aritomo travel on without him.

He caught up with the procession, dismounted and walked beside the palanquin.

'Not long now, lord,' he murmured. 'We are nearly there.'

•

The west gate stood open. Tama waited inside, with her women and retainers. Masachika contemplated their appearance with pleasure and pride – the women's layered robes in autumn hues, the men's new brilliant green hunting robes. Scarlet maples framed the view of the mountains in the east, and mandarins on a small tree by the steps glowed orange. The gardens and the house were immaculate, not a single stray leaf or unwelcome insect to be seen. The weather was perfect, neither clouds nor breeze, just the blue sky fading into pink and violet as the sun set and the first stars appeared. He felt a surge of satisfaction and, of course, gratitude to Tama, but he could not help searching for Asagao among the women.

They all bowed to the ground and murmured expressions of welcome, as Aritomo was helped from the palanquin. He stumbled a little but then regained his balance, acknowledging the greetings with a slight nod. Masachika had left his horse at the gate, and had not failed to bow to Sesshin's eyes and the gateposts. Now he came forward, not offering an arm to help his lord lest that should offend him, but alert to any sign of weakness or dizziness.

'Masachika,' Aritomo said, turning back. 'That is the gate with the famous eyes, is it not?'

'It is, lord.'

'Ah,' Aritomo sighed. 'To think I have talked with their owner. You would not guess what I have learned from him.'

He looked at Masachika with his own unfathomable eyes. Masachika tried to make his expression opaque, fearing Aritomo could see all his desires and ambitions.

'I thought I heard voices as I passed under the gate.' Aritomo was deeply interested in supernatural phenomena. 'Do the eyes have the power of speech as well?'

'There are guardian spirits within the gateposts,' Masachika said. 'They are entirely benevolent.'

'They sounded agitated,' Aritomo said, and stepped onto the verandah. A stool had been prepared for him and maids came forward to wash the dust from his feet. He did not say more, but gave Masachika another searching look. The caged werehawks were squabbling and shrieking.

Masachika bowed again, and as he rose, was approached by one of Tama's women who whispered that her mistress had gone further into the garden, and this would be a good time for them to talk. She emphasised her words in a meaningful way that irritated him. All he wanted now was to be with Asagao. She was not with the women on the verandah, but he thought he could hear snatches of music from the pavilion where she was staying. Sighing heavily, he went to the lakeside where Tama was pacing to and fro.

'Don't walk around in that unattractive manner,' he said. 'You look less than calm.'

'Calm?' she retorted. 'I hardly know the meaning of the word anymore.'

'What's the matter? Everything's going fine. The house, the garden, look magnificent. Come with me to Lord Aritomo, so he can congratulate you as I am sure he—'

She did not wait for him to finish. 'The spirits are very upset. I've been doing all I can to placate them.'

'That's the last thing we need! What have you done that's annoyed them?'

'I? I have done nothing. It is you who has outraged them. Ever since you came here with that girl . . .'

'Don't start on that again,' Masachika said, affecting a weary tone. 'I've told you, she means nothing to me.'

'Then send her away.' Tama stared at him defiantly.

'I won't do that. I need her for the entertainment I have arranged. The rest of the troupe will arrive tomorrow. We passed them on the road. I made them hide behind the bank; it was very amusing! We will hold the first hunt, and the entertainers will be ready in the evening, when we return. Do we have enough torches, and enough to drink?'

'Everything is prepared, Masachika. You don't need to supervise me, and don't try to change the subject. You, of all people, should know that the spirits should not be treated lightly. We made a vow before them, and I have had to make others to convince them that you are not lying. I have staked my life on your sincerity. I promised, if you proved untrue, I would kill myself. Look, you know the dagger I always carry with me?' She brought it out from her sash. 'I am ready to use it at any time.'

'Don't try to bully me, Tama. I will not be dictated to, by you or anyone. There is no need for such dramatic behaviour. I have told you, the girl means nothing to me, but even if she did, what of it? Men take mistresses and concubines – why shouldn't I? It is expected in my position. You should consider yourself fortunate I don't have a whole string of them.' He added spitefully, 'If I did, one of them might give me a son.'

'If you came to me more often, I would give you children,' she said in a low voice. 'And a string of women would be preferable to one who has won your heart.'

'You are completely unreasonable,' he said. 'And don't start weeping. Your tears repulse me and you must not appear before our visitors with red eyes. Go inside and take control of yourself. And then get on with the many things that need to be done. It is almost dark. We must prepare for the feast.'

'I have given you everything, Masachika, and I will take it all away from you.' She looked at the dagger in her hand, with an almost tender smile. 'Just one word in Aritomo's ear . . .'

'There is a special place in Hell reserved for women who betray their husbands,' he replied. He did not feel in the least threatened by her. If anything, her outburst proved the strength of her love for him. But he was not going to reveal to Aritomo's men how much she had always dominated him, nor was he going to yield to her. He did not believe for a moment that she would kill herself, or that she would divulge his secret conversation with the Emperor's mother. As for the spirits, he would deal with them in the morning, reprimand them and make sure they knew whom they had to obey.

He watched Tama walk away and, when she had disappeared into the house, he went to the pavilion and ran across the stepping stones, calling Asagao's name.

•

A wide plain lay to the southwest of Matsutani, between the forested mountains and the rice fields. It had no water, so was useless for cultivation, but it was a fine place for both hunting and hawking. Tama had arranged for over fifty farmers to come from the surrounding villages to act as beaters for the hunt. From dawn the next day their shouts, drumming, and the clash of cymbals echoed through the Darkwood, as they drove animals into the range of the hunters. It was dangerous work – the men were armed only with staves, one broke a leg falling from a high cliff, two were gored by wild boars that came hurtling out of the bushes – but also enjoyable. They would be rewarded with some of the meat and it was a break from the daily toil of wresting a living from the land. The tasks of autumn awaited. The rice had been harvested and women were threshing and winnowing the husks, and shelling beans into huge baskets. Manure had to be spread on the fields, the woods close to the village coppiced for flexible branches that would be used in building and basket making, rice straw dried to make sandals, reeds cut for thatching, firewood gathered for the long weeks of snow. Beating for the hunt was a holiday.

The warriors wore chaps of fur or deerskin and hunting robes stained with persimmon sap, or in colours of green and cream, printed with autumn flowers and grasses. The horses' reins were dyed blue or purple, the saddles decorated with silver lacquer, the girths braided with gold thread.

As they galloped over the plain, bringing down the panicked animals, Aritomo watched from the back of his dapple grey horse. He wore bearskin chaps and a hat of silk, with a motif of pine trees, a compliment to Masachika, to whom he had entrusted his sword and his bow. His falconers sat on horses behind him, each with a hawk on his wrist.

A little further back stood a huge man, holding the white banner of the Miboshi.

Masachika thought the lord looked better than he had for several weeks. The fresh air, the new surroundings, the excitement of the hunt, had made the blood flow more strongly through his veins. His spirits seemed high too; he was in a generous mood and the successful hunters were rewarded with gifts of land of hundreds of acres.

Masachika wore a hunting robe of light willow green, patterned with flocks of plovers. His chaps were grey wolf skins and his hunting arrows were fletched with tawny and white hawk feathers. His bow was bound with wisteria vine and he rode his favourite tall black horse, Sumi. His sedge hat was lined with pale blue silk.

Sumi was restless, pawed the ground and shook his head frequently. His skin twitched with every shout and every clash of the cymbals. Masachika was cramped and uncomfortable. He turned his irritation onto Lord Aritomo, who sat without moving, and allowed it to fester into bitter anger. As the host, he was obliged to leave the best opportunities to his guests, but it riled him to see so many of them distinguish themselves and be rewarded, while he had to content himself with holding Lord Aritomo's weapons.

He had to watch while one man killed a boar, bringing it down right in front of Lord Aritomo; another returned in the late afternoon, a huge black bear, with thick fur and gleaming teeth, slung over his horse's back. He presented it to Lord Aritomo and it was graciously accepted, and a large estate at the foot of the High Cloud Mountains granted in payment. Masachika added words of congratulations that nearly choked him.

When the sun began to descend towards the west, Aritomo indicated he would like to return. A conch shell was blown to signify the end of the hunt and his warriors began to gather round him for the ride back. The men's faces were flushed with excitement; the horses breathed heavily, their flanks heaving, white with sweat.

Masachika gave Aritomo's weapons to one of the bodyguards and let the men go on ahead, while he arranged for the slaughtered animals to be collected and carried home, where they would be skinned, some of the meat distributed to the beaters, the rest prepared for the evening's feast. As well as deer and boar, and the bear, there were serow, wolves and foxes, rabbits and hares, squirrels, pheasants, marmots, raccoons. Tusks and antlers would be removed, the larger ones saved for helmet decorations, the smaller used for knife handles and other carvings.

The number of dead deer astonished him – could there be any left alive in the Darkwood? He rode through the temporary dwellings erected for the warriors, greeting many and accepting their thanks and compliments. A wooden platform had been constructed, facing the lake, where Aritomo would eat and watch the performers. The lake had shrunk so much in the years of drought there was a wide expanse of sand on the shoreline. At one end, food was being prepared in an outdoor kitchen, at the other was the small stage for the musicians. The acrobats would perform on the sand. They had requested a boat, as well, and a small one lay at the water's edge.

Already, from behind the silk curtain that defined the end of the stage, Masachika could hear the chattering of monkeys, and a plangent twanging as the musicians tuned their instruments. He dismounted, told the groom who had been walking beside him to take the horse to the stable, and went behind the curtain.

The music stopped and everyone immediately bowed to him. There were two young men, about twenty years old, he thought, four somewhat older, and two who looked well into their thirties, already showing signs of age. Several of them had monkeys already sitting on each shoulder, tethered with braided blue silk cords, fastened to leather collars set with mother of pearl and blue gemstones. The monkeys had thick grey and white fur, their faces and rumps were rose pink and their deep-set eyes, hazel or green. They wore the same sleeveless red jackets as the acrobats.

The music group consisted of the flute player he had heard on the road, a drummer, the two women singers and a lutist. There was no sign of Asagao.

He asked where she was and one of the singers replied, 'She has gone to get the other lute; her own has a broken string.'

He was tempted to follow her, and lie with her quickly, before the night's celebrations started. The idea excited him unbearably. He checked that everything was ready and went to enter the garden by the east gate, from where it would be easy to slip unnoticed into the pavilion. But his wife was standing on the verandah, directing a flurry of maids and servants who were carrying bowls, cushions, eating trays and so on, to the lake shore.

She saw him and, giving some last instruction to the steward, stepped down from the verandah and came towards him. Her face was pale, her eyes, despite his admonitions, red rimmed.

'What's the matter?' he said sharply.

Her voice was expressionless and cold. 'Have you been to the west gate?'

'No, I came in the other way.'

'Come with me now.'

'I am busy now,' Masachika said. 'Besides, it is better not to disturb the spirits.'

'You won't disturb them,' Tama said. 'They are not there.'

She walked swiftly to the gate and stood between the posts. The evening's offerings lay scattered about as though someone had kicked them away.

'I felt them go,' she said. 'They threw the offerings at my head and rushed past me.'

'You are imagining it,' Masachika said. 'It is your own lack of composure that you are feeling. They have just decided to go quiet again.'

'I don't think so. They have escaped. They released the two werehawks Lord Aritomo brought with him.' She looked upwards. 'The birds were flying around shrieking but I can't hear them now. Well, it doesn't matter. You have lied to me and to the spirits, and now my life is forfeit. I only hope that will be enough to placate them, and that they will not ruin the estate after my death.'

'Don't talk nonsense,' he said, but more gently, for he was suddenly afraid she was losing her mind. 'You are not going to kill yourself.'

She did not reply, but gave him a look such as he had never seen before from her. Her contempt stabbed some inner part of him and he felt unexpected despair over all he was going to lose.

'Tama, I beg you. Don't do it. The girl means nothing to me. I will send her away tomorrow.'

'It is too late,' she replied.

He took refuge in anger, then, as was his habit. 'How can you bother me with your fantasies at a time like this? I have so many things to think about. We will talk tonight – I will come to you, it will be between us as it used to be, I promise you. Now, let us present a night's entertainment that Lord Aritomo will never forget.'

'And your plan to hasten his end?' she said scornfully.

'Don't speak of such things!' He looked anxiously round the garden, as though they might be overheard.

'If you do have the courage to do it, you will have to write your own poems to the Emperor,' she said, and walked away from him.

Masachika heard a bird call and, looking up, saw, perched on the roof, the strange black bird he had noticed in the rice fields. He could just make out its outline against the darkening sky. The streaks of gold glimmered in the last of the light. He waved his arms at it but it did not move.

'I will deal with you in the morning,' he vowed.

●

From the house to the lake shore, the garden blazed with light. Oil lamps, candles, torches, the kitchen fires at the northern end on which the beasts were roasting, all competed with the huge orange moon that was rising behind the mountains.

Persimmon moon, Masachika thought, with an uneasy feeling of premonition. It was the last thing he wanted Aritomo to see. Fortunately, by the time Aritomo had finished eating, the moon had changed its colour and was high enough to throw a silver path across the lake's surface.

Aritomo commented on it as he took another cup of wine. 'Even the moon conspires to make us feel at home. Masachika, you and your wife have excelled yourselves. I cannot remember a more delightful day.'

'It is nothing,' Masachika replied. 'However, still to come is a humble little entertainment I have arranged for your pleasure.'

Aritomo gave one of his rare smiles and leaned forward in anticipation.

A wide mat was unrolled on the shore and the silk curtain of the stage drawn to one side. Behind it, the musicians were seated, with a few lamps lighting their faces. Masachika could see Asagao quite clearly, her delicate features, the curve of her breast. She held the shabby old lute, which seemed a shame, but it was the only displeasing aspect. He could not believe he was being forced to give up this beautiful girl. He felt a surge of anger against his wife. He suppressed the fear he had felt earlier and took comfort in memories of how Tama had come to him in Minatogura, her pleas, her expressions of love, repeated so many times in so many nights, over the years. In the end she always yielded to him. This time would be no different.

There was a sudden clacking of sticks, announcing the beginning of the performance, and the loud pounding of a drum. As the other musicians joined in, Masachika could hear the lute. It was slightly out of tune and its notes sounded reluctant. Asagao was frowning and she glanced at the other lute player, who made a swiftly hidden grimace in response.

Aritomo, who had a fine ear for music, was also frowning.

'Well, it is, after all, country-style music,' he said graciously. 'We cannot expect the skills of the court here.'

Masachika bowed his head in response, trying to stay calm, wondering why Asagao was playing so badly. Had Tama, or the guardian spirits, cast a spell on her?

The small boat floated into the moonlight path, lit by two torches blazing in its stern. Three monkeys were perched in it, wearing courtiers' robes, with black silk hats on their heads. One held a fan, one a wine flask, and the third beat a rhythm on a small drum.

The boat nudged against the shore and the monkeys stepped out gracefully. They walked on their hind legs towards Aritomo and bowed to the ground in his direction. Then they turned to the south and bowed to the guests, and to the north, to the musicians.

Three acrobats came out of the darkness, tumbling across the mat in a series of cartwheels and somersaults. They seized a monkey each and threw them into the air. The monkeys landed nimbly on the men's shoulders and then leaped sideways from shoulder to shoulder, as if they were being juggled.

Something in the music changed, as if the lute had stopped resisting the player. Masachika heard Aritomo gasp in surprise. He followed his gaze to Asagao. Somehow, when they weren't looking, she had changed lutes. She was now holding one of rare beauty, its cherrywood frame and mother-of-pearl inlay gleaming in the torchlight. And music poured from it, almost celestial in its purity and perfection, leaving even Asagao open-mouthed with amazement.

The bird, perched somewhere unseen, sang in harmony with it.

For a few moments the audience watched and listened, transfixed, not sure if it was some magic trick or if they were witnessing a miracle.

Aritomo looked from the lute to the acrobats and back again. Then he was on his feet, his face white, his eyes blazing.

'Arrest them,' he said, trying to speak forcefully, but failing. His voice was a croak. 'Seize them immediately.'

'Lord?' Masachika said, bewildered.

'That is Genzo – the Imperial lute that has been lost since the rebellion. One of those young men is Yoshimori!'

13

TAMA

Once she had seen that the food was prepared and everything was running smoothly, Tama slipped away to her room. She performed all her tasks with a detached tenderness, knowing each one was for the last time. Haru alone noticed her leave, and rose to follow her, but Tama made a sign to her to stay where she was. Haru would try to dissuade her, and she was determined not to be turned away from her purpose.

The house was empty. All of them, servants, maids, guards, were on the lake shore, attending to guests, hoping to see the performers. A few lamps had been lit, and their flames burned steadily in the still air. She glanced almost indifferently at the cypress floors, each perfect plank selected by her, at the silk wall hangings and all the valuable carvings and vases that she had chosen and had displayed discreetly throughout the house. She marvelled that all she had once loved so much now meant nothing to her.

The main rooms of the house faced south and east. The room in which she lived was on the northwest side. The moonlight did not penetrate it, but the shutters had not been closed and the shadows the moon threw hovered in the garden. Moths were fluttering around the lamp flame and she could hear the thin whining of mosquitoes. From the garden came the melancholy chirping of insects that had only days to live.

But even that is longer than I have.

She went to her writing desk and found her ink stone and brush. There was still enough water in the dropper to wet the stone. She took out a few sheets of paper, enfolded in a silk cloth, and unwrapped them, shaking out the fragments of rue and aloewood that had been placed among them. Everything was attacked by insects, nothing was exempt from the universal rule of death. The only courageous act was to snatch control from death itself, to decide the time and manner of one's own departure. The thought made her smile.

I will compose a poem on that, but first I will write my testament so that no one misunderstands my reasons.

Matsutani no Tama, daughter of Tadahise, wife of Kiyoyori and Masachika . . .

She felt a slight movement in the air beside her.

'What is Matsutani Lady doing?'

'Is she getting ready to kill herself?'

'She has to, she made us a vow.'

'So why doesn't she get on with it?'

Tama said, 'I am writing a few things down first.' She was glad they were there with her. 'Then, I promise you, I will not hesitate.'

'We can trust Matsutani Lady.'

'Not like Matsutani Lord, so-called.'

'He's a liar.'

'Yes, he tells lies.'

'I know he does,' Tama said. 'I know all his faults. I loved him despite them. Maybe I still love him . . . now, please be quiet so I can think clearly.'

There were a few moments of silence then one of them – she still could not tell them apart, but she thought it might be Hidarisama, as he usually spoke first – said in a sulky voice:

'I feel like throwing things.'

'Oh, so do I!'

'Let's go throw things at Matsutani Lord.'

'So-called.'

'No,' Tama said firmly. 'The throwing must not start again. Not until after I am dead. Then you can do what you like.'

She wrote swiftly, putting down her reasons for dying, on this night, by her own hand. Not only Matsutani's unfaithfulness to her, but his willingness to betray Lord Aritomo and the secrets he had kept from him; the intrigue with Lady Natsue; Kiyoyori's daughter, Hina; Akihime's son.

There, that should condemn him, she thought with mingled satisfaction and sorrow. A whisper came from beside her.

'How will she do it?'

'With her knife. She is taking it out now.'

'Oh good, I want to see blood.'

'Oh, so do I!'

Tama felt the blade with her thumb. A thin strip of blood sprang out of her skin. She let a few drops fall on a new sheet of paper on which she wrote.

At the Shirakawa barrier,
The one I desired awaited me.
I called him back.
We lay together in the cattail grasses.
He gave me life's dew. I gave him death's.

'Make sure Lord Aritomo reads these,' she said, laying aside the brush and taking up the dagger. Without hesitation she put it to her throat and, leaning forward so her own weight helped her hand, cut fiercely from left to right. She felt the sudden shock in her nerves, her body's realisation that a catastrophe had taken place. Her blood felt warm on her hands.

As she fell forward she heard music, so beautiful it dealt her a further shock.

It is the Enlightened One coming for me.

Then she just had time to realise it was a lute, playing by the lakeside. Could it be Asagao who was so talented? Tears of envy and regret came to her eyes, and she wept for her own passing from this world.

14

MASACHIKA

Masachika could not believe his good fortune. The promised surprise was far greater than he could have imagined. Within moments the acrobats were surrounded. The monkeys leaped away, screaming in shock and fear. The musicians were seized, their instruments taken from them and thrown into a pile, except for the lute, which was carried reverently to Lord Aritomo.

It still played exuberantly as though there was nothing to fear, nothing to regret.

Aritomo looked at it without speaking. A murmur began to run through the watching crowd. *It is the Emperor! It is the Emperor!* One by one the servants fell to their knees.

As Aritomo reached out to touch the lute, warriors ran to get their weapons. Aritomo turned his gaze on the acrobats.

'Bring the two young ones to me,' he commanded and when they had been forced to their knees before him said, 'One of you is the son of the rebel, Momozono. Which is it?'

They exchanged a swift look in which Masachika thought he saw recognition, acceptance.

'I am!' the shorter one said defiantly.

Masachika knew he was lying. It was obvious to him which was Yoshimori; he was surprised he had not recognised him before. Without knowing it he had brought Yoshimori to Aritomo, and Asagao and her lute had revealed him. *Tama will forgive me everything now!*

'It is the taller one, lord,' he said.

'Yes, I think so too. Well, we will execute them both. Prepare the ground. You may carry out the act yourself. I cannot praise you highly enough, Masachika. You have done what no one else could do. First the Autumn Princess, now the false pretender. Name your reward. I will give you half the realm.'

'I desire nothing but to serve you,' Masachika replied. 'I will fetch my sword.'

As he went towards the house he thought he heard Asagao calling his name, but he ignored her. He would have to let her go now; he would not be able to save her. He wanted above all to find Tama and tell her the news.

At the threshold Haru met him. He could not see her clearly but something in her face, her posture brought him to a halt.

'Don't go inside,' she said.

'What is wrong? I must fetch my sword and speak to my wife, but I must hurry. Lord Aritomo is waiting.'

'Lady Tama is dead. There is a great deal of blood.'

'I don't believe you! Let me see her!'

'You should not go inside. The guardian spirits are in there. They told me to take these papers to Lord Aritomo.'

Masachika made a grab at them. 'Give them to me! I command you as your lord!'

She evaded him. 'I never served you, Masachika. My husband and I served Lord Kiyoyori.'

He was taller than she was and much stronger. She was made confused and slow by shock. He was about to overpower her and take the papers from her when the two young werehawks swooped down, striking at him with their beaks and talons. He let go of the woman to protect his face and Haru ran into the garden towards the lake shore.

Masachika hesitated for a moment but decided the most important thing was to get his sword. He stepped into the house, took it from the rack inside the entrance and drawing it said, 'I command you to return to the gateposts.'

There was a long moment of silence and then one of the spirits said, 'Who's that?'

'So-called Matsutani Lord.'

'The liar?'

'Yes, the liar and the traitor.'

'We don't have to do what he says anymore!'

'No, never again!'

'And can we throw things now?'

'Yes! Yes!'

The first thing they threw was a lamp. It fell near Masachika spilling oil on the matting. A little flicker of flame began to grow from it.

'Tama!' Masachika called. 'Tama, come out!'

'Matsutani Lady is dead.'

'She was brave.'

'Not like so-called Matsutani Lord,' they said together.

Their voices echoed after him as he ran from the house, sword in hand.

The crackle of burning followed him, the air became heavy with smoke.

Matsutani Lady is dead.

She had sworn to kill herself and she had kept her word but why now? Why had she done it when his fortune was at its peak? They could have shared everything together. Asagao was already as dead to him. But could Tama really have betrayed him? He had to get the papers before Aritomo read them.

The moon was now directly overhead, its light shimmering on the still surface of the lake, on the swords of the warriors, showing clearly the two young men kneeling on the sand.

Their hands had been bound roughly behind them. The shorter one looked from side to side, obviously very afraid, but Yoshimori was quite calm, his face turned upwards, his lips moving slightly as if he were praying. The monkeys had sought refuge with the older acrobats and were clinging to them, all except one who kept running to Yoshimori wailing like a human child. He shook his head at it, trying to gesture that it should go back to the others, and then resumed his silent prayer.

Asagao saw Masachika and called his name again. She was in a huddle with the acrobats and musicians. Armed warriors had formed two circles, one around them, the other around Aritomo and the young men, keeping the crowd back. He saw Haru struggling to get through them, waving the papers, and he could hear her voice, shouting to Lord Aritomo to listen to her.

She had not yet reached Aritomo. Masachika felt a surge of relief and then a thud of excitement in his belly. He was going to execute the Emperor of the Eight Islands. He would never be overlooked again; his name would never be forgotten. He might not have killed a single animal in the hunt, but the greatest prize would be his.

He strode towards Aritomo. The warriors parted at his approach. He saw wonder and admiration in their eyes.

'I am ready, lord,' he said, holding Jinan aloft.

Flames seemed to crackle along the blade, as a fireball shot into the air from the house. The three werehawks could be seen in its light, swirling above the roof.

'The house is on fire!' Aritomo cried. 'What is happening? Is it the work of those guardian spirits I heard before?'

Masachika said, 'I am here. Let us act immediately.'

Aritomo did not reply to this but said, 'Have the spirits escaped?'

'Don't worry about them! I can control them. We must not delay.'

'But the house is burning. Where is your wife?'

Haru had forced her way after him and shrieked in reply, 'She is dead, Lord Aritomo. She took her own life and she left this testament. You must read it at once!'

Aritomo heard her finally, and turned towards her. Before Masachika could intercept he had taken the papers and entrusted them to one of his warriors. The heat was growing intense and sparks and ash were falling around them.

'We cannot stay here,' Aritomo said. 'If Lady Tama is indeed dead I will do her the honour of reading this later. But now I must make all haste to get away, for I believe this place is accursed. Masachika, you must stay, subdue the spirits, save your house if you can, and bury your wife. I will see you in Miyako.'

'But the execution . . .' Masachika said, Jinan still in his hand, ready.

'It will take place in public in Miyako. That will put an end to the rumours and the unrest.' Aritomo looked around at his elated warriors. 'Secure the prisoners and prepare to leave immediately.' Then he could not prevent himself from giving a great shout of triumph.

'I have Yoshimori and I will live forever!'

15

HINA

Hina stood motionless. She wondered if she would ever move again. The two arrows still quivered in the boar's flesh, one in its throat, one in its back.

Chika was lying next to it, crumpled, bloody, his sightless eyes staring upwards.

She heard a voice behind her ask, 'Are you hurt?'

Could it be Take? So one of the arrows was his. Whose was the other?

Her heart, along with everything around her – the rustling leaves, the dappled sunlight, the chirruping birds – seemed to pause. She held her breath. Figures were moving out from the trees. The sunlight was behind them and she could only make out their shapes, as if they were shadows falling on a screen.

She saw the antlered outline of the man–deer.

Take said again, 'Lady, are you hurt?'

'No.' She could not take her eyes off the approaching group. She hardly registered the fact that Take had returned or questioned how he had got there. She heard him set another arrow to his bow.

'Don't shoot!' she cried.

'Do you know them?'

'It is Shikanoko, your father.'

A strange-shaped wolf-like animal walked on one side of him, and at his other shoulder an old silver white stallion.

'Nyorin,' Hina whispered, and tears began to flow down her cheeks.

There were three men on horseback, two wearing black silk coverings across their faces, showing only their eyes. The third also had a scarf wound round his head, but it was a dark red colour, madder-dyed. Behind him, his arms round his waist, was the fourth man. He made a half-wave towards them, and slid from the horse's back. He went swiftly to Chika and knelt beside him

Hina did not think she knew him, but Take returned the greeting eagerly.

Pushing past the group came another white horse, black tail and mane, its head high, its eyes huge. It gave a shrill neigh and cantered up to Hina, stopping directly in front of her and lowering its head to breathe in her face.

'Tan?' she said wonderingly, put her arms round his neck and laid her cheek against his smooth coat. She could feel his heartbeat.

When she stepped back, tears filled the horse's dark eyes and streaked his cheeks. She put out her hand to wipe them away, and then touched the salty wetness on her own cheeks.

'This is your twin,' she said to Take. 'You and he were born on the same day.' Then she dared to look at Shikanoko, who was now standing within arm's reach. 'I suppose Risu is dead?' she said. She could think of nothing else to say.

'She died years ago. We buried her in the mountains.'

His voice had hardly changed. She would have known it anywhere. She had heard it in her dreams for years.

'Lady Hina,' he said, speaking more formally, and dropped to one knee before her, bowing his antlered head.

'You do not have to bow to me,' she cried. She put out one hand and touched the broken antler. She felt something spark beneath her fingers as if the air were full of lightning. She closed both hands around the polished bones, hardly noticing the flesh sear. Her tears fell for his humility, for the pain he had suffered and all he had endured. She lifted with both hands. For a moment it seemed she was trying to move an immense weight, rooted in the earth, and then, as her tears fell more freely, the heaviness dissolved and the mask floated, of its own accord, away from Shikanoko's face.

He cried out, from pain or surprise, she could not tell. She saw the grey–white colour of the skin across his forehead, the tangled beard on his cheeks. His eyes blinked in the sudden intense light. His lips looked chapped and dry. He covered his face with his palms.

She knelt, still holding the mask, looking at its lacquered face as it became lifeless. It had been so easy, so quick, yet she knew something momentous had happened. 'What shall I do with it?'

He took a bag, many layered, brocade, from his waist and held it open. It seemed too small to contain the mask yet it slipped inside from her hands and he tied the cords.

She wanted to take his hands and look deep into his eyes, but he would not meet her gaze.

'I have worn the mask for over twelve years,' he said. 'I hardly remember what I was like before. I no longer know how to look at the world without it.'

He seemed physically affected, almost on the verge of fainting. The two men in the black face coverings dismounted, gave their horses' reins to the red-scarfed one, and came to Shikanoko, kneeling beside him, embracing him. None of them spoke, as if they did not yet understand what the removal of the mask would mean.

Hina stood and stepped back, confused by so many emotions she could not speak. Was that all that was going to happen? Why had he not taken her in his arms? *I love him*, she thought, *but he does not love me.*

The man with the red scarf tethered the horses, and began to uncover his head. Hina saw he was clean shaven, and grinning at her. When he spoke she realised it was a woman.

'Don't you recognise me, lady? And can this young man really be little Take? When I last saw you, you were a babe in arms. Lady Hina was jumping into the lake with you! You were both thought to be drowned.'

'Bara?' Hina said, hardly believing it.

'No longer Bara, lady. I changed my name. Now it is Ibara. I have become as sharp and prickly as a thorn.'

There were too many people, Hina thought, too many cross currents, from the past, from the future. She took a few more steps backwards and found herself standing next to Take, who still had the arrow set to his bowstring and who had not ceased staring at Shikanoko.

She turned to look at him, and saw he was wearing a blue jacket, and bearskin chaps. His huge bow looked ancient but his sword was newly fashioned. There was something outlandish about him as though he had come from another world.

'How did you get here? Where have you been?'

'A tengu dropped me here,' he replied lightly. 'Just in time too!'

'You saved my life,' she said.

'I did not know whether to aim at the man or the boar,' he said. 'I did not know which was the greater danger to you.'

'Poor Chika,' she said, trembling as she recalled his hands on her. 'Who was he?'

'I knew him when I was a child.' She did not want to say any more about him.

Tan rubbed his head gently on her shoulder. Nyorin also approached, whinnying at her. Standing between the two white stallions she felt their power, their steadfastness.

'Shikanoko!' she called.

He raised his head and looked at her. His eyes were already accustomed to the light but his face still wore a fragile, vulnerable look.

'Do this one thing for me and then I will never ask anything of you again.'

He rose and came towards her. 'What do you mean? My life is yours to command, however you wish.'

'This is your son, Takeyoshi. I have looked after him since he was born. Now you must promise to take care of him.' And then she added, in a low voice, 'His mother was Akihime, the Autumn Princess.'

Take dropped to his knees. 'Sir . . . Father . . . I offer you my sword. It was forged for me by the tengu, Tadashii, who was one of my teachers. The other was your companion, Master Mu.'

Mu took the blade and examined it eagerly. 'It's a good one,' he exclaimed. 'A brother to mine, which was also made by tengu.'

'And this is the bow, Ameyumi, the Rain Bow, that we recovered,' Take said, tentatively, standing and holding it out to Shikanoko.

He took it, gazing at it in wonder. 'Ameyumi! I remember it from my childhood. It was lost when my father died in the north. And you can shoot, with a bow this size, and so accurately!'

'You must keep it,' Take said.

Shikanoko handed the bow back to him. 'No, it is fitting that it should be yours. I have its echo, Kodama.' He reached out and touched Take's face. 'To meet you after all these years is more than

I could have ever hoped for! I hope we will never be parted.' He looked around. 'But where is Yoshimori?'

'He went with the acrobats,' Hina replied. 'They have gone to Matsutani to perform for Lord Aritomo, on the orders of Masachika, my uncle.'

Tan pawed the ground and let out a shrill neigh.

'Why did he do that?' Take cried. 'Why put himself in such danger?'

'He does not know who he is,' Hina replied. 'Or rather, he knows, but he chooses not to admit it. He is the Emperor, he goes where he wants to go.'

'And we must follow him,' Shikanoko said. 'Ibara, let Chika's horse carry him. Takeyoshi can ride with me on Nyorin. And, Lady Hina, I believe Tan will be happy to carry you.'

'No one else rides him, but Lady Hina can.' Ibara was smiling, but then her expression changed as she went to Chika and began to arrange his clothes, binding his own sash round the terrible wound. Mu helped her and between them they slung the corpse across the tall brown horse, soothing it as it shuddered and rolled its eyes.

Shikanoko lifted Hina onto Tan's back. She felt her body longing to soften at the touch of his hands, but she tried to make her will fierce against him.

'You know who this horse is, don't you?' he said.

'Risu's foal. I saw him being born – on the same day as your son.'

'But over and above that,' Shikanoko said, gently, 'the spirit within him is not a horse, but that of your father, Lord Kiyoyori.'

Tan's ears twitched and he whinnied as if he were laughing for joy.

'I called him back from where he walked on the banks of the river of death. Someone who owed him a great debt had taken his place on the ferry that plies between this world and the next. Your father was able to return to continue his struggle to restore the true Emperor.'

Hina leaned forward and clasped her arms round the horse's neck, laying her head on the thick, black mane. 'Now I understand why I loved you so much,' she whispered.

•

Often Take tired of riding and ran ahead. Hina wondered what the tengu's teaching had done for him to make him so tireless and so fast. Even when the horses cantered, as they frequently did, for their riders were all seized by the same sense of urgency, he could outstrip them. He had grown to his adult height and no longer had the slender limbs of a boy.

Shikanoko could not take his eyes off him, watched him almost hungrily, but he hardly looked at Hina, nor did he speak much to her though they often rode side by side.

As they approached Matsutani, and her eyes took in the scenes of her childhood from which she had been exiled for so many years, she became almost feverish. Her eyes glowed and her colour was heightened.

Ibara said to Mu, 'She was a beautiful child – I always imagined that was what saved her life – and now as a woman she is unparalleled. But maybe I am biased, having cared for her like my own child.'

'She also has wisdom,' Mu replied, 'which gives her a rare inner beauty.' He sighed. 'Ah well, things will work out or they will not.'

Ibara, who was sitting in front of him, jabbed him in the ribs with her elbow. 'Sometimes we are called on to make them work out, my friend. Our lord may have been released from the mask, but his eyes have not yet been opened to what's in front of him.'

Hina could hear what they were saying. The thought that Shikanoko probably could too made her colour rise further.

'What will we find at Matsutani?' she wondered aloud. 'Will Lord Aritomo still be there? Will Yoshimori be safe? And what about Haru, Chika's mother? Could she still be alive? What a terrible thing, to be bringing her son home, dead.'

Shikanoko said, 'We are very close now, no more than an hour or so away. I'll send the Burnt Twins ahead to see how things stand. Nagatomo was brought up at Kumayama, and is familiar with the whole area. Eisei has been to Matsutani and knows both Aritomo and Masachika by sight.'

'Why are they called the Burnt Twins?' Hina asked, eager to keep him talking, but also genuinely curious about his loyal companions.

'They were both forced to wear the mask – it seared their skin. Out of their suffering came companionship and love. They are twinned souls.'

'It burned my hands too,' she said, glancing at his face, which was slowly returning to a normal colour. He had shaved away the beard. 'Yet it did not burn you?'

'It was made for me. Only I can wear it, but in the encounter with the Prince Abbot some of his dying power condemned it to fuse to my face. I lived half-man, half-deer ever since, until you released me.'

'It is so powerful,' she said, remembering what Chika had told her.

'Powerful and dangerous,' he replied. 'So much that I fear using it. I hope I never have to place it on my face again.' He stopped abruptly and after a few moments said, 'You were able to do what no one else could, take it from me. But I am sorry about your hands.'

'They are healing fast,' she said, not quite truthfully for they were still painful. It was lucky she could ride Tan without reins.

Now he will say something, she thought, but it seemed he felt he had already said too much. He turned in the saddle, beckoned to Nagatomo and swiftly gave him instructions.

After Nagatomo and Eisei had left, the others dismounted to wait for their return. The horses grazed. Shikanoko went a little way off and sat in meditation, the wolf-like creature at his side.

Hina went in the other direction, wondering if his thoughts were as distracted as hers. Take was helping Mu and Ibara make a small fire and prepare food. Then the three of them began to spar with poles they cut from saplings in the surrounding forest.

Hina was determined not to move before Shikanoko did. Slowly her mind stilled and she succeeded in dismissing all thoughts of him. Instead she concentrated on Yoshi, holding him up to Heaven, praying for his safety.

Time crawled past, as though the whole world had slowed and thickened. Around the end of the afternoon, when the shadows were lengthening and the air growing colder, the wolf-like creature got to its feet and walked stiffly to the path, gazing in the direction the Burnt Twins had taken.

'They are returning,' Ibara said, lowering her pole, sidestepping Take's final lunge and laughing as it unbalanced him.

Eisei rode first, Nagatomo behind him, his horse slower because of its extra burden, a woman who clung to his waist.

Eisei called out, 'Matsutani has burned to the ground. Aritomo has already left for the capital. The place was deserted except for this woman.'

When Nagatomo dismounted and lifted her down, Hina saw it was Haru.

It was years since she had seen her, and Haru had turned into an old woman.

The birds had begun their evening chorus and, echoing through it, Hina heard a sharp call, echoed by another. Her heart seemed to stop and painfully start again. Was it Kon? If Kon had abandoned Yoshi, it could only mean he was dead.

Haru walked tentatively towards her, frowning as though she thought she knew her, eyes fixed on her.

Hina wanted to prevent her seeing her son's body and called to Ibara to move the horse, but her intention had the opposite effect, drawing Haru's gaze in that direction.

The woman gave a shriek, and stumbled towards the corpse, which was hanging head down across the brown horse. She knelt in front of it, touching the cold swollen lips and the limp hands.

'What happened?' she said, turning to Hina. 'Who was responsible?'

'He was killed by a boar,' Hina said. 'It was charging at me.'

'He saved your life? At least he died well. What happened to the boar, did it live?'

'Shikanoko and his son killed it,' Hina replied. She would not disabuse Haru of her belief, for Chika had been trying to save her life in his own way. Now his fate seemed unutterably sad. She wanted to weep for him and his mother.

'Shikanoko?' Haru looked around wildly. 'Shikanoko is here? We thought he must be dead.'

She saw him as he stood and moved towards them. 'You have a son?' she cried. 'Why is your son alive while mine is dead?'

She fell to the ground, sobbing, tearing at the earth with her hands.

'Haru,' Shikanoko said, his voice both stern and gentle. 'Chika is dead. We have brought his body back to bury wherever it pleases you. But there is no time for any excesses of grief. Where is the Emperor?'

At that moment two birds flew down with a clatter of wings and landed on Shikanoko's shoulder. Hina knew them at once as werehawks. For an instant, she noticed, Shikanoko flinched, but the birds were not attacking him. They bowed their heads and then whispered in his ear.

'Where did you come from?' he said. 'Who brought you to Matsutani?'

They replied excitedly in their grating voices. Shikanoko said, 'Yoshimori has been taken to Miyako. Kon has followed him. We must go after them.'

The birds squawked in approval and then muttered something else.

'I suppose you are right,' Shika replied, and then addressed the others. 'I must deal with the guardian spirits at Matsutani. We will go there first.'

16

MASACHIKA

*I*should take my own life before I am shamed publicly. No, I gave
Yoshimori to Aritomo, he will forgive me anything. Tama is dead.
If only I knew what she wrote, to what extent she betrayed me.
Maybe he will not read the papers at all. Why should he believe an
old woman like Haru? I will follow him to Miyako. I will carry out
the execution. Once Yoshimori is dead Daigen will be Emperor and
his mother already favours me. Tama is dead.

All these thoughts raced through Masachika's mind as he watched
Aritomo and his warriors leave and the house burn to the ground.
Some of the servants made futile efforts to fetch water from the lake
to douse the flames but the spirits threw fireballs at them, followed
by volleys of burning utensils and furniture. Eventually everyone
gave up and ran away.

He spent the night in the pavilion where he had lain with
Asagao a short time ago. When day broke he saw the house
was completely destroyed. Whatever had remained of Tama was
reduced to ashes. Why had he treated her so badly? Why had he lied
to her? He had satisfied his own desire even though it had wounded

and humiliated her. They had had everything and he had smashed it. She and Matsutani had been given to him once, then ripped away by his father's cruel decision, then restored to him. She had made the estate beautiful, she had been its heart. He was as guilty of her death as if he himself had plunged the knife into her throat.

He would have thrown himself howling to the ground in grief, but the sight of Haru approaching made him restrain himself. He hid himself away, unable to face anyone, least of all her.

Haru knelt in front of the smouldering ruin, her eyes not leaving the destruction, her lips moving. There was no sound other than the two werehawks, which from time to time gave their piercing call. The spirits had fallen silent.

A little later two horsemen rode up. He was afraid they might be Aritomo's men, sent back to arrest him, but he saw the black silk coverings over their faces and recognised one of them as Eisei the monk. It was like a hallucination from the past. He remembered that Eisei and the other one who had been similarly disfigured had ridden off with Shikanoko. Did their presence now mean Shikanoko himself was nearby?

The two men dismounted and spoke to Haru. Then they rode away with her. The werehawks followed.

When they had gone he left the pavilion and knelt in Haru's place. He could not decide what to do. It was as though the life force that had animated him had been abruptly shut off. All his ambition, lust and greed had been reduced to ashes along with his house and his wife. Tama had destroyed him but he did not resent or hate her for it. He admired her courage more than ever and he knew he had never loved anyone else.

'Forgive me,' he whispered. 'You were everything to me and I did not know it.' Tears burst from his eyes then.

'What should I do?' he said more loudly. He felt the spirits' presence.

'You could kill yourself,' came the mocking reply.

'But we don't care if you do or not.'

'Live or die, it's all the same to us.'

'You no longer matter.'

He drew Jinan and laid it on the ground beside him. Last night he had been prepared to take an Emperor's life with it. Now he could not even use it against himself. One part of his mind kept niggling at him that he would survive; he always did; he would find a way out. Eventually he decided to listen to it, mainly because he lacked the courage to kill himself.

Jinan: Shikanoko had given it to him, in exchange for Jato, and he had never seen another sword like it. Only its name had displeased him, reminding him as it did of his own status as second son. Yet he was alive and his older brother was dead, just as Aritomo would soon be dead. None of his rules and rituals, his codes for the way of the warrior, his ideals of honour and courage, could save the great lord from the illness that was killing him. *I will outlive them all*, he promised himself. He got to his feet and picked up his sword. The air smelled of smoke and beneath it another stench, as the piles of dead animals began to rot.

'Farewell,' he said silently to Tama. He skirted the lake and began to walk along the track in the direction of Kuromori. It was his childhood home; he had lost it and won it back. He would return there and see if anything could be salvaged of his life.

But his spirits failed to recover and he was thinking again of using Jinan to end his life when he heard a twig break, then another, the trample and splash of horses' feet ahead of him. He left the path swiftly and hid himself in the undergrowth.

A group of people on horseback were picking their way along the stream. An ungainly creature ran in the lead, its head swinging from side to side, its nostrils flaring. It was the fake wolf he had seen years ago with Shikanoko. It caught his scent and stopped dead, looking in his direction and growling.

Several horses followed in single file, the first a white black-maned stallion with no bridle, carrying a woman. It halted and neighed loudly. Masachika remembered again his dream about his brother, Kiyoyori, and a foal. He knew it was the same horse, full grown.

A rider on a brown horse pushed past the stallion, dismounted, drew his sword and approached the bushes where Masachika was concealed.

'Come out and show yourself!' The voice was curiously high, like a woman's.

He came out, his hand on Jinan. Haru spoke from the rear of the line. 'It is Masachika.'

She rode behind the man with the black face covering whom he had seen earlier and Eisei followed them, his ruined face uncovered. Then came Shikanoko himself, on an older white horse, surely the stallion Masachika had found at Nishimi and sent to Ryusonji. He looked back at the black-maned horse, and saw the young woman properly. Her expression chilled him to the depths of his being. He felt she saw through him and judged him, and so did the horse. It must be Hina. If she and Shikanoko had come a day earlier, surely Aritomo would have forgiven him everything.

He could hardly bring himself to care. He said, more from habit than any real conviction, 'Aritomo has left. He must be taking Yoshimori to the capital. An attack is being launched even now, by sea, on Rakuhara. Take me to Kuromori and I will help you plan a counterattack to rescue the Emperor.'

Shikanoko's gaze swept over him. Masachika quailed before the expressionless eyes. Shikanoko said merely, 'Ride on,' and as the others obeyed, 'Ibara! He is yours!'

The black-maned horse gave a loud cry so full of sorrow and anger that Masachika felt another wave of grief engulf him. Within moments all but two of them had disappeared down the track. He called out helplessly, 'Shikanoko! I could have helped you. We are on the same side now.'

Ibara was the one who had first spoken to Masachika. She was raising her sword. 'Go ahead, Mu,' she said over her shoulder, to the smaller man who had remained with her. 'I don't need you.'

'I wouldn't dare suggest you do,' the other replied. 'But I like to watch you in action, so I'll wait till you've finished.'

'It won't take long,' the woman said.

'I see you are going to kill me,' Masachika said. 'You don't know how great a favour you are doing me. But can you tell me why?'

'You don't remember me, do you?'

He searched his memory, but there had been so many women. He had forgotten all their faces, except Tama's.

'My name is Ibara. And the groom you murdered? Have you forgotten him?'

Now he was able to place her. 'The man who guided me over the mountains,' he said. 'You were at Nishimi. You were mad with grief. I spared your life.' It seemed almost humorous. He could have killed her then, all those years ago. Now that the end was so near his heart had lightened.

'His name was Saburo,' she said, as stern as the lord of Hell in judgement. 'We loved each other. You killed him, you caused the death of the Autumn Princess, and because of you my lord, Yukikuni no Takaakira, was forced to take his own life.'

The dead crowded round him, clamouring for justice.

'Kill me now,' he pleaded. 'Be quick!'

'With pleasure,' Ibara said.

His eyes were playing tricks on him. It seemed to be Tama standing before him with the sword. He felt profoundly grateful to her. She would punish him and then she would forgive him, be his guide across the Three Streamed River of Death as she had been in life.

The sword swept. He felt the blow but no pain.

'Tama!' he whispered as he fell.

17

ARITOMO

Once back in Miyako, Aritomo moved swiftly to secure the capital. Every road into it was heavily guarded. His warriors roamed the streets day and night, arresting anyone acting suspiciously and rounding up all those known to have had Kakizuki connections. The Imperial lute, Genzo, was locked away. The prisoners were confined in cells in Ryusonji.

He waited anxiously for Masachika for he was eager to conduct the execution. After several days passed, and Masachika still did not return he began to wonder what could have happened to delay him. Only then did he remember the testament the woman had handed over. He issued orders for it to be brought to him.

He read it in mounting disbelief at all Masachika had concealed from him: Kiyoyori's daughter was alive and was probably Lady Fuji's murderer; Akihime had had a son who also survived. Who were these people, weak and insignificant, women, children, who were undermining his rule? Who were the riverbank people who had concealed them for so long? Their existence was an affront to him. They lived beyond his regulations, they obeyed none of his laws. He set about interrogating and punishing them, starting with Asagao, Masachika's woman who had played the lute. She was only the first of them to die under torture.

It was no great surprise that Masachika had been ready to betray him: he had never trusted him. More unexpected and insulting was the Empress's plan to supplant him. The only thing that comforted him in his shock and rage was his secret: he would outlive them all. What if he did not sleep at night or eat in the day; what if his body seemed to be failing him at the time when he most needed his strength, his flesh melting from his bones; what if when he dozed briefly from exhaustion he was assailed by nightmares? He was not ill; these symptoms were the price to be paid for immortality, the way the body learned to cheat death. He continued to drink the lacquer tea and the water from the well at Ryusonji.

He let a day and a night pass after reading the testament while he reflected on all its implications. Masachika would never come back to the capital. Either he had already killed himself or more likely he had fled. Aritomo vowed to track him down. The Empress and her son would also have to be dealt with, but how would he rebuke them? He would separate them, for a start. The Emperor must move immediately into the new palace. Maybe Lady Natsue could be exiled. Now Aritomo held Yoshimori, she would have to stop her ridiculous plotting against him.

Arinori's name had been mentioned several times in the interrogations, as the protector of Lady Yayoi, who had turned out to be Kiyoyori's daughter, the one who had found her at the temple and procured the privilege of being her first lover. Aritomo longed to question him, but Arinori had sailed to the west leading the attack against the Kakizuki. No word had come from him. Aritomo did not believe the surprise attack could fail; he was impatient to hear of the annihilation of his enemies. But troubling signs began to manifest themselves.

Late the following afternoon when he went to Ryusonji a white dove inexplicably dropped dead from the sky, in front of his horse, feathers fluttering after it like miniature Miboshi banners. As he crossed a bridge, he heard a voice say, distinctly, 'The white one is spoiled. Chuck it away.' In the cloister he heard another voice, accompanied by a lute, singing a ballad about the fall of the Miboshi and the return of Kiyoyori.

It was Sesshin whom Aritomo had had confined in a room in his own palace. Wondering how he had escaped, he told two of his men to bring the old man to him. They returned, one of them carrying the lute, the other holding Sesshin by the arm. Sesshin again seemed to have forgotten who Aritomo was.

'What did those words mean?' Aritomo demanded. 'Were they a prophecy?'

'The past and the future are one,' Sesshin mumbled. 'Sometimes I sing of one, sometimes of another. But where's my lute?'

He rambled for a while in a way no one understood, before beginning to sing again.

The dragon's child
Sleeps in the lake.
Where is his father?
Where is his sister?
When the deer's child calls
He will awaken.

He broke off suddenly and sniffed the air. 'Someone is very ill. Someone is dying. But where's my lute? Who stole my lute?'

'I am not dying,' Aritomo said in fury. 'I am like you; I will live forever. Break the lute! Destroy it!'

'Shall we kill him, lord?' asked one of the warriors, while the other smashed the lute against a column and then stamped on it.

'No!' he replied, seized by superstitious fear. 'Send him away. Banish him. Let me never hear his voice again.'

He did not wait to be announced to Lady Natsue, but burst into her apartment, pushing her ladies aside and ordering them to leave.

She sat immobile, outraged, indicating with her head that he should bow. When he did not her eyes flashed in anger. She said in an icy voice, 'I must congratulate Lord Aritomo. You have found Yoshimori. You have achieved all I asked of you. But why do you delay any further? You must execute him at once.'

'I will,' he said, and then, 'Your Majesty should know that you will not see the Matsutani Lord, Masachika, again.'

She went still and lowered her gaze.

'I don't expect him to show his face in the capital, but if he does he, too, will be executed. I don't have to tell you why but we will not discuss it further.'

When she said nothing, he went on. 'I will not be overthrown.'

She sat in silence for several moments, only a faint flush at her neck revealing her rage. Then she said, 'Where are the werehawks?'

'The werehawks?' he repeated. 'They flew away.'

'They should have flown straight back to Ryusonji, if you were unable to win their obedience. One werehawk has returned but it is older and has some gold feathers. It sits on the roof above the prisoners' cells and calls in an intolerable way. The other two must have gone to someone else – the only person who could control them is one who destroyed my brother, the deer's child, Shikanoko. You will not be safe until he is dead.'

Sesshin's song came back to him: *When the deer's child calls, He will awaken.*

'Shikanoko will come here,' Aritomo said. 'And I will be ready for him. I have no more to say to you now. You will have to move away from the capital. I will inform you where that is to be. Let your son know this: his position is upheld by me. He may be the Emperor, but I hold all the power.'

Dusk was falling as he left. He saw the werehawk keeping watch on the roof and could not resist the impulse to listen to the prisoners, hungry to know all he could of Yoshimori before he put an end to his life. He told his men to go on to the gate and went silently to the outside of the cell.

At first there was only silence, then he heard one say, not Yoshimori, the other one whose name he had been told was something ridiculous like Sarumaru, 'It's true, isn't it? You really are the Emperor?'

'No!' Yoshimori said. 'It's all a mistake.'

'Then why does the lute play for you?' Saru demanded.

'I don't know,' Yoshimori said quietly.

'Don't lie to me,' the other exclaimed. 'Not after all we have been to each other. I was there on the boat when we pulled Yayoi and Take from the water. It played then. And that crazy bird, Kon, that's why it follows you, isn't it? Where did you come from?'

'I hardly remember,' Yoshimori said. 'I know a young woman took me away from a burning palace and told me to pretend I was someone else. But before that everything is confused. I don't know if it is a memory or a dream. I was carried everywhere – I wanted to run, but the women wouldn't let me. My father was addressed as Prince, my mother as Princess, but my real life, the one I do remember, only began shortly before I met you in the Darkwood.'

'None of it matters since they are going to kill us,' Saru said.

'Let's pray together,' Yoshimori whispered and he began the

words of a prayer Aritomo had never heard before. He shuffled closer to the door.

'Someone's coming!' Saru cried. 'Are they going to take us out and execute us now?'

Aritomo froze. After a long silence he heard Yoshimori say quietly, 'The Secret One is with us, just as the priest always told us. He will never forsake us.'

'But if you are the Emperor,' Saru said, sniffing as if through tears, 'you are descended from the gods. You are divine!'

'I don't dare think that about myself,' Yoshimori replied.

'Why are we forbidden to kill when all around us the beasts kill each other, men slaughter them in their hundreds, like in the great hunt we witnessed, and think nothing of taking human life. Even animals fight for their lives. If we were not forbidden to fight we could defend ourselves. A cornered rat has more courage than we have.'

'All living beings fear death,' Yoshimori said. 'That's why we should not inflict it on any of them. I suppose you are sorry that you found me in the forest? I am more sorry than I can say, for causing this suffering to you and all our friends.'

'I would die to save your life,' Saru said. 'You know that, don't you? Didn't I pretend to be you, when we were first seized? I would even kill to save you.'

'Better to leave it all in the hands of the Secret One,' Yoshimori said.

'I am not sure I believe in that god any longer,' Saru said in an anguish-filled voice.

'At least Kai is safe,' Yoshi said very quietly. 'That must be part of his plan, for if she had not been carrying our child she would have come with us. I don't fear my own death, but I dread hers.'

The silence deepened over the temple. The musicians had quietened. No one sang; no one screamed. It was almost raining.

A dank drizzle filled the air, and the eaves dripped with moisture. The bird called from the roof, startling Aritomo.

'That's Kon!' Saru said suddenly. 'It's still around. Why doesn't it go for help?'

'I don't think anyone can help us now,' Yoshimori said.

Aritomo waited for a long time but neither of them spoke again. He returned to his palace deeply disturbed by all he had heard. The bird might go for help? Help from whom? Kiyoyori's daughter? Shikanoko? Yoshimori and the other acrobats belonged to some hitherto unknown sect? He had an unborn child? Was Aritomo going to have to scour the Eight Islands all over again to find another supposed heir to the throne?

•

Messengers came that night, two of them, faces ashen with fear. Aritomo had the reputation of summarily executing bearers of bad news. There had been a sea battle. The Kakizuki had been fore-warned. Arinori's fleet had sailed into a trap, carried by the tide into the waiting warships. He was dead and most of his men drowned, the ships sent to the bottom of the Encircled Sea. Shortly after, others came from the opposite direction, from the east. Yukikuni no Takauji was in open rebellion and was laying siege to Minatogura.

'The pretender, Yoshimori, dies tomorrow,' Aritomo declared. Vomit rose in his throat, he tried to hold it down, but could not. Pain tore through him. For a moment he thought savagely that the messengers' deaths would ease it, but then he reminded himself he would need every man he had. The Kakizuki would certainly attempt to return to the capital. He must prepare an army to counteract and surprise them. But whom could he trust, now Arinori and Masachika were gone? Someone had betrayed his plans. There must be spies everywhere. He groaned loudly.

His attendants tried to persuade him to rest, but he could not lie down with any ease. He was dressed and ready before dawn and as he paced the floor waiting for daybreak he heard the steady splash of water from the eaves, a sound so unfamiliar for a moment he did not recognise it.

The Emperor is in the capital and it is raining.

18

HINA

Hina stood beside Tan in front of the west gate at Matsutani. It was the only part of the building still intact; the house, the pavilions, the stables and other outbuildings were smouldering ruins, charred wood, ash that was once thatch.

In their niche, among the carvings, the eyes gleamed. She had not seen them since she had left them at Nishimi, when she had fled all those years ago with Take.

'They are Sesshin's eyes, Father,' she murmured to Kiyoyori's spirit. She had fallen into the habit of telling him everything and, even when she did not put her thoughts into words, she felt he understood them. 'Do you remember when we found them on the ground after the earthquake? They make you see yourself as you really are, not as you wish you were.'

Ibara rode up behind her and dismounted. She said to Hina, 'It is done. Masachika is dead.'

The horse shuddered slightly and bowed its head three times.

'So soon after my stepmother died,' Hina said. 'In the end they were not parted for long. May they find peace together and be reborn into a better life.'

338

'You are more forgiving than me, Lady Hina. I don't know enough about her, but I hope he rots in Hell!'

Ibara's breath caught in her throat and then she said, 'Revenge is not as sweet as I thought it would be. Why should I feel regret and pity now, for all his mistakes and my own?'

'It is the eyes,' Hina said. 'Under their gaze, you see yourself without the armour of your self-regard, and in that light you can only feel regret, remorse and pity.'

Tan bowed his head and nuzzled her shoulder.

It was late afternoon, the sky was covered in clouds and the air felt damp as though rain might fall at any moment. Nagatomo and Eisei had fashioned torches from burning wood.

Shikanoko called to them, 'We must ride on. If the spirits have returned to the gateposts, let them remain there. Nothing is left for them to destroy. Aritomo and Yoshimori are more than a day ahead · of us. We have no time to waste.'

Hina thought she heard a whisper.

'Shikanoko is here!'

'I heard his voice, didn't you?'

'I did! I heard his voice!'

Hina wondered aloud, 'Should I bring the eyes?' There was nothing left for them to keep watch over and it seemed fitting that they should be with the Kudzu Vine Treasure Store and the medicine stone that she carried in her bag.

Tan nodded vigorously.

'I don't have anything to put them in,' Hina said.

'Here.' Ibara handed her a small bamboo box, empty apart from some scarlet maple leaves. 'I like to pick the leaves up, sometimes, I don't know why. Shake them out if you want to.'

'No,' Hina replied. 'They will make a fine mat to put the eyes on.'

She vaulted onto Tan's back to reach them, and as she lifted them down and placed them carefully in the box she heard a voice say, more loudly, 'Who's that?'

'It must be Kiyoyori's daughter!'

'Lady! Lady! You are back!'

'Welcome home!'

'Is Kiyoyori with her?'

'I feel he is, don't you?'

Shikanoko, a werehawk on each shoulder, rode up to the gate, calling her name. 'Lady Hina, are you ready?'

'Shikanoko!' the first voice cried.

'I knew it was you,' said the second.

'You have both been misbehaving again,' Shikanoko said sternly. 'You have destroyed the very place you were meant to guard. I should shut you up in a rock for a thousand years!'

'We didn't mean to.'

'Everything was so out of kilter and amiss.'

'Yes, amiss and awry and out of kilter.'

'The Emperor was here.'

'They were going to kill him.'

'So we saved his life, you see.'

'Then I forgive you and I bid you farewell,' Shikanoko said. 'Come, Lady Hina, Ibara.'

Hina sat on Tan's back and put the bamboo box in her bag. Ibara leaped onto her horse and called to Mu to join her.

'Don't leave us here!' one of the spirits cried.

'No, don't leave us here. Take us with you.'

'You belong here. Your master, Sesshin, placed you here,' Shikanoko said.

'There is nothing to guard here anymore.'

'We want to come with you.'

'How will you travel?' Shikanoko asked. 'You cannot just waft around disembodied for that length of time. I would need to put you in something.'

'I want to go in your sword.'

'No, I want to go in the sword.'

'I said it first, you choose something else.'

'I'll go in the bow.'

'No!' Shikanoko said. 'I don't want you in either my sword or my bow. I would never be able to rely on either of them again.'

'We will behave.'

'We promise.'

'We will protect you. Your sword will be the strongest.'

'Your bow, the most accurate.'

'Oh, very well,' Shikanoko said. 'I don't have time to argue now.'

He spoke a word of power. The air shimmered. Both Jato and Kodama took on a sudden glow as if they were lit from within. It faded slowly.

'And no chattering,' Shikanoko said, as he clicked his tongue to Nyorin to move forward.

'We'll be completely silent.'

'As silent as the grave.'

•

They had ridden a little way when Shikanoko called to Ibara to ride alongside Nyorin so he could talk to Mu.

'You said Kiku had offered to help us. We'll need him, but we have no way of getting in touch with him in time.'

'We'll ride with your message,' Ibara said eagerly.

'It takes days to get to Kitakami and then back to the capital,' Shikanoko replied.

'I wish I could summon up a tengu or fly myself,' said Mu. 'What about those birds? Can you send them?'

'They are young and untrained. I don't think they are reliable.' The birds croaked indignantly at him, one in each ear. 'They are eager to go, but even if they find their way, Kiku might not understand them. Worse, he might kill them, as you and he did Gessho's.'

'Send a sign with them; send the little fawn I gave you. Kiku will know the birds come from you. I'm sure he will be able to talk to them.'

'I suppose we must try it.' Shika took the carved fawn from the breast of his robe, pulled out a thread from the material and tied the tiny figure to the larger bird's leg.

'Go,' he said. 'Fly north. I will guide you with my mind.'

As the birds fluttered away he said to Mu, 'I have never done this before. I don't even know if it is possible.'

•

Most of the way they rode in single file, with Nyorin leading, but Tan also liked to be in front, and when the track widened, he pushed his way forward to canter alongside his father.

Despite being side by side, Shikanoko and Hina still hardly spoke. Sometimes she felt there was a depth of understanding between them, at other times he seemed remote and distant. Once or twice she caught him looking at her, with a kind of longing that made her heart jump with hope, but then he seemed to withdraw within himself, assuming his cold, distant demeanour.

As they came closer to Miyako they realised the roads were heavily guarded. Shikanoko decided to ride through the mountains, making their journey longer. Six days after they left Matsutani, they came out of the woods and saw the capital spread out below them. From that distance it looked as it always did, giving no sign that its Emperor was present or that he was alive.

The air was damp and cool. Around them the trees were in full colour, made more radiant by the dim light. They were not far from the eastern bank of the river, hidden by the thick woods that covered the slope of the mountain. Across the river, which had shrunk to a trickle during the years of drought, could be seen the five-storeyed pagoda of Ryusonji and the cedar-shingled roofs of its great halls. The temple bell sounded the sunset hour, its sonorous tone echoing from the surrounding hills and followed by other bells throughout the city.

Despite the hour and the rain, the riverbank swarmed with people. Their clothes were brightly coloured, glowing in the dusk. Some curious trick of the evening light brought out all the red and orange hues.

'It's the riverbank people,' Hina said. 'From the boats.'

'They have come to watch,' Take said beside her, his face riven with anxiety. 'We are going to rescue him, Yoshi, the Emperor? We are going to be in time?'

'Yes, tomorrow we will rescue him,' Shikanoko promised.

Mu and Ibara found a spring, lit a small smokeless fire and boiled water. Ibara washed the mud from the horses' legs and Hina took her beechwood comb and untangled Tan's mane and tail, brushing them out with her fingers. Then she did the same for Nyorin. The horses, father and son, stood as still as carvings, nose to nose, only their nostrils quivering as they exchanged breath.

Take disappeared with Nagatomo and Eisei and returned with two squirrels and a rabbit. Hina drank a little warm water, but refused food. There was some shelter under a ledge of rock and Shikanoko suggested she rest there.

'What about you?' she said. His clothes were already dark with moisture.

'I will stay awake. I have not told the others, but I lost contact with the werehawks. I don't know where they are or if they ever got to Kitakami. I must make one last effort to find them.'

'Then I will stay awake with you.'

He bowed formally to her and went a little way away, under a spreading yew whose thickly leaved branches gave some protection. She saw him remove his sword and bow and place them beside him, speaking a few words to them, and then giving each one a light pat. Then he drew his legs up under him and closed his eyes.

She closed hers. She heard the others whispering for a while. A night bird made a sudden jarring call. In the distance dogs were barking. Gen whimpered in response.

Hina's mind was empty for a long time. Then a waking dream came over her. She was riding Tan across the river. Someone waited for her there. She had never seen him, but she knew it was Lord Aritomo. She saw his disease revealed, the rotting lungs, the decaying bones.

I have to take the medicine stone to him to show him he is dying.

She opened her eyes and looked towards where Shikanoko sat. It was very dark. The fire had almost died down, only the embers gleamed. She thought he had put on the mask, thought she saw the outline of the antlers, but then she realised it was only shadows. There was a slight reflection from Gen's gemstone eyes.

Slowly the sky paled. While it was still the grey half-light just before dawn, Shikanoko stood and walked towards her. Kneeling beside her, he said, 'I saw you showing something to Lord Aritomo.'

'I saw it too. It seems I must take the medicine stone to him.'

'What's that?'

'It's something your mother gave to me.'

'My mother? When did you meet my mother?'

Hina wanted to tell him everything, but there was no time. She was gripped by fear that there would never be time, that they would die that day, before they had really spoken to each other. All she said now was, 'She asked you to forgive her.'

'Is she still alive? Where is she?'

'She died, but she saw Takeyoshi before she passed away; we were both by her side.'

His mouth closed in a tight line. He seemed to hold his breath for a long time before letting it out in a deep sigh.

'You must give me a full account after everything is over,' he said, so distant again. 'Let me see the stone.'

Hina drew it from the bag and held it out to him. He took it and looked curiously at it.

'It does not seem to be either precious or beautiful. Is it anything more than a rock?'

'If you are sick, it shows you if you will die or if you will recover,' Hina explained. 'It helped me read the Kudzu Vine Treasure Store. It is a tool in diagnosis and healing.'

'Does it reveal the time of one's death?' he said, peering closely in to it.

'If that time is close, it does.'

'Well, I see nothing,' he said, laughing as his mood changed swiftly. 'But I hope Aritomo will. We will ride side by side and show it to him.'

'I should go alone,' she said. 'I will be able to approach him.'

'Lady Hina, I would obey you in everything, but not in this. I will be at your side.'

The light was strengthening. From across the river came the werehawk's frantic call. Tan neighed loudly in response. Shikanoko ran to the edge of the trees and looked down.

He called back to the others, 'Aritomo has arrived! We can't wait any longer.'

Nagatomo was already preparing the horses. Shikanoko held out his hands. His bow flew into his right hand, his sword into his left.

'Thank you,' he said to the spirits. 'Now behave yourselves, I am depending on you!' Smiling a little, he turned to Hina. 'Are you ready, lady?'

Tan stood beside her, quivering with excitement. She put the stone back in the bag and tied it to her waist. Shikanoko lifted her onto Tan's back. The horse's coat was as smooth as silk beneath her fingers, the black mane she had combed out the night before fell over his neck like a woman's hair.

Shikanoko swung himself up onto Nyorin. 'Wait out of sight,' he said to the others. 'If we all appear at once, the guards will shoot as soon as we are within range.'

'And they won't shoot at you two?' Nagatomo said. 'You are riding into certain death!'

'I am counting on Aritomo's curiosity,' Shikanoko replied. 'If Heaven does not protect me now, then I'll know I faced its just punishment.'

'Let me go with you, Father,' Take begged.

Shikanoko looked at him with an expression of tenderness. 'If I die,' he said to Nagatomo, 'you and Eisei must escape with my son and serve him as you have served me. Go to the east, to Takauji.'

'We will, lord,' they promised, bowing their heads.

The temple gardens at Ryusonji spread around the lake, where the dragon's child slept, down to the river bank. The walls had once run down to the water's edge, too, but now the water had receded so much there was a wide gap on either side. Guards, armed with spears, had been placed here to keep back the throng of people who had been gathering since the previous night, drawn by rumours and premonitions that they were going to witness the execution of an Emperor.

It was misty, drizzling slightly, and the crowd was silent, with sombre, expectant faces.

Aritomo himself, hollow-eyed and stern, sat on a platform hastily erected in the garden between the lake and the river. A ginkgo tree nearby was shedding its golden leaves, and maples glowed red. Butterbur flowers were a brilliant yellow around rocks and at the foot of stone lanterns. The paths among the moss were raked smooth. The temple bell tolled the hour of sunrise.

The two white horses emerged out of the mist, picking their way through the shallows, the splashing of their feet louder than the flow of the river. A guard broke away from the others and ran towards them, shouting at the riders to stay back.

Hina thought she heard voices whispering, 'Shikanoko! It is Shikanoko!'

Aritomo rose to his feet. 'Seize them! They will be executed along with the pretender.'

She took the medicine stone from her bag and held it aloft. 'I have a gift for Lord Aritomo. It will reveal life and death to him.'

Her clear voice could be heard throughout the gardens. There was a murmur of surprise from the crowd. Aritomo, momentarily distracted, said, 'Let her come to me.'

Shikanoko dismounted and walked forward, the two stallions following him closely.

Aritomo called, 'Put down your weapons!'

Shikanoko took the sword from his sash and the bow from his shoulder and laid them down on the moss, along with his quiver. He lifted Hina from Tan and they both fell to their knees a few paces away from the platform.

Hina was aware that death might come at any moment yet, in that instant of vulnerability, she felt no fear, only a sense of rightness, of being exactly where she was meant to be, in this early morning of the tenth month, in the hour of the Hare.

Aritomo made a sign to one of his attendants, who stepped down from the platform and approached Hina. He reached out to take the stone, but she stood swiftly and said, 'It is for Lord Aritomo's eyes only.'

The man looked back to Aritomo. The Minatogura Lord, his curiosity piqued, said, 'Let her bring it to me.'

Hina stepped onto the platform and held out the medicine stone. Aritomo looked at it warily, and then looked into her face.

'It will show you if you are to live or die,' she said. 'Take it and look into it. If Heaven wills it, you will know how to prepare yourself.'

She saw the naked longing in his face, so intense it brought on a bout of coughing. As he struggled to get his breath, it was clear to Hina, even without the aid of the stone, that his illness was mortal. She watched him with calm compassion. He was a mighty lord, a general, a warrior, the most powerful man in the Eight Islands, but, like everything else, he was destined to die.

He took the stone in both hands and looked into it. His face took on an even more deathly hue.

'I am dying?' he whispered to her.

'The stone does not lie,' she replied.

His fingers gripped it with white knuckles, as he stared at his own death. Then he lowered the stone and for a few moments sat speechless. She saw the struggle within him: part of him longed for peace so he might prepare himself for death, but his iron will would not allow him to deviate from the path he had set.

'It is a lie,' he cried. 'I am not dying. I am immortal. I cannot die. But let Yoshimori look in it and see his imminent death!'

The stone in his hands gleamed as bright and dazzling as a mirror.

'Bring out the impostor!' Aritomo ordered. 'I will see him dead and then deal with this witch and Shikanoko.'

Hina was seized, dragged off the platform and thrown to the ground.

Guards appeared immediately, as though they had been nervously awaiting this command, Yoshi walking between them. He had been dressed in a robe of rough hemp cloth, a dirty brown colour. His hands were bound behind his back, his feet were bare. Hina stared first at his face, in which she thought she saw both resignation and fear. His eyes glanced once around. She thought he saw her but could not be sure. Would he recognise Shikanoko?

He stared upwards at the mountains and the ragged, white clouds that hung around them. His lips moved as if he were praying. A slight smile crossed his face. Following his gaze Hina saw Kon, circling overhead, screeching wildly. Yoshi lowered his eyes, and Hina looked at his feet. The long flexible toes gripped the earth, as though at any moment they would launch him into an acrobatic show. But where were the others? Saru, the monkeys? Surely they were not all already dead?

Yoshi was forced to his knees. An even deeper hush fell over the spectators. Hina could not believe it was truly going to happen. She could not prevent herself from sitting up and looking round, seeking help.

Aritomo stepped down from the platform and went to Yoshimori. 'Look into this,' he said, holding out the stone. 'See that you are about to die!'

The Emperor of the Eight Islands looked at the stone, then looked at Aritomo, his face calm.

Light flashed from the stone. Aritomo dropped it as though it had become red hot and took a step back.

'Now!' he said. 'Do it now!'

Hina heard the sigh of a sword being raised. A sob burst from her.

Kon swooped down, flew around the raised sword and stabbed the executioner in the eye. Tan gave a fierce neigh like a human scream and charged at the man. He stumbled, rolled on the ground, but kept a firm grip on the sword and, as the horse reared over him, thrust upwards deep into Tan's chest.

'Tan!' Hina screamed. 'Father!'

She heard Aritomo shouting to his warriors. 'Kill them all, horses and all. Don't let any one of them escape.'

Blood was staining the white silken hair. Tan lowered his head, fell to his knees. Hardly knowing how she had got there Hina found herself next to him, trying in vain to staunch the wound. The horse's body seemed to melt and fade and in its place stood her father, young and courageous, just as she had last seen him when she was a child. Kiyoyori held out his hand and the sword, Jato, flew to him from where it lay on the moss.

Shika called to Kodama, 'Come here!' and the bow launched itself into the air, along with the arrows. As soon as he held them he shot twice rapidly at Aritomo. Both arrows found their mark, one in the neck, one in the chest, but the Minatogura Lord was impervious to pain or fear. With raised sword he rushed at the kneeling Emperor.

'Lord Kiyoyori!' Shika shouted.

'I cannot die!' Aritomo cried. 'Not one of you can kill me.'

'I am returned from the dead,' the warrier replied. 'I can kill you. It is for this that I was called back by Shikanoko.' He let Jato move with its lightning speed to cut the sword from Aritomo's hand and with the returning stroke slash him from shoulder to hip, sending him to his knees. Aritomo struggled to his feet. Nothing was going to kill him. He stood for a long moment, even as his life's blood ebbed from him. Then with a cry of despair and disbelief, he fell heavily into the mud, quivered, and lay still.

Kiyoyori lowered the sword, went to Hina and took her in his arms.

'Father,' Hina said again, with sorrow for she knew he was about to leave her, this time forever.

'My work is done,' Kiyoyori said. 'Don't weep for me, my brave daughter.'

He handed Jato back to Shika and said, 'Thank you, Shikanoko. All debts between us are settled.'

Yoshi still knelt on the ground, Kon on his shoulder.

'Jato, we may need to fight now,' Shika said quietly, looking at Aritomo's men who, shocked and enraged by the death of their lord, were gathering round them. 'This is your true Emperor,' he cried to them. 'Lay down your weapons and surrender to him!'

When none of them obeyed, Kiyoyori called towards the lake. 'Come, Tsumaru, my son! I am ready to join you!'

There was a sound like a thunderclap and a crackle of flame. A cloud of steam rolled over them. The lake was boiling. Some said, afterwards, they saw the dragon child, with its wings and its talons, its ruby red eyes, take Kiyoyori's spirit in its embrace and descend with him into the lake, where father and son would dwell together until the end of time. Hina believed it was true. But she herself saw nothing until the steam cleared. Aritomo lay dead; his warriors milled to and fro, unsure whether to flee or to fight or to surrender; the crowd was running away; werehawks circled overhead crying in triumph. Down the river, from the north, came an army like nothing she had ever seen before. Warriors with one eye, with wooden legs, with hooks in place of hands, the Crippled Army, and at their head, riding on a black horse, a man who resembled Mu as closely as a twin. The guards who had not run away already tried to do so now but for most of them it was too late.

Shikanoko went to Yoshi, loosened his hands, raised him to his feet, then knelt before him, offering him Jato.

'Your Majesty may now safely ascend the Lotus Throne,' he said in a loud voice that echoed around Ryusonji. Kon fluttered down in front of them, calling exultantly.

'I don't want your sword,' Yoshi said. 'I don't want to be Emperor. You can't make me. I would rather be dead!'

As if in response rain began to fall heavily.

19

SHIKANOKO

'It is nothing to do with whether you want it or not,' Shikanoko said, making no attempt to hide his exasperation. It was a cold day in early winter. It seemed he had made the same argument a hundred times. Yoshimori had been moved to the luxurious palace that had been built for Daigen, and clothed in robes befitting an Emperor, but he still refused to start acting as one. 'You were born into this position, by the will of Heaven. The whole land, all the Eight Islands, depends on you. It's not possible for you to refuse it.'

'There must be someone else, someone who actually wants to be Emperor,' Yoshi said. 'What about the one who was ruling before I was discovered?'

'The former Emperor Daigen has been sent into exile,' Shika said, 'along with his mother and his household. He may never return to Miyako, but he will not be ill treated.'

Kuro and Kiku had offered to get rid of him, but Shika had forbidden it and had sent Daigen away before the brothers could dispatch him in the way they had the women and children at Kumayama.

'Does that mean you had him killed?' Yoshi said, eyeing Shika with mistrust. 'And you will have me killed, when I become an inconvenience.'

'I swear he is alive. As for you, you are the son of Heaven. I offered my sword, Jato, to you. I will serve you for the rest of my life.'

'As I said, I don't want your sword,' said Yoshi. 'I gave it to Take.'

When Shika merely bowed in response, Yoshi said, 'If I did agree to become Emperor my first imperial command would be to send you into exile!'

'If that is to be the price, I will pay it,' Shika replied. Yoshimori had threatened this in previous conversations, and exile was beginning to look more and more attractive. Quite apart from Yoshi's stubbornness, life in the capital, as the Kakizuki returned to take up power again and Kiku and his Crippled Army demanded recognition and rewards for their part in the victory, became more complicated every day. Everyone came to him with requests, demands, threats, promises. Lord Keita was reputed to be on his way back from Rakuhara and his old palace was being restored to all its former luxury. Minatogura had fallen to Takauji, who had declared his loyalty to the true Emperor and wrote asking for advice on how to subdue and administer the port city.

Aritomo and his warriors had to be buried with all the appropriate ceremonies lest their enraged spirits returned to haunt the capital.

Hina and Ibara were living in Lord Kiyoyori's old house, but Shika had not visited them, had not seen Hina since the day of Aritomo's death. He told himself he had been too busy, but he was not sure of his own feelings, and besides, what did he have to offer her? It was clear that she loved him, for she had been able to break the spell of the mask, but what could he do about it if he was under threat of banishment?

Who am I? he had often thought during the sleepless nights as autumn turned to winter. *Who is this person, a grown man, to whom they defer as if he knows what is right and what to do next?* He had lived for years in the forest. He knew nothing of the administration of cities, of the entire country. He saw people turn to him, but they were afraid of him. He remembered the promise of the mask. Should he take up residence at Ryusonji and become another Prince Abbot, practising that sacred sorcery that protected the realm? Or was his calling to be like Kiyoyori, a warrior lord, a great general, defeating the Emperor's enemies, pacifying the outer islands, repelling invaders? Everything was possible to him, yet without Yoshimori's trust and cooperation he could do nothing.

'Your life will not be unpleasant,' he said now to Yoshimori. 'You will never lack anything, never be hungry again. I've been told you are very fond of women – you will have all the concubines you want, the most beautiful girls in the realm, or boys if you prefer. You will marry a Princess.'

'What if I told you I was already married?' Yoshi said. 'I don't want any other woman, I want only her.'

'I am not sure she would be considered suitable,' Shika said.

'Then I will never be Emperor,' Yoshi replied.

'Maybe she could be included among your concubines,' Shika suggested.

Yoshi gave him a look of contempt as if this was not even worth answering.

'In any case, I won't be able to roam in the forest with Saru and the monkeys, will I?' he said finally.

'A forest can be put aside for you and filled with monkeys, I suppose,' Shika said. 'And Saru can join you wherever you like.

He can be given a noble rank.' He had discovered that Saru was the youngest brother of Taro, who had taken Kiyoyori's place on the ferry across the river of death. Saru deserved some reward for his brother's sacrifice. 'Where is he now?'

'He is here in the palace recovering. But he wants to go back to Aomizu with the other acrobats, those who survived. If only I were free to go with them!'

'None of us is free,' Shika said. 'We are all constrained by ties of duty, loyalty, service. You are bound to Heaven, I am bound to you, and so it goes throughout the realm.'

'On the river bank I was free,' Yoshimori replied. 'We all were. You should know this, you lived in the Darkwood like a wild animal for years, doing as you pleased, obeying no one.'

Shika did not reply for a few moments, thinking of the Darkwood, of the pleasures and suffering he had experienced there, of all its creatures, both real and magical.

'I was less free there than I am now,' he said finally. 'I was trapped, half-man and half-stag, imprisoned by another's sorcery and my own guilt and grief.' He took a deep breath and said, 'I suppose we must face what took place all those years ago.' It was painful but he would do anything to obtain reconciliation between them.

'You were going to kill me,' Yoshimori said. 'I have never spoken of it to anyone, but I have never forgotten it. I was only six years old and you were going to kill me.'

'I deeply regret it, all of it. I have spent years atoning for it. I can only ask you to forgive me.'

'I should,' Yoshimori said, with feeling. 'We are taught to forgive. But since we are being honest I will tell you I cannot. It is a gut feeling, as strong as anything I have ever felt. I cannot bear your presence. I do not even want to look at you.'

Shikanoko said nothing, feeling more alone than he ever had in his life. He could not help recalling the night he had spent with Akihime, his forbidden passion, the grief and guilt he had lived with since. He had been under the control of another's will, had been outplayed by the Prince Abbot, had come close to killing Yoshimori. He still ached from the punishment Kon and the horses had meted out to him.

They forgave me, he thought now. *But it seems Yoshimori never will.*

'Heaven saved your life then,' he pleaded. 'Surely that is an indication of its plans for you?'

Yoshimori's expression changed again. 'When you and I talk of Heaven we mean different things,' he said slowly. 'Your world is full of sorcery and darkness, revenge, conquest and death. Your Heaven is implacable and unfathomable. But I want to live in another kingdom, one where there is no killing, where Heaven is merciful. To rule as Emperor I must accept that I am divine, the son of the gods, yet I believe that only the Secret One can be divine, and we are all equal, all his children. I cannot set myself up above others or above him. I don't expect you to understand. It's how I was brought up, how I've lived till now. It could be argued that that was my destiny.'

Shika had noticed that Yoshimori would eat only vegetables and bean curd. Take had told him a little about the sect to which the acrobats belonged. It had not seemed of any great importance. Now he saw that for Yoshi it was.

'If you want the court to stop eating meat, it is within your power to do so,' he said. 'You only have to express a desire and it will be carried out. You have experienced life in a way few other emperors have. You have the knowledge and the power to do great good for your people.'

'And if I ordered you to stop all killing, would that be carried out too?'

'No one should take another's life lightly,' Shikanoko said. 'But men will always fight to defend themselves and their families; the evil need to be kept in check, the wicked punished, the realm protected. The warrior class serves you in this respect, my son and I first among them.'

'There is no point talking to you,' Yoshimori said. 'I will never be able to make you understand. But you cannot force me against my will.'

Shika knew it was true. He was the Emperor. No one could force him to do anything, not even to become Emperor.

He left the hall, and walked down a long passage, as courtiers on either side bowed deeply to him. On the verandah he paused to breathe and recover his equilibrium. Being with Yoshimori, feeling the strength of the younger man's dislike, distressed him beyond words. The sky was covered by low grey clouds. The wind was icy and damp. He thought he could smell snow in it. The last of the leaves had fallen. Gardeners were gathering them into piles. On one side of the step grew an ancient cumquat tree, its fruit forming, tiny and green.

Yoshimori must ascend the throne before it ripens, he vowed.

Take was waiting for him at the gate with Nyorin, and the brown horse that had been Chika's. He wore the sword, Jato, at his hip and the bow, Ameyumi, on his back, and carried Shika's bow, Kodama, and quiver, and Jinan, which had been recovered after Masachika's death.

Kon perched on the roof of the gate. The two young werehawks were sitting on Nyorin's back. They flapped their wings and cried in excitement at Shika's approach.

'How is he?' Take asked.

'As stubborn as ever. Between you and me I don't think I will ever persuade him. I did not realise his religion would be such a hindrance. You were brought up with the acrobats; do you share his beliefs?'

'Not really,' Take admitted. 'I admire them, but I can't keep them myself. I like swords and fighting and eating meat.'

His honest response made Shika smile. 'And the young woman he calls his wife, tell me more about her.'

'She is beautiful, clever and kind,' Take said, a light coming into his eyes. Shika wondered if he was not a bit in love with her himself. He would soon be old enough to marry.

'He shouldn't have to give her up,' Shika said.

'Her ears are not like other people's,' Take explained. 'They say it's a blemish.'

'I suppose that would be a problem for the Imperial Household. They have many arcane regulations and requirements that have to be followed.'

'I'm not surprised Yoshi doesn't want to be Emperor,' Take said. 'I would hate it.'

The horses picked their way through the rubbish-filled streets. Shika began to think about the problems of cleaning up the capital. The river was flowing freely again, but so many people had fled, there was no one left to do menial work, and when he had suggested to Tsunetomo that the Crippled Army might help, he had been met with incredulous laughter.

'We may be cripples but we are still warriors,' Tsunetomo said. 'We will never do the work of rubbish collectors.'

Take was also silent, as if preoccupied by something he did not know how to put into words. Finally he said, 'Father, you should take your sword back. It doesn't feel right that I should wear it.'

'I gave it to the Emperor and he gave it to you. It's yours now, and will be your son's.'

'I'm not sure that I can control it. Last night it danced for a long time around midnight and today when I went to pick it up it wriggled beneath my fingers like a snake.'

'It is Hidarisama misbehaving,' Shika said. He had been meaning to deal with the guardian spirits, but he had been so concerned with everything else, he had not yet had the opportunity.

'Let's ride to Ryusonji,' he said. 'I will find something there for them to look after.'

As they approached the temple Shika heard the strains of singing. Ahead of them on the long avenue that led to the main gate, a figure walked in a wavering, stumbling fashion. The werehawks squawked and cackled and flew to circle above his head, and then back to Shikanoko.

'It is a poor blind man,' Take said. 'He must be lost.'

He leaped down from his horse and went to the man's side, speaking clearly. 'Sir. Let me guide you. Where is it you want to go?'

The blind man replied in a surprisingly strong voice, 'I am on my way back to Ryusonji. Someone has to keep an eye on the Book of the Future. Aritomo sent me far away but he couldn't send me far enough!'

Shika recognised the voice and at the same time felt the bow on his back shudder and heard a whisper.

'It is our old master.'

The response came from Jato's direction. 'Now we're in trouble.'

'He'll be angry, won't he?'

'He'll be furious.'

Shika dismounted and went to Sesshin. 'Master,' he said. 'It is I, Shikanoko.'

Sesshin turned towards his voice. 'Is that really you, my boy? It's taken you long enough to get here. And why have you brought those rascals with you? They should be at Matsutani.'

'There's nothing left there,' said Hidarisama.

'Was I talking to you? Silence!'

'It all burned down,' Migisama muttered.

'Silence, I said. I will deal with you later.'

'I hope to find somewhere for them at Ryusonji,' Shika said.

'Good idea. They'll have to behave then.' Sesshin began to hum and then resumed the song he had been singing before,

At the temple of Ryusonji
Where the dragon child dwells
With his father, Kiyoyori . . .

He broke off to say, 'You know Kiyoyori dwells there now too?'

'I suppose his work on Earth was complete.' Shikanoko thought with wonder and regret of Tan, who had shared his life for so many years. 'I miss him.'

'He must have had some dragon spirit in him,' Sesshin remarked. 'Somehow I failed to notice that while he was alive, though I knew he was an exceptional man. I perceive much more clearly now I am blind. This young man is your son?'

'Yes, his name is Takeyoshi.'

'I can tell you have a kind heart,' Sesshin said to Take. 'Try not to make as many mistakes as your father.'

'He is not cursed with the powers of sorcery,' Shika replied. 'He will be a warrior, I hope.'

'Even monkeys fall from trees,' Sesshin said. 'Even warriors make mistakes. And your powers have blessed you as much as they have cursed you. Your biggest mistake was not getting rid of those imps, while you had the chance.'

'We would never have rescued Yoshimori without their help,' Shika said with assumed mildness.

'Well, it's too late now. They are in the world and you will have to live with that.'

They reached the gate, which was guarded by one of Kiku's men, who had a powerfully muscled upper body and only one leg. Shika had seen him in action and knew he hopped faster than most men could run.

Sesshin sniffed the air rudely. 'I smell one of their men here. You may find you want to deal with that as soon as possible.'

Shika was surprised and a little disconcerted to see Kiku's man here at the temple's gate. He had not known the Crippled Army had taken over Ryusonji. He felt a moment of disquiet that Kiku might know enough of sorcery to tap into the sacred power of the temple and gain access to the same supernatural skills as the Prince Abbot.

The guard recognised him and made a clumsy bow.

'You will find Master Kikuta inside, lord.'

I must order Master Kikuta *back to Kitakami*, Shika thought. *I cannot have him here.*

As they walked through the first courtyard Sesshin said, 'Aritomo's men broke my lute. I wonder if there is another one lying around. I miss playing. I discovered music late in life but it became my greatest pleasure. I used to sit just over there, facing the garden and the lake. I sang to the dragon child. I like to think it pleased him and consoled him.'

'You should have Genzo,' Take said. 'That's the Imperial lute that Lady Hina hid for years.'

'Yes, I know all about Genzo, but I think a lute that is not enchanted would suit me better.'

Shika looked over at the lake, now brimming with water, and saw Hina.

Leaving Take to accompany Sesshin to the temple he walked towards her. At the sound of his footsteps she turned her head.

Frost lay on the ground and etched the bare branches of the maples and the edge of the lake. It had grown much colder. *I should put my arms round her and warm her,* he thought. Instead he bowed formally.

'Lady Hina.'

She smiled slightly. 'I come to this place frequently. I feel very close to my father and my brother here.'

'Will you stay in the capital?'

She looked at him steadily for a few moments and then said quietly, 'I don't know where else to go. I am not sure what place there is for a woman with my past.'

'You are Lord Kiyoyori's daughter. Nothing can change that. You are the heir to his estates.'

'I cannot live at Matsutani. It has too many unhappy memories. I will give the estates to the Emperor and he can bestow them where he wishes.'

'He will not wish to bestow them anywhere,' Shika said bitterly, 'as he does not wish to be Emperor.'

'Unless you are brought up with the knowledge from childhood it must be unbearable,' she replied. 'But what else can he do? He cannot run away and live with the monkeys again. And if he did, what would it all have been for?' She gestured at the temple and the lake. 'All the sacrifices, all the deaths?'

He could think of nothing to say.

Hina looked at him with concern. 'What brings you here? Was it to talk to Master Kikuta? He seems to have settled in here.'

'I did not know that until now.'

'Does it alarm you?' she said astutely.

'A little.'

'You should beware of him,' she said.

'I know he has become very powerful.' Shikanoko sighed. 'I must talk to him, but first I have a small ceremony to perform. The guardian spirits from Matsutani are still in my weapons. I would leave them there – at least I could keep an eye on them and control them, and I am grateful for how they saved our lives on the river bank – but my sword, Jato, is now my son's, and it is too much for him. I met Master Sesshin on the way here and he agrees they should be placed somewhere safe here. They will have to obey him.'

'Sesshin?' Hina looked past him towards the temple. 'I have the eyes here with me. I did not know what to do with them.'

'Give them back to him,' Shika said.

'Yes, that seems right.' She called out, 'Ibara, would you mind bringing the bamboo box to me?'

Ibara came out of the shadow of the cloister. She bowed her head to Shika as she passed him and murmured, 'Lord.'

He hardly recognised her. The woman's clothes she wore seemed to shrink her physically, softened her features, made her submissive, turned her into a servant.

Have we all imprisoned ourselves, become captives of the roles we have to assume?

'Sesshin is on the verandah with Take,' he said to Hina, following her as she walked swiftly towards the others.

She knelt and touched her brow to the ground. 'Master, it is I, Hina.'

'Hina? Kiyoyori's child? The little girl who tried to be a healer? Well, well, what a surprise! Though I shouldn't say that, because, really, it is no surprise at all. It all turns out the way it is meant to be.'

'I have brought your eyes,' Hina said, taking his hands and placing them round the bamboo box. 'And I want to thank you for the Kudzu Vine Treasure Store.'

'You managed to read it? I thought you would. Though why I should have thought that, I don't know, as no one else has ever managed it, apart from me.' His fingers fumbled with the lid. He opened it and the eyes looked out as bright and lustrous as ever.

None of them said anything for a few moments, silenced by what the eyes showed them, the brief and fragile nature of their lives, the futility of all their striving.

But Shika saw something more. He saw his own heart, his love and need for Hina, and he knew she saw her love for him too.

'Well,' Sesshin said. 'It's taken you long enough to realise it, my boy, but it's been your destiny ever since you rode into Matsutani on that bad-tempered brown mare.'

He closed the box. 'I don't need these. As I said, I see more clearly without them. I will put them where they can make sure those rascals behave themselves.' He reached out to Hina and Shikanoko, as though he would join their hands, but he was interrupted by a voice calling down the cloisters.

'Shikanoko! You are here at last!'

Kiku hurried eagerly towards them. 'Welcome! Come inside, let me get you something to eat and drink.' His eyes fell on Sesshin. 'Who is this old man?'

'This is Master Sesshin,' Shika said. 'One of your fathers, as it happens.'

A shadow passed over Kiku's face. 'I remember now. We freed him, and in return he told you to kill us.'

'He didn't mean it, and he's sorry now,' Shika said.

'I did mean it and I'm not sorry,' Sesshin said. 'But I accept your existence now and I'll try to work around it.'

'I'm glad to hear it,' Kiku said. 'All the same, I don't think I want you here. Get moving, get out.'

When Sesshin did not stand up, Kiku called, 'Tsunetomo! Throw him out!'

'He is a great sorcerer,' Shika said. 'He goes where he wants to go, and stays where he wants to stay.'

'Does he want to go to Paradise?' Tsunetomo appeared with drawn sword.

'Haha!' Sesshin rocked with laughter. 'I'd be very grateful if you could send me there.'

'He cannot be killed,' Shika explained.

'Really?' Kiku put out a hand to restrain Tsunetomo, who seemed eager to test Shika's claim. 'That's interesting. You may stay then, as long as you don't get in my way.'

'Kiku,' Shika said, 'it is not for you to decide at Ryusonji who stays and who leaves. I want you to go back to Kitakami. You have carved out a place for yourself there; no one is going to challenge you on that or take it from you. You must leave the capital with all your men before the end of the month.'

Kiku stared at him. 'I like it here. This is a place of great power. I can use that.'

'I will not allow Ryusonji to become a centre of sorcery again. That is over. From now on, it will be a place of worship, nothing more.'

'Any power I gain here, from the dragon child or whatever other source, would be at your service. We would all work for you, as we have done till now. You could achieve anything you wanted with our help.' Kiku's voice had a faint note of pleading to it now. There was something incongruous to it, as though he were still a child, which of course, in human terms, he was, just an adolescent, not much older than Take. The thought touched Shika deeply. He had brought them up as his sons; he still felt a responsibility for Kiku, and for Mu and Kuro, who had now come silently along the verandah to stand at their brother's side.

'I am truly grateful to you all,' he said. 'Our lives have been entwined for years, ever since you were born, and there are strong bonds between us. But I do not want you in the capital, least of all at Ryusonji, certainly not with Gessho's skull. My order stands: leave before the end of the month.'

'We are your sons,' Kiku said stubbornly. 'Look, I have brought back the carving. I saw it on the werehawk's leg and knew it was a message from you. I came at once with all my men. We saved your life, we saved the Emperor.'

'I told you,' Mu interrupted. 'He has a human son. He will never need you, or love you, in that way. Let's go back to Kitakami. The Tribe, your Tribe, can flourish and be strong there.'

Kiku's gaze turned to Take, who was still kneeling beside Sesshin, the sword, Jato, lying next to him on the boards. He let the carving fall from his fingers, stepped towards him and dropped to one knee, staring intently in his face.

'Let me see what a human son looks like,' he whispered.

Take tried to cry out, then his eyes began to roll back in his head. Faster than the snake that was forged within it, Jato rose and thrust itself into the space between them, breaking the Kikuta gaze.

Kiku grasped the sword with both hands, trying to push it away, but it resisted him. Blood began to seep from his palms.

Take came half-awake and made a grab for the hilt. 'Let go!'

Kiku made no response, concentrating on dominating the sword. Shika could feel the power he possessed, emanating from him, the power that came from the skull, the sorcery and wisdom of the Old People. Shika had not realised Kiku was so strong. His heart quailed momentarily. He was not ready for yet another challenge. 'Master,' he whispered, 'do something.'

'I gave all my power to you, remember?' Sesshin said cheerfully. 'It's up to you now.'

Almost without thinking, Shika opened the seven-layered bag and took out the mask. He looked across at Kiku. Their eyes met. Jato hovered motionless.

'You don't want to use it, do you?' Kiku said. 'So give it to me.' He twisted the sword and it struggled from Take's grasp. Kiku took it, the blood seeping from the horizontal cuts across both palms. 'Give it to me or your human son dies.'

'Don't give it to him,' Hina cried.

Shika put the mask to his face and felt it cleave to him. He feared it might be for the last time, that Kiku's power would be greater than his, and he would never be able to remove the mask again. He saw years of loneliness and grief stretching away before him. But then he realised that it was more powerful than ever, that those years in the Darkwood had refined and honed it, as they had him. *Anything is possible to me*, he thought with wonder and awe. He said silently, *Put the sword down!* And then aloud, 'Hidarisama! Come here!'

Kiku's face twisted in pain, as he lost the struggle with the sword and relinquished it with an anguished cry, staring in shock at the bloody lines on his hands.

Jato, which had been about to plunge into Take's throat, flew from Kiku's hand to Shika's.

'You will obey me,' he said, and Kiku bowed his head. His eyes glistened with tears though he did not let them fall.

'What happened?' Hidarisama exclaimed. 'That was close!'

'You idiot,' said Migisama. 'You nearly made a big mistake. You were obeying the wrong person.'

'Oof! Maybe it's time to get out of this sword.'

'Before you do any harm.'

'Now I will do what I came to do,' Shika said. 'Hidarisama, you are to stay here. Choose where you want to go.'

'What about me?' said Migisama. 'Don't I get to choose?'

'Shikanoko was talking to me!'

'You're the one that did something stupid, not me.'

368

'Make up your minds quickly,' Shika said. 'How about the pagoda? Or the main gates?'

'The gates, so we can watch everyone go in and out.'

'The pagoda, so we can see the whole city.'

'If it's the pagoda, I want the top.'

'Why should you have the top? You wanted the gates.'

'You may go to the pagoda,' Shika said. 'You can share the top floor. Hidarisama will have the waxing moon, Migisama the waning.'

'Oh, very well.'

'I suppose that's acceptable.'

The voices of the guardian spirits grew fainter.

'Hey, he didn't say what happens when there's no moon.'

'We'll come down then and have fun!'

There was a slight movement of the ground like a small earthquake as the pagoda quivered. A flock of white doves that had been dozing on the roof flew upwards, with a sudden fluttering of wings. As if they had pierced the clouds, a few large flakes of snow began to fall.

Kiku looked at his palms, now marked forever with bloody wounds that would fade into distinctive scars. 'I will do as you command,' he said, 'but I will never forgive you. You and I are enemies from now on, as will be our children and our children's children.'

'Those children will all bear the mark of the sword,' Sesshin remarked. 'Long after what caused it has been forgotten.'

Kiku turned abruptly and walked away, disappearing into the main hall. Tsunetomo went after him. Kuro looked at Shika, seemed about to say something, then changed his mind and followed his brother.

Mu said, 'We will leave today to get back to Kitakami before winter sets in.'

'You may stay in the city,' Shika said.

'Do you fear me less than you fear him?' Mu looked at him with an amused expression.

'It's not fear,' Shika replied, but, in fact, it was a kind of fear, of what Kiku might become, mingled with love and regret, bringing him close to tears. 'But there is a difference between you.'

'Maybe because I was lucky enough to cross paths with a tengu,' Mu said.

Shika nodded, remembering Shisoku's words from long ago and, earlier, the fawn's form, the tengu overhead, the game of Go.

'I'll go with him,' Mu said. 'I'll try to explain everything to him. There are many things he doesn't understand.'

'I'm coming with you,' Ibara said.

'That would be most pleasant.' Mu was smiling. 'You can meet my daughter, and my youngest brother, Ku.'

'I'm sick of being a woman, and – forgive me, Lady Hina, I don't mean to offend you – a servant. I liked it in the forest when I was equal to men.'

'Maybe we will go back to the forest,' Mu said, with a trace of longing. 'We should see how things are at the old hut, and how Ima is getting on. But for a little while we must stay with Kiku.'

Hina spoke quietly behind Shika. 'Come to me. I will remove the mask.'

He turned and bowed his head, feeling deep relief as it slid easily from his face. He took it from her, feeling the cool touch of her fingers, and slipped it into the seven-layered bag.

'I was afraid he would take it from you,' she whispered, 'even kill you for it.'

'He nearly succeeded,' he said in a low voice. He was trembling with exhaustion.

'Can someone tell me what happened?' Take said, looking as if he had just woken up.

'Kiku put you to sleep with his gaze,' Mu said. 'I've seen him do it before.'

'I felt I knew nothing, had learned nothing, from you or the tengu,' Take said, shamefaced.

'Well, learn from this experience,' Mu said. 'Never let anyone from the Kikuta family look you in the eyes.'

'Hidarisama has left the sword,' Shika said, handing Jato back to Take. 'You may use it freely.' *Now I will speak to Hina*, he thought. *Now we will walk down to the lake together and discuss our future.*

As though she read his mind she looked up at him and smiled. Her hand touched his briefly. He heard his heart pounding, but it was not his heart, it was hoof beats. A horse neighed and Nyorin answered, from where he was waiting outside the gate.

'Nagatomo is here!' Take cried.

The Burnt Twins came through the main gate on horseback, allowing no one to stop them. The horses were breathing hard, eyes wild, flanks heaving. Nagatomo dismounted, approached Shika and said quietly, 'The Emperor has disappeared.'

Eisei slid from his horse's back. 'Saru has vanished too.'

'How could that happen?' Shika said with quiet anger. 'Must I look after everything myself?'

'No one expected them to be so agile, so acrobatic,' Nagatomo replied. 'They scaled the wall, leaped into a tree, and were away over the river before anyone could follow. Apparently a young woman was waiting on the further bank with a change of clothes. We found the Emperor's robes abandoned there.'

'We must go after him,' Shika said.

'I've told people he is unwell,' Nagatomo said. 'We should not let the news spread, and we cannot pursue him as if he were a criminal.'

'I'll go and find him,' Take said. 'I can persuade him to return.'

Shikanoko looked at his son for a moment without speaking. 'Very well,' he said finally. 'There's no point in me going, as he hates me above all. But you knew him in his other life. If he listens to anyone, it will be you. But who will go with you?'

'Lend me Nyorin. I will go alone. Don't worry, Father. I know both the river bank and the forest. I know where they will go.'

20

TAKEYOSHI

As Takeyoshi followed the river north the snow continued to fall, but it was not settling enough to reveal tracks. He had Jato at his hip and Ameyumi on his back. He rode at a canter, trusting the old horse not to stumble, and, if anyone greeted him, he replied it was a good day for hunting. He wore the bearskin chaps that the tengu had given him and a green robe that had belonged to Hina's father, Lord Kiyoyori. After a while the snow stopped, the clouds cleared a little and a pale wintry sun appeared. There was no wind.

The Sagigawa flowed from Lake Kasumi to the capital. Between the river and the mountains of the Darkwood lay a pattern of rice fields and vegetable gardens, crisscrossed by dykes and footpaths. Take wondered if Yoshi and Saru had run through them to reach the forest, but he then thought they were more likely to be trying to get to the lake, perhaps heading for the Rainbow Bridge or Aomizu, places they knew well and where they would be hidden. As he rode he reflected on the grief they must both be feeling. No one had considered the deaths of Asagao and several of the other acrobats and musicians as very important, but to the two young men they were friends, family, colleagues. He and Hina had rescued the survivors, tended their broken bodies and arranged for the dead to be buried. They had attended their funerals and said prayers for them, but they had followed the usual temple ceremony. Take, alone, was familiar with the prayers of the Hidden, but he repeated them only in his heart.

Kai had come to Yoshi to help him get away. She had made the journey pregnant and alone. He was amazed and impressed by her devotion, and concerned for her and the unborn child.

They are going to Aomizu, he realised. *They will seek out the old priest, the one who told me not to be angry. They will tell the families how the others died, ask for forgiveness and pray with them. They will hide, like all the other runaways and outcasts, among the people of the river bank.*

Just before the barrier at Kasumiguchi he saw Kon flying over-head. The sight of the bird comforted him. It meant he was going in the right direction. Kon would lead him to Yoshimori.

The barrier was still guarded by Kiku's men. They were stopping people and demanding, 'Red or White? The new Emperor or the old?' as though all alternatives had been reduced to a single choice: True or false? Right or wrong? How did anyone know ultimately?

They were persuaded by Take's excuse of hunting, and let him through as they did most of the common people. They were concerned only with arresting fleeing Miboshi warriors.

Yoshi and Saru would have looked like the many ragged youths who were walking in either direction, to the capital to sell produce and firewood, or going home to their villages.

After the barrier he let Nyorin walk for a while to rest him. Gradually the road became less crowded. There were fewer villages, the land was wilder and more mountainous. He had grown more used to being alone, but as night fell the solitude of the landscape began to make him uneasy. He tried to sing to raise his spirits, but all the songs he knew reminded him of the dead musicians. He seemed to hear their voices echoing from the darkness, the ghostly strain of a lute, the rhythmic beating of a drum. He felt Kai was ahead of him, and the drum was hers.

The moon rose, casting shadows of horse and rider on the frosty ground. He did not want to stop, it was too cold, so he let the horse walk on. From time to time he dozed a little, feeling his head grow heavy and his eyelids close. He smelled smoke, not sure if he was waking or dreaming, and heard a rattle and clicking of stones.

Nyorin came to a halt, pricked up his ears and turned his head. Take looked in the same direction and saw a shadowy figure silhouetted against the firelight. He recognised the bulky outline, the beaked head.

'Tadashii!' he said. Nyorin gave a low whinny and stepped purposefully towards the fire.

'Ah, here you are,' the tengu said. 'Come and sit down. Meet my friend – actually, I think you met, after a fashion, before. He doesn't have a human name but that doesn't matter. He doesn't speak and, anyway, you will never see him again after tonight. We are just passing the time until . . . well, never mind what, just passing the time in a game of Go.'

The board was carved on the stump of a kawa tree, the white stones were shells, gleaming with mother of pearl, the black ones were obsidian pebbles, river smooth. They rested in bowls of mulberry wood, reflecting the firelight.

Tadashii rattled the black stones in his bowl. His opponent grunted in irritation and rolled his eyes.

'It's considered very rude to do that,' Tadashii said. 'But I like to annoy him.'

He picked up a black stone and placed it on the board with a loud clack.

'This is you,' he whispered. 'I knew you were on your way, but he didn't. You getting the Rain Bow upset him but this will shock him, even more! Oooh, now we are in the end game!'

He laughed loudly, the sound echoing back from the cliff face as though twenty tengu were laughing with him.

'Wait,' Take said. 'Why am I a piece in your game?'

'Don't worry about it,' the tengu replied. 'Rest by the fire. I think there's a flask of cold broth and some bones left if you're hungry. Tomorrow it will all work out, you'll see.'

Take's eyelids were drooping against his will. He barely found the strength to unsaddle Nyorin. The old horse shook himself, exhaled heavily, and lay down. Take drank the broth and ate the rice balls he had brought with him. He cracked open the bones with his teeth and sucked the marrow from them. He had no idea what animal they were from. Then he lay down next to Nyorin, resting his head on the horse's shoulder. He heard the rattle and clack of the stones through his dreams.

Towards dawn he heard Kon calling and felt the beat of wings on his face. When he woke the tengu were gone. The embers of the fire were still warm and the tree stump remained but it was no longer carved into a grid nor was there any sign of the shells and stones.

Was the game over? Had they moved on to play somewhere else? Or had he just dreamed it all?

Nyorin got stiffly to his feet, snorted and let out a stream of urine, which steamed in the freezing air.

'I suppose we must go on,' Take said, lifting the saddle to place it on the stallion's back.

Something, or someone, had left a trail on the ground. At first he thought they were shells, gleaming white, but when he saw them more clearly he realised they were feathers, each tip spotted with purple.

Did tengu bleed? Had Tadashii pulled feathers from his wings to show Take the way? He was touched by this sacrifice but then it occurred to him the tengu would do anything to win the game.

The trail led to a clearing by a small pool. It was full of birds, blue and white herons. They all had their heads turned in one direction, watching two young men on the bank. Kai sat on the edge of the pool, her head turned, like the birds', towards Yoshi and Saru. Her hair covered her like a cloak. Her feet were bare. *How beautiful she is*, he thought with a surge of longing.

Yoshi and Saru were walking on their hands, reflecting each other's movements with perfect symmetry. It was a routine he remembered, but it seemed empty and sad, lacking the older men and the monkeys. He could move in and take part as he used to but he had vowed he would never do acrobatics again. That part of his life was over. It was over for Yoshi and Saru, too. No matter how hard they tried to recreate it, as they were doing now, it was gone.

A shadow darkened overhead. The birds all took off at once, crying in alarm. A huge tengu, Tadashii's opponent, swooped down and seized Yoshi by the feet with its talons.

Saru flipped over, screaming, and leaped to grab Yoshi's hands. The unexpected weight made the tengu falter, but its wings began to beat more powerfully. Kai leaped to her feet, calling for help.

Take pulled the bow, Ameyumi, from his back and fitted the arrow to the cord, with steady hands.

Kon flew screeching at the tengu's head.

Take aimed at the body, hoping not to hit the bird. The arrow thrummed loudly above Kon's cries and Kai's screams. The tengu made a hideous noise and opened its claws, letting Yoshi and Saru fall heavily to the ground. Then it pulled out the arrow and threw it away, drew its sword and flew towards Take.

Nyorin reared, striking out with his front hoofs. In that moment Take slipped from his back, dropped the bow and drew Jato. The sword came alive in his hand, just as the tengu delivered a savage blow at his head. He parried it, felt the shock run up to his shoulder, then jumped sideways as the backward sweep of the tengu's sword nearly took off his arm.

For a few moments he fought instinctively and defensively, then gradually, as time stretched out, he recalled the teachings of both Mu and Tadashii. He recovered his stance and began to notice the tengu's weaknesses. The arrow had done some damage and the tengu was losing blood – *so they definitely do bleed, purple* – and despite its enormous strength, it was slower than he was.

Kon, meanwhile, was doing his best to distract the tengu, making fluttering attacks at its face and neck. The herons returned, with their long beaks and harsh cries, and, at Kai's urging, flew at the tengu, further disabling it. It slashed out at them angrily and one fell flapping to the ground, but in that moment Jato found the unprotected chest and thrust upwards through the ribs to the heart.

Blood gushed out, purple and frothy, but still the tengu did not die. It threw its sword at Take and, with a look of hatred in its eyes, made a gesture of surrender and farewell. Its wings moved slowly, barely enough to lift it from the ground and clear the treetops, its feet scraping through the branches, blood dripping in large spots like summer rain.

A noise came from the mountains, an echo of Tadashii's laughter. *Maybe I just won your game for you,* Take thought, *but now I have my own end game to play.*

Yoshi and Saru lay on the ground, unmoving. For a moment he was afraid the fall had killed them, but then Saru moaned and he saw

Yoshi's eyes flicker open. He knew he should kneel and offer his sword to the Emperor, but his fury got the better of him.

'You nearly got me killed! The birds of the air came to my aid! You could not defend yourself or help me?'

He looked at the dying heron with sorrow. 'Even the heron knows who you are and gave its life for you. Kon has followed you loyally for years. Won't you recognise that, admit you are the Emperor and accept it?'

For a few moments Yoshi did not reply. A deep silence filled the clearing. No birds called; even Kon was mute.

Then the Emperor got to his feet and walked towards Kai. He held her in a close embrace, swept back her hair and kissed her ears. He whispered something to her and she looked at Take and nodded, tears pouring from her eyes. The Emperor glanced at the heron and at Kon and then turned to Takeyoshi.

'Kai does not want to be an Emperor's concubine. I am entrusting her to you. Bring the child up as your own. Maybe one day, if she agrees, you will marry. To honour the heron you will take it as your crest, and, as your name, Otori, like the houou that Kon has become. Now help me onto the horse.'

Otori Takeyoshi bowed and obeyed, then lifted Kai up behind Yoshimori.

'You can walk.' The Emperor turned the stallion's head and rode in the direction of the capital, Take on one side, Saru on the other, the golden houou flying overhead.

21

SHIKANOKO

The Emperor acted as he had threatened and his first act, after ascending the Lotus Throne, was to exile Shikanoko from the city. Next he granted lands in the extreme west to Iida no Saru and Otori Takeyoshi, in the wild area that would come to be known as the Three Countries. In exchange for her estates of Matsutani and Kuromori, and in recognition of her family's sacrifices and losses, he gave the domain of Maruyama, where her mother had been born, to Kiyoyori's daughter, Lady Hina, stipulating only that it should always be inherited through the female line.

It was as though he wanted no one around him who knew what he had been formerly, nothing to remind him of all he had lost.

The Kakizuki lords ran the city as they had before, taking over Aritomo's improved administration and more productive taxation system, and continuing to love music, poetry and dancing as much as ever.

Eisei became the Abbot at Ryusonji and, with the advice of Sesshin, developed a close enough relationship with the dragon child to ensure its blessings and protection. The two werehawks lived with them. He and Sesshin also composed The Tale of Shikanoko: the ballads of the Emperor of the Eight Islands, the Autumn Princess and the Dragon Child, The Lord of the Darkwood, and The Tengu's Game of Go, as they are known today.

Nagatomo went to Maruyama with Lady Hina.

In Kitakami, Mu and Kiku disagreed about everything until Mu – Master Muto by now – moved with Ibara and their children to Hagi, where Otori Takeyoshi was building a castle. Take's courageous and cheerful nature had endeared him to the natives of his new land. He knew that life was like a game of Go, complex and demanding, but still only a game, and he was determined to play it as best he could. He and Kai came to love each other, marry and have many children.

Kinpoge married her cousin, Juntaro, but her life and Take's continued to be entwined, one with the other. The tengu, Tadashii, had been wrong, for once, when he said they would not see each other again.

Shikanoko spent more than a year on a lonely island off the far southern coast, with only Gen for company, apart from the islanders who taught him ways to fish, as well as various secrets and spells that calmed storms and summoned sea monsters. It amused him that he had, indeed, straddled the Eight Islands, from north to south, as Kongyo had dreamed, but as an exile not as a ruler. Somewhat against his wishes, he gained a reputation for wisdom and power, and in his second spring on the island he began to receive many visitors seeking help and advice.

One of these came in the third month, when the island's surface was covered with tiny purple and yellow flowers and the air was filled with the cheeping of sea-bird chicks. He wore a black silk covering over his face.

Gen wagged his wispy tail and whimpered.

'Nagatomo!' Shikanoko said in delight, and embraced his old friend. 'What brings you here?'

'It seems you have been pardoned, to the extent that you may leave the island, though you may not return to the capital.'

'I hope I never visit that place again in my life!' Shikanoko replied. 'But where am I to go?'

'Anywhere you like, west of the High Cloud Mountains.'

Shikanoko was silent, remembering, reflecting. Then he said, 'So I am never to see the Darkwood again, nor Kumayama?'

Nagatomo did not reply directly but said, 'Lady Hina sent me.'

'Is she well?'

'She invites you to Maruyama. She said to tell you she must have a daughter to inherit the domain, but a daughter cannot be born without a father.'

Shikanoko smiled and said, 'She must have hundreds clamouring to be her husband.'

'She will marry no one but you,' Nagatomo said. 'My opinion is, you owe it to future generations.'

'So I do,' Shika agreed. He was imagining his daughters, as wise and beautiful as Hina, as brave as Takeyoshi. And then he remembered Hina's hands on his face, as she removed the mask, and a wave of hope and longing swept over him.

'We will leave on the next tide,' he said.

AUTHOR'S NOTE

This book was partly inspired by the great medieval warrior tales of Japan: *The Tale of the Heike*, the *Taiheiki*, the tales of Hōgen and Heiji, *Jōkyūki*, and *The Tale of the Soga Brothers*. I have borrowed descriptions of weapons and clothes from these and am indebted to their English translators, Royall Tyler, Helen Craig McCullough and Thomas J Cogan.

I would like to thank in particular Randy Schadel who read early versions of the novels and made many invaluable suggestions.